This book should be returned to any branch of the
Lancashire County Library on or before the date shown

− 9 NOV 2012		NCH 2/12
1 2 FEB 2013		
2 2 JUL 2013		
− 1 OCT 2013		
Fs 11 1/16		
~~fisher 7/18~~		
fisher 7/18		

Dear Reader

If variety is the spice of life, Mills & Boon® is definitely the spice of romance. My favourite aspect of Mills & Boon is their commitment to publishing a vast assortment of genres—something for every reader. As a historical western writer and reader, I'm ever thankful to know that while Mills & Boon continues to launch new lines and evolve with its readers, the traditional romance novels I love to read and write won't be left in the dust—*gotta have my cowboys*!

I'm honoured to write for a publisher fulfilling the needs of readers.

Stacey Kayne

MUSTANG WILD

BY
STACEY KAYNE

Stacey Kayne has always been a day-dreamer. If the comments on her elementary school report cards are any indication, it's a craft she mastered early on. Having a passion for history and a flair for storytelling, she strives to weave fact and fiction into a wild ride that can capture the heart. Stacey lives on a ranch near the Sierra Nevada mountains, with her high-school sweetheart turned husband of over twenty years and their two sons. Visit her website at www.staceykayne.com

Dedicated to

My grandmothers—women of strength and courage who've influenced my life.

Special thanks to

Lyn Randal, my dear friend, contest rival, star sister and guardian angel. My English teacher, Mr Perez, whose praise of my writing fuelled my courage to write a book. My mom—I couldn't have achieved this dream without your love, faith and support! My mother-in-law, for being my friend, cheerleader and very first proofreader. Evan Fogelman, for believing in my work, giving me confidence and keeping my spirits up. My critique partners, Sheila Rae Z Mohs, Renee Luke and Carla Hughes—who put up with my dyslexic jargle and help me find those missing words, while adding fun and friendship to my life. My angel boys, for being the best kids ever—and for letting their mom hog the computer! Last but not least, my hero, my husband, the man who has suffered through countless dinners out of a box and the untold amount of housework that is always on my to-do list. He never counted on his wife being a writer, but has adjusted well. You have to admire a man who can proudly announce, "My wife writes killer romance novels." Love you!

Chapter 1

New Mexico Territory, 1880

Skylar Daines reined her Arabian stallion beside her younger brother and surveyed the ragged, canvas-topped structures wavering in the desert heat like an ugly mirage. As long as Chance Morgan was in the area, she didn't care if the town of Black Dog was a row of outhouses.

Unfortunately, it didn't appear far off from being just that.

Fear spiraled up from the pit of her stomach, sending a wave of shivers across her skin as she scanned the parallel cluster of makeshift buildings surrounded by miles of dry dirt, sand and sage. For such a small watering hole, a fair number of horses stood along the short strip of dirt, with more staked and hobbled on open ground.

"Sis, you sure that's Black Dog? It don't look like no place to find someone trustworthy."

Straining for an encouraging smile, she met Garret's gaze. "This is it," she said in a steady tone, suddenly wishing her father's maps weren't so accurate. "Let's see if anyone has heard of Chance Morgan."

Garret's hazel eyes narrowed, his features hardened, reminding Skylar of all the violence he'd been exposed to in his tender thirteen years.

"I don't like it, Sky." He shook his head, making no move to urge his horse forward.

She didn't blame him. But they hadn't come this far to fail. Her father's last words had been to take Garret and the deed for their land in Wyoming to Black Dog and find Chance Morgan, her father's business partner. They'd just spent a month traveling across a land as unforgiving as life itself. There'd been no time to ponder the grief weighing on her soul. Her guilt, on the other hand, hung around her neck like an iron yoke.

She wouldn't fail Garret. She would get him safely to Wyoming. They'd reclaim their mustangs and have the home their father had promised them.

Fighting the tremble in her hands and an exhaustion she felt to the center of her bones, she reached over and tugged on the brim of Garret's tan hat. "There's no going back, little brother, and nothin' to go back to. Pa said to find Morgan and that's what we're gonna do. We can't make it clear to Wyoming without provisions. Pull out your rifle if it'll make you feel better."

Garret nodded and draped his long gun across his lap.

Praying there wouldn't be any call for gunfire, she urged her black stallion forward, conscious of the sun beginning to sag in the western sky.

As she rode down the center strip of Black Dog, lively

piano music carried into the street from a building occupying nearly the whole right side of town. The name Big Jack's Saloon was whitewashed across its wood front. With not a soul in sight and every other establishment appearing deserted, she imagined Big Jack wasn't low on customers.

Skylar dismounted and led her horse toward a hitching rail outside the saloon. A handsome red mare with light spots on its hindquarters was tethered a few feet away. Shifting her gaze from the large Appaloosa, she glanced at a set of double swinging doors. She'd never been inside such an establishment.

"Appaloosa," said Garret. "Pretty one, too. At least we know Morgan has an eye for fine horseflesh."

Skylar glanced up at her little brother as he reined his chestnut Arabian in beside her. "Why do you say that?"

"His name's on his saddle," answered Garret, still admiring the well-groomed mare.

Her eyes darted toward the horse's tack. Bold as daylight, the letters *M-O-R-G-A-N* were pressed into the leather. "Well, knock me over with a feather."

"If you're as beat as I am, I probably could," Garret retorted.

"Wait here. I won't be but a few minutes."

Clutching his gun in one hand, Garret jumped from his saddle and grabbed her by the arm as she turned toward the saloon. "Sky, you can't go in there. Yer wearin' a dress! I'll go in and get Morgan."

She shook his hand away from her elbow. Garret and her father had been reluctant to accept the fact, but at nineteen, there was no hiding that she was a woman, no matter what she wore. At the moment, she imagined her appearance was nothing short of obscene. The threadbare dress she'd found in her father's saddlebags was made for a woman half her size. She'd never realized her mother had been such a dainty woman. The buttons strained between Skylar's breasts were dangerously close to popping off. The blue calico skirt barely reached the top rim of her boots.

Her only shirt and pair of denims were so filthy, she hadn't had much choice but to wear the dress. Her dusty, windblown hair hung just above her shoulders like dried grass.

"You're staying here," she said to Garret. "Mount up."

"I'm going in with you."

"The Arabians are all we have left. You're going to watch them while I talk to Morgan."

"I'm not about to let you—"

"Garret, you'd get tossed out of that saloon before you stepped two feet past the door. Now do as I said."

Garret's frown deepened. His anger-filled gaze bore into her for a lingering moment. "I don't like it," he grumbled as he turned and mounted his horse. He tugged his hat low on his brow then rested the barrel of his gun in the crook of his arm. "Shout if you need me."

Skylar started toward the music and clamor, wishing for once that Garret could have been her *big* brother. *You can do this,* she soothed, reminding herself of how far they'd already come. No smelly herd of liquored-up cowboys was going to keep her from fulfilling her father's promise.

Stepping through the double swinging doors, she was greeted by the familiar stench of tobacco, whiskey and horse. The scent of cowpunchers. The scent of home for the past eight years. She frowned at the thought.

That's all about to change. She glanced around the crowded, smoke-filled room. Seemed half the population of New Mexico Territory was in Big Jack's. The place was packed with cowboys and fancy women in colorful silken gowns. She'd never seen so many vibrant colors.

She walked deeper into the crowd of festive men and women, scanning the faces of men seated at the many round tables, and others as they moved between them. Chance Morgan had worked her father's cattle drives for a couple years, but she hadn't seen him for over three years. She imagined he'd still look the same. Tall, blond and handsome, with chilling green eyes.

Hearing an uproar of voices and the name "Morgan" shouted amongst them, Skylar peered through a cluster of men and saw the tall, blond and handsome man responsible for the ruckus.

Morgan sat at the back table. His laughter filled the air as he leaned forward, wrapping his arms around the pile of money at the center of the table. She followed the crowd of folks gathering around him.

"You gonna use it, Tuck?" someone shouted as Skylar squeezed between two large bodies.

"Fifty dollars says he won't," said the slender man sitting opposite Morgan. He reached across the table and pulled a paper from Morgan's pile of coins.

"Hell, yes, I'll use it," Morgan answered as he snatched

the paper from his hand and tossed it onto his winnings. "Just as soon as a blue-eyed angel floats down from heaven and calls my name."

Skylar stepped beside his chair as gruff laughter roared around her. "Mr. Morgan?"

The man glanced over his shoulder. His emerald-green eyes grew wide. "Merciful heaven. Hello, angel," he said in a low, velvety voice. "You are a beauty."

This was Morgan all right, and he'd obviously been drinking. Her appearance was anything but pleasant. "Mr. Morgan—"

Morgan rose to stand directly in front of her. Her body tensed as he scanned her from head to toe before his gaze slowly traveled back up. Hypnotic eyes held her gaze as the corner of his mouth kicked up in a cocky grin.

Dear God, why couldn't she breathe?

His eyes were the same brilliant shade of green as Chance Morgan's, his hair the same pale blond, and damn if he didn't have Chance Morgan's handsome face. But every tingling cell in Skylar's body told her this man was *not* Chance Morgan. One of the men had called him by another name. Perhaps Chance had a twin.

"*Tuck* Morgan?"

"A deal's a deal," he murmured. His lips stretched into a full smile, revealing strong white teeth and enough charm to sweet-talk the spines off a prickly cactus. His arm shot out and hauled her against his side as he shouted, "Boys, my angel just arrived!"

He's drunk, all right. "Mr. Morgan, I—"

"Hang on, angel," said the green-eyed stranger, his muscular arm easily suppressing her struggle to move away from his side as he turned back toward the table of men. "I believe the bet's fifty dollars. Ante up, gentlemen!"

Three men seated at the table fumbled hastily through their vest and trouser pockets. A few more men standing behind them tossed their money into the center of the round table.

"By God, he's gonna do it," one shouted.

"I don't believe it," said another.

An older man dressed all in black stood up from the table. "You gotta sign the document, Tuck," he said, flattening out the paper. "It ain't no good unless you sign it."

Tucker reached over and signed his name. The older man beamed a smile at Skylar, then laved his tongue across the palm of his hand and swiped it across the top of his head, slicking back a few strands of dark hair. He straightened his posture, tugging on the sides of his black coat. "Now the lady," he instructed.

"Mr. Morgan," Skylar said again, looking away from the odd man dressed in black. "I really need to speak with you. I believe we're traveling with you to Wyoming and—"

"That's the plan, angel girl," he said, giving her a wink as he placed the pen in her hand and wrapped her fingers around it. "It's all arranged. Just sign your angelic name onto that paper and we'll be set. Angels do have names, don't they?"

He beamed another smile, and Skylar felt a tad dizzy. His arm clamped around her shoulders was all that kept her from swaying. "Sign the paper?" she asked in confusion. She glanced down at the table. "W-why do I—"

"No time for questions, angel. Are we goin' to Wyoming or not?"

"Yes, but—"

"Then sign the document, sweetheart."

"The contract?" she asked as he guided her hand toward the bottom of the paper. She and her father had discussed the contract for driving the horses in exchange for provisions. She no longer had her mustangs, but she had to get to Wyoming if she intended to reclaim them. She blinked and tried to focus her tired eyes on the words. Morgan's breath rustled her hair as his hand slipped from her shoulder and slid across the flat of her stomach. A burst of tingling shivers raced across her skin.

"Uh-huh." His voice vibrated against her ear. The hard length of his body pressed against her backside.

Damnation. Her bones were turning to jelly! Desperate to escape the situation, Skylar quickly scribed her name beside the name *Tucker Morgan* then took a step away from him.

"Hang on, angel. Don't fly away just yet." His hand slid back around her waist. Sparkling green eyes locked with hers as he pulled her into his arms. His slow smile did the most horrifying things to her insides. The noise and clatter of the room turned to a steady hum as she stared up at Tucker Morgan's sharp features; his warm gaze and charming smile paralyzed her mind.

"I do," he said, although Skylar didn't know what he meant by the odd comment. Before she could contrive a rational thought, he leaned toward her. "Say yes," he said, his lips mere inches from hers.

"Yes? But I—"

He tipped his head forward and *kissed* her, the touch of his soft lips cutting off the rest of her words. Skylar gasped as he stroked her lips, teasing them apart, filling her mouth with the hot taste of whiskey and flooding her body with a rush of fiery sensation.

A voice deep in her mind told her to pull away, yet every gentle, intoxicating touch of Tucker Morgan's mouth offered her something she'd craved for so long.

Tenderness.

His kiss was unlike anything she'd ever experienced. His mouth moved over hers in the most alluring, unde-manding way, subtly seducing her mouth into submission until she was returning his kiss.

Hoots and hollers filtered through the electrifying hum of her body. Skylar tensed, and he lifted his lips from hers. Heat rushed to her face. She was shocked to find her arms banded around his neck, her fingers twisted into the blond tufts of hair touching his collar. With her body pressed flush against his, she could feel his heartbeat hammering as erratically as her own.

"Dear God," he breathed, his eyes looking deep into hers.

"Guess I don't have to tell you to kiss your bride," said the jubilant voice of the man standing beside them.

Bride? Skylar jerked away from Tucker's embrace. She stumbled backward, but was instantly shoved back into his arms by whoever stood behind her.

"Drinks are on me," Tucker Morgan shouted, clamping her back against his broad chest, then in one swift motion, he lifted Skylar into his arms. "It's you and me, angel girl," he said as he carried her through a crowd of well-wishers.

"Wait!" she screamed, while silently assuring herself she had not just married this man.

He pushed through the swinging doors. Skylar twisted in his grip, managing to kick her legs free when they reached the road. She shoved away from him and saw her horse from the corner of her eye.

"Oh, no, you don't," he said with a rueful laugh, his arm coiling around her waist.

A shriek escaped her throat as one of his hands closed over her backside. Seeing his soft, intoxicating lips aiming for hers, she turned away, struggling to free herself from his grasp.

"Get your damn…would you…" No matter which way she twisted, she couldn't evade his hands and lips. His strong arms clamped her against his firm chest.

"Come on now, angel. I know you—" He stiffened as a loud *donk* echoed from behind him. His brilliant eyes popped wide, before he crumpled to the ground, falling at her feet as though his bones had turned to dust.

Garret sat before her, backward in his saddle, with a skillet in his hands. "Did I kill 'im?" he called over the ringing of the cast iron.

Dear God! She wasn't sure.

Skylar dropped to her knees beside Tucker. She lifted one of his eyelids, but the green eyes that had held her captive moments ago were rolled up in his possibly fractured skull. She pressed her cheek to his chest.

"He's breathing." She quickly ran her fingers through his thick blond hair, checking for injuries. One heck of a goose egg was rising from the crown of his head, but all seemed to be intact. *Thank goodness.*

"Dag blast it!" Garret cried out as he knelt beside her. "He smells like he's been steeped in whiskey!"

"Why'd you hit him?" she demanded, grabbing the iron skillet from Garret's hand.

"The man was attacking you! If I'd a had a clear shot, I'da blown a hole through his chest. I told you not to go into that saloon. You shoulda let *me* go in to get Morgan."

"Well, would you look at that," called a gruff voice.

Skylar glanced up at a pair of drunken cowboys staggering toward them. Her gaze dropped to the skillet in her hand.

Oh, Lord. She was going to get arrested!

"Tuck's bride already showed him what-for with a fryin' pan," one said, flashing a broad, toothless grin.

The other cackled with wild laughter. "Give 'im hell, honey," he called out. "He deserves every blow."

The men shuffled past, chuckling and intermittently bumping into one another, apparently unconcerned about their friend's state of unconsciousness as they searched for their horses.

"Skylar?"

She cringed at the sound of Garret's harsh tone. With slow reluctance, she met her brother's wide-eyed gaze.

"What in the hell were those men talkin' about?"

"Watch your mouth." She shot Garret a stern glance as she stood, brushing the dust from her skirt.

Garret surged to his feet. "Tell me you didn't marry this flea-bitten drunk!"

"I'm not really certain," she replied, keeping her gaze on her unconscious groom. "Everything happened so fast. If I did, I'm sure it wasn't legal." She hooked her arms under Tucker's broad shoulders.

"You weren't gone but five minutes!"

"Lord, he weighs a ton," she muttered, barely able to lift his shoulders off the ground. Already pushed to their limits, her tired muscles complained as she tried to drag him toward her horse. Lucky to be standing, she couldn't move him an inch.

What a fine mess. "How are we going to get him over a horse?"

"Over a *horse?*" shrieked Garret. "The man was attacking you! Let the coyotes and cougars have 'im!"

"I can't."

"What the hell went on in there, and where's Chance Morgan?"

Skylar gave up her struggle to move the drunken clod and lifted her gaze toward her brother, who was brimming over with anger. "*This* is Morgan. But his name is Tucker, not Chance. Help me lift him."

"*What?*" Garret looked closer at the man lying in the dirt.

"I said his name is Tucker, not—"

"I don't care what his name is. He's not goin' anywhere near our horses! What happened inside that saloon?" Her brother stood rigid as a statue, his hands planted on his narrow hips.

"Calm down, Garret. I'm sure it was a simple mistake. He obviously thought I was someone else and before I could correct him, his friend—"

"Uh, Mrs. Morgan?"

Startled by the deep voice directly behind her, Skylar spun around. A man the size of a giant with more shaggy brown hair than a grizzly stood before her. He pulled off his battered hat and held it to his chest. A broad grin parted the thick fur on his face.

"Name's Hal. Just wanted to congratulate ya on the weddin'. Never thought I'd see Tuck marry." He lowered his gaze to the man sprawled out on the ground between them. "Need a hand with your husband?"

The entire town was daft.

Skylar forced a smile, seeing as the man was being quite cordial. "Yes. If you could toss him over my saddle, I'd be much obliged."

"Not a problem." Hal gave a slight grunt as he lifted Morgan, who was none too small, and hoisted him onto her horse, belly-down. "His animal is that perty roan." Hal motioned toward the Appaloosa.

"Thank you, Mr. Hal," she said with the same plastered-on smile. "That marriage bit, it wasn't legal…was it?" Skylar held her breath, praying he'd give her reassurance that a prank had been played on her.

"It was legal, all right. Henderson's a bonafide preacher and you both signed the marriage document. You're married right and proper."

"You signed a marriage document?" Garret shouted.

I signed a marriage document? Skylar's spirits plummeted. She knew better than to sign a paper before reading it! But Tucker Morgan had…he had…she wasn't sure what he'd done.

"He *tricked* me," she said, glaring at the unconscious culprit, wishing she had lodged her boot in his ribs while he was lying on the ground.

"That's Tuck," Hal said with a coarse laugh. "Slippery as a wet otter and crafty as the devil himself. Bein' at his weddin' was well worth losin' fifty dollars."

"Fifty dollars, huh?" murmured Garret.

Hal touched his fingers to the brim of his hat and bid her a good evening before he turned and swaggered back to the saloon. Skylar shifted her gaze toward her horse and found Garret with his hand stuffed deep into Tucker Morgan's breast pocket. His face brightened with a smile as his hand emerged with a wad of greenbacks.

"What do you think you're doing?"

"I'm hungry! I'm gonna find me a mercantile."

"That's stealing, Garret."

"The hell it is. He's your husband." He turned his back to her and started down the road.

Skylar released a long sigh. Her little brother was developing a flippant tongue, although, at the moment, she had far more pressing worries. "See if the merchant knows how to get to Morgan's place," she called after him.

She glanced back at Tucker Morgan's limp body. What was she supposed to do now? Hopefully Garret hadn't caused any permanent damage, or at least not enough to prevent the handsome cowboy from helping them get to Wyoming.

Chapter 2

It wasn't all that uncommon for Tucker Morgan to wake up in bed with a strange woman and a pounding headache, but he wasn't suffering from an ordinary hangover. The fierce throbbing in his skull wasn't the only thing out of sorts this morning. He lifted a wet cloth from his forehead and glanced again at the woman sleeping beside him.

Hell. Plenty about this morning was out of sorts. The fact that he and the woman next to him were fully clothed being the most troubling. They even had their boots on!

Her boots weren't the laced or buttoned-up version most women wore, but the same leather tug-on boots he was wearing. Her uncommonly short hair couldn't reach past her shoulders. Lying on her side, the golden strands swirled across her face. But her body, now that was all in proper order, with all the right curves in all the right places, and encased in a hideous blue dress that might have fit her once upon a time. The fabric of her bodice molded to the round swell of her breasts like a second skin.

Tucker closed his eyes, the pounding in his head increasing. His headache wouldn't even let him enjoy the view. He needed coffee and a shot of whiskey. Hell, with this headache, he needed a pint of whiskey.

Groaning, he forced himself to sit up and glance around his bedroom. How had they ended up here? He'd never brought a woman back to this run-down cabin.

Trying to jar his memory, he stood and slowly shuffled toward the kitchen.

"'Morning."

Tucker jumped at the sound of the unexpected greeting. A young boy with pure white hair sat at the little table that occupied the left half of his cabin. He gave the cotton-topped kid a quick once-over before muttering, "Who the hell are you?"

"Your bride's brother."

"My *what?*" Tucker countered, his headache suddenly forgotten.

The kid's white eyebrows pinched inward as his eyes narrowed. "Your *wife's* brother. I…am…Skylar's… brother." He dragged out each word as though he were talking to the town idiot.

Stunned, Tucker glanced toward the bedroom.

I married a saloon girl?

He knew all the girls at Big Jack's. Skylar wasn't a name he'd heard before, and he would have remembered that short, golden mane. He rubbed a hand over his stubbled jaw, trying to recall the events from the previous night. Surely this was some kind of misunderstanding between the woman and the boy.

"Skylar?" he said aloud, the name sounding no more familiar than the kid looked sitting before him.

"Yes?" called a feminine voice, just before the slender woman appeared in the doorway. Deep blue eyes held his gaze. Sunlight streaking in from the bedroom window glimmered in the tangled golden hair wisped around her oval face. A vision from the saloon flashed in his mind.

He'd just won a hand of poker when he'd heard a woman say his name—then there she was, an angel with gilded hair and the purest sapphire eyes gazing straight into his soul. He'd jumped to his feet and...

Dear God, I married an angel!

Not a true angel, his sober mind reasoned. He'd met her in Big Jack's, after all. Despite her threadbare clothes and bedraggled hair, she was a pretty thing. *Damn pretty.*

"Are you new at Big Jack's?" he ventured.

Hearing the metallic click of a gun hammer, Tucker shifted his gaze toward the kid. The boy sat at the table, calm as you please, holding a rifle aimed straight at Tucker's chest.

"Mister, I believe you just called my sister a whore."

"Garret!" called the woman. "I'm sure that's not what he meant. Is it, Mr. Morgan?"

Of course that was what he'd meant. Why else would she have been in a place like Big Jack's? Tucker met the kid's hard gaze. His hazel eyes revealed a boy well beyond his young age. This was a kid who'd seen his share of hardship, but, hell, who hadn't?

"I need some coffee," he groaned, his head again pounding, the pain increasing by the second as the prior evening's events came flooding back into his mind.

Tucker turned his back on the boy and his rifle. He was surprised to find a pot of coffee already steaming on the stove. He filled a cup and took a few sips of the strong brew. What could have possessed him to actually *marry* the woman standing behind him? A man could find plenty of other ways to torture himself besides taking a wife.

"I'm sure it was a farce," he said, mostly assuring himself as he stared into the steaming, dark depth of his coffee.

"Not what I was told," she answered in a stiff tone. "You tricked me into signing an actual marriage document and I'm pretty sure your preacher friend muttered some vows."

Tucker bit out a curse, feeling the disgust he heard in her voice. He had laughed as hard as everyone else when Henderson threw that marriage document into the pot, but it seemed the joke was on him.

He took another gulp of coffee then turned back toward the mess waiting behind him. Seeing the kid with his rifle still trained on him, he smiled.

"Boy, you better put that away before you hurt yourself."

"Garret, lower your gun."

"Who *are* you?" Tucker asked, his gaze again taking in the woman's short, tangled hair and strange attire.

"A full name would be nice," he added, his voice clipped. "You said my name when you entered the saloon last night, so you knew who I was."

"Not exactly. I was looking for *Chance* Morgan. My father never mentioned any Morgan by the name of Tucker."

"You knew I wasn't my brother. You called me Tuck."

"I heard a man call you by that name and when you stood up, I knew you weren't Chance."

"How?" he challenged. He didn't know a single living soul who could recognize him from his twin.

"You look…different."

"The hell I do!"

"He's got a point, Sky," the kid put in. "He sure looks like Chance to me."

"Only Chance isn't a drunk," she said in a harsh tone. "Chance worked with my father for two years when we drove stock in Texas and I never once saw him in such a state."

Hearing her harp on Chance's choirboy character only increased Tucker's anger. His twin truly was his other half. His boring half. Just because Chance couldn't stomach the taste of whiskey didn't make him a saint. No more than blowing off a bit of steam before heading out on a long drive made Tucker a drunk. "And your father would be?"

"Zachary Daines."

Ah, hell. I'm in trouble. If Chance returned this afternoon and found him married to Daines's daughter, he'd have a holy fit. Chance had assured him Zach Daines was one of the best horse trainers around, which was why Tucker had agreed to purchase Daines's mustangs and hire him on as foreman for their new horse ranch in Wyoming. He'd also heard that Daines was a sizable man and hard as stone, which made Tucker wonder why Daines wasn't doing his best to beat the life out of him right at this moment.

"Where's your father?"

Her blue eyes narrowed. "Where's Chance Morgan?"

Tucker didn't like the direction of their conversation. If Zach Daines were alive and kicking, he'd be standing inside this shack, keeping his belligerent daughter in line. Now that he thought about it, he wondered what she was doing here at all.

He'd been told that Daines was bringing his two sons, along with a crew of men and a few dozen horses, none of which he heard milling about outside the cabin. Tucker's gaze moved between Skylar and her brother. "What happened to your father?"

"He was kill't," the boy informed him baldly. "Four weeks back in Arizona. Randal, one of our own men, turned on us. His buddies rode into our camp with their guns blazing. I heard gunfire and came runnin' to see what all the ruckus was about. Sky grabbed me and said Randal kill't our pa and was after the deed. She threw me on a horse and…here we are."

Damn it! He had told Chance it was a fool idea to send their deed off with Daines. "Who has the deed?"

"I do."

Tucker shifted his gaze to Skylar Daines's cold blue eyes. "I'd like to see it."

"I'd like to see Chance Morgan."

Tucker took a step forward, glaring at the woman who

stood only a few inches shorter than himself. "You're looking at him."

"No, I'm not."

"Sky," the boy interrupted. "He does look just like Chance."

"No, he doesn't," she insisted.

The close view of her sapphire eyes brought another image to Tucker's mind. He seemed to recall those big blue eyes up close, right before she wrapped her arms around his neck and kissed him wildly.

A smile tugged at the corner of his mouth, which broadened when he saw a tinge of red rising into Skylar's cheeks before she dropped her gaze and took a step back. He wasn't the only one remembering that kiss.

What the hell am I smiling about? I'm married to this woman!

I'll fix one mess at a time. He turned toward the door. First he'd make sure Henderson didn't validate his legal tie to this woman, then he'd get his deed back and send her and her kid brother on their merry way. Without their father and his horses, they had no reason to ride all the way to Wyoming. Chance wouldn't be back from Santa Fe until late this afternoon. He wouldn't even have to know about the accidental marriage.

"Where are you going?" Skylar called as he yanked the door open.

"To find the wolf in shepherd's clothing who got me into this mess!"

The door slammed shut, rattling everything inside the small cabin, including Skylar's nerves.

"Sky, why didn't you just show him the deed?"

Skylar looked away from the rotted door and glanced at her brother. "I don't trust him."

"He's Chance's brother. Pa trusted Chance, didn't he?"

Her father had also put his trust in the man who shot him in the back and stole their stock. She bit back those words, saying, "Did you see the glint in Morgan's eyes when you told him our pa was dead? Did he spare a breath to offer us any condolences? He's no better than Randal, all too eager to leave us to choke on his trail dust while he steals us blind. Tucker Morgan won't lay a finger on that deed until our feet are on *our* Wyoming soil."

Garret's eyes clouded with fear. "You really think he's like Randal?"

Skylar released a deep sigh, trying to ease the tension Tucker's intense gaze had caused. His six-foot-plus frame certainly wasn't lacking in brawn, but she didn't truly believe he posed a physical threat. Despite his anger, he'd been quick to smile, the softness in his eyes revealing a sort of lightheartedness she wasn't used to seeing in men.

"No," she admitted. "He's not like Randal." Wade Randal was evil to the core. A chill shivered down her spine as she recalled the man's dark, unflinching eyes when he'd turned on her after shooting her father, giving her an ultimatum that was as unexpected as it was appalling—certain death or a life of sin at the right hand of the devil.

Choosing neither, she'd lashed her bullwhip across the chiseled features of his smug face, parting bronze flesh with a thick trail of blood. He had reared and howled with pain, giving her the opportunity to sprint toward Garret and the saddled Arabians.

"Don't fret," she soothed, seeing Garret's face still creased with concern. "Chance is bound to show up shortly and we'll straighten this whole thing out. Go on out and check on our horses. Make sure they get some oats and I'll cook us some breakfast."

"You think they'll let us ride with them to Wyoming?"

"They don't have a choice."

Garret beamed a smile as he stood to go do as she asked, his confidence seeming fully restored.

Her little brother's faith helped to ease her frazzled nerves. She wished she could share his confidence, but Tucker Morgan's reaction to the news of her father's death told her their battle was just beginning. If he thought they could be brushed aside, he was in for an awakening.

Skylar's tense muscles began to relax for the first time in weeks as she eased into the small wooden tub of fresh, warm water. She had already washed her filthy clothes and the dishes she'd used during breakfast. Now it was her turn to be scrubbed clean.

She quickly ran the soapy cloth over her arms as she drew in a deep breath and held it in her lungs. Lord, she loved the smell of soap. If she had a home, she'd take a warm bath twice a day. She'd have one of those long porcelain tubs she could stretch her legs out in and lie in warm, sweet-scented water until her skin shriveled up.

But I don't have a home, she silently reminded herself. During the last eight years she'd bunked in only a few wooden structures, for a couple months at a time. The dark sky or tattered tarpaulin tents were her common source of shelter at night. Her far-too-infrequent baths were taken in cold streams. Imagining her life any other way had been a waste of time and energy. During the last few years, she'd wasted a good deal of time daydreaming about having a real home…and a husband.

Her brief experience two months back had forced her to reconsider those naive dreams. She'd been a fool to think the intimate touch of a man would be any different from their brawny handling of livestock. Had she known allowing that smug bastard the liberty of a single kiss would have resulted in bruised lips and countless other bruises, she certainly wouldn't have stood there in the dark, leaving herself vulnerable to Wade Randal's sudden advances. Had Garret not come over the rise and shouted her name, Skylar was certain Randal would have attempted much more than the mauling she'd been powerless to fight off.

Thank God I don't have to learn the same lesson twice. Not that anything could excuse her gross stupidity.

She'd never even liked Randal, but having never been the object of any man's desire, she hadn't discouraged his attention. She'd let curiosity get the better of her, and she regretted it. She should have seen the black-haired demon for the snake in the grass he truly was. Instead, she'd been caught up in her embarrassment over their scuffle and had done all she could to avoid the man during the following month, as he secretly plotted to betray her father. Had she kept her guard up, her father might still be alive.

Leaning forward, she dunked her head into the water

and ferociously scrubbed the soap from her hair, trying to wash away the shameful memories. As she lifted her head, warm tears mingled with the cool water dripping across her face.

"You can't turn into a crybaby now," she scolded, swiping at the hot trails, fighting off the overwhelming sense of helplessness that had plagued her since she'd watched her father die.

She had to be strong for Garret. She had to focus. Too much was at stake. Yesterday she'd been exhausted, hungry and wholly unprepared for...*what?* Tucker's charming good looks and kissing skills?

That about summed it up. With a groan, she sank deeper into the soapy water, not wanting to believe what an utter fool she'd made of herself and quite thankful that Tucker had been in such an almighty hurry to undo their hoax of a marriage.

Brutality and guns she could have handled, but one ludicrous compliment, a dashing smile and Lord have mercy, the way he'd kissed her...it wasn't any wonder he'd sent her mind into a haze of confusion. He had held her with a gentleness and kissed her with a tenderness she hadn't believed a man was capable of, especially not a man of Tucker's size and strength.

He also muscled you out of the saloon. He certainly hadn't been flashing any smiles this morning. She'd seen the spark in his eyes before he'd left, and knew he'd been calculating just how fast he could get rid of them. She couldn't let that happen. It wouldn't happen, not while she had the deed in her possession.

The sound of a horse's heavy hoofbeats coming into the yard jolted Skylar from her thoughts. Tucker must have blazed a trail to town and back, because she'd not expected him to return so soon. They were a good hour's ride from Black Dog, yet she could swear he'd hardly been gone two full hours. Judging by the hard language carrying through the rotted wood of the cabin, things hadn't gone well in town, but she didn't have time to concern herself with Tucker's mood, her main concern being her state of undress as she sprang from the small washtub.

The door began to squeak open as she reached for the drying sheet she'd laid on the table. Frantic, she grabbed the clean skillet instead and flung it toward the door.

"What the—" Tucker's deep voice dropped off just before the door slammed shut and the skillet banged against it. "Skylar!"

"Stay out," she shouted. "I'm not dressed!" Wrapping the linen around herself, she hurried into the bedroom.

Standing outside, Tucker heard the bedroom door slam shut.

These Daines kids were a menace to society, and obviously hell-bent on busting his head open! After being laughed out of Big Jack's, he was in no mood to dodge frying pans. He didn't find one damn bit of humor in the news of his bride's assault against him, but the whole town of Black Dog sure did.

He waited a moment then carefully peeked into the cabin. The strong scent of soap hung in the air as Tucker scanned the perimeter for danger of flying kitchenware. Seeing that all was clear, he stepped inside.

"Is an iron skillet your weapon of choice?" he called toward the bedroom as he picked it up and dropped it onto the table. He didn't have a hangover, he had a *concussion*.

"You could have knocked first," Skylar called from behind the bedroom door.

"It's my cabin!" Although, it sure as hell didn't look like it. She'd taken over the place. Damp clothes hung from a rope she'd secured across the corner where the stove stood. More were draped over the two chairs she'd placed in front of the stove. She'd also been cooking. He didn't see any trace of bread or biscuits, but he detected the faint scent of baked goods amidst the scent of soap. Some fresh biscuits or maybe a couple of flapjacks could certainly help to ease his headache.

"Did you take care of the marriage?" she asked from the bedroom.

"Not exactly," Tucker bit out. He picked up a rag from the table and dropped it on a puddle of water beside the small, water-filled washtub. His gaze followed Skylar's wet footprints across the dingy wood floor to the door of his bedroom.

This woman is trouble. The sooner he unloaded her, the better. He turned his attention back toward the stove.

"Seems we'll have to ride up into Santa Fe to have it annulled," he said, scouting around for possible left-over baked goods. "Being a railroad town, they have a telegraph office. You can contact a family member from there. Since you're a friend of my brother's, I'd be happy to pay for your fare to wherever you need to go."

The bedroom door banged open as Skylar's sharp tone

shot through the cabin, echoing in Tucker's throbbing skull. "So you can conveniently steal our land?"

Tucker spun around. "*Your* land?" he countered, just before his eyes made contact with a sight that nearly brought him to his knees in a hard rush of unexpected desire.

The woman was half-naked! Standing there in nothing but one of *his* blue button-up shirts. *Dear God*—she had legs for a mile.

His eyes slowly worked back up those long, ivory limbs, then stopped on the hard piece of metal aimed at his chest. *Where the hell did she get a revolver?* Her thumb slipped over the hammer and pulled it back. Her steady hand and hard gaze told him she might know how to use the blasted thing.

"The only place we need to go is Wyoming, Mr. Morgan. Now, I suggest you wait outside until my clothes have dried. We can discuss our business arrangement then."

The Daines family certainly had a fetish for firearms and frying pans. But then, he had been gaping at her. What the hell did she expect with what she had on? "Don't worry, Miss Daines, I am a gentleman."

Her slender, arching eyebrows called him a liar, and Tucker felt downright insulted. "As soon as your clothes are dry, we'll ride into Santa Fe and get that annulment."

"No."

"No?" Tucker repeated, certain she hadn't comprehended his meaning.

Skylar drew a deep, calming breath as she felt the tables

beginning to tip in her favor. Her weak-minded mistake suddenly began to glow with appeal. Morgan couldn't cast her and Garret aside while she was married to him. "No. I won't consent to an annulment," she said, the cold grip of fear easing as she watched his face contort with surprise. "I believe I'm starting to like the sound of Skylar Morgan."

"Lady, what are you trying to pull? You don't want to be married any more than I do!"

True. But she knew leverage when she was married to it. "You can have your annulment the moment my feet are on *my* Wyoming soil."

"Damn it, woman! You don't seem to understand the situation. Chance only has one partner, and you're lookin' at him. The only reason your father had that deed is because he asked for it. He gave my brother some cockamamy story about needing proof that we intended to buy his horses and Chance trusted him enough to hold on to *our* deed."

He was lying! He had to be lying. Her father had plainly stated he and Chance were partners.

"It's going to take us weeks to get to Wyoming," said Tucker. "And besides the dangers from the land itself, there's plenty of bushwhackers and hostile territory between here and there. We'll have our hands full enough with my horses, without having to worry about a woman and a kid."

"My name is Skylar," she said, taking a step toward him, keeping her revolver aimed at his chest and damn near mad enough to shoot him. What kind of a fool did he take her for?

Tucker's eyes drew wide as he stepped back.

"You're the one who doesn't understand," she continued, struggling to keep a steady tone. "I know more about long drives and horses than you could ever hope to. I don't need to be looked out for by you or any other man. Garret is *my* responsibility. I look out for him, which means no green-eyed, gambling drunk is going to swindle us out of a partnership. Good day, Mr. Morgan."

Until the door slammed in his face, Tucker hadn't realized she'd chased him outside.

"Partnership?" *What kind of deal did Chance make with Zach Daines?* Either Daines had lied to his quick-draw daughter or Chance had lied to him, and that wasn't likely. Chance wouldn't have taken on another partner without telling him. So what the blazes was she talking about?

Tucker turned, gathered his horse by the reins and stomped across the yard toward the barn and corrals. Until he talked to Chance, he wasn't about to start the war promised in Skylar's bone-chilling glare. On the other hand, he had half a mind to march back into that shack and remind Mrs. Skylar Daines-Morgan whose cabin she was washing her laundry in, and whose shirt was draped over her long, shapely body.

Problem was, he was pretty sure which half of his brain was giving him those ideas. He'd never been so blessed mad, and fully aroused. She'd pulled a gun on him, insulted his honor and integrity, and still he found her sexy as hell.

He had to get a grip. "Knock it off!" he ordered, glaring down at his traitorous body.

"Tucker?"

Tucker's eyes snapped up and met the twisted expression of the boy standing on the other side of the fence.

"Who you talking to?" he asked as he hopped up and flopped a long leg over the rough wood.

Tucker felt heat rising up from under his collar as the boy straddled on the fence gazed down at him. "What are you doing in that corral?"

"Sky said to check out the stock, so I's doin' just that."

"Oh, she did, did she?"

"Yep," the kid replied, not the least bit intimidated by Tucker's hostility. Damn but that annoyed him! Where did these Daines kids get their grit?

"We're gonna be drivin' them together, so we need to be familiar with them."

"We haven't settled on—"

"Mr. Morgan, don't think you'll be able to brush us aside 'cause our pa got kill't. It'll take a whole lot more than yourself to keep my sister from claimin' what's ours."

The boy sure held a whole lot of confidence in his bossy sister, Tucker thought as the kid paused, shifting the brim of his hat and regarding him through squinted eyes.

"She's washin' our clothes, so you ought to steer clear of the cabin for a time."

"Last I checked, it was still my cabin."

The boy grinned. "She already kicked you out, huh?"

"She didn't kick me nowhere." Tucker scowled, still mad as hell that he'd been tossed out of his own house. "I don't take orders from overrighteous females."

"If you got a problem with girls givin' orders, you bes'

get over it. Sky knows her business about horses. She won't be buffaloed by no man."

"So I was told," Tucker quipped. And he had more than a problem with girls giving orders. He'd watched his stepmother lead his father around by his nose for too many years to let some parasite of a woman sink her hooks into him. Winifred Morgan had damn near sucked the life right out his father. Tucker had been twelve years old when his father joined the rebel army ranks, despite his wife's adamant protest. He and Chance didn't stick around to watch Winifred rave and pout; they'd set out after their father.

Something just isn't right when a man seems happier on a battlefield than he does in his own home.

"If them old mules is all you have, you ain't got shit for horses," the boy said, glancing into the corral at Tucker's packhorses.

"I have a nice harem of mustangs and a fine stallion grazing a couple miles out."

The kid flashed a grin. His eyes sparkled with interest. "Catch 'em yourself?"

"Sure did."

"They wild or green broke?"

"Wild as your sister," Tucker said with a wry smile. "They can be bridled, but I wouldn't put my hide on one unless I wanted my brisket cracked open."

The boy lost his smile. "You're right lucky I didn't have a clear shot yesterday, or I'da kill't you for handling my sister the way you did."

"Sorry about that," Tucker said, trying to suppress another smile. Garret glared at him, true anger burning in his eyes. Tucker held no doubt the boy would have shot him to protect his sister. "I was drunk," he said, as though that explained everything.

"Yeah, we noticed. I still don't see how you managed to marry Sky without her deckin' you."

Tucker knew how. He'd shocked the hell out of her, then he'd kissed her until neither one of them could see straight. Seemed getting unmarried was going to be the real trick. "You want to go take a look at those horses or not?"

"Yes, sir," the boy exclaimed, hopping down from the fence.

"Call me Tuck."

The kid's lips stretched into a wide grin, and Tucker's mood began to brighten. Seemed he'd won over one of his adversaries.

Tucker and Garret rode back into the yard a couple hours later. He spotted Skylar leading her saddled Arabian from the barn. The horse she held by the reins was one of the finest stallions Tucker had ever seen. His sleek black coat gleamed in the sunlight as she led him farther into the yard. Like Garret's chestnut-colored mount, the black Arabian had a look of speed and strength about him that would draw the interest of any horse rancher, yet Tucker's attention quickly strayed to the woman.

"Garret," Skylar said as they reined beside her. "We're in need of firewood if we plan to have a warm supper. Can you take care of it?"

"You bet, Sky," Garret replied without hesitation.

Tucker and Garret continued past her, dismounting in front of the cabin. Tucker glanced back at the slender woman adjusting her saddle, the revolver she'd pulled on him strapped to her hip. A shapely hip, presently bound in faded denim, as was her sweetly shaped backside. *She has no right to look so good in denim britches,* he thought, annoyed by the instant stir of his body.

Her golden hair glimmered as her gaze whipped toward him. The straight, clean strands hung just below her chin, encasing her pretty face. Realizing she was glaring at him, Tucker smiled and gave her a wink as he touched his fingers to the brim of his hat. Her gazed snapped back to her horse.

For all her fine physical features, Tucker imagined there was more fun to be had in a pocketful of rattlesnakes than any time spent with Skylar Daines-Morgan. "She always so damn bossy?" he asked, pulling his gaze away from her.

"Yeah," said Garret, his expression glum. "But it ain't her fault. There's no room for a soft trail boss in a cattle outfit."

Tucker felt his face twist with shock. The kid was serious. "She's a *woman.*"

"Yeah, well, that didn't start till a few years ago. My pa sure wasn't happy about it."

"He wasn't happy about what?"

"Sky bein' a girl and all."

Tucker was amazed at his comment as he followed

Garret toward the woodpile beside the cabin. "Kid, I can pretty much guarantee you, she's always been a girl."

"Yeah, but she ain't always looked like one. A couple years back, her and my pa got into a big fight. Sky said she couldn't help how she looked and that she wusn't gonna cut her hair no more. That's why we stopped drivin' cattle and started rounding up mustangs on our own."

Again Tucker glanced across the yard as Skylar lifted a pointed boot to a stirrup. She mounted her horse with a grace that echoed pure femininity, the swell of her breasts clearly visible beneath her ivory shirt and leather vest.

Boots and britches sure as hell wouldn't keep him from seeing that she was one shapely woman. A woman who had a profound and discomforting effect on his pulse.

"She told Pa she wanted to wear dresses and things of the like," Garret continued as Tucker watched Skylar guide her horse across the open ground. "She said she was sick of herding cattle and sleeping in pastures and she wanted a real house where suitors could come to call on her."

The boy let out a long whistle, drawing Tucker's attention away from Skylar. Garret's white eyebrows shot up as he shook his head. "I ain't never seen my pa so steamed. He wouldn't have it. They hadn't got along too well these last couple years. When Pa said we were goin' to Wyoming, she told him he could herd his horses straight to hell for all she cared. She was done with long drives. She refused to come with us until Pa showed her the deed and promised we'd have a home when we reached our land."

Was the kid trying to make him feel guilty? Hell, he wasn't responsible for the lies their father had told them. But the boy wouldn't let up. When they'd ridden out to check on the mustangs, Tucker had tried not to notice the tears in Garret's eyes or the tremble in his voice as he filled him in on the night his father had been killed.

All this sentimental rubbish made him...*nervous.* Not that he didn't feel for the kid. He and Chance had been twelve years old and standing right beside their father when he'd gotten shot in the chest during the War Between the States.

"How old is your sister?" Tucker asked, suddenly curious.

"Nineteen," Garret said as he picked up a log and set it on the chopping stump. "That dress she wore yesterday is the first one I've seen her in since our ma died." He shifted the ax in his hands as he met Tucker's gaze. "I used to feel bad for Sky, our pa not lettin' her wear dresses and all. But after what happened yesterday, I can see he had reason for doin' what he did."

"Let's get this wood chopped," Tucker said, avoiding Garret's hard look. "I sure wouldn't want to get on Skylar's bad side."

Chapter 3

The woman didn't have a bad side, Tucker decided upon close observation. She was damn beautiful from every angle.

He stood just beyond the cabin, where he'd been stock-still for the past ten minutes as he gazed across the yard, his eyes continuing to move over Skylar, watching her stretch, reach and bend as she groomed her horse inside the stable.

"I was gonna harass you for staring, but damn if I can pull my eyes away from her."

Tucker jumped at the sound of his brother's voice then glared at his own reflection. "By God, it's about time!"

"Who the hell is that?" Chance asked as he stepped beside Tucker. His eyes never wavered from Skylar, watching her work the brush over the stallion's shiny black coat.

"I should be asking you," Tucker replied, certain this entire mess was all his brother's fault. "According to the information you gave me, that would be Zach Daines's oldest son."

"You must need spectacles. That shapely creature is no boy."

"Didn't you know your buddy Zach had a daughter?"

Chance glanced over at Tucker. "Hell, no! I only knew his two sons, Sky and Garret."

"Sky is short for Skylar, and as you said, *she's no boy.*"

Chance's gaze whipped back to Skylar. "If *that's* Sky, she's had one hell of a growth spurt. I can't believe she's the same skinny kid I knew three years ago." He glanced back at Tucker. "I don't see why you're in such a snit. They're Zach's kids, let him worry about them. Or is it Zach's wrath you're worried about, if he catches you eyeing up his daughter?"

"I can't fear a man who's six foot under."

Surprise lit Chance's features. *"What?"*

"Skylar and Garret said they were hit last month by rustlers—killed their pa and stole their stock. They arrived with themselves and two Arabian studs, or didn't you notice all those empty corrals?"

A heavy sigh broke from Chance's chest as he pulled off his brown Stetson and shoved a hand through his hair. "Hell."

"My sentiment exactly." Tucker nearly smiled as panic replaced the amusement that had lit his brother's eyes.

"So now *we're* supposed to look after his kids?"

"Hell if I know. He was your friend. I never even met the man. I got sick of chasing the south end of longhorns at the age of eighteen."

"We're going to have our hands full with your mustangs, not to mention every horse thief between here and Wyoming."

"Don't I know it," Tucker said, nodding his head in full agreement.

Alarm tightened Chance's features. "Who has the deed?"

"She does." Tucker smiled, knowing the relief in his brother's eyes would be short-lived. He'd have an easier time getting their deed from the belly of a live grizzly than he would from Zach Daines's daughter.

"So, why didn't you just give your condolences, ask for the deed and send them on their way?"

"I tried, but she won't consent to an annulment."

Chance arched an eyebrow. "Come again?"

"You heard me."

"You *married* her?"

"By accident."

"By *what?*"

"Are you hard of hearin' all 'a sudden? I said I married her by accident."

"No, Tucker. You break a window by accident. You step in horseshit by accident, but no one gets *married* by accident!"

"Well, I did! I was over at Big Jack's—"

"Drunker than a skunk in a barrel of whiskey," Chance cut in, shaking his head.

"—and the reverend threw a marriage document into the pot."

"Gambling with a man of the church, no less."

"I had just won the hand when this angel appears outta nowhere."

"*An angel?* Damn it, Tuck, I told you bounty hunting was no way to make a living! Your conscience is affecting your brain."

"My conscience is just fine! I've never killed anybody

in cold blood, and we both know I shot more men at the age of fourteen than I have in the last twelve years."

A glittering glance from Chance revealed memories neither one cared to discuss. Memories of a childhood spent spying for military camps during the War Between the States after the death of their father. With a loyalty to no one but each other, they had moved with ease through military camps on both sides of the enemy line, relaying information and documents. But it didn't matter what color coat you wore in hell. Caught with incriminating documents, they'd been tossed into a place that made hand-to-hand combat on the battlefields seem inviting.

"She caught me off guard is all," Tucker said after a moment of heavy silence. "I'll admit I'd had a few shots of whiskey and Henderson stirred things up with that marriage document, and then this pretty blonde showed up beside me—"

"And you accidentally married her," Chance finished for him.

Tucker frowned at Chance's disapproving gaze. "Would you shut up and let me finish? Why do you always have to put a downward spin on everything?"

"The only one creating a downward spin is you, little brother. By the rate you're spinning, the heels of your boots must be gettin' close to the fires of hell. You better cut that angel loose before you drag her down with you."

"I tried! I rode into Black Dog, but Henderson had already caught the first stage out of town. So now we've got to have the damn thing annulled, but Skylar refused. She said she won't agree to an annulment until we reach

Wyoming, claiming our ranch is half hers. I explained the dangers of traveling through wild country, but the woman's stubborn as granite rock."

"And cunning as a fox," Chance ground out, shifting his hard gaze toward Skylar. "I've worked too damn hard these past ten years to give away half our land to a pretty lady." He paused, shifting his gaze to the Arabian. "That sure is one handsome stud she's grooming."

Tucker wasn't surprised by Chance's distraction with the horse. "The chestnut Garret's riding is just as impressive."

"Where did Zach find such rare horses in the States?"

"How the hell should I know?" Tucker scowled as he slumped back, leaning his shoulders against the rough wood of the cabin. "You said you worked with Zach and his boys down in Texas. How could you think his daughter was his son?"

"That was three years ago. I'm sure none of the other men suspected Sky to be anything other than what she appeared to be. A fine kid who could rope and ride with the best of us. Her hair was short and her shape was, ah...I guess you could say, *undeveloped*. Zach worked Sky as hard as the rest of his men."

"Her father had her driving stock?" Tucker still struggled to believe that fact. "Where was her mother?"

"From what I recall, Zach's wife took sick and died seven or eight years ago. Being the stock-drive foreman, Zach's kids came along. Garret rode on the chuck wagon, but Sky collected pay like the rest of us and he, or rather, she, earned it. Where's Garret?"

Tucker flashed a slight smile. "He insisted on rounding up the mares alone. I figured I'd give him a good hour to wear them out a bit before I go help him."

"Don't look like he needs much help to me."

Tucker followed his brother's gaze across the mesa. Garret was riding the chestnut stallion toward the cabin and holding three leads, each attached to a mare. "Well I'll be damned."

"Don't I know it. But it's your own fault. Marrying angels by accident," Chance muttered in disgust, shaking his head. "Seems we've been spotted by your angelic wife," he said, waving to Skylar as she walked toward them.

Tucker pushed away from the cabin wall and leaned close to his brother. "One more thing, Chance, before you rush off to greet her. Remember when I said it was a fool idea to send our deed off with Daines? Seems he told his daughter you and him were partners. Married or not, as I said just now, she believes half our land is hers."

Chance's eyes widened as Skylar approached them. His surprise confirmed it. Zach Daines had lied to his daughter.

"Chance," Skylar said, stopping in front of them.

Chance was quick to recover. "Sky." He extended his hand. "It's been a long time."

"It has," she replied, shaking his hand, her lips twitching with the hint of a smile. "I never knew you had a twin brother."

"I never knew Zach had a daughter."

Her frown deepened. She gave a slight shrug. "Minor family details, I suppose."

"Tuck mentioned you were hit by rustlers, lost your father and your stock. You have my condolences, Sky. Your father was a good man."

The instant shadow of sadness in Skylar's blue eyes surprised Tucker, and he realized he hadn't offered her any such sentiment in regards to her father's death. Another area where he hadn't handled himself very well. *Damn.*

"Thank you," she said.

Her thick tone pricked at Tucker's skin. She cleared her throat, visibly fighting moisture from her eyes. The show of emotion didn't last but a second.

"We need to discuss the agreement you had with my father," she said in a firm tone.

Any sentiment she felt over her father's death didn't compare to her determination to claim what she believed to be hers. Since Chance was the one who had hired Daines, he'd damn well better find a way to set her straight.

"I believe Garret could use my help," Tucker announced, and quickly started across the yard, leaving Skylar and Chance to hash things out.

A half hour later, he and Garret had the horses corralled. Chance and Skylar had gone into the cabin. Concerned, Garret headed inside, but Tucker opted to keep out of rifle range. He'd had his round with Skylar, and lost. He mounted his horse, preparing to round up his white stallion and the last of his mares when the cabin door slammed.

Tucker couldn't hold back a burst of laughter at the sight of Chance's rage-reddened face. He had to give Skylar credit. It took a stubborn soul to get a rise out of his twin. By the murderous look on Chance's face, he was mighty ticked off.

"I don't see a damn thing funny about this, Tuck!" Chance shouted as he stomped toward him. "I've never met a man with more determination than that woman. You do know what she's determined to get, don't you? Our land!"

"I know. Did you tell her about your contract with her father for the horses and employment?"

Chance stopped beside him and planted his hands on his hips. "I sure did."

"And?"

"She demanded to see the contract."

"Did you show it to her?"

"It's on our ranch, in Wyoming!" he shouted, sounding frantic. "She said she'd take a look at it when we get there, but until then, she'd take her father's word over mine. I swear, if Zach wasn't dead, I'd kill him! I trusted that man!"

"Skylar seems to share your good faith in him."

"And to compound our problems, you had to *marry* her. What the hell were you drinking? I thought Winifred had cured us both of ever seeking any prospects of marriage."

"She did," Tucker insisted. An instant tension seized his spine as the memory of his stepmother's yipping voice calling their father's name echoed in his ears, along with the unpleasant recollection of his father's simpering replies. *Sorry, Winifred. Right away, Winifred.* It was enough to make a grown man sick.

"Could have fooled me," Chance retorted.

Tucker imagined his twin felt slightly betrayed by his marital slipup. Not only had he broken their pact by getting himself hitched, he'd managed to marry a woman with a stubborn streak as wide and wild as the Rio Colorado.

"What are we supposed to do now, Tuck?"

He followed Chance toward the cabin where his horse was tethered. "She wants proof, we'll give her proof. Once we get to Wyoming she'll see she's wrong and we'll have the marriage annulled. If we gussy her up a bit she could land the first Wyoming man we meet for a husband. Problems solved."

Chance's scathing glare told Tucker he wasn't the least bit convinced. "It's a long way to Wyoming, little brother."

Chance hadn't calmed down one bit when Tucker finally led Rosie into the stable. Sick to death of his brother's obsessive complaining, Tucker felt his jaw clench with tension. Straining to control his temper, he focused his attention on the sunlight streaming through wide cracks in the west side of the barn. The bars of light flickered across his Appaloosa's spotted coat.

The old barn wasn't much in the way of shelter, having cracks just as wide in the rotted wood overhead, but he'd paid next to nothing to occupy this abandoned farm. He'd spent a week reinforcing the fragile shell of the barn just to be sure the whole shooting match wouldn't collapse on his horses when the wind kicked up.

"You've really done it this time, little brother," Chance continued as he led his horse into a stall.

"Would you stop calling me that," Tucker said with a scowl. He led Rosie into the neighboring stall. "You don't know which of us was born first. It wouldn't matter even if you did," he said as he started to remove his saddle. "We've been mixed up so often, neither one of us knew what name to answer to until we were old enough to decide for ourselves."

"It was me," Chance said with infuriating finality. "Did you know Zach was ransacked by one of his own men?"

"Yeah. Garret mentioned that. Backshot him, too."

"Sky seems to think Randal is still headed for Wyoming and plans to squat on our land. She says he knew we were waiting on Zach for the return of the deed and is hoping she got lost in the Arizona desert along with the document. He has big plans to keep those horses and our ranch. Maybe we ought to sell off your mustangs or set them free so we can get back to the ranch as quickly as possible. We're short over a half-dozen men, we don't have—"

"I'm keeping my horses," Tucker cut in.

"—Daines to break your mustangs or the manpower to drive them."

Tucker lifted his saddle from Rosie's back and tossed it onto the railing before he looked back at his brother. "I'm keeping my horses. I didn't just ride out one sunny afternoon and pick them at random, Chance."

"They're vicious and wild as hell!"

"*You* were the one who suggested we wait for Daines to gentle them!"

"That spotted mare nearly whipped you clean out of your saddle when you lassoed her," Chance continued, obviously trying to take the focus off the fact that this whole mess was all his fault.

Despite his irritation, Tucker smiled as he began to brush his horse. "That skewbald is a spirited one, and the best of the herd. She'll gentle."

A short, rueful laugh broke from Chance's chest as he tossed his saddle blanket and sheepskin over the wood railing. "By the time you gentle that mare, snow will be filling the Colorado passes. Your white stallion's no better. In the two weeks you've been working with him, he's given you more lumps and bruises than you've given him manners."

"He's coming around just fine. We'll get started with the mares first thing in the morning."

"We need to get back to our ranch, Tuck," Chance shouted. "We need to leave within the week!"

Tucker straightened, meeting his brother's hostile gaze. "I don't know why you're shouting at me. *You're* the one who hired Daines, then sent our deed off with him."

"At the time, it seemed the safest option. I was headed into the badlands to help *you* with that band of outlaws, remember? Zach had a whole crew of men for protection and I knew he'd get the deed back to us. He signed the contract. I never once doubted he'd be keeping the deed for anything other than collateral for our buying his horses. You're the one who married his daughter. Hell, Tuck, you *married* her!"

"Do you have to keep saying that?"

"I can't turn my back for ten minutes without you pulling some reckless stunt that lands us in a heap of trouble!"

Tucker glared over his horse at his brother. "We haven't been together a full two weeks and I'm already sick to death of your mothering. Well guess what, Mother Chance, me and my recklessness raked in the pile of money that started the horse ranch we've been dreaming about having since we were twelve."

"True, but there's more to running a ranch than playing with horses. You couldn't hold on to that place for a full year if I didn't do all the tasks that require sitting still for more than five minutes. When I arrived in Wyoming, you were nearly flat broke and didn't even know how many men you had working for us, or any documented financial records."

Yeah. And his system had been a hell of a lot more fun before Chance showed up with all his business protocol and bookkeeping journals. But, truth be told, Tucker wasn't keen on long-term responsibilities. He could read, write and tally numbers just fine, he just didn't like doing that sort of stuff, and he'd never been too good at making himself do things he didn't enjoy. Life was too damn short.

"Things will work out," he said.

"Things will work out?" Chance parroted in a dull tone.

Tucker sensed another fire-and-brimstone lecture coming on. Lord, his brother had surely missed his calling to be a preacher. He turned his back to Chance and focused on grooming his horse.

"I'd feel more at ease if I thought you were the least bit concerned about our situation, or haven't you noticed that all our planning has been shot to hell?"

"Would you stop being such a damn wake-chaser. So we've had a few shifts in our plans," Tucker said with a shrug. "Life doesn't always play out like those long, boring cattle drives you're so fond of, and a bunch of fussing and fretting isn't going to solve our problems."

"I have plenty of cause to be fretting, Tuck. You don't seem to be in a hurry to get back to Wyoming. A few months ago you couldn't wait to get off our place. Frankly, I'm beginning to wonder if you'll be able to handle being tied down to one place for more than a season."

Tucker's gut tightened in a painful knot as he continued to run the brush over Rosie's smooth coat. He'd been asking himself that very question, and he knew Chance sensed his restlessness. After spending the fall building a bunkhouse, stables and fences, he'd developed a serious case of cabin fever over winter. By the end of spring, he was all too happy to spend his summer hunting the band of horses he'd spotted while traveling through New Mexico the year prior, leaving Chance to run their newly constructed ranch for a few months.

But he was committed to his brother, to the pact they'd made to each other. He'd find a way to make it work. Leaving Rosie fed and dry, Tucker went to stand before his brother's stall.

"We may drive each other insane, but we're in this

together. I'll do what I can with the horses and we'll start for Wyoming within the week. We'll need supplies for the four of us. You want to take care of that?"

Chance gave a sharp nod and resumed grooming his horse.

"You better send word to the ranch when you go for supplies and let Zeke know Randal may be on his way. Trouble's a tad easier to spot when you know it's coming."

"Will do."

Tucker glanced through the open doors to the cabin across the yard. Cold, hard dread settled in his chest. "Chance, is she really as impossible as she seems?"

Chance met his stare. "As a ramrod no one questioned Sky's authority or skill, though none of us knew we were taking orders from a girl."

"Hell."

"Hey, Tuck?" shouted a voice from outside.

"In here, Garret," he called back.

Garret came through the wide double doors with a bedroll tucked under each arm. He stopped as he stepped into the shadows of the barn, his eyes widening as his gaze moved between Tucker and Chance. "Wow. That's plain spooky. One of you should grow a beard or somethin'."

Tucker glanced back at his twin standing inside the stall and realized he, too, had a day's worth of stubble on his chin. "We tried that, but neither one of us could stand having a furry face. What's with the bedrolls?"

Garret shrugged. "Figured I'd find a spot in here for us to bed down tonight."

"You can sleep in the cabin."

He tossed the bedrolls into an empty stall. "Nope. Sky said we're sleeping out here. She also said you two can come in and have supper."

Tucker whipped his gaze toward his brother. His lips stretched into a tight smile. "You hear that Chance? Skylar says we can go eat in our own cabin."

Garret snickered as he walked from the stable.

"What the hell are we gonna do, Tuck?"

"About the only thing we can do. Go eat supper with Skylar Daines-Morgan, our new trail boss."

Chapter 4

Skylar sat atop the fence outside the stable, watching a small beacon of white light blossom in the darkness. The orange sun began to slowly crest the eastern horizon, magically chasing shadows from the land. Pale streamers of light sprayed across the sky, replacing the nighttime stars with the warm glow of early morning, and transforming hidden patches of white into brilliant pink clouds.

Skylar saw no beauty in the colorful sunrise, only deception. Pink clouds were merely an illusion of light, just as her father's promises had been an illusion to lure her to Wyoming. The bitter reality of her father's lies crashed through her spirit with devastating force, filling her chest with such pain she hardly had room for breath.

Life seemed to be one big deception after another. Her father had never intended to build them a home. Zachary Daines had caused her plenty of disappointment in the past few years, but to her knowledge, he'd never flat out lied to her. *Why did he lie?*

To get the only thing that's ever mattered to Zachary Daines, her mind answered. The chance to see and roam a new stretch of ground. To do that, he'd needed her to tame his horses and look after Garret.

She didn't want to believe Chance Morgan's word over her father's, but when she stared into Chance's cold green eyes, she knew he was telling her the truth. The deed she'd safely sealed inside the rear facing of her father's Bible belonged to the Morgans alone, yet she couldn't let them have it. Not yet.

Drawing a deep breath, she shifted her gaze into the corral at Tucker's small band of anxious mustangs. She'd spent the last two years turning wild ponies into fine horses many cattle or cavalry outfits had paid top dollar for. Yet here she sat, with nothing to show for all her hard work and a little brother to raise on her own. How on earth was she supposed to take care of Garret without a job or a penny to her name? How could her father do this to them?

She had to get their horses back. She and Garret could at least make a start with the money from those mustangs. If they made good time and followed the trails marked in her father's journal, they could catch up to Randal in Wyoming. Although even if she recovered her horses, she still had the Morgans to worry about. As Tucker's wife, they could try to claim her horses without paying her one red cent.

Tugging at her leather gloves, she jumped down into the corral. There didn't seem to be a man on this earth who could be trusted, and Tucker Morgan had proven to be as deceitful as the rest. She and Garret had overheard every word of Tucker's plans to gussy her up and marry her off to the first Wyoming man they came across. Fuming, she had served a bowl of stew for herself and Garret, then dumped a handful of salt into the rest. She was here to train horses, not cater to a man who planned to trade her off like livestock.

She shrugged her lariat from her shoulder, catching the coils of rope in her gloved hand. Tucker Morgan had a thing or two to learn about women. By the time they reached Wyoming, he'd be begging her to stay on and work with his horses.

"Okay, ladies, who's gonna be first?" She scanned the mares, all of whom were stamping and snorting, making it clear they had no desire to tote a rider on their backs. Time they learned life didn't have a damn thing to do with what anyone wanted. If she was going to beat Wade Randal to Wyoming, they had work to do.

Pulling some slack through the knot at the end of her rope, opening her lasso, she glanced at the saddled brown-and-white mare she'd separated from the herd the night before. She'd spent most of the past evening assessing Tucker's mares, allowing them to become familiar with her and the sound of her voice. The spirited paint had caught her attention right off as she moved through the corral, pushing the others out of her way. Skylar had seen a few nips and cuts on some of the other mares, and figured the dominating brown and white was responsible for those injuries.

The headstrong mustang had been a handful just to haul into a solitary pen. She'd been a snorting, stamping beast while Skylar slung a saddle onto her back during the early-morning darkness.

I'll save the best for last, she thought, shifting her gaze back to the other horses.

Tucker stood in the cabin doorway watching Skylar lead a mustang with a light golden coat away from the corral. He wondered what she planned to do with the wild mare. The sun hadn't been up for a full half hour, yet she had already saddled two of the mares and apparently had plans to take an early-morning ride on one. A pair of fringed chaps clung to her long legs, the fawn leather encasing her shapely backside like a picture window.

He had a notion to tell her she'd be better off mounting an untamed horse inside a corral, but as he watched his wild mustang trot along beside her, showing no signs of protest, he decided to remain a silent spectator. The faint, soothing sound of Skylar's voice drifted back as she guided the horse farther away from the ranch.

As they walked deeper into the vast expanse of dry dirt, sage and chaparral, Tucker saw Garret riding bareback on his chestnut Arabian, all bright-eyed and ready to assist his sister. Skylar stopped a few yards away from him. Within the space of a breath she was on the mare, sitting tall in the saddle as she waited for the mare's reaction.

The mare seemed to be as stunned as Tucker by Skylar's quick jump into the saddle. The buckskin stood perfectly still for a moment, then began to sidestep, steadily working toward an all-out fit. Twisting to the right, the horse bucked its hind legs up off the ground.

After a few more sharp kicks, the horse planted its hind quarters on the ground, trying to dump the extra weight. Skylar stuck to the mare's back as though her denim pants were sewn to the saddle. She leaned forward and touched her heels to the horse.

The mare shot up and took off across the desert. He could see Skylar was trying to nudge the stubborn horse to the right. When the mare didn't respond, Skylar's left arm shot out, and to Tucker's surprise, a bull whip uncoiled from her hand and pierced the air with a sharp *snap*.

The horse veered right.

"I'll be damned." A smile tugged at his lips as he watched the woman and mare in sheer amazement.

"What the hell!" Chance bumped Tucker away from the door frame as he barged outside with his gun drawn. "I heard—"

"Skylar riding a mare," Tucker finished for him as he glanced at his brother's half-shaven face. "You might want to pull your jaw shut. All that sweet lather's bound to attract flies."

"She's riding one of your mares."

"She is," Tucker said, shifting his gaze back toward the open desert.

"She's got a bullwhip," Chance said as the whip cracked again.

"She certainly does."

Skylar continued maneuvering the horse in different directions, only cracking the whip when the horse didn't respond to her nudges. Garret stayed close by, riding a short distance behind her. After a few minutes of zigzagging, the mustang was catching on, taking its cues without being prompted by the crack of the whip.

"That's the damnedest thing I ever saw," said Chance as he holstered his gun. "Has she whipped the horse at all?"

"Nope."

"I told you Daines was known to be one hell of a horse trainer," Chance said, sounding smug.

Tucker laughed at the jubilant gleam in his brother's eyes. Seemed they had their horse trainer after all. "Maybe you ought to finish shaving before your lather starts to crack." Still needing a shave, Tucker followed Chance inside.

When Tucker returned to the yard the buckskin Skylar had ridden was tethered outside the corral, the saddle already pulled from its back. Not seeing any sign of the boss lady, Tucker approached the tethered buckskin.

"Easy, girl," he murmured, running a hand across her thick, golden coat. He inspected the horse's flank for any abrasions caused by Skylar's spurs.

The mare didn't have a mark on her.

"I didn't bloody your horse, Morgan."

Tucker glanced back at the woman standing behind him, her hands firmly planted on her hips, a coil of rope over one shoulder, her bullwhip coiled around the other. Narrowed blue eyes bore into him as he turned to face her.

Daines had either been a desperate man, incredibly brave or just plain stupid. If Daines hadn't been killed by horse thieves, he surely would have had hell to pay when Skylar reached Wyoming and discovered he'd lied to her. Thanks to Zach Daines, Tucker was left to deal with her wrath.

"I didn't accuse you of any such thing," he said in an easy tone. "In fact, I'm impressed as hell by the way you handled this mare."

"I'm just getting the job done. If you have a preference as to which horses you want gentled, say so now."

"After watching you, I wouldn't be surprised if you broke them all before we leave."

"I don't break horses, I train them."

Tucker didn't miss the sharp edge in her tone. "There's a difference?" he asked, fully aware that there was and quite certain of her position between the two. Yet he was curious to hear Skylar's take on the subject. Or maybe he enjoyed the incredulous expression that eased her harsh frown.

Her big blue eyes widened a fraction, her lips parted. *Full, pink lips.*

For a shrew, she had the most kissable lips he'd ever seen.

"You say you own a horse ranch?" she asked.

"It's a new business venture," he explained, which was true. He'd gentled a few horses in his day, but he was far from being a skilled trainer. His field of expertise was tracking vermin. "Are you going to enlighten me or stand there and silently call me an idiot?"

She took her time in deciding. Then those pretty pink lips shifted into a slight grin, and Tucker felt a true sense of caution.

"A spirited horse with good training," she said, "knows its job, can execute routine tasks with little to no prompting, and most importantly, has enough sense to know when a useless lump is riding on its back. A real intelligent horse will unload that useless baggage at the soonest opportunity. Pleasant creatures, really."

Skylar's tight smile told Tucker he'd been lumped into her *useless-baggage* category of riders. Although judging by her hostility, men in general occupied that category.

"A horse that's been broken," she continued, "has been bullied into doing its master's bidding. Convinced it's too stupid to think for itself, it relies on the rider for guidance. Unfortunate, and frequently disastrous. From my own observations, I'd choose horse sense over a cowboy's any day."

Tucker didn't doubt it. "Why didn't you take the spotted mare out first?"

Her blue eyes narrowed and Tucker had to fight a grin. She didn't like being questioned. He was suddenly overwhelmed by curiosity, his mind filling with questions he couldn't wait to have answered by his new horse trainer.

"She's the strongest, most ill-tempered of the lot. But don't worry, Morgan, she'll be gentled. I'll take her out just as soon as she wears herself out a bit more warming to that saddle. Like I said, if you have a preference with the others, say so now."

"Miss Skylar, you can go ahead and pick and choose as you see fit."

"Good." She turned her back on him and opened the

gate. Tucker watched her shrug the rope from her left shoulder and open her lasso as she spotted the mare she wanted. She tossed her rope, snaring the mare with an ease that came from years of practice. The kid hadn't been exaggerating when he'd said his sister knew her business.

"Morgan, are you gonna come take this mare or am I working alone today?"

He tensed at her impatient tone. *Lord, my brain must have been floating in whiskey when she walked into Big Jack's.* He wasn't about to let her walk all over him.

He entered the corral and held his hand out to take the rope. "Is calling me 'Morgan' a shortcut so you don't have to figure out which one of us you're talking to?"

"No, Tucker." She turned, leveling her gaze on him. "It's supposed to keep things formal between us."

Tucker couldn't fight his smile, a small part of him liking that she recognized him from Chance, and mostly amused that she felt she needed anything other than her sweet disposition to keep their relationship strictly business. He quickly tied the mare to the fence outside the stall and went to retrieve another.

"So, what's on the agenda, boss lady?" he asked, certain she had one.

"We'll separate twelve horses to be gentled. One of you can help Garret rig them with cinches so they can get used to having their barrels strapped before we toss a saddle on them." She grabbed another rope from a bundle on the fence. "The other can work with me."

Tough choice. But he'd never been one to take the easy way out. "What are *we* gonna do?"

Her gaze flickered up, and Tucker swore he saw a smile in her eyes.

Seemed he wasn't the only one who enjoyed a challenge.

"We get to teach your mustangs some manners," she said.

"And we'll work with the other eight tomorrow?" he asked.

Taken aback by his question, Skylar wondered just how much this handsome cowboy truly knew of horses. "No. We'll work with the same twelve tomorrow."

His pinched expression told her he didn't like that answer.

"Morgan, you can either have twelve well-mannered horses, or twenty that won't ride worth a damn. Your choice."

"I hope you don't think I'll be leaving the others behind."

Skylar hoped he didn't plan on arriving in Wyoming with all twenty of his mares. They had plenty of wild territory to cross, and his band of horses would slow them down, making it nearly impossible to travel without being detected. Four measly horsemen certainly wouldn't intimidate a band of thieves or hostile Indians into keeping their distance. Unsure of how Tucker would react to the prospect of such situations, she decided not to mention it. He'd catch on soon enough.

"You won't have to leave any horses. The others will follow the more dominant of the group, but we need horses we can ride. I won't put Garret on a wild mare, and I won't kill our two stallions by pushing them too long and hard. When I'm finished, we'll each have four horses, including our own mounts."

Tucker's eyebrows shot up. "You're planning on doing some hard riding."

"I plan to head out in two days and keep as fast a pace as possible."

"Two days?"

"I already went over this with Chance, and he didn't have a problem with leaving in two days. In fact, he seemed real pleased and said he'd ride out tomorrow to get supplies."

"You'll have twelve horses ready in two days?"

"I will." She waited to hear him say she couldn't. He surprised her by saying, "Then we bes' get busy," before he beamed one of his smiles.

She wished he wouldn't do that. With his freshly shaven face all bronze and shiny, and the scent of shaving lather strong on his skin, Tucker was already plain delectable.

Skylar turned away from him, her face warming from the ridiculous thoughts fluttering through her mind.

Delectable?

Good Lord. She'd gotten carried away with a single kiss and now she was thinking like a harlot. She'd been working and bunking with men most her life, yet not one of them had ever caused her pulse to stir or mind to spin by simply looking at her. But she didn't want a repeat of her encounter with Randal. She'd make it perfectly clear she had no such interest in Tucker.

What she needed was to get her hide on a wild mare and focus on work, not the green-eyed cowboy with a fallen-angel smile.

Tension eating at his spine, Tucker sat anxiously in his saddle, watching Skylar in silent fascination. After working with most of the mares they'd separated from the herd, he wasn't proud to admit he'd eaten far more dirt than she had. In fact, she was presently sitting on the only horse that had managed to toss her from its back. More than once.

The first time he'd watched Skylar's body slap against the unforgivably hard earth, his initial reaction had been to make sure she was all right. Before he could dismount, she'd jumped to her feet, dusted herself off and marched toward the mustang with a determination Tucker couldn't help but admire.

Hang on, darlin', he thought as the spotted mare dipped her head, digging her front hooves into the ground and whipping Skylar to another sharp stop. To Tucker's surprise, the mare didn't kick and thrash, but stood stock-still. Skylar appeared relaxed, her eyes narrow with concentration as she dug her boots into the stirrups and tightened her hold on the reins, preparing for another round of bucking.

The woman was amazing. She seemed to be able to predict the horse's movements. And her voice… Tucker damn near melted off his mount every time she used that soft, sensual voice of hers to calm the mares.

As if cued by his thoughts, Skylar began talking softly to the mare, attempting to reason with a creature that had proven to be as strong-willed as she was.

Tucker's muscles tensed as her sultry tone grated over his skin and curled around his senses. Needing a distraction, he glanced out at the wide streamers of pink streaking across the western sky, and doubted Skylar had even noticed the blush of sunset, her sole focus being the wild horse.

"Skylar," Tucker said when she was quiet once more. "You've got to be exhausted. What do you say we call it day?"

"I'd like to ride her back to the ranch." Her frown deepened. "But what I'd like don't count for spit, or I'd be chin deep in a long tub filled with sudsy, warm water."

Tucker chuckled. That had been another surprise. Though it was as dry as the desert floor, Skylar had a sense of humor, and she wasn't as impossible to work with as he'd feared. In fact, they'd worked really smoothly together all day. Of course, the only time she seemed aware of his presence was when they switched mounts, and even then, their verbal exchange was minimal, each knowing what needed to be done without prompting from the other.

"Suppose I should be happy she's letting me sit up here without trying to get me under her hooves," she said with a heavy sigh.

She clearly wasn't happy with the progress she'd made with this particular mare. The horse had only one direction in mind, and that was toward the setting sun.

Skylar had managed to work her in circles, but they'd been steadily moving west for the last hour despite Skylar's efforts to urge the horse in the opposite direction.

Tucker rode slowly toward her. "Put the lead back on her and you can stay in that saddle while I drag her back to the ranch. Perhaps after we walk her through the routine, she'll catch on."

Skylar did as he suggested and tossed him the rope.

When they reached the yard, Tucker dismounted and grabbed the mare by her harness. "I'll take her," he said as Skylar stepped down from her saddle.

"She'll be the first to go out in the morning."

"You got it, boss lady," Tucker said as he led the horse toward the corral.

A short while later he walked from the stable after finishing with the horses. He spotted Skylar leaning against the small single corral on the opposite side of the stable from the mares, where he was keeping one rowdy white stallion. Tucker had eaten quite a bit of dirt and sand trying to gentle that stud. "I hope you're not planning to tackle him before supper," he said, coming up behind her.

Skylar glanced back, surprising him with a slight smile. "Nope. He's all yours."

"Your face is starting to sunburn," he said, noticing how her relaxed expression enhanced the delicate features of her pretty face.

Skylar blinked, appearing confused by his comment. "What?"

"Your face, it's sunburned."

She dropped her gaze, clearly perturbed by the off-handed comment. "I'll borrow Garret's hat for a while tomorrow."

"You don't have one of your own?"

"I lost it the night we were ambushed."

"I'll have Chance pick one up for you when he goes for supplies in the morning."

"I don't want any favors from you, Morgan," she said, eyeing him skeptically. "I only want to get to Wyoming." She turned away from the fence and started toward the barn.

"Chance," she said as she passed his brother, who'd been walking toward them.

"Sky," he greeted in return, touching his fingers to the brim of his hat, but she didn't pause for pleasantries. She marched her tight little butt right past him and into the barn.

"Your wife sure don't like you a'tall," Chance said as he followed Tucker toward the cabin.

"So I keep being reminded. She keeps working miracles with those horses and she can cuss me clear to Wyoming."

"Amen to that," Chance agreed.

"Where's the kid?" Tucker asked, glancing about the yard.

"He headed in a little while ago to check on supper."

Tucker stopped in his tracks. "Who fixed our supper, you or him?"

"The kid. Stewed meat and potatoes again."

Tucker groaned. "If he cooks like his sister, we'll be better off heading to the stable and eating oats with the horses."

"Don't worry. I hid the salt. And I thought our cooking was lousy."

"It is," Tucker said as they reached the cabin. "But there's a hell of a difference between lousy and plain inedible."

While Tucker and Chance washed up, Garret set four places at the small table and began serving stew into the bowls.

"Go get your sister," Chance said as he sat down at the table. Garret set the pot of stew back on the stove then hurried out to fetch Skylar.

With only two rickety old chairs in the cabin, Tucker grabbed an empty crate from the floor and flipped it up on its side, placing it before an open spot at the table. "How'd things go with you and Garret today?" he asked, taking his makeshift seat.

"The kid talks too damn much. But other than that, he's just like his sister. He doesn't have any quit in him. You and Sky seemed to do all right."

Tucker reached toward a box of matches at the center of the table beside the kerosene lantern. Removing the glass globe, he lit the wick, spilling golden light across the darkening room.

"Only because she was too busy with the horses to hiss and spit at me."

"Then you bes' keep her busy, because we need her."

Tucker agreed, but hadn't expected Chance to come right out and say so. "Glad to hear your approval. As of this morning, she and Garret are on the payroll. Skylar needs a hat. See that you pick one up for her when you get our supplies."

"Fair enough. I'll put it in the ledger. I wish they'd hurry up," he said with a scowl, glancing at the door. "I'm half-starved."

Tucker's stomach grumbled as he looked at the bowl of steaming meat and potatoes in front of him. "You and Garret ate something at noon, didn't you?"

"Apples and dried beef don't fill a man's gut."

Tucker nodded an agreement, having inhaled the same dinner in between saddling horses.

Both glanced up as the door squeaked open.

"Sky won't be comin' in for supper."

"Why not?" Tucker and Chance asked simultaneously.

Garret's mouth dropped open, his gaze moving between them as he eased into the chair across from Chance.

"You'll get used to us," said Tucker. "Is she so put out by me that she doesn't want to eat in my company?"

Garret shook his head. "It ain't that. She's asleep. I tried to wake her, but I couldn't."

"Couldn't?"

"She ain't dead, but she's sleeping pretty solid. Can we eat?"

"She worked her butt off today," Chance said, then nodded toward Garret. "Bow your head, kid," he instructed as he propped his elbows onto the table and folded his hands. "Lord, we thank you for this food we're about to eat and for seeing us through another day. Amen." Chance grabbed a spoon and dug into his bowl of stew. Garret followed his cue, taking two heaping bites before Chance managed one.

Tucker muttered an "Amen" then stood. "Skylar should eat. I'll go see if I can wake her."

"Be careful," Garret called after him. "She can be a pistol when she's tired. She never opened her eyes when I tried to wake her, but she did try to kick me."

"I'll keep that in mind," he said, shutting the door behind him. With darkness quickly claiming the sky, Tucker walked across the shadowed yard. Stepping lightly into the barn, he spotted Skylar in one of the stalls across from their horses. Not certain if he should wake her, he crept quietly up to the gate.

Lying belly-down, she was stretched out on some fresh straw, her jacket balled up under her head, her face hidden beneath the folds of her arms. He wondered why she hadn't at least laid out her bedroll.

His gaze swept across the length of her slender body. After the way she exerted herself today, she didn't need to miss a meal.

He started to enter the stall then paused, noting a fine tremble in her shoulders. He heard a sharp gasp of air from beneath her folded arms and felt an instant tension move across his own shoulders.

Ah, hell. She's not sleeping, she's—

Skylar shifted onto her side. Tucker took a quick step backward into the shadowed corner of the barn as she sat up.

Sniffling, she shoved her hair away from her face. Tears twinkled like stars as they slid down her cheeks, capturing gleams of light filtered through the cracks of the barn.

He had to get the hell out of here! Two years of witnessing Winifred's frequent tearful tirades had given Tucker a healthy fear of fitful women.

Skylar drew a deep breath and closed her eyes, releasing a stream of silent tears.

After a few moments of listening to her even, steady breaths, it occurred to Tucker that not all women may be prone to tearful theatrics. Despite her glistening cheeks, Skylar appeared rather peaceful. And vulnerable.

She's got one hell of a poker face. Looking at her now, she hardly resembled the woman full of confidence and sass who'd spent the day working his horses. His gaze skimmed across long, golden lashes resting against pink skin that had seen too much sun.

Why am I still standing here?

With her eyes closed, he was wasting his chance to escape. He backed up as quickly and quietly as he could, and bumped hard into something solid. The rafters overhead creaked as he turned toward what should have been a clear path to the open door. In the dim light, he couldn't make out what he'd hit, until a large canvas sack swung back from the shadows and clocked him right between the eyes.

Pain shot across Tucker's face as the familiar sound of cast iron pounded stars into his eyes.

"Goddamn it!" he shouted, staggering backward. He clamped a hand over his nose as he slammed against the stall behind him.

Tucker blinked several times to clear his vision, his mind still registering the pain. He eased his hand away from his throbbing face. Crimson droplets of blood dripped steadily into his palm. *Son of a bitch!* Skylar's skillet had likely broken his nose!

Remembering she was also in the barn, Tucker suppressed a groan and glanced over his shoulder.

Skyar's wide, glistening eyes stared into his. Sitting on her knees, her lips parted, she looked as stunned as he felt.

Too late to run now. His gaze focused on tears still bright in her eyes.

"You okay?" she asked, swiping her hands across her cheeks as she stood up.

"Just dandy." He pinched his nose and tipped his head back to slow the flow of blood drizzling down his chin.

"How long have you been standing there?"

"Long enough to get a nosebleed," he quipped. *And a black eye.* The flesh around his left eye was growing tighter by the second.

A light trickle of laughter danced across his senses, distracting him from the pain. Opening his eyes, he was stunned to find Skylar directly in front of him, her blue eyes bright with amusement. She tugged a handkerchief from her pants pocket. "Let me see," she said in the sultry voice she used with the horses as she reached toward his face.

Tucker reared, keeping his hand clamped over his nose. "I don't—"

"Stop fussing and put your hand down."

Feeling like an idiot, biting back a curse, Tucker did as she said. He was instantly rewarded by the soothing glide of gentle fingers against his aching face. Watching the intent look in Skylar's eyes, he wasn't sure which made him dizzier, the blow to his head or the tender slide of her fingers across his nose.

"It's not broken."

"No thanks to your pack," he grumbled, while wondering how hands tough and calloused as his own could feel like velvet against his skin. "How many frying pans do you own, anyhow?"

Her light, musical laughter coiled down his spine, tensing his entire body as she examined the left side of his battered face. "I hung our gear from some old nails to keep it out of the way, but you seem to have struck up a courtship with our skillet."

Her smile was like her voice. Warm, sultry, *alluring*.

She must be too tired to be hateful, he thought, knowing her red-rimmed eyes were caused by more than tears. His gaze drifted across her face. Her skin looked as soft and pretty as a rosebud. And those lips… Standing so close, he could feel her breath mingling with his.

Tucker pinched his eyes shut. It would be wrong to make a pass at his new horse trainer, the woman he intended to unwed.

A woman who's after my ranch.

He suddenly wished she had kept her poker face on and hoped she'd be getting it back soon.

Focus on the pain. Not that he could feel anything beyond the fire pooling in his groin as her fingers tentatively probed his rapidly swelling eye.

"Luckily, you have a thick skull," she said, wiping a fresh trail of blood from his upper lip with her handkerchief. "Here. You may need this for a while longer."

Tucker opened his eyes and took the bloodstained cloth from her hand. "Thanks," he said, his voice so thick it barely scraped past his throat.

"No problem. You can keep it."

"I meant for the doctoring. You've got a healing touch that could make a man want to get hurt just to be petted by you."

Something flashed in her eyes, something close to fear. Her gaze narrowed, and Tucker realized his choice of words must have given her the wrong idea. Not that he was against the idea of having her soothing hands all over him, but he hadn't meant to announce it.

"You shouldn't go creeping about in shadows," she said, her features firming. "A man could get shot that way."

His gaze dropped to the gun still holstered at her hip.

Fun was over. *Thank God.* Much more of her coddling and he would have gotten himself shot for sure. "I wasn't creeping about in the shadows. I came to tell you supper's on the table."

She stepped back into the stall and latched the gate behind her. "I'm not hungry." She grabbed a bedroll and released the ties. "Shut the barn door on your way out," she said as she tossed the heavy blanket across the bed of fresh straw.

Even as Tucker told himself he should get out while he could, he lingered, knowing she should eat. "Skylar, you need to eat."

She flopped onto her stomach, fluffed her jacket under her head, then shut him out completely by covering her face in the folds of her arms.

What was he supposed to do now? Just walk away?

Beats standing here like a bleeding idiot, his mind answered. He turned away, careful to miss her pack this time, and left the barn. What did he care if she didn't eat?

Reaching the house, he was still pinching his bloody nose as he stepped inside. Garret burst into laughter before Tucker shut the door behind him.

"I told you to be careful," he squealed.

Not feeling up to giving any explanations, Tucker walked past the table and into the bedroom. Silently cursing the muffled laughter following him from the other room, he tossed himself onto the bed.

"Is it broke?" Standing in the doorway, his evil twin flashed a wide grin.

"No," Tucker answered, annoyed by what it took to put an upward curve in Chance's lips.

"What were you doing within arm's reach of her? You know she's a spitfire. The kid even warned you."

Tucker gaped at his brother over the top of the rag pressed against his nose. "She's a woman, for criminy sake!"

"She's a cowhand. You better realize she's used to being treated as such. Commenting on that pretty face of hers will only get you into trouble, and treating her like some delicate piece of frippery...well, it seems that sort of foolishness will get you a busted nose."

"Skylar didn't give me the bloody nose."

"Uh-huh. Am I supposed to believe you walked into the barn door?"

"She hung her pack from one of the nails in the rafters. I didn't see it until the damn thing hit me in the face."

Chance's grin returned. "This woman's damn hard on your health."

"Go to hell," Tucker mumbled.

"I'll be on your heels the whole way, little brother. Is she coming in?"

"No. She's…sleeping."

Chance turned and walked back to the table, telling Garret he could have extra stew.

Tucker stared up at the dark ceiling, knowing Chance was right. Despite her pretty face, sultry voice and shapely body that tied him in knots, Skylar was just another cowhand. He'd be doing himself a favor to think of her as such.

Hell. He'd being doing himself a favor not to think about her at all.

Chapter 5

Huddled over the tiny kitchen table with Tucker and Chance as they went over her father's journal, Skylar continually found her gaze drifting from the sketches of terrain to the sharp lines and intriguing planes of Tucker's face.

The swollen tissue across the bridge of his nose was hardly noticeable anymore, leaving only a dark streak beneath his left eye; a constant reminder of her humiliating display of weakness. It was bad enough he'd caught her crying; then she had to go begging for more trouble by constantly looking at him. She'd been chastised enough over the last few years by her father to know better.

You go flashin' smiles to the men and you're gonna find yourself under some rutting bastard and your belly swollen with child.

Her run-in with Randal had proved his point.

Randal had been full of crocodile smiles and smoldering stares. She hadn't thought she'd behaved in a promiscuous fashion toward Randal, but she hadn't blatantly discouraged his attention, either. During the few minutes he'd wrestled her to the ground, she hadn't liked his hard kisses or groping hands one single bit. She shuddered at the recollection as self-contempt churned at her insides.

She couldn't allow any such confusion between herself and Tucker. Fortunately, he hadn't looked at her in such a way since the night before last or mentioned the incident. For some reason, Garret and Chance seemed to think she'd been the one who'd bruised up his handsome face. They had harassed him all of yesterday, none of which seemed to bother Tucker. He made light of the incident, flinching dramatically whenever she was within three feet of him. But then, Tucker seemed to make light of life in general. She'd never known anyone who was so quick to smile.

She needed to get out of here. She found it impossible not to stare at him when they were in the same room, intrigued by his similarities to Chance, as well as their differences, which was why she tried to avoid being in the small cabin at all.

"Have you found a problem with my suggestion?" she asked.

Tucker turned the page and pored over the next two maps with the same intensity he had the others. "Not exactly."

"This is some journal," said Chance.

The slight upward tilt of Chance's lips caught Skylar's attention. Chance's personality was such a contrast to Tucker's. If they had any physical differences, she hadn't been able to pinpoint them. It amazed her that two men could be physically identical, yet so very different at the same time.

"What are we waitin' on?" Garret called as he barreled in through the open door. "The gear's all packed. Hey, that's my pa's journal." He stepped beside Tucker and dropped his elbows onto the table as he leaned toward the center.

"Kid, your head makes a better door than a window," Chance said in a dull tone.

Garret eased back and Tucker gave him a firm shove, knocking Garret off balance. Garret quickly found his footing and retaliated by slamming his body against Tucker, nearly knocking him off the crate.

Tucker laughed as he straightened and looked back at the journal.

Another difference, thought Skylar. Tucker was particularly kind to Garret, and *playful*. He didn't show the impatience she saw in Chance's expression when Garret hounded them with questions or rattled on the way Garret was prone to do. Tucker was—

Blast!

Realizing she was staring at him *again,* she shifted her gaze toward the open doorway. "We're burning daylight," she said with impatience. "Are we settled on heading northeast or not? We can bicker about specific passes on the way."

"You're sure these drawings are accurate?" asked Tucker. "I've spent a good deal of time picking my way across Colorado territory, yet this map is littered with passes I've never seen or heard of."

"My grandfather was a surveyor by trade and my father did some scouting for the military before he married my mother."

Tucker's sharp green eyes flickered up, making brief contact with Skylar's before he glanced back down at the journal.

Skylar felt as though she'd been physically touched. Something in the way the man looked at her sent a charge through her body that affected her mind. *Like a steer on loco weed.* She hadn't forgotten how intoxicating those green eyes could be, or how incredibly soft and gentle his lips had felt against hers. As hard as she tried over the past two days, she couldn't get the recollection out of her mind.

"Sky?"

"Yeah?" Skylar blinked, and simultaneously realized Tucker was staring at her and Chance had been talking to her. She dropped her gaze away from Tucker. "Yeah, that's the pass," she said, noticing Chance's finger on the narrow channel through the San Juan Mountains, hoping that was what he'd been commenting on while her mind had been off chasing rainbows.

Dear God, how long had Tucker been watching her stare at his lips? "If we take that pass, I estimate we could cut a good four days of travel," she said, trying to ignore the burning in her cheeks.

"I'm willing to give it a shot," Tucker replied. "What do you say, Chance?"

Chance muttered an agreement. Skylar closed her journal and glanced up. Tucker's eyes lingered on hers long enough to cause a series of flutters in her stomach, which spiraled up through her body and straight to her head when he flashed those pearly white teeth of his.

In a burst of motion, Skylar grabbed her journal and straightened away from the table. "Let's get to Wyoming." She started for the door, silently cursing the tingling surge she felt clear to the soles of her feet. Did he realize how incredibly charming he was?

Skylar groaned inwardly, disgusted by her thoughts. "Lord, I must be touched in the head."

He's not charming. He's arrogant, and he knows exactly what he's doing. The man was a flirt, plain and simple. He was the sort who flirted with anything female. She'd make it known she didn't care to be a part of any such behavior.

She stopped beside the spotted mare tethered outside the corral. The mustang snorted and flattened her ears. "That's the idea," she said, smiling at the hostile signals coming from the ornery mare. She'd keep it clear that she wasn't interested in Tucker's fallen-angel smiles.

"You're going to ride that paint?"

Skylar jumped at the sound of Tucker's rich voice then spun to face him. Damn the man! She shouldn't be feeling the strange sensations that swirled inside her whenever she caught his gaze. "Do you have a problem with my riding this mare?"

"No, ma'am," he said, raising his hands and backing away from her as though she'd drawn her gun on him. "You go ahead and lead the way."

Listening to his low laugh as he walked toward his horse, Skylar wondered what she was so worried about.

In the past three days they'd covered far more desert ground than Tucker could have imagined possible. Finished roping off the mares, Tucker followed Chance toward their saddled horses staked near one the few patches of sand not littered with cacti and scrub. In the distance, white dunes rose up against an opaque sky, making it impossible to tell where earth ended and sky began.

"Who's taking care of supper tonight?" Chance asked as they began removing their saddles. "You or me?"

"I'll give it a shot," Tucker said, figuring Chance could use the break after handling the chore for the past two nights. Skylar had made it clear that her job pertained strictly to the horses.

"Garret, *wait!*"

Tucker's gaze whipped around at the sharp sound of Skylar's voice. She ran toward the packhorses. Fifteen yards away, Garret stood beside a mule, releasing the ropes over a sack of supplies that more than doubled his weight. Skylar reached over the boy's head, grabbing a heavy pack before it took the kid to the ground. Together they eased the large canvas sack down.

Garret flashed a sheepish grin as his sister gave him a light scolding. The kid's smile brightened as she reached out and ruffled his white hair, saying something Tucker couldn't make out. Garret gave a sharp nod before running off to do whatever she'd asked of him.

Tucker grinned and turned back to his horse. He'd never

seen a kid idolize his sister the way Garret did. But then, he'd never known a woman like Skylar. A born taskmaster, she didn't have a speck of trouble maintaining his herd and distributing orders, all while riding circles around them and keeping a constant eye on Garret.

Two nights back she'd surprised Tucker again by relieving him of his night watch just after midnight. He and Chance had been splitting the late-night and early-morning shifts, but Skylar didn't cut herself any slack.

"I'll get a fire started," Chance said as he walked away with his saddle slung over his shoulder.

As Tucker finished with his horse, Skylar approached the saddled Arabian staked beside him. She drew a long breath as she stroked her hand across the horse's black mane.

Tucker figured three days of grueling riding and little sleep had to be catching up with her. As her hand drifted away from the stallion, her horse stepped back and nudged her arm with its muzzle, clearly wanting more of her touch.

"Spoiled rotten," she murmured, and stretched her arms around his big head, giving him a petting embrace she seemed to enjoy as much as the stallion. Her gentle smile didn't hide the exhaustion Tucker could see in her eyes.

The horse gave a snort of protest when she withdrew her caressing hands and stepped toward her saddle. "Chores first, you big hound," she said, tugging at the cinch.

"Can I give you a hand?" Tucker asked, moving beside her.

The second she met his gaze, her soft expression soured right up. "No. Why would I need help removing my saddle?"

"I just thought—" Tucker snapped his mouth shut, realizing he'd thought wrong. "Never mind."

Just another cowhand, he silently repeated. Normally, he wasn't so slow.

She turned her back to him. "Garret and I can handle the horses. You should probably get started on camp."

"Right." After three days of the same routine, he was beginning to catch on. He'd clearly blown any chance they'd had at being friendly that night in the barn. If she wasn't giving him orders, he was all but invisible.

Too bad she wasn't.

By sundown, Chance had set up camp and Tucker had charred a couple of batches of biscuits and scorched a few jackrabbits. He certainly hadn't done anyone any favors by volunteering to cook.

Serving what was left of the food onto two plates, he covered the second with a tin and left it by the fire for Skylar. He took his plate and sat beside Chance. Garret sat on the other side of the fire, reclined against an embankment of sand, his face fixed with a frown as he tapped his fork against a piece of overcooked rabbit.

"It's meat, kid," said Chance.

"You sure?"

"Fairly," Chance answered, in the midst of some extensive chewing.

Garret took a bite and grimaced.

Tucker didn't see how the kid could complain when their ramrod couldn't do any better. Hearing the sound of Skylar's approaching footsteps, he glanced through the darkness. Despite his efforts not to, Tucker watched as she walked into the warm firelight, not paying them any notice as she tossed her hat and gloves onto her pack and began removing her chaps.

She stood a mere five feet away with her back to him, completely unaware of how her feminine curves and long, graceful limbs were driving him to distraction. Her fingers worked the buckle just above the curves of her backside. Successfully freeing the clasp, she bent forward to unlatch the straps around her thighs.

Good God. He shifted his gaze back to the unappetizing food on his plate. Grabbing his fork, he began picking at the rabbit meat.

"Your plate's by the fire," he said when she'd folded her gear and tossed it toward her pack.

Firelight flickered across her blond hair as she whipped her gaze toward the fire. She spotted her plate then shifted her wide blue eyes toward his gaze.

Apparently she hadn't expected him to fix her a plate. "I figured if I didn't set some aside, your little brother would inhale the rest."

"Thanks." She picked it up and walked around the fire to sit beside her brother.

"Not a chance," Garret replied. "If I gotta eat this stuff, she does, too. Is this meat or bread?" He wrinkled his nose as he tapped his fork against a charred biscuit.

"It's a biscuit," Tucker answered.

"Tucker, I don't think the boy cares much for your cooking," said Chance.

"No offense or nothin'," Garret quickly put in. "I'm just not used to crunchy…*biscuits?*"

"I never claimed to be a damn trail cook," said Tucker. "I suppose you can do better?"

"*Me?* No. But Sky—"

Skylar's boot tapped against Garret's. Her stern glance instantly cut off the kid's words.

"Sky what?" Tucker prodded.

"Nothin'." Garret dropped his gaze to his plate and shoved a hard clump of flour into his mouth.

"Boy, are you gonna let her shut you up like that? What's she gonna do? Take you over her knee?"

Garret glanced up at his sister, a grin pushing high into his cheeks. "Maybe."

Skylar cracked a slight smile at her brother's answer.

The kid obviously didn't have any real fear of his sister, but he didn't offer any further comment.

Knowing Skylar planned to take the first watch despite her clear exhaustion, he said, "Why don't you have Garret take first watch so you can—"

"Garret won't be doing night watches," she interrupted.

"Why the hell not?" Tucker inquired.

"I could take a watch, Sky," Garret protested.

She ignored him. "Because I said he's not. It's not open for discussion. The three of us splitting the watch should be sufficient for all of us to get enough sleep."

Tucker glanced at Chance sitting beside him, who only shrugged his shoulders in response. Tucker's gaze moved between the disappointment in Garret's eyes and the sheer determination crackling like blue embers in Skylar's.

The kid wouldn't be doing night watches.

"Fine. I can take—"

"I'll take the first watch," she cut in again. "You two can debate the rest."

Skylar dropped her gaze, disengaging herself from further conversation. She didn't have to glance beside her to know her little brother was angry with her for interfering, but Garret hadn't buried any inexperienced cowhands who'd found themselves on the underside of a spooked herd. She had. As long as she was in charge of her little brother, he wouldn't be doing any night watches.

The weight of something dropped onto her shoulder. Skylar glanced to her right. From the corner of her eye, she saw a long black leg stretch across her tan vest.

Tarantula!

With a shriek she was on her feet, smacking the spider from her shoulder. Her gaze pinned to the spot of black she'd flung across the low-burning fire, she drew her revolver and fired a single shot. The bullet pounded the spider into the ground, spraying bits of sand toward Tucker, sitting a mere foot away.

"What the hell!" he shouted, jumping to his feet with Chance clamoring up beside him.

"Did you get it?" Garret asked.

Skylar's lungs burned as she tried to catch her breath, while silently berating herself for creating such a scene. She'd actually screamed. Her father would have had a fit over such a reaction.

"Get what?" Tucker asked, leaning over the tarantula she'd shot into a sandy grave. "It's a damn spider!"

Skylar cringed as she watched Chance's and Tucker's identically twisted expressions glance up at her.

Realizing she could have spooked the horses that were barely a hundred yards away, she stilled, trying to hear past the pounding of her pulse for sounds of disturbance and retreating hoofbeats. *It would serve me right.* The fact that she heard no such sound was pure luck. There was no excuse for the way she'd overreacted.

"Sky don't have much tolerance for tarantulas," said Garret, still sitting calmly on the ground, grinning up at the others.

Damnation, but she hated those hairy critters! More than the tarantulas, she hated having a fear she couldn't control. Anything with eight legs made her stomach churn and her skin crawl.

"You nearly shot me over a goddamn spider?" Tucker shouted. "If you'd have flung that thing a foot to the right, I'd have a hole in my chest!"

"Don't shout at me," she said, holding his stern gaze.

Don't shout at her? Tucker was two strides away from reaching out and shaking her until her teeth rattled. She'd scared the holy hell out of him. The woman was a lunatic! "You go popping your gun at every damn tarantula in this desert, and you'll bring every horse-thieving outlaw down around our ears."

"I think she hit it right between the eyes," said Chance as he squatted beside the spider.

Tucker bent down and scooped the spider into his hand and held it toward the fire to get a better look. The dead tarantula filled his palm, its twitching legs even hanging over a bit. Damn if Chance wasn't right. Seemed their ramrod was also handy with a side iron. Seeing Skylar take a step back, he said, "Hold your fire, boss lady. You killed it."

Skylar turned and ran from the campsite.

"What the hell is she doing now?"

"Sounds to me like she's puking her guts out," Chance said mildly, the unmistakable sound echoing back from the darkness.

"I saw her turn her nose up at a diamondback rattle-snake today when we stopped to rest the horses, yet she can't stand the sight of a spider?"

"You ever have one of those spiders crawl up your pant leg while you were sleeping?" asked Garret.

Tucker tossed the tarantula into the fire then shifted his gaze toward Garret sitting with his plate resting on his long, folded legs. "Sky did? No kidding?"

"Yeah. A few years ago. She woke up and swatted at something itchin' her leg, and that's when it bit her. She let out a scream and whipped her pants clean off, right there in the middle of camp. My pa gave her a real hard time for carryin' on like she did in front of the men. The crew made cracks for weeks about Sky dancin' and screamin' like a girl. Which was sorta funny," Garret said with a grin, "'cause she is a girl."

"Hell, having a spider that size sink its fangs into you would cause any man to howl and jump about," Tucker said as he sat back down and picked up the plate he'd tossed aside.

Garret shrugged. "Don't matter. Bein' smaller than most

the men, Sky has to keep her wits about her if she intends to keep their respect."

"From what I recall," said Chance, "Sky never had trouble keeping any man's respect. After the way she beat the tar out of that smart-mouthed cowhand who knocked her from her horse after she fired him, no one could question her ability to throw a good punch. If I'd known she was a girl, I'd have been real impressed."

Tucker couldn't believe his ears. "She fought a man?"

"Sort of," said Chance. "The kid she fired couldn't have been more than eighteen. Your typical wiseass who thinks he knows it all and can't follow orders. He'd been harassing her for days, challenging her authority. He may have gotten in the first punch, but once she was on her feet, he didn't do nothin' but bleed. She pulled his saddle from the mare he'd been riding and said she'd fire any man who had a problem with leaving him behind." Chance grinned. "Zach had to be glowing with pride that day."

"She couldn't have been but sixteen," Tucker protested.

"There about," Garret agreed, his pale blond hair glowing in the firelight.

"I'm sure Zach would have stepped in if he thought she couldn't handle herself," Chance said as he tossed another log into the fire, sending a spray of orange embers swirling up into the night air. "Wouldn't have looked good for Sky, though, and it's not like we all haven't had a few busted lips and bruised ribs from working with cattle."

Chance's reasoning didn't keep Tucker from being appalled by the thought of Skylar having to defend herself against a man. He'd worked a few cattle drives and knew how rough-and-tumble a crew could be. As a young girl, she had to have been terrified when her father tossed her into such a mix of men. Rage warmed his blood at the thought of Skylar fending for herself with rowdy cowhands with her father standing idly by, allowing such incidents to take place.

"You look like you're about to murder someone," Chance said as he sat beside him.

"The more I learn of Daines," Tucker said in a low growl, "the less I like him. What kind of a father raises his daughter around a bunch of cowpokes? What made you hire Daines, anyhow?"

"I said he was good with horses, not kids. We needed a horse trainer, not a damn nanny. You're mighty worked up over something that had nothing to do with you. What's gotten into you?"

Tucker wasn't really sure. He guessed being responsible for Skylar and Garret for the time being made them his concern. The woman *was* his legal wife.

But Chance was right, he thought, noticing the tension in his muscles. What difference did it make to him if Skylar had boxed with cowpunchers? He was allowing his mind to be jumbled by a woman who'd just as soon shoot him than look at him.

From the corner of his eye, he saw a figure emerge from the shadows. Skylar walked into camp, her narrowed eyes pinned on Garret. Tucker gathered she'd heard part of the conversation and wasn't happy about having any of those past incidents revealed.

"You all right?" he asked, noticing her chalk-white complexion, then realized he'd done it again. He was starting to act like Chance, fussing and fretting about every little thing.

"I'm fine." She grabbed her hat and chaps and started in the direction of the horses.

"You haven't eaten," he called after her.

"Worry about someone else, Morgan," she called back as she disappeared into the darkness.

Chance's low chuckle put the pinch back in his muscles.

He wasn't worried! It was an observation. Anyone could see the woman was exhausted. The last thing he needed was for her to get sick from malnutrition.

She's capable of looking out for herself. He needed to get that through his head.

His gaze collided with the pot of coffee beside the fire.

"Kid," he said to Garret, "you better take your sister her plate and a canteen full of coffee. I don't want her falling asleep during her watch."

Garret shot to his feet, and Tucker told himself he was concerned about his horses, not Skylar…but he wasn't sure he believed it.

Chapter 6

Riding a wide stretch of ground between straight cliffs and a deep gorge, Tucker reflected that the Colorado countryside took some work out of herding the horses. His gaze swept across the land as his white stallion plodded along the left side of the herd, shadowed by the steep ridge. As they rounded a sharp bend in the cliff, he spotted a dozen or more tall wooden structures adorned with feathers and strands of beads rising up from the flat land on the other side of the ravine.

Indian burial ground.

Not seeing any buzzards flocking overhead in the clear sky, he figured the bodies laid out on the high trellises had been there for a time. Hopefully they'd been left behind by a migrating band of Indians who'd long since moved on.

Glancing back toward the horses, his gaze homed in on their trail boss heading up the herd. They'd been traveling together for over a week, but Tucker had a feeling he could travel with this woman for years and never get used to her presence.

No matter how hard he tried to think of Skylar as just another foreman, he couldn't do it, being all too aware that she was a woman. A damn pretty and desirable woman. A woman who took offense to any type of offered assistance from a man. He continued to irritate her by showing her the slightest bit of courtesy.

I need to find myself some female company, he thought, his gaze following the slight sway of Skylar's body. It wasn't healthy for a man to be in a constant state of arousal. He'd never had the problem before, but then he'd never been in the company of a beautiful woman for any length of time, either. In fact, the only time he was around women at all he was usually naked or about to get naked.

Damn. That had to be it. His body expected some gratification, and not even Skylar's cold attitude toward him had convinced it otherwise. Finding some relief in a woman could certainly help to take the edge off.

Aw, hell. I'm married to Skylar. Would finding company for the night make him an adulterer? What the hell good was having a wife if he couldn't bed her!

"Amazing, isn't she?" Chance said from behind him.

"Yeah," Tucker answered absently, his gaze still locked on Skylar's slender back.

"Stay away from her, Tuck."

Shocked by the low warning, Tucker whipped his gaze toward his brother, who sat relaxed in his saddle, his expression dead serious. "What's that supposed to mean?"

"Just what it sounds like. She's not a pretty widow lady itching for a quick tumble or a seasoned temptress whose company can be bought. She's a woman with a legal claim on our name and bent on claiming half our land. Be sure you keep that in mind."

"I don't need to be told."

"By the way your eyes have been stuck to her this past week, I say you do."

"The heat must be getting to your head. I'd have better luck roping the moon than bedding that shrew. Her eyes spark with a lethal glint every time she looks in my direction."

Chance wanted to trust Tucker's reassurances, but he'd seen Sky look at Tucker with a glint in her eyes that didn't have anything to do with anger, but could be twice as lethal. "Has she once called you Chance or mixed us up in any way?"

"No."

"Don't you find that strange?"

"Yeah. But I also had a black eye last week, taking the guesswork out of who's who."

"You're sure nothing happened between you two before I got to that cabin?"

A bark of laughter leaped from Tucker's chest. "I'm still living, ain't I? Why would I fuss with her gnashing teeth and sharp claws when I can have the delicate flower of my choice in any town from here to Wyoming?"

"Maybe because you *married* her. Don't try to convince me that you're not taken by her."

"That's the only way any man would bed her, with *her* doing the taking. If you'll recall, I was drunk when I married her, before she opened her mouth and started calling all the shots. Not that I have a problem with a woman having her turn in the saddle, but the only place that woman would ride me is straight to hell."

Chance started to speak then snapped his mouth shut. He'd be a damn fool to point out that he'd caught Sky watching Tucker damn near as often as he'd been watching her. That knowledge would only give Tucker the confidence he needed to pursue her, and screw things up worse than they already were. Discretion had never been Tucker's strong suit, and Chance held no doubt that the *only* reason Tucker wasn't trying to seduce the feisty beauty was Skylar's harsh attitude toward him.

That wasn't enough to ease his worries. "I want your word, Tuck, that you'll keep your hands off of her."

Tucker reined his white stallion to a hard stop and gaped back at him. "Are you serious?"

Chance reined in beside him. "She's not a fast woman who'd take a roll in the hay lightly. I wouldn't doubt that she's completely untouched. I don't want you getting a mind to tame her."

"You talk about her like she's a wild mare. Although now that I think about it," Tucker said with a wide grin, "she behaves more like a wild mustang than a woman."

"Then you'll have no problem giving me your word."

"Fine, I give my word," said Tucker, laughing as he urged his horse forward.

Chance has lost his mind.

As Tucker caught up with the horses a glint of sunlight coming from the steep hillside caught his attention. He spotted a man crouched in a thick patch of low shrubs on the hillside, aiming a rifle toward the herd.

"Sniper!" Tucker shouted the warning as he reached for the rifle in the scabbard at the side of his saddle and fired off a shot as the sniper did the same. Another gunshot from farther down the hillside pierced the air like an echo.

Tucker whipped his gaze toward the horses just in time to see Garret's horse go down, tossing the boy from his saddle.

Son of a bitch! Someone had tried to shoot the kid!

Chance began returning gunfire as Tucker set his white stallion into a hard run, weaving through the mares stampeding toward Garret.

At the center right side of the herd, Garret was in the direct path of the spooked mares. He struggled to his feet, doing his best not to get trampled. Tucker saw the relief in Garret's wide eyes as the kid spotted him riding toward him. He instantly widened his stance, preparing to leap onto the back of Tucker's mount. Tucker wrapped his hand around his saddle horn. Leaning down, he grabbed the kid by the arm and yanked him up. Garret shifted into place behind him.

"Hang on," Tucker shouted.

Garret latched an arm around his waist and pointed straight ahead. "My horse took off into that ravine."

Tucker guided his stallion down the steep slope, into the muddy bottom of the deep gulch. "Get down," he said to Garret as they jumped from the saddle. Garret landed right beside him in the mud, his thin arms sinking into the thick sludge clear up to his elbows.

They weren't going to have too much trouble rounding

up the other horses. Most of them had taken shelter in the ravine and were headed upstream.

In the midst of the gunfire, Tucker climbed the steep incline to check the positions of Chance and Skylar. As he reached the top, Chance tumbled over the side.

"There was two of them," Chance said, crawling up beside him. "One left."

"Where's Sky?" asked Garret as he moved between Tucker and Chance.

"Keep your head down, kid!" Tucker placed his palm on the boy's scalp before he could peek over the ridge. "Did you see Skylar?" he asked his brother.

"She dived off her horse the second you shouted 'sniper.' She popped up with a rifle in her hands and shot down whoever had taken a crack at her."

"Was she hit?"

"I don't think so."

"You don't know for sure?" asked Tucker.

"Hell, I was busy trying not to get shot myself! The way she responded to your warning and took out that gunman told me she's not new to being ambushed."

Hearing rifle fire he thought to be hers, Tucker looked over the ridge.

Skylar stepped out from behind the wide trunk of a lone oak tree a good thirty yards from the ravine, firing her rifle as she sprinted across the open ground. Instead of moving toward safety, her long strides were taking her closer to the location of the other gunman.

"Damn crazy woman!" Tucker shouted.

Firing another shot, she dived behind a large boulder.

Tucker dropped down as a bullet kicked up dirt just a foot away, letting him know the sniper hadn't forgotten about them.

"That rotten bastard is shooting at my sister!"

Tucker grabbed Garret by the back of his shirt before he could stick his head up again. "Damn it, kid, I said stay down! One crazy Daines is all I can deal with!"

The next three shots that rang out didn't sound like rifle fire. "She's using her revolver," Tucker said.

"Her rifle must be out of ammo," said Chance.

Tucker's gut began to burn with tension. Things were going from bad to worse. "Stay down," he said to Garret before he lifted his rifle to the top of the ridge and added to her gunfire.

Scanning the hillside, shooting at the clusters of sagebrush and manzanita, he couldn't see the gunman, but he didn't have to know the man's exact location to know he had the upper hand. From his high vantage point, he was out of range of Skylar's revolver, and without her rifle, Skylar was a sitting duck.

"You happen to notice we're near a burial ground?" Chance asked as Tucker dropped back down to reload his gun.

"Yeah," Tucker said, glancing at the opposite side of the gorge.

"All this gunfire is bound to attract attention," Chance said in a low tone. "Disrespecting their dead is sure to stoke some rage. We'll be lucky not to all end up staked out in some Ute or Apache camp."

"Not if we get the hell out of here," Tucker said, passing his rifle to Chance. "You and Garret lead the horses farther up the ravine. I'll help Skylar."

"How are you going to—"

Before Chance finished his question, Tucker scrambled over the edge of the ravine shouting, "Cover me!"

"Tucker!" Chance gave a curse and started shooting.

Chapter 7

Her back pressed against the boulder, fire burned inside Skylar's left shoulder. Morgan's rifle fire was giving her a bit of a reprieve from the fragments of rock that showered off the top the boulder when the gunman began shooting. With her target out of range, her long gun out of ammo, and a revolver that was doing little more than making noise, she figured she might as well check her wound.

Gritting her teeth, she lifted the side of her leather vest and glanced down at the bloodstained hole in her shirt. The bullet had whizzed right under her vest as she dived from her horse, lodging itself deep in her shoulder. The wound hadn't bled much. Her shoulder burned, but the pain was surprisingly tolerable, which she took to be a good sign. She tugged her bandanna from her neck then ripped at the bullet hole in her shirt.

She poked the cloth into her wound to prevent any further bleeding and swallowed a cry from the sting. Hearing what sounded like someone approaching, she dropped her vest and raised her revolver.

"Tucker!" she shrieked as he collided against her.

Despite the jolt of pain, Skylar felt a rush of relief as Tucker's arms closed around her, clamping her against his broad chest as he gained his balance.

"Hey, darlin'," he said, easing back as he sat beside her. "That shotgun out of shells?"

His light tone didn't belie the true irritation burning in his eyes. "Yeah," she said with reluctance.

"Then what the hell do you think you're doing trying to rush that gunman?" He dipped his hand into his vest pocket and held out a handful of ammo.

Skylar ignored his stern gaze as she loaded her gun. "Where's Garret?"

"With Chance, down in the ravine about thirty yards east of this rock. You really should be worrying about yourself right now." Counting off Chance's shots, Tucker peeked up over the rock and scanned the dense patches of shrubs tapering down the hillside. He didn't spot a damn thing before he was forced to drop back down.

Skylar's gaze locked with his and he knew the intense worry in her eyes had nothing to do with concern for herself. "The kid's not hurt," he assured her, although he hadn't exactly stopped to ask the boy if anything was damaged or broken.

"Thanks for going after him the way you did."

Fragments of rock scattered over their heads as more gunfire rang out across the sky. Tucker grabbed her and shifted their positions. When the gunfire ended, Skylar lifted her head and found herself sitting between Tucker's raised knees, his arms clamped around her middle. He'd been holding her against him as he curled forward, shielding her with his body.

Stunned, she looked up at the man behind her and realized anew just how large Tucker truly was. No wonder he'd pulled her between his legs. The breadth of his shoulders was twice the span of her own, making the large boulder barely wide enough to give him adequate shelter.

"So, what's his position?" Tucker asked.

"Do you think he'd still be chipping away at this damn rock if I knew that? I can't exactly pop my head up to see which patch of scrub he's hiding behind when he starts shooting."

The sound and feel of Tucker's low chuckle confused her. She hadn't been joking.

"Now that you've got that rifle loaded, let's see if we can't flush him out," he suggested. "You shoot, I'll scout."

Skylar nodded. Shifting position, she raised the barrel to the top of the boulder. She fired in the direction she believed the man to be hiding. She fired off a few rounds, her shoulder burning with each blast. Just before dropping back down for cover, she paused, seeing a single spray of light flash from a thick cluster of brush high on the ridge. Higher than she would have guessed him to be.

"Tucker—"

"I saw it," he said, tugging her back down behind the shelter of the rock. He hugged her against the center of his body as more bullets pounded into their boulder.

"Hand me your rifle, angel," he instructed.

Without question, Skylar set her rifle into the palms stretched out on either side of her and prayed Tucker's skill matched the confidence reflected in his deft movements as he shoved another shell into the chamber. In the next second Tucker sprang up and fired a single shot.

Skylar peeked around the rock as a man began to tumble down the cliff. The large body rolled end-over-end down the steep hillside before dropping some thirty feet and thudding against the hard ground a couple yards away from them. If Tucker's bullet hadn't killed the man, the fall certainly had.

Tucker reached back, grabbed her by the hand and tugged her to her feet, pulling her after him as he strode toward the unmoving body. His eyes widened with surprise as he stopped.

"I'll be damned," he said, staring down at the man.

"You know him?" Skylar's gaze flickered across the mangled face long enough to recognize him as one of Randal's men. He'd ambushed her camp the evening her father was killed.

"A mercenary," Tucker said. "We crossed paths a couple years back when we were after the same bounty."

Skylar's head snapped up. "You're a bounty hunter?"

"Past tense, honey. I used to *apprehend* outlaws for bounty. I wasn't a murderer like this one. Did you recognize the other gunman?"

Skylar looked into Tucker's hard green eyes and realized she'd never seen him truly angry before. For the first time, she saw how folks could mistake him for Chance. The thought sent a chill across her skin. "No," she answered. "I was running for cover when I shot him."

"What about this one? You recognize him?"

"He's one of Randal's men."

"That explains why they had you and Garret in their sights. Let's hope Randal only sent two of his cronies to tie up his loose ends."

Before Skylar could respond, a rumbling sound coming from overhead drew her attention. *Horses.* Judging by the rumble rolling down from the hillside, their gunfire had drawn quite a crowd.

Tucker heard it, too. A look of deep concentration came into his eyes. His large hands gripped her waist and hauled her against his side. Skylar was yanked off her feet as he darted toward the cliff. Tucker took a few long strides before he brought her feet to the ground. "Run!" he ordered, his eyes scanning the broad side of the cliff.

"What about Garret and—"

"They should be down far enough in that slick ravine to not be spotted."

"The two bodies—"

"They can have their scalps," he said, tugging her by the sleeve so she didn't fall behind, "but I'm quite partial to mine."

They ran along the steep drop of dirt and rocks, none of which would provide any cover from the riders nearing the edge of the ridge.

"There," Tucker said, pointing to a crack in the hillside. A large slab of stone stuck out over the top of the gap.

Skylar gauged the width of the narrow crevasse and doubted they'd both fit into such a small space. "There's no room."

"We'll make room."

Tucker placed her into the crack and piled in behind her. Skylar growled his name. Right now Skylar's temper wasn't nearly as threatening as a band of hostile warriors looking to see who was disturbing their dearly departed. Although, the mumbled curses falling from her lips did give a man pause.

"Darlin', I'm not enjoying this any more than you are," Tucker whispered near her ear, hoping the Lord wouldn't strike him down for lying straight through his teeth. His temporary wife had the power to bring out the evil in him because he was enjoying the hell out of having her snuggled up against him, knowing full well he was the last man she wanted to have pressed against her tight little butt.

Sweet God, but her long body was a perfect fit to his. *Too perfect.* The swell of her backside pressed against his groin was far too arousing.

"If you plan to breathe, you might want to turn around," he suggested.

"No!" she whispered.

"Turn around here before you get a mouthful of the mountainside." Taking a firm hold on her waist, he turned her so that she faced him.

Wide blue eyes locked with his. Her eyes grew even wider as he pressed her back against the cliff until their bodies were meshed together, her cheek pressed against the bend of his neck. Skylar's startled expression flooded his mind with the memory of the kiss they'd shared all those days back, the taste of her sweet mouth, the feel of her hot little tongue moving over his.

Holy hell.

Tucker heard the catch in her breath, felt her body shudder, and knew she'd felt the rapid stir of flesh he was powerless to hide.

"Sky—"

"*Shut up,* Morgan," she breathed against his neck. "Just…don't talk."

Tucker decided to follow her advice and hoped she'd do the same. But the feel of her breath against his skin wasn't doing a damn thing to discourage his aroused response.

To Skylar's relief, Tucker remained motionless and silent. The pain in her shoulder was a welcome distraction from the startling feel of Tucker's masculine body. Her breath stilled in her lungs as she heard voices coming from directly above them.

"Shh," Tucker whispered, obviously feeling her tension. Skylar closed her eyes, listening to the low mumble of voices, feeling Tucker's steady heartbeat against her chest and hoping that the pain in her shoulder wouldn't get any worse. But as minutes continued to drag by, her hopes dwindled, the voices faded, and not even Tucker's bulky presence could distract her from the pain that seemed to increase by the second.

When Tucker finally took a step back, she had no idea how long they'd been huddled against the mountain. She stumbled forward into the sunlight and would have fallen had Tucker not reached out to steady her.

"Stay here," he whispered, easing her back against the cliff.

Skylar nodded in agreement, content to watch as Tucker

ventured back to scan the top of the ridge for spectators. She flipped up her vest and peered at the hole in her shirt. Her shoulder felt as though a hot poker was buried inside it, but at least it wasn't bleeding. She shifted her vest, letting the leather conceal her wound.

"Looks clear," Tucker said after a moment. "I don't want to chance it, though. We'll follow the ravine until we catch up to Chance and Garret."

Skylar groaned as she pushed away from the hillside.

"What's wrong?"

"Nothing," she said with a shallow breath, walking past him.

Tucker stepped in front of her. His hand slid under her chin and tilted her face so he could see into her eyes. "You're hurting," he said plainly.

"I'm fine."

"You're white as a bedsheet." His narrowed eyes locked on her lips.

"I said I'm fine." She slapped his hand away from her face and stomped past him. "Let's get out of here before we're stuck in that damn crack all night."

Tucker caught up to her in a few long strides.

After following muddy horse tracks for a good mile down the narrow riverbed, Skylar felt a shudder of relief when they spotted Tucker's white stallion lined to a lone tree growing from the side of the deep gorge. Trudging through the thick mud had sapped her energy.

Tucker mounted his horse then pulled his left foot out of the stirrup, preparing to assist Skylar onto the back of his saddle. Skylar knew there was no way she could mount his horse from the left side. She could barely move her left arm, which was a good thing. The slightest movement sent stabbing pains through her shoulder.

"Climb up, darlin'. Where'd you go?" Tucker asked, twisting in his saddle.

"I'm right here," Skylar said, stepping up to the right of his saddle.

Tucker gave her a questioning glance before he reached an arm out and kicked his right foot from his stirrup.

Skylar grabbed his forearm with her right hand, lifted her boot to the stirrup and swung up behind his saddle. "Don't call me darlin'," she said, shifting into place.

Tucker whipped around. Shaded by the brim of his hat, his sharp green eyes gleamed with annoyance. "Must have slipped. All those soft curves can confuse a man. I almost thought you were a woman."

His words stung in a way that took Skylar by surprise.

"Hold on if you don't want to fall off."

His stallion lunged forward.

Skylar gripped Tucker's lean waist, the jolt of pain in her left shoulder taking her focus off her wounded pride. She leaned against his sturdy back and did her best not to pass out.

They'd traveled for what seemed like forever before Tucker guided his horse out of the ravine and into a patch of thick woods. Neither spoke a word as they rode through the tall aspen.

"Get off," Tucker said a while later as he reined his horse to a stop.

Skylar eased away from his back. To her right, Chance

was crouched beside a fire, his eyes locked on his brother. Garret sat near a boulder a few feet from the fire with a plate on his lap.

Chance stood up and started toward them. "We roped the horses off in a clearing of aspen about fifty yards farther north. We're short three mares."

"A fair exchange for keeping our skins. I suggest we move out at first light if we don't want to be visited by curious locals."

Skylar folded her knee tight against her chest and turned away from Tucker to dismount.

"There's a creek farther down where you can wash up," Chance informed them.

"I'll do that," Tucker answered in the same stiff tone and started riding away the moment Skylar had her feet on the ground.

"Supper's in the skillet," said Chance. He left camp, taking brisk strides to catch up with Tucker.

Hurting and exhausted, Skylar continued past the fire, toward Garret.

"Everything okay, Skylar?" he asked.

"Yeah. How about yourself? You took a hard fall."

"I'm all right. Just hungry," he said, dropping his gaze back to his plate as he picked at what appeared to be some type of charred rodent. Garret glanced up with imploring eyes as she approached him. "Sky, couldn't you make supper? Just once?"

"You've eaten worse."

"Not by much," he muttered.

Too tired to think about food, she slumped back against

the boulder her brother was leaning against and slid down until her bottom hit the ground. The slight bump sent a shaft of pain straight through her shoulder, causing her to suck in a swift hiss of air.

She saw the white flash of Garret's hair as his gaze whipped toward her. "Skylar, you sure you're feelin' all right?"

She nodded, the sharp pain temporarily stealing her breath. The pain seemed to worsen with each one she took.

"Honest?"

The last thing she wanted was her little brother fussing and fretting over her. As long as her wound wasn't bleeding, it wouldn't attract anyone's attention. She'd known a few men who'd harbored a bullet and recovered just fine. "I'm okay," she said, just as she felt a warm gush of blood spill from her shoulder.

Oh, no.

The bullet must have shifted. She wished Chance would have stayed in camp. She didn't want to spook her brother.

"I'm going to bed," she muttered. By the time she got to her feet, a warm trail was oozing down her chest. A bit of pressure would stop the bleeding. She'd get a compress and find a nice, flat piece of ground to lie down on until the Morgans returned.

"Sky, if you're—"

"Finish your supper, Garret. I've told you. I'm fine."

She pulled her bedroll from the pile of supplies. With the slight shift of her body, a sharp stab of pain radiated to every point. A cry ripped from her lungs as she slumped to her knees and gripped the wound.

"Skylar!" Garret was at her side in a flash. "What's wrong?"

She drew blood-covered hands away from her shoulder. The bullet had definitely shifted. "Go get Tucker."

Garret's only answer was the sound of his boots beating a hard, fast path in the direction of the Morgans.

Suddenly light-headed, Skylar clamped her jaw against the pain and opened her bedroll, spreading it out across the rocky ground where she'd dropped it. Grabbing another blanket, she pressed it to her shoulder and lay down.

Pressure.

She needed pressure to stop the bleeding. Curling up on her left side seemed to ease some of the pain as she held the blanket in place.

By the time she heard Garret calling her name, she opened her eyes to a darkening night sky. She drew in a ragged breath and wondered how many minutes had passed—it had felt like an eternity.

"Sky?" Garret said again.

In the next moment she was blinded by the light of a lantern. "Skylar, what's hurting?" Tucker asked as he knelt behind her.

"Her left shoulder was bleeding," Garret said before she could respond.

She felt Tucker's hands moving over her forehead and hair. "You're damp with sweat and cold as a wet fish. Hell!" he cried, leaning over her. "Your bedroll's soaking up all your blood!"

Skylar opened her eyes and was startled by the amount of blood soaked into the gray wool.

"Lie on your back," Tucker ordered.

The thought of shifting the slightest bit sent a shudder through Skylar. It hurt too much just lying still, but Tucker didn't wait. His large hands clamped onto her and twisted her onto her back. She sucked in a hard breath as pain seared her entire body.

He began unfastening the row of buttons on her shirt. She winced as he peeled her shirt back, disturbing the handkerchief still embedded in her wound.

"God." His whispered word came out in a rush of air.

"Is it bad?" Garret asked in a trembling voice.

"No," Skylar groaned, her eyes pinched tight as pain consumed her.

"Yes!" Tucker contradicted. "You've got a hole in your shoulder big enough to hold your whole handkerchief, yet that rag's not doing anything to stop the bleeding. Skylar, why didn't you say something?"

"Can you get the bullet out?" Chance asked from somewhere behind them.

Horrified by the idea of Tucker digging in her shoulder, Skylar's eyes flew open. The panic she saw in Tucker's expression increased her fear.

"Hell, I'm no doctor. If I tug that rag from her shoulder, she's liable to bleed to death on the spot." He closed her shirt. "I'm taking her into town."

Having someone else carving on her didn't sound any better. "With pressure—"

"Honey, *it's no good*. That bullet's got to come out and the wound closed."

"I'll saddle your horse," Chance said, taking the lantern light with him as he walked away.

"This is gonna hurt," Tucker said as he began to ease the blanket under her shoulder. "I have to tie it tight to keep pressure on the wound." He wrapped an end over the top of her shoulder and pulled it toward the end coming from under her arm.

Skylar's breath grew choppy as she felt him entwine the two ends. He tugged. She screamed. Pain pierced her body in a blinding flash as he pulled the knot tight.

"Sorry, angel," he said, lifting her into his arms.

"I'm comin' with you," Garret said, hurrying after them as Tucker carried her toward his horse.

"No," said Tucker. "Chance will need your help with the horses."

Skylar was shifted from one set of brawny arms to another. She heard the creak of Tucker's saddle.

"Hand her here." Again she was wrapped in his arms. He positioned her on his lap with her feet dangling to one side. "I figure we can't be much more than an hour's ride from Glenwood."

"In the light of day," said Chance. "It's liable to take you two hours in the dark."

Tucker's arm jostled her shoulder. Skylar bit her lip to keep from crying out, but a sharp squeak escaped her throat.

"Skylar?" he said, unmoving. "You all right?"

She nodded, pressing her face against his shirt.

"Hold on, honey," he said as he spurred his horse into motion. "We'll get you patched up."

Shards of pain cut through her shoulder with each hard stride of Tucker's horse. The constant, heavy thrusts of motion were too much to bear. *"Tucker,"* she said in a gasp, clutching his shirt. "Slow down. I can't—" Her voice ended in a wince.

Every fiber in Tucker's body urged him to ride like hell, but he instantly slowed his horse's pace, not wanting to increase her pain. The heart thundering in his chest had practically stopped beating when he saw Skylar's blood-soaked bedroll.

"Skylar, how long has that wound been bleeding like that?"

"Not long," she said in a shallow breath.

"Are you lying to me?"

"Maybe."

Despite his concern, Tucker smiled. "Honey, we've got to teach you how to complain once in a while. You should have said something."

She drew a ragged breath. "Tucker?"

"Yeah?"

"I'm scared."

Her admission intensified Tucker's fear. He figured it was rare that Skylar admitted to any type of weakness. "Don't be scared. You'll be all right."

"Garret—"

"Will be driving you crazy with his constant chatter by tomorrow morning, just like he does the rest of us."

"He's got nobody."

"He's got you, and you're gonna be just fine." He'd make sure of it.

The next hour felt like an eternity. Where the hell was a full moon when he needed one? The partial moon and starlit sky gave just enough light for Rosie to keep a steady pace without running into trees and mountainsides.

By the time Tucker made it to town, Skylar was shivering and growing lethargic. He shouted down the first man he spotted on the street, asking where he could find the town doctor.

Reining in in front of the large white house at the end of the main strip, he leaped from his saddle and raced up the front steps with Skylar in his arms. Praying Doc Perkins was home, he thumped his boot against the door then tried the handle. Finding the door barred, he gave a few more kicks, rattling the tall windows of each side of the wide door.

"Coming," someone shouted, just before the door jerked open. A short, gray-haired man held up a globe of light and shifted his spectacles. A woman stepped beside him clutching her white robe together at the throat.

"My wife," Tucker said in a rush, "she's been shot."

Chapter 8

Tucker paced the parlor like a caged cougar, nearly insane with worry. He had no sooner set Skylar on the doctoring table when he'd been grabbed by the arm and rushed out of the room by the doctor's wife. She assured him they would take good care of "Mrs. Morgan," then shut the door in his face and stayed inside to assist her husband.

That had been nearly an hour ago, a half hour since the last time he'd heard Skylar cry out in pain.

If she died, it would be all his fault. He should have checked her for injuries. He knew the numbing power of adrenaline—had seen men come back from battle during the war thinking they'd only been nicked, some never realizing they'd been shot. Most were dead by sunrise. He'd seen pain in her expression, but he'd let her harsh attitude bruise his ego and he had let it go.

Damn her stubbornness! She should have told him she'd been shot! But it seemed she'd have rather died than ask him for help. And if someone didn't poke a head out of that room soon and let him know what was going on, he was going to claw the damn door down!

The door behind him squeaked open and Tucker spun around. Doc Perkins flashed a slight smile as he peered up at him through spectacles on the tip of his nose. Tucker thought that to be a good sign, until his gaze locked on the blood smeared across the front of the doctor's white smock.

"Mr. Morgan—"

"Is she all right?" Tucker interrupted.

"She's had a rough go of it, but I did manage to remove the lead—"

"But she's okay?" Tucker asked, wishing the old man would answer the damn question!

"We finally convinced her to take some laudanum, which helped with the pain while I finished closing the wound. I believe the worst is past, but the shock of it all seems to have triggered an emotional release."

Emotional release?

Hearing a sob coming from the other room, Tucker shifted his gaze toward the closed door.

Skylar was crying. He heard the soft, consoling voice of the doctor's wife. The muffled sounds seemed to be moving farther away.

"I've never seen a woman become so agitated about shedding some tears," the doc said in a tone of bewilderment. "She's certainly entitled, after all she's endured. Wouldn't you agree?"

"Sure," Tucker said, dragging his gaze back to the doctor. "So, she's gonna be all right?"

"Your wife has lost all the blood she can spare. A bit of rest and she should be back to her normal self in no time.

Jane is moving Mrs. Morgan to one of our extra rooms where she can rest comfortably for the night. I'm sure she'd like to see you."

Tucker was sure she wouldn't, but as the doctor walked back into his surgical room, he followed, needing to see for himself that Skylar was okay. The repugnant scent of burned flesh stung his nose. The sight of the doc's scalpel and other surgical instruments spread across a silver tray beside a bundle of bloodied linens tightened the knots in Tucker's gut.

They walked through a door on the opposite side of the room and continued down a dimly lit hallway. A door at the end of the hall opened and the doctor's wife slipped from the room, closing the door softly behind her.

"The poor dear," she said as he and Doc Perkins reached the end of the hall. "She's terribly upset. She mentioned her father recently passed away."

"Yes, ma'am," Tucker said, twisting his hat in his hands, and feeling lower than dirt. He hadn't thought much about the grief she might be feeling over the death of her father. "He was murdered by horse thieves a little over a month ago."

"Good heavens," Mrs. Perkins exclaimed, pressing a hand to her chest. "I'm so sorry. And then to be shot herself by ruffians, my goodness." The woman made a tsking sound as she shook her head. "She'll soon be resting peacefully. I'll leave you with your wife."

"Thank you, ma'am, and Doc Perkins. I appreciate all you've done."

Long after the generous couple had said their good-nights and left him alone in the hall, Tucker stood there, staring at the closed door, listening to the sniffling sounds on the other side, not knowing what to do. Skylar was hard enough to handle when she was cold and vicious. He hadn't forgotten the sight of her tear-streaked face in the barn. The thought of facing those tears, her vulnerable blue eyes...it scared the hell out of him.

Stop being such a coward and open the door.

Placing a palm on the door handle, he drew a deep breath. Light spilled out into the dim hallway as he eased the door open. An oil lamp burned brightly on a night table beside a single-wide bed. Skylar was crumpled forward, crying into the bedcovers. A long white nightdress was draped over her slender body.

Tucker stepped into the small bedroom and closed the door behind him. He inched toward the bed then sat beside her. Her body shook with her soft cries. Knowing he couldn't do or say a damn thing to make her feel better was a personal torture.

Tentatively, he placed a hand on her back and lightly stroked the length of her spine. When she didn't respond to his presence or his touch, Tucker tossed his hat onto the floor and slid an arm under her legs as he eased her onto his lap.

"Don't cry, angel," he soothed, holding her against his chest, wishing like mad he could ease her pain.

Skylar slowly became aware of the large palm stroking her back. The soothing sound of Tucker's voice drew her from the haze of grief that had engulfed her. Unaware of when he'd even entered the room, she was stunned to realize she'd been lifted onto his lap and wrapped in his arms.

"I'm sorry, Skylar," Tucker whispered, his voice thick with emotion.

"I don't know what's wrong with me," she sniffled, burying her face against his chest as another wave of tears surged for release. "I don't usually cry."

"You don't usually get shot either, honey. Hell, I'd probably be bawling my eyes out too if that doc had been digging in my shoulder."

"Please don't tell Garret."

"Shh," he soothed. "Don't fret, angel girl. I won't breathe a word."

The deep vibrations of Tucker's voice and his tender embrace didn't help to slow the flow of Skylar's tears. She'd not been held so gently since before her mother died. Needing the security of his strength, accepting the comfort of his embrace, Skylar gave up trying to fight her tears and cried against his shoulder.

Tucker's hand continued to move across her back in soft, soothing strokes as he whispered against her hair. When she finally managed to dry her eyes and catch her breath, she eased away from his damp shirt. Warm green eyes held her gaze. His lips twitched with a hint of a smile.

Dear God, he was handsome.

With the doctor and his wife continually calling her Mrs. Morgan, she couldn't help but wonder what it would be like to truly be the wife of Tucker Morgan. She imagined those thoughts had started her tears. Regardless of Tucker's scorn toward marriage, she'd decided he would be a good husband. He was sweet, patient, funny and kind. If he wasn't so damned attractive and didn't make her feel so fuzzy-headed every time he flashed a smile, she'd probably really like him.

The thought nearly made her smile...*or cry*, she realized, her eyes burning again. She shook her head and dropped her gaze to her lap. She couldn't think straight.

Must be the elixir. It was working, she realized. The pain in her shoulder was nothing more than a dull ache.

"I'm tired," she said, certain she'd never felt so drained in all her life. "No wonder my father didn't tolerate tears," she muttered. "Producing all that moisture is damn exhausting."

Of course, if her father had been true to his word, she would have had a home years ago instead of winding up at the butt end of nowhere, crying her eyes out to the most handsome man she'd ever known.

"I'll help you get under the covers," Tucker said, easing her onto the bed and tugging the blankets back.

Skylar didn't argue, allowing him to help her into bed. He pulled the blankets up to her chin and tucked them in around her shoulders, all nice and cozy like, and she couldn't help but grin. Tucker constantly did little things that surprised and annoyed her, like saddling her horse in the morning, warming water just for her to wash up with at night, making sure she always got her share of the meals when she came into camp late. *And coffee*. He'd fill her canteen full of coffee when she had the evening watch.

The man's infernal tendency to care for her had made

her realize all that her father had never done, the consideration he'd never shown. She wondered why her father had even come for her and Garret after their mother died.

Pride and obligation, she figured. Zachary Daines had definitely considered himself to be a righteous man. So why hadn't he kept his word?

We can't quit driving stock until I've saved enough money to buy my own ranch.

That was always his excuse, yet she'd never been able to uncover any type of savings. Like an idiot, she'd handed over all the money she earned that wasn't spent on food and clothing for herself and Garret, thinking it was going toward her home. All she ever got were new assignments, more calluses and empty promises.

After breaking his leg two years back, her father's ambition had taken a serious dive. He'd become real good at barking out orders then disappearing for days at a time, and Skylar gave up on waiting for him to fulfill his promise. Handling most of their business affairs herself, she'd started her own savings, all of which was in her saddlebags that had been left behind in Arizona.

She'd never really discussed her plan with Garret, knowing he couldn't keep a secret to save his sweet soul, but she'd been so close to taking her brother and pulling up stakes, until her father waved that damn deed in front of her face, saying, *Didn't I tell you I'd get you a home, Sky?*

He had. And she fell for his illusion, again. If she couldn't trust her own father, who could she trust?

No one.

With another surge of tears burning at her eyes, Skylar fixed her gaze on the ceiling and drew deep, steady breaths, determined not to lose her composure again, knowing Tucker was standing nearby. She glanced beside her as he leaned over the night table. Lamplight gilded the blond strands of hair flipped up over the top of his ear, giving a halo effect to the circular ripple his hat had pressed into the thick golden waves that swirled around his head. His halo faded as he turned down the wick, reducing the bright light to a warm glow.

"Are you all right, Skylar?" he asked, his eyes looking deep into hers as he stepped closer to the bed.

Tucker's voice saying her name seemed to echo off the four surrounding walls as she settled into the soft mattress, burrowing into the warm covers. She liked the way he always called her Skylar. Her father had shortened her name and her hair when she'd begun to drive cattle.

"The bed linens smell of soap," she said, turning her face toward the fluffy white pillow, and drawing in a deep breath. "I like the smell of soap."

Tucker stared down at her, not sure how to respond to such an odd statement. But then, he supposed a girl who'd spent most of her life on cattle trails would be partial to the scent of soap.

"It's so quiet," she continued. "It's nice to be inside. Don't you think, Tuck?"

"Yeah," he said lamely, sure this was the laudanum talking. The bleakness in her red-rimmed eyes tore at his heart. He sat on the edge of the narrow bed and stroked a hand through her sweat-dampened hair, watching her eyelids lower halfway.

"I don't recall the last time I slept in a clean bed, surrounded by four walls." She pulled in a deep breath and slowly released it. "I want to go home...but I don't have one."

Tears swelled into her large blue eyes, and Tucker felt his heart shatter, the broken shards ripping through his chest. How was it that this woman had the power to make him feel so damn much?

He didn't like it.

"He promised us a home," she said.

Giving in to the powerful urge to comfort her, Tucker eased farther onto the bed and stretched out beside her. Lying on his side, he folded an arm under his head and reached out to her with the other. Gently, he brushed a few golden strands of hair away from her face and tucked them behind her delicate ear. He was amazed she didn't pull away from his light touch.

She met his gaze with glistening eyes. "I want to go home," she whispered.

"I'll take you home," he said, wanting desperately to ease the pain in those sapphire eyes. "I swear it, Skylar."

"I'm so tired," she said again.

"I know you are, darlin'." He inched a bit closer and draped his arm across her waist. "Rest. I'll watch over you."

She blinked sleepily. The smile tugged at the corners of her mouth. "Like a guardian angel?"

Tucker couldn't help but grin, seeing her lips stretched

in the sweetest smile. "More like a fallen angel. But I'll keep you safe, sweetheart."

Skylar's eyes widened a fraction. "You called me sweet-heart."

Tucker held her gaze for a long, silent moment. "So I did. You're not gonna sock me in the nose for being fresh, are you?"

Her bright smile warmed his chest.

"I can't," she said, her smile dropping into a frown. "You've packed me in so tight I couldn't scratch my nose if I wanted to."

"So I have," he said, laughing as he eased up to loosen her covers.

"I like that about you, Tuck," she said, pulling her right arm free from the blankets as he folded them back. "How do you do it?"

"Do what, angel girl?" he asked, amazed she liked any-thing about him, and thinking he'd been a fool to fold back those blankets, exposing her feminine curves beneath an all-too-thin veil of white.

"Smile so easily?" she said. "Make light of life when it's so blessed hard?"

Tucker lifted his gaze to her solemn eyes, not knowing how to answer, wishing he had the power to continually bring smiles to her pretty lips and warmth into her eyes. Aching to give her comfort, not knowing how, he lowered his head and brushed his lips across her pouting lower lip in a light caress.

He hadn't meant to actually kiss her, but when he felt her lips part beneath his, he couldn't bring himself to pull away. A single touch of her tongue to his and he was lost. He slid his hand behind her head, tilting her face up as he melded their mouths in a seamless bond. Fire roared through his veins as he yielded to her slow, contented exploration.

Drowning in the heady taste of her warm, welcoming mouth, his hand followed the graceful curve of her neck down to her shoulder. His fingers probed the bulk of her bandages under the thin cotton nightdress, and reality lashed him like a whip.

He was fully taking advantage of her hazy state of mind! And she was shattering his with every timid stroke of her velvety tongue.

Tucker tried to pull away, but was distracted by her plump lower lip. With a groan of growing need, he drew the delicate flesh gently between his teeth. When Skylar nibbled back, her fingers threading into his hair, their mouths became locked in a wild mating of tongues.

He needed to stop. He had to stop!

Struggling for clarity and restraint, Tucker forced himself to release her mouth and ease back.

Skylar looked as dazed as he felt. "What was that?" she asked, her breath rushing in and out in short gasps.

Tucker was asking himself the same question. He'd never kissed or been kissed more fully in his life. "Angel kisses," he said, certain he'd just been kissed by a heavenly being.

Her lazy grin caused him to chuckle. Lord, she was the most beautiful woman he'd ever seen when she smiled like that, with warmth shining in her glazed eyes.

"I like the way angels kiss," she said, her fingers still twirling in the hair at the back of his collar.

"So do I, angel girl."

He'd been entertained by a few women whose kisses were nice enough, but he'd never been one to dawdle with such foreplay. Yet just kissing Skylar was an exquisite pleasure in itself.

She flashed a seductive smile, then tugged on a strand of his hair, pulling him back to her lips. Tucker groaned, knowing he shouldn't, even as he took her mouth as completely as she took his.

Overwhelmed by the sheer wonder of her passion, his hand slid from her waist to the curve of her hip. The supple flesh beneath her thin nightdress burned his fingertips. His body ached with the need to caress more of her. *All of her.*

He swallowed her soft moans as she continued to devour his mouth. She shifted against him, and his hand slipped from her hip to the lush swell of her backside.

A torrent of fire exploded within Tucker's body. He smoothed his hand over the soft rounded pad, so tempted to haul her against his hard, aching flesh.

No woman had ever gotten him so hot with just kisses.

Groping for restraint, Tucker reminded himself that Skylar was heavily medicated. Any further advances and he'd be taking blatant advantage of her. Hell, he was already taking advantage of her!

"Skylar," he said in a heavy breath, lifting his head to gaze up at the spot of light on the ceiling. "Honey, *we have to stop.*"

She didn't release her sturdy grip around his neck, holding him close as she nuzzled against him. Her warm breath swirling across the skin of his throat wasn't helping to cool his violently aroused body.

"You taste…nice," she said, sounding drowsy.

Tucker felt her smile as she pressed her cold nose against the bend of his neck. She was torturing him! He'd dreamed of having his hands and mouth all over her sweet body, but her sensuality surpassed anything he'd conjured up in his mind.

Too bad she doesn't know what in hell she's doing, he thought, knowing she wouldn't be lying pliant in his arms if she weren't injured and drugged.

Employing a control that had to be deserving of sainthood, Tucker eased away from Skylar's body and lifted her arm from around his neck.

Before he could place her hand safely at her side, Skylar reached toward his face and grazed her fingers across his cheek. She flashed a crooked grin as she gazed up at him with tired eyes.

She definitely wasn't in her right mind. "Feeling better?" he asked, kissing her fingertips as she traced his lips.

"Uh-huh," she murmured, lowering her hand to his chest and snuggling against him. "Thank you, Tucker."

At least she's aware of who she's snuggling against. He had a feeling she wouldn't be so appreciative of his advances come morning, but as Skylar settled against him, a contented smile on her soft lips, Tucker felt a burst of satisfaction in knowing he'd given her some comfort.

He watched her eyelids slowly drift down until her long golden lashes rested against the soft skin of her face.

"Do you really think I look like an angel?" she asked a moment later.

"I sure do," he said, pressing his lips to her forehead and dusting his fingers across her silky hair, while forcing his body to relax as he held her.

"Sometimes," she said, her eyes still closed, "your smile, it makes me dizzy."

Tucker chuckled low in his throat, ridiculously delighted by her unexpected confession, and knowing full well she'd be mad as a wet hen in the morning if she recalled telling him such things. "Angel girl, everything about you makes me dizzy." Hell, she'd been knocking him for loops since the moment he laid eyes on her.

She never opened her eyes, but he was rewarded with another smile.

"Skylar, do you want me to hold you while you sleep?" he asked, thinking he should probably have her permission before taking any further liberties.

"I can't," she said, even as she wrapped her arm around his waist.

That hadn't been the answer he wanted. "How 'bout I hold you anyhow?" he whispered against her hair, wondering how the real Skylar had somehow surfaced for a moment in her clouded mind.

Skylar's only answer was her deep, steady breathing.

Clearly not a protest.

Tucker's mouth drew into a hard line as he glanced down at their bodies.

I shouldn't be lying on this bed in these dust-filled clothes. Her clean sheets wouldn't smell fresh for long with his large body sprawled all over them. But Skylar looked so peaceful sleeping in his arms. Anyhow, he was dog tired.

Chapter 9

Surrounded by colorful feminine clothing, strange sweet fragrances and frilly haberdashery, Tucker wondered what in the hell he was doing. He could feel his palms sweating as his fingers worked around the brim of his hat. He'd never bought a gift for a woman in his life, yet he'd entered this shop intending to buy a dress for Skylar.

As the tiny dark-haired woman before him continued to rattle off the different colors, fabrics and styles, Tucker discovered this wasn't going to be as simple a task as he'd originally thought.

"Is there a certain style your wife prefers?" asked Miss Kelley. "This is a lovely gown," she said, pulling a deep pink dress from one of her racks.

I'll take it! he wanted to shout. Skylar would look stunning wrapped in the satiny, pink fitted bodice and the long flowing skirt accented with swags of white fabric and satin ribbons.

But he couldn't see her driving horses in something with so much fluff. He should have gone to the mercantile. What she needed was a new pair of denims and long underwear. After feeling every square inch of her delicate body pressed against him this morning, he'd realized the woman needed warmer clothing.

Not that he'd groped her in her sleep. He'd awakened with Skylar's head resting on his chest and her sweet body stretched out practically on top of him. That thin nightdress didn't do a damn thing to hide the long, shapely woman beneath it. Getting out from under all that softness had been a painfully tricky task.

Despite certain curvy features that would haunt him clear to his grave and the rugged strength he knew she possessed, there wasn't much to her long slender frame. No bulky layer of muscle or thick layer of fat to keep her warm when the sun dropped behind the mountains. Nothing but a hundred and twenty pounds of sheer stubborn beauty.

"Mr. Morgan?"

Tucker shook off his stupor and realized Miss Kelley had tossed the pink gown over a green cushioned chair and was presently holding up a blue dress of similar design.

"Those are both real nice, Miss Kelley," he said, flashing a polite smile, "but don't you have something more basic? You know, something…durable." He snapped his fingers. "Something made of wool, suitable for riding."

"Your wife enjoys riding? The countryside is beautiful this time of year."

"She'll be riding from here to Wyoming on horseback," Tucker explained.

The woman's smile faltered. "Oh."

"Like I said when I came in, we're just passing through."

"Perhaps we should start with your wife's size."

"Her size?" Tucker asked, scratching at his hair.

"Yes. I'll need some estimation of your wife's measurements to choose something suitable."

"Well...she's about so high," he said, holding his hand at eye level. "I'd say a little over a hundred pounds. Thin, but not scrawny."

"Goodness. That does narrow the selection down a bit."

"How so?" Tucker asked, not sure if he should take offense to the surprise in Miss Kelley's large brown eyes.

"She's rather tall."

At well over six feet, Tucker hadn't thought of Skylar as *overly* tall, but gauging by Miss Kelley's petite body, he supposed Skylar could be perceived as such by a woman's point of view. "Is that going to be a problem?"

"Heavens no. I have a few un-hemmed gowns. I'm certain we can find a dress that will enhance her beauty."

"I believe it's the other way around, Miss Kelley. Her soft beauty is what makes the clothes look good."

Did I just say that?

The moon-eyed look on Miss Kelley's face suggested he had.

Well, hell. A few innocent kisses and she had him talking like some dolt-headed sap.

"I do believe that is the sweetest thing I've ever heard a man say about his wife."

"Yeah, well," Tucker said, rubbing a hand across the tense muscles at the back of his neck. "She's a right special woman."

Good God. Chance would split his side laughing if he caught wind of him spouting such sentimental banter.

More likely he'd beat the tar out him, Tucker decided upon second thought. He was pretty sure he'd broken his word to Chance last night, but it hadn't been a full betrayal. He'd promised to keep his hands off Skylar, and he hadn't bedded her, although Tucker was well aware that *that* wasn't Chance's real concern, their land was.

What had he been thinking, to promise Skylar a home?

Perhaps she wouldn't remember his late-night proclamation.

Unfortunately, *he did.*

"I believe this skirt will be more to your liking," Miss Kelley said as she held up a skirt. She fluffed the long folds of gray wool. "With her petticoats layered underneath, this skirt will be quite lovely."

Petticoats?

Hell. Skylar didn't have a damn thing to wear under any dress. That thought didn't help to prevent the heat presently rising up from beneath his collar. But if he was going to outfit the woman, he was going to do it proper.

His gaze was drawn back to the fancy pink gown with all the trimmings. Although practicality wouldn't permit it, that was the dress he'd truly like to see on Skylar. Course, the sight of Skylar all bound up in satin and lace would probably knock his eyes clean out the back of his head. *Not that it would matter much*, he silently commented, reminding himself he was standing inside a ladies dress shop. She'd already knocked him clean off his rocker.

Tucker reached out and took the wool skirt from Miss Kelley's hands and held it near his waist to judge the length. "This is perfect. I'll take it. And I'll be needing all the under-stuff to go with it."

"You wish to purchase undergarments?" asked Miss Kelley, looking as though she'd swallowed a toad.

"Yes, ma'am. Everything it takes to cover a woman from her chin to her toes. Bein' that you're such a fine example of feminine propriety," he said with a wink, "I'll trust your judgment in choosing what's appropriate."

That seemed to put the wind back in her sails. She lifted her pointed little chin as her lips quirked up in a smile.

"If we're in agreement," Tucker continued, "I'll take myself down to the bathhouse and stop back in here in an hour or so."

"I'll have everything ready," she assured him, her shoulders squared like such a good little soldier, Tucker half expected her to give a salute.

Chapter 10

Skylar woke to the sound of a woman's voice, the scent of oranges and a mouthwatering aroma that sent her stomach into fits. Forcing the heavy lids of her eyes to open, she spied the wooden tray sitting on the table beside the bed and a tall glass of orange juice. Her stomach growled as her eyes slowly focused on the plate piled with a mound of fried potatoes, thick ham and two slices of fluffy, white bread.

"You're awake."

Having forgotten she'd been roused by Mrs. Perkins's cheerful voice, Skylar sat up in a flutter of bed linens. Pain pierced her shoulder, reminding her of where she was and why. The room spun, and she closed her eyes. She leaned back against the wall and tried to breathe through the shaft of pain burning in her shoulder.

"I'm sorry, dear," said Mrs. Perkins. "I didn't mean to startle you. I do hope you're hungry."

"I'm starving," Skylar said, opening her eyes, meeting the warm, friendly gaze she recalled from the night before. Mrs. Perkins wore a crisp white apron over her light blue dress. The long auburn braid flecked with tiny bits of gray that Skylar had admired the night before was now pinned in a tight coil at the crown of the woman's head.

"That's good to hear, dear." She lifted the tray and placed it on the bedclothes covering Skylar's outstretched legs. "You were sleeping so soundly before breakfast I didn't want to wake you, but my husband said not to allow you to sleep through dinner, insisting you need to eat."

"I slept past breakfast?" Skylar glanced around the room, stunned by the afternoon sunlight streaming through the window on the far side of the bed.

"With good reason, dear. A body needs rest after sustaining such injuries. Your husband had a few more errands to run but should return shortly."

Her husband? *My husband.*

Tucker had been in this room. *In this bed,* her mind shouted. *With her!*

The fork she'd been lifting toward her mouth slipped from her fingers and clanked against the plate as she remembered just how close she and Tucker had been. She couldn't seem to recall their specific conversation, but she certainly remembered having her tongue inside his mouth, and not wanting to stop kissing him, even when he pulled away from her.

Oh my God!

"Mrs. Morgan? What's the matter, dear?"

Everything! She had thrown herself at Tucker! How could she face him?

Seeing Mrs. Perkins starting to move toward her, Skylar

flashed a quick smile. "I'm just a little groggy," she said, lifting the fork from her plate.

The older woman eyed her skeptically for a moment. "If your shoulder is hurting terribly, I can give you something to ease the pain."

"No!" That was how she'd gotten herself into trouble. "I'm fine. Really." She could take the ache in her shoulder. It was the ache in her pride she was worried about.

"You'll feel better after a warm bath. Mr. Morgan asked to bring the tub into the room. It's in the corner. I'm still warming the water, but it should be ready by the time you've finished eating."

Spotting the long tin tub sitting in the far right corner of the room, her aches and pride were all but forgotten. A real bathtub, long enough to stretch her legs out in and then some. It was beautiful, all silver and shiny.

Thirty minutes later warm water was steaming in the tub and Mrs. Perkins was helping Skylar ease her left arm out of her sleeve.

"I'm sorry about your gown," Skylar said, noticing the red splotch of blood that had seeped from her bandages. She winced as she freed her arm.

"Think nothing of it, dear. A bit of baking soda and that little spot should come right out. I'll be right back. I nearly forgot the soap Mr. Morgan bought for you this morning."

Skylar blinked from surprise as she scurried out of the room. Tucker had bought her soap? Shifting her gaze toward the tub, the white vapors rising from the warm bath quickly stole her attention from fretting over Tucker.

Taking advantage of her moment of privacy, she whipped the nightdress over her head, tossed it aside, and stepped into the tub.

Hissing air through her teeth, she eased down into the bathtub, the heated water stinging her cold skin. Skylar leaned back against the warmed metal, her tense muscles melting like butter as her skin adjusted to the temperature of the water.

Sweet heaven. Nothing in her life had ever felt so good.

She smiled, wiggling her toes, way down at the end of her private pool of warm water. She'd bathed in plenty of hot springs, but there was something so domestic about bathing indoors, and in a real tub meant for bathing. She'd be sure to thank Tucker for providing the experience.

"Careful, dear," Mrs. Perkins called out, shattering Skylar's tranquility as she entered the bedroom. "You don't want to get those sutures wet."

Skylar eased up, glancing down at the water steaming above her breasts, close to the cotton bandages wrapped around her shoulder and the top of her chest. Mrs. Perkins handed her a small white towel as she knelt on the floor behind her. "Press that against your shoulder, dear, and tilt your head back."

Realizing the woman intended to wash her hair, Skylar leaned forward. "You don't need to—"

"Piddle Posh," Mrs. Perkins interrupted before she could finish her protest. "We want to have you looking fresh before your husband returns," she said as she dipped a tin cup into the water and tilted Skylar's head back as she wetted her hair. "He was in such a panic when he brought you in last night, and hovered over you so, John could hardly get close enough to look at your wound. He is quite protective of you, dear, coming in here to check on you every hour or so. He's quite particular about your care. All the way down to this soap," she said her hands began to massage her scalp. "It warms my heart to see a man so devoted to his wife."

Skylar's mind reeled as she listened to Mrs. Perkins and breathed in the strong floral scent of the soap she was scrubbing into her hair. Both dizzied her mind. Tucker had bought her special soap? Had she been such a pathetic sight last night that he felt sorry for her? She cringed from the thought.

Mrs. Perkins continued chatting away as she washed and rinsed her hair, talking about her two sons, a lawyer and a rancher, and her seven grandchildren.

"All finished," she said in her cheerful tone as Skylar felt a towel being wrapped around her head. "Take your time, dear. The damp bandage across your back won't harm anything, but be sure to keep that shoulder dry." She scuttled backward through the door and pulled it to.

Skylar's teeth closed over her lower lip as she reclined back against the tub, her stomach fluttering something awful as she tried to remember all that transpired between herself and Tucker the night before.

She didn't recall much of their ride into town or even entering the Perkins' home. Her first recollection was the searing pain in her shoulder and opening her eyes to see Doc Perkins standing over her.

It was what happened afterward in this room that

troubled her. She recalled babbling something about her father, but she couldn't recall Tucker's words. His warmth, however, was quite vivid in her hazy mind. Curling against him had taken the chill right out of her. Or had kissing him warmed her?

Both, she decided. He had kissed her back, but she distinctly recalled him pulling away.

Surely Tucker realized the elixir she'd been given had caused such promiscuous behavior. After the way their marriage had come about, he couldn't begrudge her that. She'd made it perfectly clear in the past couple of weeks that she couldn't stand him. She could only pray he'd not bring up her deplorable behavior when he returned.

An hour later, she sat on the side of the bed, the skin of her fingers and toes shriveled up from her long bath, and her mouth again hanging open as her wide eyes moved over the clothes Mrs. Perkins had just announced belonged to *her*.

"Mine?" Skylar asked, certain the woman was mistaken.

"Yes, dear. Mr. Morgan bought them this morning from Miss Kelley. She's an excellent seamstress." Mrs. Perkins carefully laid the light blue waist and gray wool skirt on the end of the bed.

Tucker had bought her a new *dress?* Why?

She grimaced, recalling the blood-soaked clothes Mrs. Perkins had helped her out of the night before. But why had he bought a dress? Not that she didn't like the gray skirt and blue waist. Her skin prickled at the thought of wearing such feminine clothing.

Mrs. Perkins grabbed another garment from the end of the bed and smiled brightly as she held up a white camisole with shiny pink ribbons to be tied at the neck and waistline.

Skylar's heart stopped beating as heat flashed across her face. Tucker had bought her more than a skirt and waist.

Mrs. Perkins draped a pair of drawers over her arm with a matching satin ribbon threaded through the waistband. Apparently getting dressed was another task the motherly woman planned to assist her with.

Once Skylar got past her initial embarrassment and had donned the camisole and drawers, she decided she was grateful for Mrs. Perkins's help. She'd forgotten what a chore simply getting dressed could be, and would never have known which of the five petticoats to pull on first or last.

"Are you sure you wouldn't like me to pin up your hair?" asked Mrs. Perkins as Skylar sat on the bed drinking the last of the tea she'd brought her.

Skylar appreciated her offer, but the dress was more than enough change for one day. The heavy feel of so much fabric bunched around her legs was going to take some getting used to. She hadn't taken more than a few steps around the room, but with every step she felt like a staggering drunk, the weight of the skirts swaying to and fro with each stride.

"I'm sure," she said, handing Mrs. Perkins the empty teacup.

Mrs. Perkins nodded, smiling gently. "You should rest,

dear. I'll go and see if your husband has returned," she said as she walked from the room.

Skylar hoped not. She wasn't ready to face Tucker. The bath and all this gussying up had taken a lot out of her.

The thought spurred the memory of something Tucker had said back in New Mexico.

Gussy her up a bit and she could land the first Wyoming man we come across.

Her eyes stung as she dropped her gaze back down to the long gray skirt, her mind registering exactly why Tucker had bought her a dress instead of the denims she needed.

"What has gotten into me?" she whispered, closing her eyes against the burn of tears. She knew the score. Tucker had his agenda, and she had hers. There was no reason to cloud up, and all the more reason to stay focused. Her injury had been a setback, costing her a full day of travel. She couldn't afford to lose any more time.

Reminding herself that hers and Garret's future depended on getting their mustangs back, she opened her eyes. Her breath caught at the sight of sharp green eyes looking back at her.

How long had Tucker been standing in the doorway?

"Hey," he said, his lips twisting into a slight smile. "How are you feeling?"

The rich sound of his words caused a swirling rush of sensation in her belly. "Fine," she said in a thick voice that seemed trapped inside her throat.

He'd also bathed, and had recently shaved. He seemed pleased with the clothes he'd chosen. She knew the clothes were a ploy to unload her at his first opportunity, but that didn't extinguish the fact that he'd spent a good sum of money on them. She didn't like being indebted to him.

"Thank you for the clothes. I'll pay you back."

"Do you like them?"

Did she like them? She hadn't worn such feminine garments since she was a young girl. She loved them.

He stepped into the room, his eyes moving over her with such intensity, Skylar found it hard to breathe. She nervously crossed her arms as his gaze lingered on her midsection as though trying to penetrate the fabric to see if she'd donned the underclothes he'd bought for her.

"Yes," she managed to squeeze past the lump forming in her throat. "They're real nice."

"Consider them a gift."

"I don't accept gifts," she countered quickly, while thinking they needed to get out of this tiny room. She couldn't keep her thoughts straight with him being so close.

"When's the last time you were given a gift?"

Stunned by the unexpected question, Skylar drew a blank. She honestly couldn't recall.

"That's what I thought," Tucker retorted in a sour tone. "Don't worry, I picked up a few things for Chance and Garret, too."

"You did?"

"Yep. And if you're still having trouble with that, chalk it up to necessary supplies. You needed new duds. If you don't mind me sayin' so, they look real nice on you."

Skylar prayed her cheeks weren't as red as they felt.

"This skirt wasn't exactly practical," she said, nervously swatting at the layered mass of cotton, crinoline and wool.

"Yeah, but wearing that skirt and all them petticoats might slow you down for a while. The doc says you're to rest for a few days, and I plan to make sure you do just that. But don't worry. I bought practical stuff, too."

"You did?"

Tucker laughed at her expression of surprise. Seeing her delight in the dress alone was enough to make the shopping worthwhile. "I did. But I could sure get used to seeing you in a dress. You look beautiful, Skylar."

Her eyes widened. Her scarlet blush deepened.

"You smell pretty, too."

"I should thank you for that."

She flashed a quick smile, and suddenly the sweet-scented air felt thick in his lungs.

What the hell did he have to feel nervous about? *You spent the night holding this woman, and her kiss damn near burned you alive!* And though she hadn't yet accused him of doing so, he had taken advantage of her hindered state of mind by allowing things to go as far as they had. Hell, that was enough to make any man nervous.

The caution in Skylar's eyes told Tucker she wasn't planning on discussing any of those subjects. Being none too proud about his lack of self-restraint, that suited him just fine. "Are you feeling up to heading out or should we stay put for a while?"

"We can leave," Skylar answered, seeming more than eager to be on her way.

"If you're tired or sore, I don't mind waiting."

"I've cost us enough time already. The sooner we get out of here the better."

Good enough. Tucker took a step forward and lifted her into his arms.

"Tucker!"

"Did I hurt you?" he asked, making sure it was her right shoulder he'd pressed against his chest.

"No. But I'm—"

"My wife," Tucker finished for her. "You damn near bled to death last night. I'm carrying you to the wagon."

"Wagon?"

Tucker stared at her with a measure of disbelief, watching her expression go from embarrassment to surprise. She barely had the energy to stand, yet she actually expected him to put her on a horse. Had her father treated her with such neglect?

Knowing the answer, his lips twisted down. "Honey, you're in no condition to ride."

The embarrassment was back. Tucker was finding those pink cheeks quite becoming.

"Don't call me honey, and stop being so damn nice to me."

"Come on now," he said as he started down the hall. "You're wearing a dress. It's time to start behaving like a lady. I believe that entails graciously accepting the help of a gentleman, and no swearing."

"I've never met a gentleman," she said staring him straight in the eyes, "and you can go straight to hell."

Tucker laughed and carried her toward the foyer. Her medication was wearing off all right. His angel was back to behaving like a hellcat, hissing and spitting. Spotting Doc Perkins and his wife near the front door, he pressed his lips to Skylar's ear, whispering, "At least pretend to like me in front of the doc. I doubt he's heard many wives wishing their husbands to hell."

"Oh, I'll bet he has," she mumbled under her breath, but she behaved herself all the same while Tucker carried her out to the wagon he'd rented from the livery. As he gently deposited her on the seat her eyes widened and he knew she saw the pile of packages in the back.

"Tucker?"

"We'll talk about it in a minute, honey." He turned to the doctor and his wife, who had stayed on his heels since they'd entered the foyer.

"Thank you again for taking care of Skylar. I'm eternally indebted to you for saving her like you did."

"Happy to help, young man. Mrs. Morgan, you get plenty of rest and keep that wound dry for a good week or so."

Fifteen minutes later, as they rode toward camp, Skylar hadn't said a single word to him. She sat with her arms crossed, keeping her gaze on the stretch of rolling hills on her side of the wagon.

"Are you going to talk to me?" he finally asked.

"No."

"We're enemies again, is that it?"

"No need to be harsh. I prefer to think we've agreed to simply tolerate one another until we reach Wyoming."

"I sort of liked being friendly, Skylar."

"The only reason we were *friendly* last night is because Mrs. Perkins gave me that elixir."

Tucker grinned to himself. She didn't know it, but she'd been given another dose of that elixir. Knowing she'd refuse to take something for her pain and damn certain her shoulder was hurting more than she'd ever admit, he'd asked Mrs. Perkins to slip something into her tea to take the edge off her pain for the ride back to camp. The older woman had been only too happy to comply. Already weak from blood loss, he figured Skylar would be sound asleep within the next fifteen minutes.

As they veered off the main road into rougher terrain, Tucker kept a close watch on her. Her eyelids began to droop as she fought her drowsiness. When her chin finally dipped toward her chest, he slipped his arm around her waist and eased her against his side. As he slid her across the wagon seat, she jerked awake and pulled back.

"Don't fight me, honey," he said, holding fast to her waist. "You were half-asleep and about to fall over the side of the wagon."

"I'm awake now," she said, pushing against him.

"Damn it, Sky, you can barely hold your eyes open! I'm not taking the chance of you toppling off this seat, so relax."

She stayed stiff against his side.

"You had a rough night. For criminy sake, you had a bullet dug out of your shoulder!"

She relinquished her struggle, but he could feel the tension in her body. He glanced beside him and saw her blinking sleepily, trying to focus her eyes.

"She must have put something in that tea," she muttered.

Tucker decided it would be best not to comment on that and silently guided his horse through a thick patch of pines. As the wagon jostled along, he felt Skylar slowly relax. Ten minutes later, she was sound asleep with her head resting on his shoulder.

By the time he approached their campsite, over an hour later, she was snuggled against him, her arm strapped around his middle. Tucker reined his horse to a stop and eased back in the seat, reluctant to wake her, enjoying the feel of her body relaxed against him and the fresh scent of her clean hair. He pulled in a deep breath, bathing his senses in the floral scent of her. She smelled sweet as a rosebud. And the second she woke, she'd expose her thorns.

Stubborn ramrod of a woman, he thought with a smile. He had news for her. He could be just as stubborn.

Tucker brushed a few strands of hair away from her peaceful expression. Those soft pretty features were going to stone over the moment she realized the doc's orders meant no working with the horses until well after her sutures came out.

She can kick and cuss all she wants. She wouldn't get the better of his patience again. She damn sure wouldn't be lifting a rope, whip or saddle until her shoulder had healed. He'd make sure of it.

"Rise and shine, angel girl," he said a few moments later.

Skylar jerked up as if he'd slapped her. She glanced up

at him then blinked her wide eyes before she looked out at their surroundings. "We're here?"

"Yep." Tucker hopped down then turned to assist Skylar. "Com'ere, I'll help you down."

She stared at his outstretched arms. Tentatively, she turned her head toward the other side of the wagon.

"You try to jump out the other side, and I swear—"

"Oh, all right." She released a huff and put her hands on his shoulders as his hands circled her waist.

The second he set her feet on the ground, Garret came barreling from the trees at a full run. Spotting his sister, he skidded to a hard stop.

His wide eyes moved over her, taking in the drastic change of attire. "Wow, Sky! You look…*pretty.*"

Tucker smiled, watching Skylar's cheeks flush. Garret walked up and leaned toward her, sniffing loudly. "You smell good, too."

"Thanks," she muttered, her expression heavy with discomfort and *exhaustion.*

"Are you feeling better? Did you see a doctor?"

"She did," Tucker answered for her. "He patched up her shoulder."

"So, you're better?" asked Garret, his eyes narrowed with concern.

Tucker knew her pale complexion and heavy eyelids had the kid worried.

"I'm fine, Garret," she said with a slight smile.

"The doc says she's to take it easy for a week or so," said Tucker. "We're staying put for today. Skylar had a rough night and should catch up on her lost sleep."

"I don't need sleep," she protested.

"Garret," he said, staring into Skylar's guarded blue eyes, "the doc said she's to stay off her feet the rest of the day. I'm counting on you to make sure that happens."

"Yes, sir!"

"You," he said, wagging a finger at Skylar, "go plant your butt on a bedroll and stay there."

"You can lie down on mine." Garret took her by the arm. She glared at Tucker, her lips flattened in a tight line as she turned away. Garret trotted along right beside her, asking questions a mile a minute, giving her the attention she didn't have the sense to know she needed. The woman surely hadn't been doted on nearly enough in her lifetime.

"Where's Chance?" asked Tucker.

"With the horses," the kid called back.

Confident Skylar would be under excellent supervision, Tucker started toward the cart, wanting to unload the other packages before Chance came into camp. The fact that he'd bought Skylar a dress was sure to raise Chance's eyebrows. If Chance found out how much of a spending spree he'd gone on, his brother would have a fit and hound him with questions Tucker wasn't ready to answer, or even certain he could.

Gathering up the pile of paper-wrapped parcels, he carried them toward their packs and quickly stuffed them into various canvas sacks.

Chapter 11

In the last five days, Skylar couldn't sneeze without Tucker's palm sliding across her forehead and him wanting to investigate her sutures. She'd never been touched and prodded so much in all her life, or felt so utterly useless. After being deposited in camp by her brawny nursemaid and ordered to rest, she decided she would busy herself by making supper as she enjoyed the absence of a man who was steadily driving her insane.

Five days of feeling useless had been enough. Holding the bowl with her left arm, she whipped the cornmeal batter as a skillet warmed over the fire. She'd planned her mutiny the night before, filling a sack of beans with water while Tucker was on night watch. A smile tugged at her lips as she glanced up at the pot of simmering beans.

Tucker was all too content to work circles around her while she sat about like a useless lump. At least while they were traveling, she could ride a horse without assistance. During the past few days she and Tucker continually fought, him insisting they should slow their pace, while she refused to cost them more time. This morning she'd finally convinced him she didn't need his help to mount and dismount her blasted horse, his hands on her waist being far more distressful than any pain in her shoulder.

And what had she done when they stopped to make camp? Collapsed like a rag doll. In the space of a heartbeat, Tucker had been towering over her, hauling her to her feet and *looking down her shirt*.

Granted, he'd been checking her shoulder, but that hadn't made the experience any less humiliating or jarring to her senses.

Biting out a curse, she crouched near the fire and poured some of her cornmeal mixture into the skillet she'd placed on some stones over the campfire. She wasn't the only one adjusting to the change in altitude!

But she'd been the only one who fell to the ground the moment she stepped down from her saddle. He'd been gone for nearly two hours, riding with Chance and Garret farther into the tall pines to take the horses to the river, and still Skylar's jaw was clenched with tension.

He was going to be furious when he discovered she'd set up camp in his absence and started the two fires.

Tucker was going to rant, but Garret would be delighted. Garret was the only one she was concerned about. In a few more days, they would be in Wyoming territory and she could start scouting for Randal. If she'd chosen the right passes, they should cross trails at some point.

"What in the hell do you think you're doing!"

Skylar looked up at the green-eyed tyrant marching from the trees. "Don't start with me, Morgan," she warned, pointing her fork at him.

"Damn it, Skylar, you were supposed to be resting."

"I hardly do anything as it is," she said, turning her attention back to the corn cakes cooking in the skillet.

"You collapsed just two hours ago," he said, his booted feet stomping up right beside her.

She dragged her narrowed eyes up his long, muscular body. "From the altitude! We've all been short of breath since we rode up into this high country. I'm fine so stop behaving like my nursemaid."

"Somebody's got to! You've been pushing yourself too hard the last few days. If you don't…" His voice trailed off as he caught sight of the skillet in her hand. His blond eyebrows shot up. "Is that corn bread?"

"Yes. Haven't you ever made corn cakes over a fire?"

"No. We, uh…damn that looks good," he said, crouching beside her.

"Chance bought the cornmeal," she said, amused by Tucker's fascination as he peered into the skillet.

"Hell, he probably didn't know what it was. Either it looked like cooking supplies or the merchant suggested he might need it." His gaze shifted to the pot hanging from a tripod she'd arranged over a small fire beside the larger campfire. "Are you cooking beans in that pot?" he asked, sniffing loudly.

Before she could answer, his long arm reached toward the neighboring fire and lifted the lid from the pot.

She saw the question in his crooked grin as he glanced over at her. "Go ahead. There's a spoon in that sack right beside you."

Tucker didn't waste any time, quickly digging out a

spoon and dipping it into the beans while Skylar started another batch of corn bread. Hearing the sound of him blowing, she glanced beside her and grinned at the sight of his puckered lips as he cooled the heap of steaming beans on the large spoon.

His soft lips stretched wide as he guided the spoon into his mouth, setting the metal utensil upon his tongue before his lips closed around the narrow handle. When he slipped the spoon from between his lips, Skylar realized she was licking her own lips as she stared at his mouth, *remembering*. She lifted her gaze.

"Too spicy?" she asked, concerned by his deep look of surprise as he chewed in slow motion.

Tucker set the spoon aside and replaced the lid. "You've been eating our pathetic attempt at cooking these last few weeks when you can cook like this? Your stubbornness must run bone deep."

His teasing grin nettled under her skin. Skylar fought a smile as she dropped her gaze and tried to focus on the corn bread she was about to burn.

"No wonder you had to keep Garret quiet with those harsh glares. The boy knew what he was missing. What did you put in those beans?"

Skylar shrugged. "Salt, some dried peppers—"

"Stuff from our supplies?"

"Yes," she said, trying to swallow the short laugh that escaped her throat.

"You ought to do that more often."

"Since you won't let me near the horses, I might as well make myself useful by taking over the cooking duties."

"I was referring to that little laugh, not chores. You have the prettiest smile."

In the midst of turning the corn cakes, Skylar nearly flipped one of the flat, round breads into the fire. She gaped up at Tucker. His eyes were focused on her shoulder.

"Have you changed that bandage since we left the doc's place?"

"Not yet," she said in a clipped tone, wondering if he'd meant to shock her. How could he say such a thing to her and then act as though he'd said nothing?

"Didn't he give you fresh supplies and say to change it every few days or so? If you need help—"

"I don't. And I don't need your pity."

"Pity? I can hardly have pity for someone who's so damn mean and snippy. Do you intend to stab me with that fork?"

Skylar dropped her gaze to the fork she was holding like a dagger. The thought had promise. Having meaningless compliments slung at her felt much like being jabbed with a fork. Realizing she was burning the corn bread, she returned her attention to her task at hand. "Go away, Morgan."

"Why does everything have to be a fight between us?" he asked, staying crouched right beside her. "You're not nearly so short with Chance and Garret."

"They don't hover over me, making me feel helpless and weak." Skylar regretted the words the moment they left her lips, hardly able to believe she'd admitted to feeling weak and helpless. Tucker seemed just as surprised. His wide eyes searched hers.

"Is that how I make you feel, Skylar?"

"No. But that's how you're trying to make me feel."

"The hell I am!"

She gave a huff of disbelief. "Why else would you be treating me like a child?"

"I haven't either! I don't know what type of half-blind men you're used to riding with, but I'm very much aware that you are pure female. I've been treating you like what you are. *A woman.*"

"I want you to stop."

"Well I'm not going to. Not as long as we're married and you're my responsibility."

"*Wrong.* I am my own responsibility."

"According to your mind maybe, but not the law."

"Whose law, Tucker?" She looked away, carefully lifting the corn cakes onto a plate. "I don't see any sheriff out here forcing you to hover over me. As far as I'm concerned, that marriage document holds no validity between us." She set the skillet aside as her gaze snapped up to his. Tucker wasn't glaring at her as he should have been. His face inches from hers, his green eyes stared at her mouth.

Skylar recognized the heat in his gaze. Knowing it had nothing to do with anger, Skylar's own mouth suddenly felt dry as a desert floor as butterflies erupted in her stomach. Her breath stilled in her lungs as he leaned toward her.

Oh no.

His breath dusted her lips, sending a wave of fiery sensations crashing through her body. He breathed her name and her eyelids drooped, her thoughts scattering in a rush of anticipation.

"Boy, does something smell good," Garret called out from the pines in the distance.

Freed from the spell of Tucker's luminous eyes, Skylar jerked away from him and shifted her gaze back to the fire. Tucker pulled in a deep, ragged breath before he stood.

"You cooked!" Garret exclaimed, running across the small clearing. He skidded to a stop across the fire. For a moment, Skylar thought he was about to burst into tears. "Praise Almighty God," he said, dropping to his knees. "Is it ready? Can we eat now?"

Skylar smiled, loving his eagerness, thankful for the distraction. She could feel Tucker's eyes watching her from a few feet away. "As soon as Chance gets here, we'll eat."

Chance strode into camp a few moments later.

As they all sat around the fire eating their supper, Skylar couldn't look up. Her cheeks blazed every time she glanced at their smiling faces. Smiles that beamed even as they chewed.

No one had ever expressed such appreciation for her cooking. Even Chance had complimented her a good five or six times. Despite her discomfort, Skylar noticed the lack of tension in the atmosphere as they devoured her food.

Finished eating, she stood and carried her plate toward

the fire where a kettle of water was being warmed to wash the dishes.

"I'll scrub up the dishes," Garret said, jumping to his feet.

"You don't have to, Garret," Skylar countered, certain Tucker had assigned the chore. "I'm feeling better."

"I want to." Garret dropped his plate into the kettle then banded his long arms around her. "I sure love you, sis," he whispered near her ear.

Stunned by his unexpected burst of affection, it took Skylar a moment to return his embrace. As Garret stepped back, she felt a light nudge in her back and she glanced over her shoulder.

Chance flashed one of his rare grins. "If I give you a hug, will you keep cooking for me, too?"

Skylar laughed out loud, clearly seeing the fear in Chance's expression, that she might require such payment. "Don't worry, Chance, no hugs required. I don't mind cooking with all of you doing the work with the horses."

Tucker sat by the fire watching the friendly exchange, certain that if he'd have wrapped his arms around Skylar or even suggested such a thing, she would have socked him in the nose. He decided he'd be better off keeping his mouth shut and his hands to himself. She obviously didn't know how to take a compliment anyhow.

Every time one of them made the slightest positive remark about her cooking, her pretty face turned ten shades of pink. The woman acted as though she'd never received a compliment. For some reason, that bugged the hell out of him.

Grabbing his long coat from the ground, Tucker stood and went to start his night watch. Being so close to Skylar was hell on his mind and damn hard on his body.

Shimmering rays of moonlight streaked through the trees from a full moon overhead as Tucker started through the woods, toward camp. Hoping there was coffee still on the fire, he'd left his horse in the clearing with the herd. His breath streamed out before him in white, misty plumes as he shoved his gloved hands into his jacket pockets.

He didn't know what was more exhausting, the change in altitude and temperature, the rigorous pace Skylar insisted on keeping or his growing attraction for a woman who acted as though she hated him. Yet, she had watched his mouth in a way that told him she was more interested in him tasting her than her beans.

He'd actually managed to catch Skylar with her guard down, and her response to him was anything but hateful. If Garret hadn't come running into camp, she would have let him kiss her. But he didn't know what that meant, if anything at all.

And I don't need to find out, he curtly reminded himself. He'd promised Chance he would keep his hands off her.

"Sonuvabitch."

He paused, hearing the softly spoken curse. He was still a good fifty yards from camp. When another curse followed, he decided to investigate. He walked only a short distance before finding Skylar in a small clearing, bathed in moonlight.

His heart leaped into his throat at the sight of her. She sat on her knees in the pool of her gray skirt, with her light blue waist puddled on the ground behind her. Silver moonlight illuminated golden hair brushing her beautiful bare shoulders and the ivory skin of her slender back.

He began tugging his gloves from his hands as he silently stalked toward her, fully aware she hadn't sensed his presence, her focus on the binding she was trying to wrap across her shoulder and around her back. Her curses drifted through the tall pines as she fumbled with the clean binding that didn't appear to be cooperating.

"Need a hand?" he asked, shoving his gloves into his jacket pocket as he knelt behind her.

Skylar's head whipped around. Her warm breath curled out into the cold night air in a burst of white clouds. Startled, she nearly turned to face him, but quickly thought better of it, clamping the long piece of cloth to her breasts as she put her back to him. Wide blue eyes peered up at him over a lily-white shoulder. "W-w-what are you—"

"I was heading to camp for some coffee when I heard a foul-mouthed forest critter cursing from the bushes." He smiled, ignoring the surprise in her eyes, and trying to ignore the heated stir of his body as he reached over her shoulder to take the end of the binding she hadn't managed to wrap around herself. Skylar immediately jerked away from him.

"Let me help you."

"No. I don't need any help."

"You'll catch your death from the cold before you get that long cloth wrapped around you. I won't peek at you, Sky. Now toss that binding over your shoulder or I'm going to reach over and get it."

"Tucker—"

Her breath rushed from her lungs as his hand took the binding. "Keep that patch in place," he said, spotting the thick pad of cloth she was holding against her sutures. "Lift your arms, angel," he instructed as he reached around her. Trembling, she did as he asked. He leaned forward, passing the cloth to his other hand, and breathing in the strong sweet scent of her. The discomfort in his britches doubled as the floral scent curled around his senses and clouded his mind.

She smells incredible. He'd been a fool to buy her scented soap. If he dipped his head just a fraction, he could taste that sweet, petal-soft skin. But if he did that, she'd find his hands moving over her body instead of the cloth and they'd both end up with their bare skin exposed to the frosty night air; not that they'd be cold.

Wrapping the cloth over her left shoulder, then back across her front, his wrist accidentally brushed the tip of a strained nipple. Tucker heard the quake in Skylar's breath, and felt a sweat break out over his entire body. "Relax. I'm not trying to take advantage of you," he said, reassuring her as much as himself, and being extra careful not to touch anything he shouldn't with his next pass.

Skylar knew she was shaking something awful, but

was powerless to stop the shivering. The night air is cold, she reasoned, yet the moment she watched Tucker kneel behind her, the crisp mountain air had been suddenly replaced by midday Arizona heat. Her skin burned. Her overly sensitive breast still sizzled from Tucker's light touch.

After one more pass around her body, he tucked the end of the binding in behind her left shoulder. "Slip an arm in here, honey," he said in a deep whisper.

From the corner of her eye, Skylar saw that Tucker was holding her waist out for her. Unable to get a word past her dry throat, she shoved her arms into the sleeves. As she pulled the sides closed, she heard Tucker stand, his boots scuffing the ground as he turned away from her. When she glanced over her shoulder, nothing stood behind her but dark shadows and streaks of silver moonlight.

Her shaky hands quickly fastened the row of buttons. She took a few moments to catch her breath—which wasn't easy.

After several deep, controlled breaths, she picked up her camisole from the ground in front of her and stood, feeling none too steady on her feet. "He must have lightning in his veins," she muttered. She turned and ran right into Tucker's large body.

Skylar shrieked and stumbled back. Tucker reached out, grabbing her by the wrist to steady her.

"You're gonna wake the whole mountainside," he said in a low voice laced with amusement.

"You scared the life out of me, creeping up on me like that. *Again*."

"I didn't creep nowhere. You were breathing so hard, you wouldn't have heard me if I had skipped up behind you."

His smug, smiling face did wonders to ease her start. The skin of her wrist tingling beneath his warm fingers, she jerked it from his gentle grasp.

"Here," he said, thrusting a brown package toward her.

"What's this?" she asked, accepting the paper-bound parcel.

"Levi's, a flannel shirt and long underwear. I had mentioned that I'd picked them up for you. I just forgot to give them to you."

She recalled him mentioning the denims and shirt, but he hadn't mentioned long underwear. "Thanks," she said, hugging the package tight against her stomach which refused to stop flip-flopping as he gazed down at her. She stepped around him and hurried toward camp before she could embarrass herself further.

"Good night, Skylar," he called after her.

Hardly. She increased her strides, pretending not to hear him, knowing she'd never get any sleep now.

Chapter 12

The cove of rock made a perfect corral. Surrounded by high cliffs of dirt and granite, the horses grazed leisurely on patches of tall grass. With the only entrance to the secluded meadow roped off, and camp just a few yards away, nothing would be going in or out without their notice.

Skylar smiled in approval and tucked her gloves into her back pocket as she turned toward camp. They'd all be getting some sleep tonight.

"Hey, Sky!" Garret shouted excitedly from beyond the tall pines he and the Morgans had walked through. "Come look at this river. It's wide as a lake!"

A lake, huh?

She'd stood downwind of Garret a few times earlier in the day, and although he washed up a bit before each meal, her little brother and his clothes were well overdue for a good scrubbing. After traveling through the high country for a few days, the fall climate of these lower ranges felt like springtime.

She reached into her saddlebag and withdrew a bar of soap bound in a white cloth and started toward the veil of pines on the edge of the grassy meadow. She'd have her own laundry to wash later. Thanks to the second pair of denims Tucker had given her, she no longer had to wear her dress. As much as she liked the gray skirt and blue waist, all that flapping fabric had been downright cumbersome and inconvenient in the saddle. But beneath her men's work clothes, she took secret pleasure in her soft, feminine underclothes. She'd found a second pair with the denims and flannel Tucker had bought for her.

As she cleared the trees, she saw Garret, Tucker and Chance standing atop a large bolder, looking over the edge at a swollen gentle stretch of the river.

"You think it's deep enough to jump in from up here?" Garret was asking as Skylar stepped out onto the giant rock.

"Why don't you find out," Tucker answered, and shoved Garret over the edge.

"You sure the kid can swim, Tuck?" Chance asked off-handedly as Garret splashed into the clear, deep water below.

Tucker's eyes surged wide. With a muffled curse, he tossed off his hat and dived over the edge after Garret.

Skylar laughed out loud, reaching the edge in time to see Tucker's boots disappear beneath the water. Chance glanced over at her, his emerald eyes twinkling with amusement.

"You know Garret can swim," she said.

Chance shrugged his broad shoulders. "Apparently Tuck doesn't."

The sound of laughter and splashes echoed up from

below, assuring them neither Tucker or Garret were too disappointed about swimming in their boots and britches.

"Figures they'd enjoy it," said Chance.

Skylar glanced up at the man beside her, surprised by the blatant affection she heard in his tone.

"Little brothers, huh?" he said as he met her gaze. "Can't live with 'em, can't shoot 'em." Grinning, he winked at her.

The casual response was so much like Tucker, it stunned her, reminding her that the two men truly were identical.

Chance knelt down and picked up Tucker's hat then started down the cliff tapering to the rocky shoreline. Skylar stared at his retreating back for a moment before following him down the hillside. Her eyes moved over his strong body.

A mirror image of Tucker, Chance was no less attractive and far less annoying, yet she didn't feel the volatile mixture of sensations that crowded her body when Tucker was near. She liked Chance, had worked closely with him in the past few weeks, but his touch didn't make her skin tingle. Strange, that the man she could hardly stand was the one who caused her body to go haywire.

"Since we're needing to restock our supplies," Chance said as they neared the base of the cliff, "Tuck and I thought this would be a good spot to spend an extra night. Someone could ride into the nearest settlement tomorrow for supplies."

Skylar released a hard sigh, not wanting to give up a full day of travel, but knowing she had to. They were running low on nearly everything, and the horses could use a full day of rest and grazing. "Sounds good," she agreed.

"Liar," Chance shot back at her.

Skylar smiled. She wondered again why she wasn't physically attracted to Chance. His no-nonsense attitude and rugged work ethic was far more in tune with her own.

"Do you want to be the one to head into town?" he asked.

"I'd rather not. How about I write up a list of supplies?"

Chance nodded in agreement and continued toward the river's edge. Tucker and Garret were still floundering in the water. Garret's white hair surfaced, his lungs pulling for breath. Tucker shot up in a spray of water beside him and dunked Garret back under.

Garret resurfaced, laughing wildly as he latched onto Tucker's strong shoulders and did his best to push the much larger man under the water.

Garret's laughter filled Skylar's chest with a warmth she was becoming more and more accustomed to feeling. Having someone to horse around with had done wonders to rekindle the youthfulness Skylar liked to see in her little brother, and he and Tucker did plenty of horsing around. There had been a definite change in the chemistry between all of them. She supposed everyone was becoming accustomed to one another and feeling less on edge, but Skylar wasn't sure that was a change for the good.

She had to keep reminding herself that she had a job to do, and being friendly with the Morgans didn't mean they wouldn't up and claim the horses they had intended to buy.

The sound of Tucker's deep laughter captured her attention. Garret waded toward shore. Behind him, Tucker stood waist-deep in water, his thin cotton shirt plastered to his firm body. The muscles in his arms flexed beneath the blue fabric as he pushed his hands through his wet hair.

She quickly shifted her gaze back to Garret, annoyed by Tucker's effortless ability to fluster her.

"Here," she said, tossing Garret the bar of soap wrapped in a cloth as he waded toward her. "Might as well wash up while you're wet. Scrub those clothes while you're at it."

"Remember when we swam in that underground lake in Arizona, Sky?"

Skylar climbed onto a nearby boulder and sat down. She crossed her arms over the dusty chaps covering her knees. "Yeah, I remember," she said, recalling one of the few times they'd sneaked off while they were supposed to be working.

"I thought you were gonna be furious with Duce for tossing you into the water like he did."

Skylar smiled at the memory.

They'd been scouting for horses when Garret and Duce, a wiry horse wrangler and a man she'd considered a good friend, had discovered the cavern with a clear green pool hidden inside. It didn't take much to convince her to escape the Arizona heat and spend the afternoon splashing and swimming. She closed her eyes, silently praying Duce hadn't been killed by Randal.

"How long ago was that?" asked Tucker, his rich voice intruding on Skylar's thoughts.

"Last year," Garret answered.

Hearing a thud, Skylar opened her eyes and looked down at the rocks beside her. Tucker's wet clothes were sprawled across them. Without thinking, her eyes darted up and sought him out. Her gaze locked on glistening bronze skin.

She had been exposed to a fair number of bare chests, but nothing so spectacular as the male body moving toward her. Droplets of water caught in the golden hair of Tucker's torso sparkled in the sunlight as he waded closer to shore. His broad chest tapered down to narrow hips. Each movement flexed the hard rippling muscles. Her eyes followed the thin trail of gold hair across the center line of his body, until it disappeared beneath the veil of shimmering water.

"Toss me that soap, would you, Garret?" he called out, shaking her from the trancelike state. Her gaze moved back up his body. Tucker flashed a mischievous grin, and Skylar lost her ability to breathe. He wasn't wearing anything beneath the shimmering water. Another step and…

Feeling a blush from her face to her toes, Skylar jumped up and turned away from the river.

"Hey, you don't have to rush off," Tucker called after her.

He grinned, watching her fast retreat. He hadn't planned on coming any farther out of the river, but it was just as well that she'd gone. Too much more of watching the approval in her smoldering eyes as she soaked up her fill of him would have kept his overheated body in this cold river till dark.

"You do like to goad that woman, don't you, Tuck?"

Tucker glanced up at his brother reclined on a large boulder near the edge of the water. "She makes it too easy. Sometimes she reminds me of Cora Mae."

"Now there's a name I haven't heard in a long while," Chance said as he laid back, folding his arms under his head.

"Who's Cora Mae?" asked Garret, busily shucking his own clothes.

"Pure mischief," said Chance, "packaged in a pint-size body and topped with wild orange hair. And a set of big brown eyes camouflaged by such sweet innocence, you could have a gaping hole in your chest, Cora Mae standing before you with a smoking gun, and you'd still not believe she pulled the trigger."

Tucker chuckled, saying, "She's our stepsister. We haven't seen her in some fifteen years. She must be a full-grown woman by now."

"And most likely a self-absorbed, high-society bitch," Chance said in a cold tone. "Just like her mother."

"Winifred sure would have had her work cut out for her if she managed to refine the mulish tomboy who used to go for late-night swims and have mud wars with us on the riverbank."

"She also tattled to her mamma when the mood struck her, knowing we'd get whupped."

"She was nine," Tucker said with a shrug. "I liked Cora

Mae. So did you," he reminded Chance. They had both felt real guilty about leaving their stepsister behind, but she was Winifred's daughter. They'd already had more trouble hanging over their heads than they knew how to handle. Kidnapping was not another charge they'd needed against them.

"I liked her well enough when she was nine," Chance said as he tipped his hat forward to shade his face from the late-afternoon sun. "But you know what they say—the apple never falls far from the tree. And her family tree don't grow nothin' but sour crab apples."

Tucker looked away from his brother napping on the boulder, his mind refusing to give up thoughts that didn't have a thing to do with their stepsister. Knowing he was a fool to ask, he tossed the soap to Garret after the boy dived back into the water. "So, this guy Duce I keep hearing mentioned, was he murdered the same evening as your pa?"

"Sky told me they had him tied up," Garret said, scrubbing the white bar of soap over his skinny arms. "She was thinkin' Randal probably needed him and the others to help with the horses. I sure hope she's right."

"Maybe that was a cover and he was in with Randal. Had he been working with your outfit long?"

"Two years," Garret said, whipping his stone-serious gaze toward Tucker. "He wouldn't betray us. Me and Sky were closer to Duce than we was to anybody. He'd never hurt us."

"How old is he?" Tucker asked, the boy's answers not

doing a damn thing to ease the tension he felt building inside him.

"Probably around the same age as you," Garret said before dunking his soaped-up hair into the water.

"Hell, if she's got a beau headed for Wyoming," Chance called out from his rocky perch, "you won't have to worry about her finding a man. But you might have some heavy explaining to do."

"Not to Duce, you won't," Garret said with a laugh, brushing his wet hair back with his hands. "My Pa woulda fired anyone who tried anything fresh with Skylar and he made sure every man knew it."

Issuing that sort of challenge was begging the men to seduce Daines's feisty daughter. Tucker didn't see how any man could romp through the water with Skylar, be subjected to her pretty smiles and soft skin, and not take her. Walking away from her that night a week back had damn near killed him.

The way the kid talked, Skylar and Duce had actually been friendly with one another. Tucker had seen Skylar's big blue eyes cloud over when her brother mentioned the man's name. She wouldn't show such emotion over just another cowhand. If Duce was any kind of man, he would have been all over her.

With his teeth clenched tight and a tension tugging at his back, Tucker waded up to the shore and grabbed his wet clothes from the rocks. He twisted the denim and cotton, wringing out the water and popping threads.

What am I so worked up about?

He eased his grip on his shirt before it was ripped to shreds. He didn't have a damn thing to be jealous about.

I'm not jealous! he silently defended. The thought of him being jealous over a woman was laughable. Possession worked both ways. He just didn't like the idea of Skylar being in the arms of another man.

He didn't like it one damn bit.

Chapter 13

The morning sun sparkled like twinkling stars atop the surface of the gently flowing water. After she scrubbed her clothing in a shallow pool along the shoreline, Skylar's sun-warmed skin prickled as she waded farther into the wide river with the soap and cloth clutched in her hand.

Taking a deep breath, she dived beneath the glittering surface and swam toward the clear, deep pool where Garret and Tucker had frolicked the day before, hoping the swim would help her body adjust to the cold water. With each broad stroke of her arms, a dull ache tugged at the tender muscles in her left shoulder. She'd removed her stitches a couple days back. Most of the swelling and bruising had faded, leaving an ugly red seam of flesh in the hollow of her shoulder.

Surfacing in the sheltered cove of deep water, she shivered and realized Garret and Tucker may have been smart to jump into the stream still wearing their clothes, saving their bare skin from the bite of the frigid water. With her clothing strung out across surrounding boulders to dry, she didn't have that option. As desperately as she needed a bath, she wouldn't complain if she had to bathe in freshly melted snow.

By the time she swam back to the shallows, the water didn't feel quite as cold and the stiffness in her shoulder was easing. She quickly scrubbed up with the soap she'd used to wash her clothes, wishing all the while that she had brought her sweet-scented soap. But today she was finally Morgan-free and she didn't want the floral fragrance causing her thoughts to stray to Tucker. When she'd set off for the river nearly an hour ago, Tucker and Chance were saddling their horses to ride toward town. By now they were miles from camp and wouldn't be returning until nightfall.

A smile stretched her lips as she started toward shore. With the Morgans out of her hair, she finally felt relaxed, and she'd have some time alone to spend with Garret.

She grabbed the drying sheet from a rock and glanced at the clear blue sky and towering pine trees as she dried herself. Snowcapped mountains rose up in the background in all directions. It was beautiful here, surrounded by the tranquil chirping of birds and the whisper of the gentle river flowing beside her. All that was missing was a cozy cottage nestled beyond the pines in the sun-sprayed meadow, and a man to share it with. An old dream, yet reinvented Skylar realized, for that man now had a face.

Realizing it belonged to Tucker, she released a low groan and closed her eyes. Cursing silently, she shook her head, disappointed in herself for thinking such foolishness.

I might as well be chasing rainbows. Tucker didn't hold

more than a passing interest in her, the same as he held in anything else.

Not today. She would not allow herself to think about Tucker Morgan. Wrapping the thin strip of cotton around herself, she stepped into her boots and started back to camp. Her new denims, shirt and undergarments were spread across the warming rocks and would likely take half the day to dry. Although she'd enjoyed the chance to wear something feminine, she looked forward to the freedom that came with wearing denims.

As she spotted their camp in a meadow of green grass littered with giant boulders, her eyes locked on the low-burning campfire. Expecting the fire to be extinguished, she was elated to find a source of warmth and increased her strides until she stood before the low flames. Leaning over the rising heat, she shivered as tendrils of warmth moved across her chilled skin. She splayed her hands over the currents of warm air. Boots scuffed the ground behind her. A pile of mended rope landed near her feet.

"Garret, could you grab my saddlebags?" she asked, hoping she wouldn't have to leave the fire to get her clean clothes. When he didn't respond, she turned around.

"Tucker!"

He stood a few feet away, stiff as a statue, his wide eyes riveted on her chest. Every nerve in her body jolted to full alert. Her hands flew to the top of the damp sheet precariously covering her body.

"What are you doing here?" she demanded.

"I, uh, I was… Damn if I can remember." His eyes lingered on her chest, increasing the heat in Skylar's face before he again met her gaze. "You shot my mind to hell by sashaying into camp, wearing that little bit of cotton. It's not much of a cover, Skylar." His eyes dropped back down to her chest, and lower still. "You're killin' me," he said in a hoarse whisper.

She tightened her arms around her breasts and twisted slightly away from him, salvaging what little modesty she could, while wishing she could wrap the mountainside around her. "I thought you rode to town."

Tucker drew a deep, ragged breath then turned away from her. Relief vibrated through Skylar as he strode toward their supplies. She remained by the campfire, debating whether to make a run for cover behind a boulder or risk ignoring any sense of caution and marching toward Tucker so she could retrieve her clothing.

She was surprised when Tucker returned with her saddlebags. He reached into one of the deep pockets and pulled out her old pair of denim britches and the other white camisole with pink ribbons he'd purchased for her.

"Here you are, angel girl. Cover up," he said as he tossed them to her. "Do it quick."

Tucker continued to stand there, gaping at her.

"Turn around!"

"I don't want to. You're the prettiest thing I've ever seen."

"Damn it, Tucker!" If her face burned any hotter, her skin would catch fire.

"You sure don't know how to take a compliment," he grumbled, and turned his back to her. "Your shoulder's healing up nice. When did you remove the sutures?"

"Why didn't you go to town?" she asked as she shrugged on the camisole and quickly tied the ribbons. Dropping the drying sheet, she kicked off her boots so she could pull on her pants.

"Garret was looking all down in the mouth before we set out," said Tucker. "I figured he could use a ride into town. You should have seen his eyes light up when I offered him to ride along with Chance."

"You could have alerted me to your presence."

"I would have, but Garret said you were bathing, so I didn't dare set foot anywhere near the river, and when you came back…*the sight of you knocked the breath clean out of me.*"

She noted the rich timbre of Tucker's voice as she worked the buttons on her denims. Alarmed, she peered through the strands of her damp hair. Tucker's sharp eyes were boldly fixed on her. Her shirt was tossed over his wide shoulder. Meeting her gaze, his mouth slowly tipped up into a wry and utterly masculine smile. His eyes radiating like embers of an evergreen fire. Flutters rose up from the pit of Skylar's stomach.

"Do you have any idea how beautiful you are?" he asked.

She felt a sudden ache in her breasts, and shoved her hair away from her face. Her nipples strained against the thin camisole. She silently cursed Tucker's control over her traitorous body. "You have no more decency than the devil. Give me my shirt."

Tucker flinched, appearing wounded by her words, but she recognized the glint of humor shining in those green eyes of his. "Two weeks ago you were calling me your angel and now I'm the devil?"

"I never called you my angel."

"You did, too. When we were cuddled up in bed at the doc's place, right before you kissed me. You said my smile made you dizzy."

He flashed that devastating smile of his as though trying to prove his point, and damn him, she felt it clear to her wobbly knees. "I, you…that elixir Mrs. Perkins gave me must have been some kind of brain-drainer! You can't hold me accountable for things I may have said or done while under its influence. And *you* kissed me first."

A thick blond eyebrow shot up as he took a step toward her. "So, you do remember."

"Hardly," she lied, the confidence in his smile increasing her nervousness and the heated swirls twisting in her belly.

"Those were some memorable kisses, Skylar," Tucker prodded, stepping toward her.

She retreated, taking a cautious step back for every step he took. "I wouldn't recall."

"You sure, honey?"

She stepped from the soft grass onto gravel and dirt, and realized she was backing up into a pile of rocks with a giant boulder at its center. "Tucker, what are you doing?"

"Bringing you your shirt, and thinking about your kisses. I've never experienced anything quite like them. Perhaps if I cuddle you a bit, I could spark your memory."

"I don't need to be cuddled by a flirtatious cowboy," she

said, her voice unsteady as she bumped into the massive wall of stone behind her.

"A bit of cuddling is good for a person from time to time," he countered.

Terrified by the rush of fiery sensations crashing through her body, Skylar's heart thundered in her chest as Tucker slowly closed in on her. How could Garret desert her like this? Her response to Tucker's presence was hard enough to control even with her little brother standing between them.

Tucker could see Skylar's pulse beating rapidly in her neck as she gazed up at him with wide eyes.

She's remembering those kisses, all right.

He'd been able to think of little else. He wanted her until his whole body ached with need, and he was sick to death of fighting it. Chance wouldn't want him to uphold a promise that would kill him to keep, and keeping his hands off this woman was slowly but surely killing him. If his brother couldn't understand that, then he'd never tasted the kiss of a woman like Skylar.

Zach Daines must have had a powerful presence to keep his cowhands from pursuing his daughter. Tucker wondered if Duce was the only man who'd risked his hide to hold Skylar. He imagined Skylar's hostile attitude discouraged such advances and figured she was mighty particular about who she permitted to get close to her. But if she'd been with a man, there was no reason they couldn't ease one another's hunger and still keep things in perspective. Skylar didn't want to be tied down any more than he did, but that didn't have to keep her from burning in his arms.

"I don't believe you've had enough cuddling in your lifetime," he said, not stopping until his boots were touching hers. She flinched as he lifted his hand to touch her cheek.

"You're afraid of me."

"I am not!"

"No?" He planted his hands on the stone wall just above her shoulders, his body all but making contact with hers. He saw fear in her eyes, heard the startled squeak that escaped her throat, yet she made no attempt to push him away. "Then what are you afraid of?"

"Nothing," she said in a whispered breath. She squared her shoulders and hardened her gaze.

A grin tugged at his mouth. She was terrified, and if she was feeling anything near the passion presently ripping through his veins, he couldn't blame her one bit.

Tucker dipped his head, brushing his cheek against hers in the lightest caress. A violent tremor shook Skylar's body, the vibrations moving clean through him. She swayed and her hands shot out, grabbing at his waist, inadvertently tugging him against the length of her body. Tucker shuddered with barely restrained desire.

"I have a confession to make," he said in a gruff whisper, passion constricting his throat. "You scare the hell out of me."

He'd never wanted anything the way he wanted her. He eased back, meeting her gaze. Skylar's eyes widened with blatant surprise.

"Tucker."

"Angel girl."

The corners of her mouth twitched with the hint of a smile, and he felt an explosion of warmth. The endearment pleased her. Dear God, how he wanted to please her. Since he'd spent the night holding her in his arms, he'd craved her smiles.

Lifting a hand, he threaded his fingers into her hair. "So soft," he said, loving the feel of the damp strands sliding through his fingers. "Golden silk. The perfect frame for such a beautiful face. You're so pretty, Skylar."

Skylar stared up at Tucker in sheer amazement, willing herself not to be moved by his words, even as her eyes felt the burn of tears.

She wasn't sure which one of them closed the distance between their mouths. The instant she felt the gentle pressure of his lips against hers, she didn't care. She only knew the sleek probing of his tongue gliding against hers helped to ease the aching of her body.

But she soon realized that like the first lick of a peppermint stick or nibble of rich, smooth chocolate, the alluring taste of Tucker only left her craving more. Like a kid cut loose in a candy store, she took it, heedlessly lapping and nibbling at his mouth as her hands feasted on the muscular ripples along his sides and back in greedy exploration.

Every touch and taste seemed to increase the insatiable hunger welling inside her. Her insides ached for something she couldn't name, until Tucker used his body to press her against the boulder. Heat shot through her in a wild torrent of sensation as he rocked his hips against hers, the solid proof of his arousal caressing her so intimately, he electrified her blood.

The sharp reality of what all his kisses were leading to sent a spike of fear across her scattered senses. She suddenly recalled the force of Randal's body pinning her to the ground, and her father's warning that the coupling between men and women was no different from the breeding of horses.

A girl didn't spend her life around horses and not witness the wild, frequently brutal act of mating.

"Tucker," she said, turning away from his kiss, determined to end this madness. But his lips only shifted course, moving down the side of her neck, distracting her, blurring reality with desire.

"Tuck, stop, I can't think when you're…"

He dusted tender kisses across her face.

Perhaps my father was wrong, she thought as Tucker's mouth again settled over hers, evaporating any thoughts of protest. Tucker wasn't anything like Randal.

He's a special kind of fire.

His long, gentle fingers caressed the back of her neck while his other hand stroked her side, steadily burning away the ugliness of life as his fiery kiss consumed her, breathing life into her soul. By the time he released her mouth, she was clinging to him, straining for clarity as her lungs strived for breath.

"Let me love you, Skylar," Tucker said, his lips pressed against her ear.

"I can't!" she gasped, panicked by his brazen request, and her body's willing response. Tucker must have been listening to her body and not her words, because in the next moment, he was kissing her again, with overwhelming intensity. The rhythmic caress of his hips pressing her against the boulder set her ablaze, the cloth barrier between them taunting her superheated flesh.

She didn't understand her body's reaction to Tucker, any more than she could deny the streams of fire coursing through her veins. She raked her fingers through his hair, needing to be closer to him, wanting everything his kiss and caress were promising. She wanted it now, before she expired from the volatile sensations swelling inside her.

"Tucker," she gasped, pulling away, not knowing how to say what she wanted.

He groaned as his lips moved across her throat. "If you tell me to stop, I will. But I may lose my mind."

"Don't stop."

He reared back, his eyes wide, his chest rising and falling with each rapid breath. "I hope you're serious."

Apparently finding the answer in her gaze, his look of surprise was quickly replaced with a twisted grin. "You won't regret it, honey," he promised, and swooped her into his arms.

Skylar shrieked his name.

"Shh," he soothed, pressing his lips to hers. "I don't intend to take you against this rock and I can't make love to you here in the dirt."

Make love to me? Skylar swallowed hard as she gazed up at him, his choice of words adding to the chaos raging within her, and then he was kissing her again, dissolving everything in her mind but the taste and textures of his wonderful mouth.

A moment later she felt soft, cool grass against her back, contrasted by the warmth radiating from the man above her. She released a soft cry of protest as he pulled away. When she opened her eyes, Tucker's knees were straddling her hips, his hand reaching toward her camisole. Her breath caught as she watched him tug on the pink ribbon at her waist. Enigmatic green eyes locked with hers as his hand moved to the top ribbon.

"I've been dreaming about unwrapping and unraveling you for weeks."

She closed her eyes and held her breath, shivering as his hand pushed the thin garment aside, exposing her breasts to his gaze. "They're a nuisance," she said, annoyed by the heat she felt in her face. She gasped as he buried his face between them.

"They're heaven," he breathed against her skin.

"Tucker," she choked in a rush of air. She glanced down at the golden crown of his head as his lips brushed across the sensitive skin between her breasts. Skylar winced, every nerve ending in her body feeling exposed.

"Skylar, you are pure perfection."

Her breath caught at the sight of him looking at her body with a mixture of awe and admiration. He lowered his head, his breath dusting her breast before he flicked his tongue over the tight peak.

The light caress seared her body like a lightning bolt. Skylar cried out, her back arching off the grass.

"Easy, honey," Tucker soothed, her unrestrained cry increasing his desire. He rubbed his palm across the smooth skin of her torso and got a similar reaction. He'd never been with a woman who was so responsive to his touch.

It ain't a wonder, he thought. The way she keeps herself at arm's length from everyone, her body must be starving to feel a man's caress, and I'm a man who's been dying to caress her.

He turned his attention to her other breast. The pink crown beaded beneath his tongue as he drew her into his mouth. Again Skylar gasped and bucked as though he'd burned her. Her fingers plowed into his hair, and Tucker wasn't sure if she was encouraging him or trying to stop him.

He released her and eased back. "Didn't your beau love you like this?" he asked, somewhat confused by the shock and uncertainty he saw in her eyes.

"No!"

Tucker settled on the grass beside her, regarding the pure disgust in her expression. "Do you like it?" he asked, truly concerned. When her eyes only widened in response he pressed her for an answer, damned if he'd do anything she found offensive. "Skylar?" He propped up on his elbow and reached across her and brushed the warm skin of her waist.

"I don't know," she said in a soft voice, shielding her eyes with long, golden lashes. She flushed from her forehead to her beautiful breasts glistening in the morning sun from his caresses. He was pretty certain she'd like it.

Skylar eased onto her side and inched toward him, which Tucker took to be more of an act of shyness than actually wanting to get close to him. Watching her face, he stroked his palm across the soft skin of her stomach, moving slowly up her body until her breast filled his palm. Skylar shivered and moaned. When he stroked his thumb across the firm peak, her eyes widened and glazed with undeniable pleasure as her breath unraveled in a long, languid sigh.

"Tucker?" she said, her voice trembling.

"It's okay, angel girl," he soothed, plying her lips with gentle kisses. The realization as to just how innocent she was to this sort of play stunned him, and fueled his passion. "We'll take it real slow," he murmured against her lips.

She answered him with a kiss that caused him to question his own restraint. *She'll like it all*, he silently vowed. He'd pour over her with the gentle subtleness of sunlight, taking her the way dawn takes the night sky, leaving no part of her untouched.

Chapter 14

Slow was another word for torture. Tucker's gentle touch and soft lips moved across her body like molten molasses, caressing her bare skin and drizzling pleasure from the tips of her fingers to her toes. He melted her muscles as he singed her soul with his sweet, hot fire.

She wanted to feel more of him, but he kept himself just out of reach, constantly shifting above her. A cry of passion and impatience rose up from her throat. Tucker responded by returning his mouth to hers, treating her to a kiss which only fueled the fire building inside her. She trembled from the frightfully wonderful feel of his body again moving over hers, bringing him back into reach of her eager hands.

She was delighted to discover he'd removed his shirt. Before she could enjoy her discovery Tucker's hand stroked across her belly, trailing down until he jolted her body with a rush of hot pleasure. His gentle strokes stripped everything from her mind but the wondrous feel of his intimate caress. Consumed by pleasure and the mounting tension pooling at her center, her body arched, seeking. As if answering her silent plea, Tucker's warm, wonderful mouth closed over the tight peak of her breast.

She gasped, the wild sensations welling inside her becoming almost painful, frightening. "Tuck, no more, I—"

The slow, deliberate swirling of his thumb over her sensitive flesh ended Skylar's words in a deep moan as pleasure pulsed through her body. He repeated the caress, his mouth loving her breast in the same sensual rhythm, and Skylar's world exploded in a burst of shimmering sensation.

She gripped his shoulders as waves of fire burst through her, shaking her, consuming her. When Tucker finally moved over her, Skylar banded her arms around him, needing his weight to soothe the violent tremors racking her body.

He murmured something against her ear, but his words escaped her, her mind still splintered by the effects of his sensual touch. Aching to touch him as completely as he'd touched her, she slid her hands down his lean back. Just as her fingers slipped beneath his denim waistband, his slick, corded muscles slid from her grasp as Tucker eased down her body, his lips blazing a trail of fire across her abdomen. His teeth grazed her stomach, stinging her with a rush of rippling sensation before he pulled away from her completely.

"Come back," she said in a shallow breath, frustrated by his evasiveness to her touch. Her eyes fluttered open and gazed up at the bluest sky she'd ever seen.

"Patience, love," Tucker answered, his voice thick, his

breathing sounding hard and forced. "I'm only trying to give you what you're asking for."

Asking for?

Skylar propped herself up on her elbows. The sight of her own nudity stunned her. Tucker had distracted her so completely with his touch and undressed her with such subtlety that she hadn't fully realized she was lying in a meadow wearing nothing but sunlight.

Tucker towered over her, his spectacular bronze skin glistening in the sun. His tousled hair hung in his eyes as his hands worked at the buckle of his belt.

Skylar sat up in a rush. Drawing her knees to her chest, she banded her arms around them. Tucker's pants dropped from his hips to his ankles. He kicked them aside, leaving him just as naked as she. Skylar's breath lodged in her throat. Her body tingled, her skin prickled as her gaze traced his broad shoulders and the sculpted muscles of his abdomen tapering down to narrow hips, and below.

"Oh my," she breathed, suddenly quite nervous about the physical details of coupling.

Being raised around a bunch of men prone to relieve themselves whenever they felt the urge, she'd witnessed a fair amount of indecency. Tucker's powerful body didn't resemble the flashing glimpse of any cowhand she'd ever seen.

She didn't realize she was gaping at him until he placed a finger under her chin and tilted her face up to meet his gaze as he knelt beside her. His eyebrows cinched together. "Skylar?"

"I—I didn't realize…I've never seen…I just didn't realize," she said again.

Tucker's lips quirked with a slight grin. "You've never seen a naked man?"

"None like *you*. You're very…"

"Horny," Tucker supplied, silent laughter shaking his chest.

His disarming smile reminded Skylar of the gentleness he possessed. The laughter in his eyes began to soothe the nervousness he must have sensed. Instead of crowding her, he eased back.

Her gaze slid down the sculpted lines of his chest and torso, to the very male part of him that no longer seemed so different from the rest of his body. *Skin over steel.*

"Masculine," she amended, her throat closing over the word. "And beautiful," she said in a gruff whisper as she slowly sought his gaze.

The approval Tucker saw in Skylar's eyes washed over him like a caress. "You're very feminine," he said, smiling as he pressed his lips to her raised knee. *And shy.*

She was wrapped up tighter than an armadillo. Her shyness continued to amaze him. He scooted a bit closer. When she didn't back away, he reached out to either side of her and stroked his hands up the smooth skin of the thighs she held tight against her chest.

"Are you hiding from me?" he asked, leaning forward to brush his lips across her blushing face and timid smile. As his lips met hers, her arms curved around his neck. Tucker slid his hands between her raised knees, meeting no resistance as he gently eased them apart, bringing their bodies closer. Skylar returned his light kisses, allowing him to ease her back onto the grass.

Her slender body felt so delicate beneath him. He pulled back to gaze down at her. The warmth in Skylar's eyes stole his breath, the uncertainty he'd seen a moment ago now lost in a glow of raw desire. He shuddered as she smoothed her hands across his chest.

Hell. He was about to lose control just looking at her. Combined with her touch, things looked grim. He'd done his damnedest to avoid the feel of her hot little hands, her touch burning through the short rope he had on his control the way a flame takes to kerosene.

"Kiss me," she said, her hands sliding around his neck, drawing him to her.

More than eager, Tucker did as she asked. He brushed a trail of kisses down her neck, across her narrow shoulder. His name left her lips in a deep sigh, sending a tremor of sensation through his body. Tension strained between his shoulders as his body burned with an urgency he'd never felt with any other woman. He groaned as his shaft brushed against the sultry entrance of her feminine core then pressed into the satin heat.

"Skylar," he sighed, clenching his eyes shut as his slight penetration jolted his body with fiery sensation.

He rocked gently against her, taking her with agonizing slowness. Skylar's soft moans clawed at his resolve, the tight passage of her body caressing him so completely, he couldn't breathe. Damn it all, he wanted this to last, but his body wasn't going to cooperate.

He took her mouth in a deep kiss. Skylar folded her legs around his hips, demanding fulfillment.

On the verge of losing control, Tucker gripped her hips and sheathed himself deep inside her.

Skylar winced, tensing beneath him as he felt a delicate barrier give way to his intrusion.

"Sky?" he said in a ragged breath, afraid to move. But even as his mind reeled from shock, his body shuddered with a tingling rush of pleasure. "Honey," he began again when he managed to pull in a full breath. "You're a—"

His words ended in a groan as Skylar's hips rocked forward, taking more of him as her hands slid up the corded muscles of his back. Helpless against the pull of her body, Tucker brushed his lips across her temple, whispered her name and sank farther into the sweet, satin paradise.

Any pain his breaching may have caused her had abated. The constricting proof of her pleasure was about to undo him.

Shaking from the shimmers of sensation cascading through her body, Skylar tightened her legs around Tucker as he filled her to the point of bursting. And then he was moving, each thrust sending streamers of fire racing down her spine, pooling at her center until she cried out.

Her body arched, trembling as pleasure pulsed through her. Tucker held her tight, her name echoed in her ears as her world splintered in a shimmering array of wild sensation. Moments later, Tucker collapsed on top of her, his breath rushing out in hard gasps near her ear.

As Skylar's breathing started to ease, her muscles began

to relax, leaving her with no more strength than a puddle of warm mud. "Oh my." She sighed against his shoulder, enjoying the salty taste of his skin. "I had no idea anything could…Tucker, what did you do to me?"

He would have laughed at her innocent comment, had his mind not been so heavily weighted by the intensity of what he'd just experienced.

A virgin. She had been a virgin! Yet she'd taken him with a hot, sensual passion that burned him clear to his soul. He buried his face in her hair. Bracketing his arms on either side of her head, he lifted more of his weight off of her without giving up the complete contact of their bodies. Skylar's long, lean body was a perfect fit to his, from her sweet lips, to her soft breasts pressed against his chest, to her delicate feet rubbing at the backs of his calves.

"Tuck?"

"Hmm?" he replied, kissing the shell of her ear. She was sweet.

"Are you going to let me up?" she asked.

The rumble of Tucker's laughter touched Skylar in a hundred intriguing places. She never imagined a body could feel so much.

"I wasn't planning on it," he said, his seductive tone tightening the wonderful sensations still burning deep inside her. He released a low groan, and she wondered if he, too, had felt them.

More of his weight shifted off her as he began to ease back. "Is your shoulder hurting?"

Deciding she liked him where he was, Skylar's arms wrapped around him, holding him in place. "It's not hurting."

"Do you want me to let you up?" he asked.

Skylar was sure she should say yes, but she couldn't. It felt so soothing to have his warmth and his weight pressed against her, their bodies still joined. She slid her hands across the slick muscles of his back, loving the feel of his strength, knowing he was presently using those corded muscles to keep all his weight from crushing her as he sheltered her from the sun.

"Skylar?" Tucker's lips dusted the pink scar on her shoulder, then her collarbone.

"Why do you call me that?" she asked, tilting her head to give him full access to the sensitive skin of her neck.

Confused by her question, distracted by the wild sensation building within his body, Tucker lifted his head. The openness in her questioning gaze seized his full attention. She was beautiful when she was guarded and stubborn, but with her defenses down, her beauty was breathtaking. He could get damn used to staring into those soft blue eyes. "Why do I call you Skylar?" he asked.

She nodded.

"Because that's your name, sweetheart. You made that real clear the first morning in my cabin. 'My name is Skylar'" he mocked, "'and I'm queen of my own mountain! I don't need you or any other fumbling cowboy.'"

A giggle trickled up from her throat as she smacked her hand against his shoulder. "That's not what I said."

"Close enough." He brushed light kisses across her smiling lips. "You were the prettiest woman I'd ever seen, standing there in my shirt."

Skylar shivered as she felt his body stir deep inside her. "Tuck? I thought you, er, we…were done."

"Done." He met her gaze. "After the way your sweet body burned through my control? You have to give me a chance to do better."

"Better?" Skylar said in a faint voice, growing dizzy from the thought as her body seemed to cry out in anticipation.

He flashed a teasing smile. "Just what did your beau do with you, anyhow?"

Skylar couldn't believe he'd asked her such a question while they were still intimately joined. But then, she'd not expected any of Tucker's lovemaking surprises.

"Duce must have had ice running through his veins."

"*Duce?* You think I did this with *Duce?*"

"Not anymore. You should have told me you were a virgin."

"*Told you?*"

"Yes. *Told me.* If I'd known, I would have—"

"Stopped?" she suggested, torn between insult and flat-out irritation. He was obviously worrying about the implications that came with taking a woman's virginity. Expecting him to become defensive, she was surprised when his lips curled into another smile as he settled more of his weight on top of her.

"Not likely," he said.

"You don't have to worry about me crying holy matrimony just because I'm inexperienced. This changes nothing."

Skylar's stern expression slammed Tucker back into the harsh reality of the present moment. *Hell.* He hadn't even thought about that. He should have been worrying about his freedom, yet getting away from Skylar was the last thing on his mind. Nor was she showing any signs of wanting to be left alone.

Her fingers lightly traced his shoulders, moving down his arms, turning his blood to fire as desire filled her eyes. The depth of her passion had been as surprising to him as the depth of her innocence. Her unbridled response had blazed through his control, burning him until he was shaking with the eagerness of a weak-kneed greenhorn who'd never had a woman. And he hadn't. Not a woman like Skylar.

Tucker shifted slightly within her.

Sighing, Skylar slid her hands around his sides and down his back. The slight sound of satisfaction sent a wild shudder of pleasure crashing through him. He trembled as the tight heat of her body constricted around him. He groaned, and repeated the slow deliberate movement.

Hell. He was about to do it again.

Chapter 15

Her eyes closed, lying on the cool grass in a tangle of sweat-dampened limbs, Skylar didn't know illusion from reality anymore, and it was a glorious, delirious feeling. She listened to the tranquil chirping of birds and Tucker's deep, steady breaths. A light breeze whispered across her bare skin, causing her to snuggle closer to the warmth of Tucker's body.

He stirred at her movement, lifting her head higher on his shoulder. Skylar pressed her lips against his neck, tasting his warm salty skin. She smiled as his arm tightened around her waist, holding her securely against the length of his side.

"You awake?" he asked a moment later.

"I'm not sure I'm alive."

The low rumble of his laughter vibrated against her skin. Easing from her embrace, Tucker sat up then stood. "Come on," he said, smiling at her as he reached down to help her up.

Skylar sat up and stared skeptically at his outstretched hand.

"Honey, you look like a woman who's been thoroughly ravished. But I know a fun way we get you spiffed up."

"Spiffed up?"

"Yep. We're gonna have a bath in the river." He grabbed her by the hand, pulled her to her feet and began leading her toward camp. "You flash me one of those sweet, seductive smiles and I might even let you scrub my back."

"Tucker, I don't—"

"No arguments," he said as he picked up the soap and washcloth she'd set on top her saddlebags.

Skylar's mind reeled as he tugged her after him, walking naked, toward the river. "Tucker?" she finally managed to get past her lips.

"Oh, all right," he said, again taking her by surprise as he stopped and lifted her into his strong arms. "I'll scrub your back first."

"Put me down!"

"Not on your life, honey. It's time you learned how to lighten up and have a bit of fun."

She realized he wasn't heading down to the shoreline, but rather walking out to the rock perch she'd found him on yesterday. Her eyes darted back to his. She recognized that evergreen glint. "You wouldn't."

"You wanted to romp in the water with us yesterday," he said, never slowing his powerful stride. "Admit it."

Skylar whipped her gaze back toward the river coming into view below. She tightened her arms around his neck. "Tucker—"

"Too late for second thoughts, angel girl." He leaped, and Skylar gasped at the instant feeling of weightlessness, just before she splashed into the cold river. Tucker's arms released her as they both swam up to the surface.

"Tucker Morgan!" Laughing, she clung to him with one arm as she pushed her wet hair away from her face. "You're crazy!"

"So I've been told. I suppose that makes us an even match. You're definitely the most mind-bending woman I've ever known."

Skylar eased back.

"That wasn't a complaint," he assured her, pulling her back against his chest. "You've been drivin' me wild ever since you pulled your gun on me."

She smiled and felt his body tremble as she coiled her legs around his waist, allowing Tucker to tread water for the both of them.

"The water's deep here," he said, his legs moving in an easy, steady rhythm to keep their heads above the water.

"You don't think I can swim?"

He smoothed his hand across her thighs. "A man can hope. I like having you cling to me."

Skylar smiled and brushed a kiss across his mouth.

"I'm starting to think I might have jumped over the wrong cliff by mistake," he said against her lips, "and this is heaven. You better pinch me so I know you're real, sweetheart."

"I'd rather kiss you," she admitted, and kissed him deeply. When the kiss ended, she drew his lower lip between her teeth. She skimmed her tongue across his lip before releasing the captive flesh, drawing a low groan from Tucker.

"Now I'm certain of it," he said in a thick voice. "I'm in heaven."

This isn't heaven, it's another illusion. A wonderful, beautiful illusion she intended to embrace, for it would be over too soon. "Do you still have the soap and cloth?"

Tucker grinned, enjoying the playfulness in her tone and the open desire in her gaze. He held up the soap and cloth, showing that he did.

She flashed a sinister grin, and before Tucker could figure out what she was up to, she snatched them from his hand and slipped under the sparkling veil of water.

She could swim, all right. She glided beneath the water's surface like a fish. Tucker swam after her, not knowing what her game was, but ready and willing to play.

He caught up with her in the shallows, and damn near swallowed his tongue when she stood and turned to face him.

Her wet skin glistened in the sunlight, the pink crowns of her breasts beading into tight peaks. Her ivory skin blossomed to a soft pink. She sank down, shielding herself beneath the veil of water. He grinned at the sight of her shy smile, realizing again just how innocent she truly was, or rather, had been.

"Started worrying about that deep water after all, huh?"

Skylar lifted her hand from the water and extended a single finger, then curled it toward her, beckoning him to come closer.

Tucker swallowed hard, but the lump in his throat didn't budge. "You really gonna scrub my back?" he asked as he stepped closer, his voice thick.

She straightened, soaping the cloth as she waded toward him. Stepping close, she smoothed the cloth over his chest and up to his shoulder, leaving a trail of soapy lather, igniting a trail of sparks beneath his skin. The smile she flashed was anything but shy, and sent his pulse soaring.

"I intend to touch you as completely as the river has."

His heart thudded heavily against his chest, the water surrounding them suddenly feeling hot against his skin. Despite his feet being firmly planted on the sandy river bottom, he had the sudden revelation that *he* was the one in way over his head. Looking into the warm, bottomless pools of Skylar's eyes, he didn't give a damn if he drowned.

Crouched by the fire, Skylar kept her eyes fastened on the trout frying in the skillet. Flames licked over the edges of the cast iron, lighting up the shadows of dusk. In the distance she could hear the sounds of approaching horses.

Chance and Garret were still a good ways from camp, and already a blush was creeping into her face. Despite her silent assurance that neither of their brothers would be able to tell what she and Tucker had been up to, she hadn't convinced herself.

She felt different. She and Tucker had worked together all afternoon, taking care of chores and herding the mares to the river for a drink. Whenever their gazes met, she hadn't been able to fight her grin, or the surge of warmth she felt deep in her chest when he smiled back.

After ushering the horses back to their temporary holding pen, Tucker had returned to the river to catch fish for supper. She had stayed in camp to prepare the rest of their meal.

Kneeling beside a warm, steady fire, she spooned clumps of dough into a skillet, while trying to block the memory of Tucker's tender lips and magical hands from her mind—but never quite succeeding. Their brothers would be back soon and she couldn't go on blushing every five minutes to the fanciful thoughts flirting through her mind.

Setting the skillet of dough aside, she glanced up as Tucker walked back into camp, a line of cleaned trout in his hand, a smug grin on his handsome face. He placed the fish on an empty plate beside her, took her by the hand and hauled her up. She was wrapped in his arms and lost in his kiss before she knew what hit her. Only when their lips parted did she realize the liberty he'd taken, and how easily she'd been overcome by his presence.

He couldn't do that!

"Are you, uh…feeling okay?" The concern in his gaze ignited another strain of panic. She supposed he was referring to her lost virginity.

She turned away and reached for the fish. "Just fine." She grabbed the sack of flour, settled near the fire and began to batter the trout, but she was far from fine. She had completely lost her damn mind. It wasn't like her to act without thinking about the repercussions of her behavior, yet she'd done just that.

The fish met a warm skillet with a loud hiss. Tucker sat beside her and began working on the tangled and frayed rope he'd abandoned earlier. It seemed he needed some clarification about their future interaction with one another.

He couldn't tip her world off-kilter whenever he pleased. This morning's escapade was an isolated incident. She couldn't imagine he'd contest the annulment. There was no reason to think they wouldn't be granted one, as long as they were both in agreement—today never happened.

They'd had their fun and now it was time to get back to business, *reality*. She was headed to Wyoming to get her horses back and build a future for herself and Garret, not tumble in the grass with cowboys who were too handsome for anyone's good.

Handsome, sweet, and gentle, her mind added. Goodness but the man had tender lips. Lips he'd used to sip every last drop of water from her skin after they'd walked from the river.

Her flesh prickled at the memory, her body shivered.

"Skylar!"

She jumped, feeling the bite of a flame on her wrist just as Tucker shouted her name.

His hand closed over her arm and jerked it away from the fire. "Honey, watch that flame."

Honey? Damnation. He couldn't be calling her such things in front of their brothers! "I think I can fry fish without falling into the fire."

"You damn near caught your shirt on fire." He twisted the bottom of her singed sleeve so she could see the black marks in her new shirt. "Let me see your wrist."

Skylar tried to tug her wrist from his grip. "Listen, Morgan, I hope you don't think—"

"Morgan?" Tucker's look of shock quickly transformed to one of anger. "What the hell, Skylar? You can't—"

"At least they didn't kill each other."

Skylar and Tucker spun around at the sound of Chance's voice as he walked into camp leading a packhorse. "Garret, it looks like you won yourself five bucks. I was sure one of them would be skinned out and tacked to a tree before we made it back."

"Not quite," Tucker said in a dull tone.

"If you're hungry," Skylar said, tossing Tucker a hard look, "supper's about done."

"I'm starving," said Garret.

"Kid, you must have eaten a pound of dried beef in the last hour, not to mention the sack of sweets you hauled out of that mercantile."

Garret grinned at Chance as he crouched beside Skylar's saddlebags. "I'm still hungry," he insisted. "But I need to scrub up a bit."

Skylar forked the fish onto a plate then reached for the skillet she'd filled with clumps of dough.

"Hey, Sky?" said Garret. "Where's the soap?"

"The soap?" she repeated, recalling the exact moment she and Tucker had realized it was missing. They'd lost it somewhere between their extensive bath in the shallow waters and making love on the riverbank.

"Yeah, and the cloth."

"Oh, yeah. The soap and the cloth." She strained for a casual tone, sure that her voice was a few notches too high. "I lost them."

"You lost them?"

She tossed a quick glance over her shoulder at her brother. "Yeah. In the river."

"It was my fault," said Tucker, and Skylar's heart stopped beating. Her gaze locked with his mischievous green eyes.

He wouldn't! She'd kill him!

"I borrowed them," Tucker said. "You wouldn't believe the chewing she gave me over it." He flashed a grin.

Knowing he had actual bite marks hidden under his shirt and the bandanna tied around his neck, Skylar felt the flush in her cheeks shoot clear to the soles of her feet.

"I have spares," Tucker said. He stood and walked toward his own supplies, saying, "I'll replace what I lost."

After serving up the food she'd prepared, Skylar ate her supper in silence, too conscious of Tucker sitting barely a foot away from her as the others talked casually about horses and ranching. She could have kicked him for sitting beside her. He was fully aware that she didn't want him near her. Twice his elbow had bumped her arm as he ate his meal.

"What do you say, Sky?"

Skylar glanced up at Chance, not having a clue what they were discussing. "About what?"

"Breeding," Tucker supplied.

Skylar choked on her last bite of trout. With a strangled cough, she unclogged her windpipe. Tucker's hand repeatedly thumped her between her shoulder blades as she sucked in a gasp of air.

"Helps if you chew, darlin'," he said, handing her a cup of coffee, his palm now moving caressingly over her back.

She glared up at him as she took the cup, not the least bit amused by his teasing—in front of their brothers!

"I'd sure like the chance to pin either of your studs up with one of our mares," Chance said, forking his fish, not seeming to pay them any notice. "We could have some fine colts."

Hit by a startling realization, Skylar sucked down a scalding gulp of coffee, hardly noticing the pain of her throat.

Dear God! Coupling makes babies.

How could she have made such an oversight? They hadn't done it just once. Did that mean he could have made three babies? *No. People don't have litters.* But... Tucker and Chance were twins.

Oh God. What had they done?

"Sky," Garret said, pulling her from her thoughts. "Are you okay?"

She glanced up and found three sets of eyes focused on her. "Just fine," she said, forcing a light smile.

"So, what do you think, Sky?" asked Chance.

She twisted away from Tucker's hand on her back, thinking she couldn't have any babies. She had Garret to raise!

"Arabian sires could be big business," he added.

"That's the plan." She shot to her feet. "I'm sure we can work something out, Chance."

"Where are you going?" Tucker called after her as she started out of camp.

"To find the outhouse," she said without looking back. *And to be sick.* Her stomach cramped at the thought of the new mess she could have gotten herself into. How could Tucker do this to her? She'd trusted him!

Your first mistake, her mind shot back.

When an hour passed and Skylar didn't return to camp, Tucker began to think her departure had more to do with being peeved than having to pee. *Bet she's with her horses.*

He stood and started toward the meadow where the stallions were staked, leaving Garret sleeping in his bedroll and Chance fiddling with his ledgers beneath the lamplight. As Tucker neared the horses resting in the darkness, he saw Skylar's blond hair in the soft moonlight. She sat in the grass near her Arabians, probably telling them what a bastard he'd been.

Spotting him, she jumped to her feet.

"Thought I'd find you here."

Her pinched expression and tightly crossed arms confirmed his assumption. He'd done something to ruffle her feathers.

"Stop threatening me," she said as he reached her.

"*Threatening* you?"

"Dropping those hints in front of our brothers."

"Honey, I haven't been threatening you. Chance and Garret don't have a clue as to what's going on between us. I just love seeing your rosy cheeks."

She flinched away as he lightly brushed his finger across her cheek. "Tucker—"

"You're so beautiful when you're mad," he said, tugging her into his arms, silencing her with a kiss.

Caught up in the sudden taste of him, distracted by the

feel of his body and a rush of masculine scent, Skylar returned his kiss, but only briefly before she gained some clarity and pulled away.

"Tucker," she growled, careful to keep her voice low, not wanting it to carry back to the others. "You can't do that!"

"Why not? No one's around. Don't tell me you weren't enjoying that kiss as much as I was."

She stepped farther away from him, chagrined by her lack of control. "I'm stopping it right now. It ended at the river."

He stuffed his hands into his pants pockets. "Is that so?"

"Yes."

"It's hands-off from here on in?"

"I—"

"Had a great time, but the fun's over. It's back to business."

Skylar felt a rush of relief. "Exactly. I'd like to forget it ever happened."

"That's not likely. A man doesn't forget your kind of passion."

"I'm sure you'll manage," she said, certain he'd forgotten such experiences with countless women.

"Don't bet on it."

She tensed at the sight of Tucker's irritation. What did he have to be mad about?

"What we shared wasn't your run-of-the-mill roll in the hay."

Something very close to hope sparked inside her. She wanted so much to believe their joining had been special to him, something more than mere physical fulfillment. But she knew better. She'd overheard him and Chance discussing their take on marriage more than once, a loathing so deep in their tone she'd felt it. "What would you call it, Tuck?"

"Hell, I don't know!" he scoffed, taking a step back. The combination of caution and confusion in his eyes added to the wariness welling up inside her.

Tucker didn't want any permanent attachments. She'd been aware of the fact long before she'd given herself to him, but that didn't keep the slow slide of pain from crashing against her heart. If she became swollen with child, it would be her burden, not his. She was already bearing all she could handle.

"We have a long day ahead of us tomorrow and a lot of ground to make up," she said, turning toward camp. "Good night, Tucker."

Chapter 16

"Do you plan to ignore me the rest of the way to Wyoming?"

Skylar glanced over her shoulder as Tucker rode up beside her. "I do," she said with flat honesty. She'd been doing her best to do just that for the past two days.

"Well, I don't intend to make that an easy option."

Heaven help her, she'd noticed! His heated gazes and intentional bumps and nudges throughout the day had been driving her mad.

Determined to get her point across, Skylar kept her gaze straight ahead, but she could feel his eyes burning into her. After a few minutes of listening to the cool breeze rustling in the trees and the steady rhythm of moving horses, she gave in and glanced at the man riding beside her. His lips curved into a seductive smile.

"Stop looking at me like that," she ordered, the swirling sensations deep inside her driving her to distraction.

"Like what?"

"You know very well *like what.*"

Tucker leaned toward her, his green eyes shining with mischief. "Like we're lovers?"

Skylar's body tensed with alarm. Blood rushed to her face in a wave of heat. *"We are not!"*

Tucker laughed, holding her gaze as his horse trotted along beside hers. "Honey, we're lovers three times over. Ain't no two ways about it."

Horrified by his candid statement, Skylar glanced about, checking the location of their brothers. Both were well over thirty yards off, separated by the moving herd, but Skylar felt self-conscious of Tucker's proclamation being overheard by the wind and horses.

"Damn you, Tucker! Don't say things like that, and stay away from me." She urged her horse into a faster pace. Tucker followed suit, staying right beside her.

"I don't see what you're so bent about, Sky," he said, all humor gone from his voice. "We both had a good time. There's no reason we can't be friends. I think we should give it a try. What do you say?"

Skylar took one look at his handsome face, saw the seductive smile hidden in his eyes and said, *"No."*

"Why not?"

"Because I know what being *friends* means to you. I'm not proud of my behavior the other day, nor am I some harlot you can throw to the ground whenever the mood strikes you."

"I don't see you as any such thing! I see you for what you are. A strong, intelligent, desirable woman. You don't have to treat me like I'm invisible to discourage further intimacy between us."

She risked looking up at his luminous green eyes and

knew he sure as heck wouldn't be the one to discourage any further intimacy between them. "I think I do."

Hearing the huskiness in her voice, a grin tugged at Tucker's mouth, but he had better sense than to let it break free. "Am I that much of a threat to you?"

"Don't flatter yourself. I tend to be overcautious is all. It's already been proven that I can't think worth a handful of spit when you're touching me, so I aim to stay away from you. You'll have to find some other easy woman to be your passion fancy. The *last* thing I need is to arrive in Wyoming jobless, penniless and with a randy cowboy's babies in my belly."

Skylar flicked her reins and urged her horse into a hard pace. Tucker watched her ride off, feeling quite put in his place, and fully insulted.

Did she truly hold such a low opinion of his moral character? Hell, he had more integrity than to turn his back on a woman carrying his child. He wouldn't have seduced her if he feared it was her most fertile time of month. Not about to be caught in a paternal web, he'd sought out an education on how to avoid such situations early on. Never accused of being shy, he had no trouble finding an experienced widow willing to share her bed and wisdom on the matter.

As Tucker watched Skylar, it dawned on him that she may not have a clue as to when a woman was in the most danger of conceiving.

No wonder she's mad. She thinks I put her at risk of bearing a child.

Tucker twisted against a tension that seized his spine. He didn't like knowing Skylar thought ill of him.

* * *

Finished with her evening watch, Skylar walked into camp just after midnight. She was surprised to find the fire still burning.

"Evening."

She jumped at the sound of Tucker's casual greeting. He sat in the shadows beyond the glow of the fire. "What are you doing up?"

"Waiting for you. Sit and talk with me for a minute."

She eyed him warily as he patted the ground beside him. "We don't have anything to talk about."

"Yes, we do. I've been thinking about what you said today, and I'm wondering how much you know about a woman's fertile time of the month."

"Tucker!" Her gaze darted to her brother in his bedroll on the other side of the fire. "Garret is sleeping not four yards away."

"Come sit down and I won't have to talk so loud. Either way, we're going to talk about this, Skylar. I won't have you thinking I bedded you without regard to you becoming pregnant."

He'd lost his mind! Skylar glanced again at Garret sleeping beside the fire.

Tucker shot to his feet. "Fine, let's take a walk." He grabbed her by the hand and tugged her after him before she could refuse.

Walking off into the dark with Tucker was a bad idea. A real bad idea, but Skylar didn't have much choice. The man seemed determined to speak his mind. She silently followed him, trying not to focus on the warmth of his large hand wrapped around hers, dreading whatever he was set on telling her.

They'd walked a good distance, weaving past trees and thick bushes, nearing the location of the horses before Tucker stopped.

"Tucker—"

"No," he said, pulling her toward him. "You had your say, now I'm gonna have mine. Just how much do you know about reproduction?"

"What?"

"You know, how and when a woman gets pregnant and all."

Skylar felt her mouth drop open, the blood draining from her face. Did he truly expect her to answer such a question? She was fairly certain she had a handle on the *how*, but she wasn't about to say so.

"After what you said to me today," he continued, "I'm thinkin' you don't know a whole lot, so let me fill you in on a few details."

Speechless, she stared up at his stern expression. Her mind reeled as Tucker began explaining the reproductive cycle of a woman, and how her monthly bleed determines her period of fertility. She tried to pay attention, certain this was all useful information, but she was somewhat distracted by his hand on her back, the feel of his hip pressed against hers, his gaze, so intent on her.

"So, you see?" he said. "If I thought there was a high risk—"

"How do *you* know there wasn't?"

"I pay attention, sweetheart. Wasn't hard to figure out

why you were taking twice as many trips into the bushes this past week and had suddenly become religious about washing laundry."

Skylar gaped at him, her mind wavering between horror and sheer embarrassment that she'd been so transparent.

"I'm sure no one else noticed," Tucker assured her.

"*You* did."

"I also made a living at paying attention to the minutest detail. Outlaws don't exactly *want* to get caught."

His other arm moved around her, imprisoning her in his strong embrace. Skylar felt a rush of panic and instantly pulled back. "Tucker, don't."

"Skylar, you're making me feel damn guilty, and I don't think I did anything to feel guilty about. I didn't force you."

"I know that." She stood stiffly in the circle of his arms, desperately trying not to feel the sensations caused by his light embrace, silently commanding her body not to respond to him.

"Do you think I'd force myself on you?"

"No," she said, annoyed by the tremble in her voice.

"Then why are you shaking?"

"Because you…you're touching me."

His eyes gleamed like emeralds in the moonlight. "I'm barely touching your coat," he pointed out.

It was true, yet the heavy canvas barrier didn't keep the slight pressure of his hands from burning into the small of her back.

"I haven't even tried to kiss you," he said with a slight grin. "Do you want me to kiss you, Skylar?"

"No!" she lied, infuriated by her body's refusal to co-operate. Tucker nuzzled her hair, causing her breath to quake and sending a violent tremor through her body. All of which she was certain he heard and felt.

"You sure, honey?"

She wished he wouldn't call her that. She held her breath as his lips moved over the shell of her ear. Her traitorous mind remembered the feel of those soft lips roving over her bare skin.

"I'd sure like to kiss you," he whispered.

Not about to force her, Tucker loosened his hold on her and eased back. She was fighting it, but he saw passion in her gaze. Fighting his own urge to tug her against him, he carefully placed his hands on her shoulders then slowly slid them across the length of her arms and he gently took her hands in his.

"Tucker?"

Hearing her voice as a plea, Tucker dipped his head and brushed his lips across hers. She stood stiff as a rooted tree, allowing him to kiss her, yet not participating, but she wanted to. He felt it as his tongue glided across the trembling seam of her lips, heard it in the quake of her breath. He parted her lips with his tongue, tasting her sweetness and the passion she was trying not to reveal.

He felt the moment she gave up her internal struggle. A deep contented sigh broke from her throat. She slipped her hands from his and coiled her arms around his neck. Her body relaxed against him as she angled her head, fitting her mouth to his, sending a shock wave of passion crashing through his body as she took full possession of his mouth.

By the time he lifted his mouth from hers, they were both shaking, their lungs pulling frantically for breath. "Damn," he sighed. Skylar rested her forehead against his chest. Her quick breaths swirled inside his open shirt with each labored rise and fall of her chest.

"I can't do this, Tucker. It doesn't make sense."

He smiled and brushed his lips across her soft hair. "Sure it does." His hands slid under the back of her jacket and tunneled under her shirt. She moaned, leaning into him as he caressed the warm skin of her slender back. "You need to be touched, as much as I need to touch you."

"We shouldn't," she said, meeting his lips as he lowered his head for another soul-searing kiss. She shifted against him, making a muffled sound that could have been a protest.

Tucker instantly ended the kiss, and silently berated his lack of control. "Honey, if you want to stop, I—"

Her tongue quite effectively cut off his words as she tugged him back against her body, which was fine with him. He was far too busy returning her kiss to be bothered with words anyhow.

Dear God, she was killing him, one kiss at a time.

Tucker pulled his hands out from under her shirt and reached for the buttons, needing to feel her skin against his. He brushed open her shirt and camisole and hugged her against his bare chest. She trembled in his arms, her gasp lost inside his mouth as he kissed her.

He listened to every catch in her breath as he caressed

her fully, enjoying each sigh of pleasure he drew from her, repeating each caress that made her tremble.

"You're so soft."

Skylar's teeth closed over the tense muscle in his neck. Her short fingernails scored across his back, biting into his skin as she rubbed hotly against him. Tucker began to wonder who was seducing whom. She was burning him alive!

The ache in his britches becoming nearly unbearable, he reached between them and jerked at the steel buttons. "Don't panic, honey," he said, feeling a rush of relief at loosening the strained confines of his denims. "I'm just easing some tension."

Her hand closed over him, shaking him with a wild rush of desire as she measured him from tip to base and back again.

"Better?" she asked, her smiling lips pressed against his neck, just before she opened that sassy mouth and treated him to a kiss that sent his mind and senses reeling.

"Damn," Tucker groaned.

Weakened by the pounding rush of pure fire, he sank down to the ground, taking Skylar with him. She didn't protest their change of position. She shoved him onto his back with an aggressiveness he found to be damn exciting. She stretched out on top of him, stoking the fire raging through his veins, beneath his skin.

"*Tucker,*" she said, the tremble in her voice telling him she was burning just as badly for him.

Their hands collided in an effort to unfasten her denims. She used her hands instead to lever herself up and give him better access, urging him to hurry as her tongue traced his lips. His fingers fumbled with her button fly as she kissed him nearly unconscious. He didn't think he'd ever get his fill of her kisses. Damn the inconvenience of her britches!

Through the pounding of his pulse and their heavy breathing, Tucker heard a rustling sound beyond the brush they were lying behind. Someone was approaching. A horse, he thought, hearing the creak of a saddle.

Skylar's wide eyes locked with his. She wrenched herself from his arms and darted through the brush with the speed of a startled doe, disappearing into the darkness without disturbing so much as a leaf.

Struggling with the loss of her body pressed against his, Tucker closed his eyes for a moment. Blinking to clear his vision, he forced himself to his feet. He was still puffing like a freight train, trying to catch his breath when Chance rode through the scrub and trees.

"Tuck, what the hell are you…" Chance's eyes widened in the moonlight as his voice trailed. "Hell! If Sky has you that worked up, you bes' ride into the nearest town and get yourself a woman. Two or three if you have to."

Tucker cursed and quickly adjusted his clothing. "I wasn't—"

"I don't want to hear it," Chance said, holding up his hand. "There are some things a brother just shouldn't have to witness," he grumbled as he rode back to his post.

It was on the tip of Tucker's tongue to set Chance straight, and tell him he'd been rolling in the dirt with the hottest woman he'd ever come into contact with, but he doubted Skylar would see such praise as a compliment, any more than Chance would approve of their affair.

Skylar's words echoed back in his mind.

I am not some harlot you can throw to the ground whenever the mood strikes you.

Hell. He hadn't done a fine job of proving her wrong. He'd pulled her into the dirt with no thought of anything other than easing into her sweet body and fulfilling a mutual hunger that refused to stay sated.

He didn't get it. Having had Skylar should have cooled his fire. But until Skylar, he'd never kissed a woman who made his blood roar in his ears and his heart thunder in his chest.

Tucker collapsed onto his butt and propped his elbows on his raised knees as he raked his fingers roughly through his hair.

What in the hell is wrong with me?

She'd been right to try and push him away. He didn't have a sliver of control when she was in his arms. He couldn't go back to camp, not with Skylar stretched out in her bedroll, in plain view beneath the moonlit sky.

He had to get a grip.

Glaring at his reflection in the round shaving mirror he'd hung from the broken limb of a cottonwood tree, Tucker continued to silently berate himself for his behavior the night before. Skylar hadn't made eye contact with him once all morning, and he couldn't blame her one bit. He hadn't shown her an ounce of respect last night, damn near bedding her not fifty yards from camp, without regard of being caught by their brothers.

A light breeze rustled the dry, copper leaves still clinging to the limbs of the old cottonwood as he dragged the straightedge razor across the last patch of shaving lather on his jaw. Hearing the leaf-crunching sound of approaching footsteps, Tucker angled his head as he looked in the mirror and saw Chance coming toward him.

"Oh my God," Chance said in a low growl.

Tucker glanced over his shoulder at his brother standing a few steps behind him.

Chance's wide green eyes quickly narrowed. "You couldn't leave her alone, could you, Tuck?"

"What are you talking about?"

"Either you were mauled by a mountain cat, or you had a late-night tangle with a blue-eyed wildcat. I hope all those cat scratches were worth risking our ranch over."

Tucker dropped his gaze to his bare chest. *Hell.* He hadn't thought about the marks left by Skylar's short nails scoring across his back. Tucker plucked a small towel he'd tossed over a limb, swiped his razor across it before folding the blade up then swabbed the specks of shaving lather left on his face as his mind raced for some justification he could tell his brother.

Coming up short, he took his shirt from the limb and shrugged it on as he turned to face Chance, not sure of what he could say in his own defense.

"What's the matter, Tuck? Cat still got your tongue, or did she swallow it whole?"

A flash of anger warmed his blood. "Drop it, Chance."

"Damnation. I knew something had happened between you two when me and the kid came back from getting supplies." Chance shook his head. "But I figured you'd be crowing to the trees if you'd actually bedded her. And I didn't believe Skylar was a fast sort of woman."

"She's not! She was…" The words lodged in his throat. Somehow, it didn't seem right to be discussing Skylar's lost virginity, not even with Chance. Judging by the anger in his brother's expression, that bit of information would explode his temper.

"She was what?" Chance prodded.

"Nothing. Just drop it." Tucker reached back, collected his mirror and dropped it into his shaving case. "What goes on between me and Skylar is none of your business," he said, preparing to walk past him.

Chance's eyes flared with rage as he took a step forward, blocking his brother's retreat. "None of my *business*? Damn it, Tucker," he roared, shoving him hard in the chest.

Tucker's back slammed against the tree. Dry leaves rained down on him as he regained his balance.

"Have you forgotten about our ranch? I'm just as involved with that woman as you are! You agreed to keep your hands off her! If she gets her hooks into our land, she's likely to put us out of business!"

"Skylar is no threat to our ranch!" Tucker shouted back.

"I'm sure that's what the brain in your britches is telling you! Does Sky know you have no intentions of staying married to her?"

"She knows," he said, annoyed by the pang of guilt his

brother's condemning glare was causing in his chest. "She doesn't want to be married any more than I do."

Chance didn't look convinced. "You sure about that? She doesn't seem the sort who'd take to being used, and you've all but sealed her claim on our land."

"I'm not using her!"

"The hell you're not."

"What's your problem? You've bedded more than your share of decent woman. Were you using them?"

"Yes. Just as much as they were using me, but I damn sure didn't leave them feeling used and defeated."

Tucker's free hand fisted at his side. "Neither am I. I haven't forced myself on her."

"Right," Chance said, folding his arms across his chest. "I'm sure she came on to you all hot and heavy and you did your best to fight off her advances. Is that how it happened, Tuck?"

Watching anger narrow Tucker's eyes, Chance figured that wasn't how it happened at all; and mindfully widened his stance, seeing that his twin was a breath away from throwing a punch.

If throwing a few punches was what it took to pound some sense into Tucker's thick skull, he was willing to take his share of bruises to oblige him. "Just how do you think Sky's gonna feel when we arrive in Wyoming and show her the contract I signed with her father, proving she doesn't own a single blade of grass on our land? Your little affair will only be adding insult to injury. This may be a game to you, Tuck, but you better remember she's on the losing end. I've worked with that woman too long to underestimate her. You think Winifred pulled a number on our pa? Well she didn't have an ounce of Sky's tact and skill."

Tucker opened his mouth to respond, then snapped it shut, his anger lost in the deep concentration Chance now saw in his eyes. Seemed he'd given his little brother something to think about, other than the ache in his crotch.

He reached out and grabbed the shaving supplies from Tucker's hand. "Unless you plan on taking a shine to married life, I suggest you concentrate on getting your horses to Wyoming and keeping your fly buttoned up."

Tucker shot Chance a hard look as his twin turned on his heel and walked away. It was just like Chance to rake his conscience over hot coals!

He waited until Chance was gone from his view before slowly starting back toward camp. With every dragging footstep his conscience told him he should feel guilty for breaking his word to his brother.

As he neared camp, he spotted Skylar sitting on her knees by the extinguished campfire. Watching her lithe movements, her silky blond hair hanging in her face as she loaded the rest of her cooking supplies into a canvas sack, he couldn't muster the guilt. Given the chance to love Skylar a hundred times over, his response would be the same. He couldn't regret what they'd shared, but his brother's words had him wondering if Skylar felt the same.

She'd been the one who plainly stated she still wanted the annulment. Why should he believe any differently? He hadn't used Skylar. She'd given herself freely and had enjoyed every damn bit of their time together. If anything, he'd given her a reason to smile and laugh, something she'd done more of in the few hours they'd spent together than she'd done in the past weeks combined.

He could still hear the soft, trickling sound of her laughter, see the light of her smile, the life that lit her eyes. He'd given her the freedom to let go and enjoy a moment of life. Give and take. It was called *sharing*. Surely Skylar saw it as such.

So why does she look so damn sad, he wondered as he drew closer. Skylar stood with the heavy pack in her arms, a frown firmly fixed on her face.

"I'll take that," he said, rushing forward and plucking the heavy sack from her grasp.

Solemn blue eyes flickered up before she quickly looked away.

"You're mad at me about last night," he said in a low voice.

"I'm mad at myself," she answered in a flat tone.

"It was my fault," he said, fully aware that he'd pressured her last night. "Listen, Skylar—"

"I tried that last night," she interrupted as she lifted her hat from her back and tugged it onto her head, hiding her face beneath the wide ivory brim. "Right now we have horses to drive."

Okay, so maybe I should keep my distance for a while. Tucker watched her walk toward the ornery spotted mare she'd taken a liking to. He turned and strode toward his packhorses. After securing the pack, he glanced back at

Skylar. Her eyes were staring back at him, blue lightning striking right into his veins.

Distance?

Hell. Tucker knew he'd be ticking off the minutes until he could hold her again.

Chapter 17

She was going to nip this wonder-lust in the bud. Perhaps with her marital tie to Tucker severed she'd be able to convince herself she had no business being in his arms.

While the others were busy with the horses, Skylar threw a fire together as quickly as she could, then plopped down beside the growing flames and opened her father's journal. She recalled a letter her father received a few months back from an old friend who happened to be a judge in a town that had recently built a new courthouse. A town in Northern Colorado.

Reedly, Freely… She tried to recall the name as she flipped through the journal, looking for the right sketch of terrain.

"Greeley!" Excitement bubbled up inside her as her finger tapped the dot marking the little town. They were close. A two-hour ride, maybe less. Surely Judge Simmons would be willing and able to clear up her marital bind to Tucker. By nightfall he'd be legally off-limits. *And he'll have no legal claim to my horses.*

"What'cha doin', sis?" Garret asked as he walked into camp.

"Help me saddle the Arabians," she said, slamming the journal shut and jumping to her feet.

Garret's expression pinched. "Sky, we just finished staking the stallions. Chance and Tuck are still roping off the mares."

"I'm getting the annulment today," she said as she hurried past him. "I know of a judge not far from here who can take care of it."

Garret shrugged his shoulders. "Okay," he said, following her toward their horses staked out in the grass.

Tucker and Chance walked into camp as Garret and Skylar returned from saddling the Arabians.

"Don't bother sitting down," she said to Tucker. "You and I are riding to Greeley."

Tucker's eyebrows shot up in surprise. "We are?"

Skylar bristled when he flashed a smile. "We're only a few days' ride from Wyoming territory. I want the annulment now. I know a judge in Greeley. The town can't be more than a two-hour ride from here. Being a friend of my father's, Judge Simmons shouldn't have any trouble granting an annulment."

"How can you be sure this judge is there?" Tucker asked. "I've been to Greeley a few times and I know for a fact that their judge travels to other small towns scattered around this region."

"I'll take my chances," she said. She needed their farce of a marriage annulled now. "The sooner we leave, the sooner we get back."

Tucker shifted his gaze toward his brother.

"Sounds like a fine idea to me," agreed Chance. "Garret and I shouldn't have any trouble. This area is crowded with clustered folks. You can't ride but a few miles in any direction without tripping over train tracks or running into some sort of settlement."

"I've already saddled the Arabians," Skylar said, motioning toward her horses.

"Keep your shirt on, boss lady," Tucker said as he turned away from her and started back toward the horses. "I need to pack a few things of my own."

Two hours later Tucker and Skylar were standing outside a big white courthouse, having just been told Judge Simmons had been called to Fort Collins the day prior and wasn't due to return for three to four days. Tucker felt a touch of disappointment for Skylar's sake. He knew she wasn't about to give up another full day of travel to track down Simmons.

Without so much as a look in his direction, she turned and started walking toward their tethered horses, her gloved hands fisted at her sides. Her tan hat, hanging from the long chin strap, bounced against the back of her jacket. Tucker stayed a few paces behind, not certain if she was about to well up and cry or explode with pent-up rage.

When she had her guard up, the woman was damn impossible to read. She'd been an impenetrable wall of stern indifference during their long, silent ride into town. She obviously had her heart set on getting the annulment.

A streetlamp blinked on across the road, capturing Tucker's attention. Beneath the shining globe, a lamplighter walked from the pool of light toward the next lamp. Tucker shifted his gaze to the soft light fading on the edge of the western horizon.

With the dark cloak of night falling fast around them, he wasn't about to ride back to camp. Even if the judge had been in town to annul the marriage, Tucker had every intention of spending the night in town and taking Skylar out for a nice meal. Greeley had a number of fine restaurants. He glanced back over his shoulder at the hotel on the corner of the block.

"I'll head over to the hotel and get us a couple rooms for the night," he suggested.

"I'm not staying in town with you." Skylar stopped beside her horse. "I'm riding back to camp."

"I'm not. If you'll recall, I had the last night watch and have been up since midnight. I'm beat. No way my butt can handle two more hours in the saddle. If you're worried about expenses, I have more than enough to cover hotel rooms and supper."

She spun toward him, her hand planted on her hips. "That's not the problem, and you know it!"

"Evening," said the lamplighter, startling Skylar as he stepped behind her, spilling light all around them by touching the flame on the tip of his pole to the wick of a lamp. Tucker smiled and gave a nod as the man continued past them.

Skylar's cheeks flushed as Tucker stepped toward her. Damn if she hadn't just admitted the power of her attraction to him. The reaction of Tucker's body was all that kept him from laughing at the desperation in Skylar's expression.

"You don't have to act so horrified. I don't have any plans other than buying you a nice dinner. The thought of bedding you hasn't even entered my mind."

She held his gaze for a long moment before her eyes trailed down the front of him. "Liar."

Despite his effort to fight it, a smile broke across Tucker's lips. Okay, so he was aching to bed her with every fiber of his body. Truth be told, he wasn't any more comfortable with the power she had over *his* mind and body, but watching her suffer from the same effects had hardened his body in a rush; not that he expected her to welcome him into her arms. Tucker couldn't have read her cold attitude toward him any clearer if she'd posted a No Trespassing sign on her forehead.

That didn't change his plans. But he wouldn't be getting her anywhere near a hotel if he didn't make his intentions official. "I give my word," he said. "I won't make advances, Sky. We can both have a warm bath and a nice supper. If you want anything more than that, you'll have to do the asking."

"I won't."

"Then you've got nothing to worry about." He walked the short distance to the hitching rail and started untying the horses. "The livery is at the end of this strip," he said, guiding the horses toward the street and pointing to the south end of town.

Skylar sucked in a long, silent breath as she glanced

down at the parallel row of shops and buildings. A block and a half away a thick wedge of light poured out onto the shadowed street from the open doors of the livery.

"Take our horses to the livery," Tucker continued, "and I'll head to the hotel across the street and get our rooms."

She still wasn't sold on the idea when he took her hand and wrapped it around the reins of their horses.

"You know you can trust me, Skylar," he said, giving her a nudge toward the street.

Oh, she trusted him all right. To be so damn irresistible she couldn't stand herself unless she was kissing him.

"Tuck!"

Hearing Tucker's name said in a high-pitched squeal, Skylar whipped her gaze toward the boardwalk. There beneath an ivory glow stood a short slender woman in a stunning gown of green and gold. She was beautiful, and Skylar suddenly felt quite ill. The golden thread embroidered into the dark velvet of the woman's gown twinkled in the lamplight. The fancy fabric parted at the center of the full skirt. Drawn back like drapes, the ends were tacked up at the woman's hips while black ruffles cascaded down the open triangle.

"I thought that was you," said the dainty woman. The excited kick in her tone was matched by the radiant smile lighting up her pretty face.

Tucker, on the other hand, looked as though he'd been hit in the face with a shovel. *"Amanda,"* he said, his voice sounding strangled as he sidestepped toward Skylar. Not about to offer him shelter from the tiny woman, Skylar stepped farther into the street.

The woman lifted her hands to her heavily padded hips, accentuating her minuscule waist. Thrusting up her tightly bound breasts, she pouted prettily. "Don't tell me you were going to breeze through Greeley without stopping by to say hello."

"Well, I, ah…" Tucker clamped a hand over the back of his neck as he glanced at Skylar.

Annoyed by the tinge of red high on his cheekbones and not caring to witness Tucker's reunion with the embodiment of feminine primness, Skylar tugged at her horses and started toward the livery. She gasped as Tucker's long arm coiled around her waist and hauled her against his side.

"Honey, I don't believe you've met Amanda Lowery."

As her gaze collided with Amanda Lowery's, the woman's coffee-shade eyes flared wide. "Oh my," she said, pressing a lily-white hand to her chest. Light streaked from the diamond wedding band on her ring finger.

Skylar wondered if the black shawl draping over the bends of her arms and the black ruffles signified that she was a widow. The woman didn't look a day past twenty, the ivory skin of her flawless face young and radiant, the mahogany ringlets piled on her head completely void of gray.

"I beg your pardon," Mrs. Lowery exclaimed, obviously just as stunned by the unexpected introduction. "I didn't realize you were a—"

"Amanda," Tucker interrupted. But Skylar had the distinct inclination Mrs. Lowery was about to say "a woman." "This is Skylar—"

"*Daines,*" Skylar put in quickly, managing a slight smile as she shoved Tucker's hand from her side. "Nice to meet you, Mrs. Lowery," she lied. She truly could have gone a lifetime without meeting one of Tucker's mistresses.

"Likewise, Miss Daines," she replied, although her thin smile was a clear contradiction to her words. "What brings you to Greeley?"

"Horses," Skylar answered.

"I believe I mentioned back in July that my brother and I were starting a horse ranch in Wyoming," Tucker added.

"Yes, yes you did." The woman's expression brightened as she met Tucker's gaze. "I have a few new colts at my place. Perhaps you would like to come by later this evening and take a look at them?"

Skylar thought to tell the flirtatious woman that she had a nice little Colt of her own, *holstered at her hip.*

"I appreciate the offer, Amanda," Tucker said as his arm curved back around Skylar's waist. "But Skylar and I have all the horses we can handle right now."

Skylar felt the blush rising into her cheeks as she stood stiffly against Tucker's side, uncertain of who had given her the greater insult. Amanda Lowery for dismissing the possibility that she and Tucker could be lovers or Tucker for openly implying that they were.

Disappointment tightened the young woman's features. "I see. Well," she said brightly, "if you should change your mind, you know where to find me. Now, if you'll excuse me, I really must be going. Miss Daines," she said in parting, though she never met Skylar's gaze before she turned in a whirl of green velvet.

Still wrapped in Tucker's arm, Skylar held her tongue and her temper as Mrs. Lowery scuttled quickly down the walk. The moment the woman was gone from her view, she rammed her elbow into his ribs.

"Ouch!" he exclaimed, flinching away from her.

"Don't ever do that to me again."

"Do what?" he asked, rubbing at his side as he held her gaze with wide, innocent eyes.

"Stick me between you and one of your...*woman* friends."

"All I did was introduce you!"

"You used me to dodge that woman, Tucker."

"I was being polite," he argued.

"How many times did you say you've passed through Greeley?"

Tucker's jaw flexed with tension as he held her gaze for a moment before saying, "I didn't."

"Then I'm asking."

"Hell, I don't know. Maybe three times. Why?"

"I'll take that to mean there are at least two more women in this town I don't care to be acquainted with. I suggest you find one of them to take to dinner or you'll be dining alone. Once I get into a hotel room, I won't be leaving it till dawn."

Tucker frowned as she shoved past him. He wasn't about to give up his plans for the evening. "Guess I'll go get our room."

"*Separate* rooms," Skylar clarified.

"Right. Separate rooms." As he watched her walk away, an unexpected cold wave of emotion covered his conscience like a dark cloud. "Hey, Skylar?" He rushed after her and took her arm.

Skylar yanked herself from his light hold then batted a dust-filled chunk of hair away from her face as she glared at him. "What?"

"I am sorry about that."

"I'm sure you are, but if you get lonely in that room all by yourself, you know where to find some company." She flashed a smile sharp enough to cut steel.

"I'm trying to apologize about Amanda and you know it!"

"And I do wish you'd stop." She turned away and continued down the street. "No need to apologize for being yourself, Tucker."

What does she mean by that? Cursing under his breath, he stomped across the street and onto the boardwalk. This evening wasn't working out at all how he'd planned it, and the truth in Skylar's assumptions about his visits to Greeley bothered him more than it should.

"What do I have to feel guilty about?" he grumbled under his breath. He thought he'd handled the situation with Amanda quite well. It wasn't as if he could control who they ran into on the street!

Tucker quickly checked them in to separate rooms then went to help Skylar with the horses. By the time he made it to the livery, Skylar had already removed both their saddles and supplies and was grooming the horse he'd ridden to town. Judging by her soft, unguarded expression, it was a chore she found relaxing. Her lips bore the hint of a smile as she brushed out the chestnut stallion's shiny brown mane.

He loved watching her work with the horses. Lord, she was beautiful. Even in her dusty trail clothes and dirt smudged across her right cheek, she was attractive as hell.

"Stop staring at me."

Skylar's biting tone pulled Tucker from his thoughts. *She's still mad.*

"Did you get our rooms?" she asked, keeping her attention on the horse.

"Yep. You want some help with the black stallion?"

"No. I'll finish here and find my own way back to the hotel."

"You have two of the finest horses I've ever seen," he said, his gaze moving over the chestnut. Flecks of orange gleamed in the Arabian's coat as Skylar led him into the narrow stall. "How long have you had them?"

"About two years," she said as she latched the gate.

"Do they have names?"

"That one is Araba," she said nodding toward the chestnut. "The black is Zarad."

"Do you know how rare they are here in the States?"

"I've been told," she said, turning her back on him as she went to tend the other horse.

She clearly wasn't in the mood for conversation.

"I'll take the gear," Tucker said, walking toward the saddlebags Skylar had slung over the side of the stall. "I'll drop these off at our rooms. Go straight through the lobby, to the end of the hall. Your room is on the left and mine's directly across the hall to the right. If I'm not in my room when you get to the hotel, I'll be at the bath-house. It's just around the corner from the hotel. There's a restaurant—"

"You don't need to give me a detailed account of your plans for the evening," she interrupted, glancing over her shoulder.

"I thought we—"

"All I care about is meeting in this livery at sunrise. I don't intend to see you again until then."

She wasn't going to cut him an inch of slack. Well, he didn't plan to cut her any, either. She'd be seeing him a lot sooner than sunrise, he'd make sure of it.

Tucker grabbed their saddlebags, slung them over his shoulder and started toward the door. She couldn't be reasonable when her dander was up, so he'd wait until a warm bath had slicked back her ruff.

Chapter 18

Goodness, I could get used to this.

The longer Skylar soaked in the tub of warm water, the sweet scent of roses filling her senses, the more Tucker didn't seem like such a bad guy. How could she stay mad at someone who treated her to such luxuries?

Why had she been so angry with him anyhow? She'd seen Tucker for what he was the moment she'd laid eyes on him. He charmed everyone he met, a personality trait as natural to him as his smile. Nor could she begrudge others for admiring the same qualities in Tucker that appealed to her.

So why had she been ready to claw that woman's eyes out after her suggestive remark?

Because part of me wants to have Tucker all to myself, she silently admitted.

Not smart.

Glancing at the shriveled pads of her fingers she was reminded that too much of a good thing could be hazardous, and *good* didn't begin to describe the warm bursts of sensation that consumed her when she was in Tucker's arms.

I'm far too inexperienced to handle his sort of fire. She had no defenses against the tender flames of his caresses, flames that consumed her as gently as the bathwater surrounding her now. But the response he ignited within her was anything but gentle. She'd all but attacked him the other night.

Skylar bit her lower lip, recalling the salty taste of his skin. A shudder swept through her. The sheer violence of her desire startled her.

She stood, breaking away from the memory as she reached for the drying sheet hanging from the tall changing screen the tub had been placed behind.

A few minutes later she stood beside the bed, dressed in her clean undergarments. Her stomach grumbled as she turned back the bedcovers. Once she was between those inviting white sheets she'd fall right to sleep, despite her hunger. As she reached toward the lamp to put it out, a knock sounded at the door. She groaned, hearing Tucker's voice call her name.

"Go away, Tucker."

"I can't. I've brought your supper. Open the door, Sky."

"I'm not hungry! Go find some other woman to pester."

Skylar jumped as the door banged open. How had she managed to forget to lock it?

He stepped into the room, saying, "I don't want to pester any woman but *you*."

"Tucker!" she shrieked, stunned by his intrusion.

Holding a large tray piled with covered bowls, plates and glasses, he kicked the door closed behind him.

"You can't just barge in here!" She reached into the saddlebag beside the bed and pulled out her clean waist and quickly shrugged it on.

"You should have locked the latch, but I guess I could have asked if you were dressed." He flashed a smile, and she reached back into her bag and pulled out the skirt. "You sure smell sweet."

"Cut it out. I didn't invite you in."

"Yeah, well, this tray was gettin' heavy, and you'll never convince me that you're not hungry." He walked to the far side of the room and set the tray on the chest of drawers near the small table with two chairs in the corner. He tossed a brown-paper package onto the bed then turned back to the tray of food. Lifting a folded white cloth from the tray, he flapped it high in the air then let it float down onto the small round table.

Skylar stood near the foot of the bed in stunned silence as Tucker began dealing plates and silverware with the card-dealing deftness of a professional gambler.

"You might want to pull that skirt on, honey," he said, keeping his focus on the silverware he was arranging, "unless you plan to come to the table in your underclothes." He flickered a glance in her direction. His green eyes shone with approval. "Either way is fine with me."

Releasing a huff of frustration, Skylar stepped into her skirt. She paused as a mouthwatering scent flooded the air, curling around her nostrils. Glancing at the table, she saw that Tucker had uncovered a dish filled with pieces of steaming fried chicken. Her stomach complained loudly as she watched him load a heap of long, slender green beans onto a white porcelain plate.

"What was that, darlin'?" Amusement laced with his voice. "Something about not being hungry?"

"Oh, do shut up."

Tucker laughed as she tied her waistband. Glancing back at the table she wasn't pleased to find two plates sitting on the nicely laid table.

Oh Lord.

Tucker took a slender vase filled with wildflowers from the tray. He set the colorful arrangement in the center of the small table. Then he plopped down on one of the chairs and smiled up at her, appearing quite proud of himself.

Skylar's heart swelled against the walls of her chest. His handsome face was freshly shaven. Blond hair floated across his scalp in thick golden waves, curling up at his collar and around his ears. She'd even detected the faint scent of cologne when he had walked past her.

She glanced warily toward the door she had hoped he'd be walking out of at any moment. "Tuck?"

"Come on, Sky. It won't kill you to have dinner with me. Let me make up for some of your disappointment. I truly am sorry your judge wasn't in town. We can still get the annulment in Wyoming."

Was that supposed to cheer her up?

He stood and walked around the table. He pulled out the other chair. "I promise to behave myself," he said with a slanted grin, then made a sweeping motion with his hand, inviting her to sit.

Feeling very much like a lamb walking into a lion's den, Skylar reluctantly walked the short distance to the table and sat in the chair.

"Aw, hell," he said as he pushed her chair in, preventing her escape. "I forgot the candle."

Skylar glanced up at Tucker's frowning expression and laughed. He amazed her. How could he think this table, filled with decorative plates, sparkling glasses and silver, and a floral centerpiece bursting with nearly every color of a rainbow could be lacking anything? A candle wouldn't have made a flip of difference. She'd never seen a more beautifully set table. In fact, she'd never seen a complete set of matching china and silverware.

"You keep smiling, and we'll have all the warm glow we need," he said, his rich tone sending shivers down her spine.

"Tucker," she said in warning as he walked around the table.

He smiled and claimed his seat. He grabbed a white linen napkin from beside his plate, shook it out and draped it across his thigh.

Skylar followed his lead, collecting her napkin and draping it across her lap. The bright light from the lamp beside the bed twinkled on the silverware spread out on either side of her plate, more silverware than she knew what to do with. Thank heavens she hadn't let him talk her into eating in a restaurant.

"Relax, honey," Tucker said as he reached toward her

glass with a clear decanter of tea. "You sure do look beautiful in that dress."

He wasn't helping her relax by making such comments, and she was well aware that her clothes were a wrinkled mess from being jammed in her saddlebags.

"Not that you don't look real nice in your denims," he quickly added.

The rich timbre of his voice and the look in his eyes sent tiny tendrils of sensation spiraling up from the pit of her stomach. "Tucker, you promised to behave."

"Skylar, that was a civilized compliment."

"There's nothing civilized about that velvet voice of yours."

He laughed out loud. "Am I really so transparent?" His gaze moved slowly from her face, down to her neck.

She was all too aware of the rapid beat of her pulse.

His smile broadened. "I can't help the effect you have on me, sweetheart, any more than you can help your attraction to me."

"Have you always been so arrogant?"

"I'm just being truthful, honey. Are you gonna just sit there and drive me wild or are you going to eat?"

Skylar picked up her fork, stabbed at her green beans and shoved them into her mouth, thinking the sooner they were finished with the meal, the sooner he would leave—a strategy forgotten the moment her mouth closed around her fork.

Coated in the savory flavor of butter, her taste buds sprang to life. She nearly groaned in delight as she chewed, tantalizing her pallet with a combination of lightly seared green beans, onions, butter and salt. *Butter.* She couldn't even recall the last time the creamy substance had passed her lips.

"Good, isn't it? Marie is a damn fine cook. Almost as good as you. Her restaurant is a few doors down the boardwalk."

"And she let you bring all this to the hotel?"

Tucker flashed one of his fallen-angel smiles. "It took a bit a sweet talking."

"Which happens to be your God-given talent."

Tucker's expression soured. "It is not."

"It is, too," she countered, amused that he'd find her comment offensive. "Don't act as if you don't know the beguiling effect your smiles have on women."

His eyes widened with blatant surprise. "For your information, Marie happens to be a sweet woman in her fifties and happily married for the better part of thirty years."

"Then it would seem your charms have no boundaries."

"I didn't charm her," Tucker said with a scowl. "I just asked politely."

"Uh-huh." Skylar grinned and took another bite, enjoying the hint of red in Tucker's cheekbones as he dropped his gaze to his plate and shoved a forkload of chicken into his mouth.

"I've never seen such beautiful dishes," Skylar said at length, her eyes tracing the rim of her dinner plate and a smaller plate holding slices of bread. A thin stripe of light blue outlined the shiny white rim, with dots of silver beading running along the inside of the blue circle. A matching serving bowl of the same elegant design sat on the table. "Is it just me, or do these plates make the food even more appetizing?"

"You're just hungry," Tucker said in a dull tone. "Dishes are dishes. They all serve the same purpose."

Skylar didn't agree. There was a world of difference between battered tin and fine china, between serving bowls and a matching place setting and an iron skillet and tin plate. Eating beside a campfire opposed to dining at a table covered by white linen. To Skylar, it was the difference between drifting and having a home.

"I take it back," said Tucker. "After watching your eyes, I can see I was wrong. Don't look so downhearted, honey. Pretty dishes aren't so unattainable."

"For you, maybe." She knew just how hard it was to obtain such simple luxuries. She'd spent her whole life working for such simplicity, yet it seemed to slip further from her grasp with every passing day.

Watching Skylar, Tucker had the unnerving suspicion that the sadness in her eyes was derived from more than her fancy for decorative dinnerware. He saw an ache in her soft expression that pained him clear to the bone. He'd never been so affected by anyone else's pain, aside from his brother's. It tore him up to see Skylar so miserable.

"I suppose you miss sitting down at a dinner table at mealtime, huh?"

"It's more than that," she said, anger firming her features. She stabbed her fork at the chicken on her plate and peeled off a chunk of white meat. "I want my own table, in my own home, with my own dishes. I've worked hard to have all those things. For years, I turned over every dollar

I earned to my father, trusting him to follow through on his promise to provide them."

"Perhaps he had intended to buy a place in Wyoming."

Her eyes burned with anger and frustration as she met his gaze. "Then why did he sign a contract with you for employment?"

She believed them. Tucker was taken back by the admission. If she believed them, why was she holding on to their deed?

He'd thought quite a bit about Zach Daines during the past weeks. Chance had told him he had a hard time believing Daines would intentionally deceive Skylar. Perhaps Daines *had* intended on providing her with a home. The man had to know how badly his daughter desired to have one.

"You don't have to own your own ranch to make a good living and buy yourself a patch of land for a house," he pointed out.

"I suppose," she said, her sullen expression unwavered.

"What about your Arabian studs? A man doesn't buy horses like that just to prance them around the desert. It wouldn't surprise me if they cost your father nearly as much as I paid for my land."

"You think so?" she asked, her eyes widening with surprise.

"I know so. That black Arabian is a real prize, and the chestnut is just as impressive. Any breeder would sell his own teeth to pen them up with a couple of his mares. I know I would. I'm sure your father was aware of that. I wouldn't mind finding out how he came across them."

"I'm not really sure," Skylar said as she spread a thick layer of butter onto a slice of bread. "He rode out one evening and came back a week later with the stallions." She took a bite of her bread and shrugged. "He was never big on conversation."

"Somehow that doesn't surprise me," Tucker said, while trying to hide yet another flash of anger he felt toward a dead man. What the hell was Daines doing leaving her alone for a week! "Getting more than a few sentences out of you at a time isn't exactly an easy task," he said.

Skylar smiled before lowering her gaze to her plate.

He liked that reaction. "So, tell me about those mustangs of yours, angel."

They fell into easy conversation as he asked various questions about the mustanging she'd done in Arizona and New Mexico, characteristics of the different bands they'd followed, and the range of clients she'd dealt with, from cattle ranchers to cavalry officers.

Skylar was shocked when she glanced down and her plate was empty. The bowls on the chest of drawers were just as bare, and they'd polished off the decanter of tea. They must have been eating and talking for well over an hour, yet the time had passed so quickly.

Tucker stood and began collecting their dishes, stacking them back on the tray. "I should head out of here and let you get some sleep. I told Marie I'd have her stuff back before she closed, and I sure don't want to get stuck doing these dishes. Not that there's much to clean. We did everything short of licking our plates."

Skylar laughed as Tucker snatched up her shining plate,

which she'd scoured clean with the crust of her bread. "Everything was delicious," she said, rising from her chair. "Thank you for the meal."

"My pleasure." He lifted the vase of flowers, tugged the linen off the table then replaced the vase. Tossing the tablecloth over the dirty dishes, he picked up the large tray with one hand and started toward the door.

Skylar stepped in front of him, opened the door and moved back so he could pass through.

"Lock the latch when I leave," Tucker said as he walked past her.

"Yes, Father," she said with a grin, amused and flattered by his protectiveness.

"I'm not your father, Skylar." He reached back with his free hand and cupped her chin, tilting her face up to meet his gaze. The deep green of his eyes sparked a swirl of sensation in the pit of Skylar's belly. She didn't resist when he leaned forward and pressed his lips to hers. She met his kiss, feeling a rush of anticipation. But the brief caress ended too soon.

"Good night," he whispered.

Primed for a thoroughly intoxicating kiss, disappointment resounded through her as he dropped his hand away from her face and stepped back into the hall. "Sweet dreams, angel girl," he said, then quickly slapped the door shut.

Skylar stared at the back of the door, her lips tingling from his light kiss, her body wound with the odd tension caused by his touch.

Of all the rotten times for him to keep his word!

Chapter 19

Churning with restlessness, Skylar walked toward the bed and flopped onto the mattress, shifting the brown-paper package still sitting where Tucker had dropped it when he'd entered the room. Lying on her back, her eyes narrowed as she focused on the thin bundle. She hooked her finger around the twine tied over each end and dragged the light package onto her lap as she sat up.

Had Tucker meant to give it to her?

She found the seam in the brown wrapping and peeled the edge back, revealing something made of white cotton. Another shirt, she thought. About to toss it aside, she spied a speck of pink thread. She peeled the paper farther back. Her breath caught as she revealed a long white sleeve, and a row of tiny pink and yellow flowers embroidered into the cuff. Tugging twine and ripping the paper, she pulled a long nightgown free of the packaging.

"Tucker," she sighed, tears burning at her eyes as her gaze moved over the prettiest nightgown she'd ever seen.

What was he trying to do to her?

More flowers were stitched along the collar and in between the tiny white buttons running from the high neck to the waistline. It was beautiful.

Within seconds she stripped off her clothing and pulled on the soft white gown. The thin garment did little to put her in the mood for sleep. Wide-awake, she paced the room, the long gown brushing the top of her bare feet with each step. She paused, hearing the door across the hall open then close.

Why had he purchased a gown for her? She couldn't stop the question from repeating in her mind. The gown was lovely, yet accepting such a gift from Tucker was completely inappropriate.

Not that she intended to give it back.

She sat on the bed thinking he must have had a motive. It wasn't fair to seduce her with items of clothing he knew she'd love. He really had no right to be buying her such things! She'd damn well tell him so!

She rushed across the hall and pounded on his door.

"Who's there?" Tucker called.

"Open the door, Tucker."

"Skylar?"

"Expecting someone else?" she asked as he slid the lock back.

"No," Tucker answered as the door swung wide, spilling light into the dark hall, light that reflected like golden sunshine upon the hard, chiseled planes of his naked chest. Clad only in his unfastened denims, he flashed a smile of pure mischief. His widened eyes skimmed down the front of her gown to her bare feet poking out beneath.

Skylar forgot all about the reason she'd convinced herself of for coming to his room. She forgot how to breathe, too caught up in the rush of desire caused by the sight of Tucker's approving gaze and half-clothed body. She wondered if it was normal for a woman to want a man the way she wanted him.

"Skylar, you—"

"I hate you," she sighed as she stepped into his welcoming arms, cutting off his words with her lips.

Tucker chortled low in his throat and pulled her firmly against his body, returning her passionate kiss. He had been two seconds away from leaving this room and pounding on her door before he'd heard her knock.

Moments later, Tucker realized he was ravishing his woman in an open doorway, and blindly kicked the door shut. "Damn, Skylar," he whispered against her lips, "if this is how you greet someone you hate, I don't think I'd survive your affection."

Her trembling smile hit him low and hard, reminding him of the passion they had shared and how much he'd missed the upward curve of her lips in the past few days. He bent and swooped her into his arms. "I really don't think you hate me," he said as he carried her toward the bed.

"I do." She raked her fingers through his hair, her eyes dark with the desire he felt burning in every cell of his body.

He laid her on the mattress and moved over her. "Then why are you here?"

"Because you're making me want you! So you can at least do something about it."

"I think—"

"I don't want to think, Tucker. You win," she breathed against his lips.

Her whispered words stopped him cold.

I win? Chance's warning of Skylar feeling defeated played back in his mind. Tucker braced himself up with his arms, meeting her gaze.

"I don't want to *win*. You're not here because I won."

"It doesn't matter."

"*Yes,* it does."

Her slender golden eyebrows pinched together in annoyance. "Would you shut up and love me?"

Tucker pushed further up with his arms. "No."

She blinked with surprise. "No?"

"Not until you smile."

Her wide blue eyes stared up him.

"Smile for me, honey." He laughed as her expression hardened with a frown. She had a stubborn streak a mile wide, which happened to drive him wild.

"No!"

Tucker arched an eyebrow. "Oh, I think I know a way to make you smile."

Skylar's gaze turned wary. "What are you doing? *Tucker!*" Her sharp laughter pierced the air as his fingers tickled her sides.

"I knew you'd be ticklish," he crooned, her clawing hands not slowing his fingers from wiggling into her sides.

"Stop it!" she shrieked as they thrashed across the bed, both of them laughing.

"Admit you like my company!"

"No!" she managed to squeak out through her wild laughter.

"You can't get enough of me," he added.

Skylar screamed and tried to jerk away from him, sending them both over the side of the bed. Tucker twisted, taking the impact of the fall. Skylar landed on top of him, her cheeks flushed, her smile bright, her eyes sparkling with laughter. He pushed her soft clean hair away from her face, tucking the silken strands behind her ears.

"So beautiful," he said, his own smile aching in his cheeks.

"You don't fight fair, Morgan."

"That's because I'm not fighting at all, angel girl. Do you like the gown?" he asked, running his finger across the flowery collar.

Her lips blossomed into a shy smile, and his chest expanded with a sudden rush of warmth. Lord, he loved this side of her.

"Yes, I like it. But I don't like you buying me things."

"I enjoy it," he said, and it was true. He'd never found so much pleasure in giving gifts to someone. "I like making you smile. Did it make you smile?"

Skylar visibly stiffened. "I never know what to expect from you," she said in a strained voice, her eyes slowly hazing with tears. "I don't usually like surprises."

"I believe you just said you like me."

"No, I didn't," she argued, even as her lips stretched into a grin. "I said I like your surprises." Her hands moved down his body, scattering his thoughts in a torrent of fiery sensation.

Tucker retaliated by tugging on her gown, bunching fabric at her waist as his hands slid beneath to her smooth skin. He caressed her back, then slid his hands lower, and was shocked when his fingers curved around the smooth skin of her bare bottom.

"Hell, Sky. You're naked under there!"

She pushed her hands against his chest, rising to meet his gaze. "Aren't I supposed to be?"

Tucker couldn't fight his laughter, seeing the true concern in her eyes. "Hell yes, you're supposed to be," he said, not having a clue as to what women deemed proper for bedtime attire, but damn sure any man would agree with his answer. To prove his point, he tugged on Skylar's hips, gliding the slick folds of her feminine core across the hard length of his arousal. Skylar trembled as pleasure speared Tucker's body. He shifted her hips again, repeating the intimate caress. Skylar whimpered, clutching at his chest.

"Tucker," she gasped, "the bed."

He sucked in a deep gasp of air, struggling to slow the beat of his heart hammering against his chest. He wrapped his arms around her and stood.

If Skylar wanted to be loved in a bed, he'd damn well love her in a bed, and take his time doing so.

Some time later, her head resting on the pillow of Tucker's arm, Skylar listened to his steady breathing. Lamplight glimmered like tiny streaks of gold across the patch of hair with each rise and fall of his chest. She couldn't close her eyes, too aware of his damp skin pressed against hers, his long fingers twisted in her hair, and his other hand resting heavily on her hip.

Somehow, just lying with him like this seemed far more intimate than the intense lovemaking they'd just shared. She knew she should go back to her own room, but couldn't summon the energy or the will to leave the warm security of Tucker's arms. As much as she yearned to give in to this state of bliss he so easily put her in, she knew she shouldn't. She was only a temporary fancy.

She smoothed her hand up Tucker's bronze arm to his wide shoulder, wanting to believe that it was the same for her. She'd be a fool to allow herself to fall in love with Tucker Morgan.

Her fingers raked across his strong chest, stopping over the steady beat of his heart. *It's just physical*, she told herself. Smiling sadly, she tilted her face up and pressed her lips against Tucker's sharp jaw, and silently called herself a *liar*.

"You keep that up and we won't be getting any sleep."

"I should go back to my room."

"No." His arms tightened around her. "Let me hold you."

He hadn't given a command. She could easily pull away from his embrace, but as he hugged her against his warm body and pressed his lips to her forehead, she didn't want to move. He released a deep contented sigh as she continued to lie quietly in his arms.

Tucker shifted as he reached toward the lamp beside the

bed and turned down the wick, surrounding them in darkness. He instantly folded her back into his strong embrace. Skylar nestled against him, and again reminded herself that this closeness between them was only temporary. She was one of many women in Tucker's life. Amanda Lowery had been testimony of that.

The thought of the pristine young widow sent an ache twisting through her heart.

She wished she was like Tucker, able to separate physical intimacy from emotional intimacy, but she wasn't.

She was a fool.

Tucker shifted in his sleep and stretched his arm out beside him, searching for the warm, smooth skin he'd cradled against his body throughout the night. When his hand found nothing but the cold mattress, his eyes popped open.

"Skylar?"

Even as he called her name, he knew she wasn't in the room.

What had he expected? What the hell was he doing?

"Hell if I know," he muttered, and sat up in the twisted tangle of sheets. Digging his fingers into his hair, he hunched forward and dropped his elbows on his raised knees. He squinted as he leaned into a bright ray of light streaming in from between the window coverings. What time was it?

Judging by the warm glow coming from the window, he'd missed sunrise by an hour or more. He rubbed at his eyes, wondering why Skylar hadn't woken him. But then he supposed he knew why.

She didn't want to face the fact that she'd come to him. Not that he hadn't done his damnedest to make sure that happened. Hadn't that been his reason for dining her and giving her the gown?

He wanted to believe it was, but in truth, he never fathomed she would actually come to his room. Skylar's resistance to his advances tested his confidence, an obstacle he'd never faced in his dealings with women.

Perhaps that's the reason my attraction to her is so damn strong.

Skylar was a challenge, and he always enjoyed a challenge. Whenever life became routine and mundane, he never hesitated in changing course to stir things up. Skylar was about as predictable as a loose cannon, and if he had simply wanted company for the night, he could have easily found another willing woman.

During the short time he'd been in Marie's restaurant, he exchanged glances with a few attractive women who'd flashed him a welcoming smile, yet the thought of bedding any of those women hadn't appealed to him in the slightest. All he could think about was getting back to the wild woman who'd wanted nothing more than to kick him out of her room.

He had worked his butt off to put himself back in Skylar's good favor. Marie hadn't relinquished her good china, fine food and fresh flowers without a great deal of groveling on his part, and he'd bought that gown from Miss Kelley, hoping he'd come upon just such an occasion to give it to Skylar. Hell, if he didn't know any better, he'd think he was courting his wife.

"Shit." Tucker yanked at the sheets tangled around his legs and swung his feet to the cold wooden floor. He had to stop doing that, referring to Skylar as his wife.

No woman was worth that lifetime penance.

They were lovers, plain and simple. He reached for the pants piled on the floor, where he'd kicked them off the night before. He quickly pulled them on and walked toward the dresser and snatched up his shirt. Shoving his arms into the sleeves, he reminded himself he'd never held an interest in any woman for more than a few days.

Yet he couldn't deny that loving Skylar was nothing like his past relations with other women. With Skylar, each time was different. Each time was *better*. She consumed him so completely, he couldn't get the feel of her smooth skin out of his mind, her taste from his mouth.

And at this very moment, she was undoubtedly denying he had any such effect on her, when he'd seen the proof in her passion-filled eyes. He wasn't about to settle for her stern indifference.

Tucker quickly finished dressing, tugged on his boots, grabbed his saddlebags and started for the door. If Skylar thought he'd accept her cold-shoulder treatment, she had another think coming.

Finding her room empty, he headed to the livery, hoping she hadn't left him to ride back alone. He approached Mr. Cobb, the white-bearded man who ran the livery, and a few of his stable hands standing outside the large barn.

"Your woman's inside," said Cobb, nodding toward the

open doors of the livery. Tucker didn't miss the grins tugging at the mouths of the other men. He glanced past Mr. Cobb and saw Skylar standing beside her black stallion, tightening the cinch of her saddle, and dressed in her dusty denims, flannel shirt and work coat.

My woman.

That didn't sound so bad.

He handed Cobb the money he owed him and went inside. The chestnut Arabian was tethered beside Skylar's black stallion. Both were saddled and ready to go. Judging by Skylar's stiff movements as she tightened the binding holding the pack behind her saddle, she was aware of his presence. Yet she didn't offer him any type of greeting.

"Good morning," he said, fighting not to reveal his irritation.

Skylar drew a deep, silent breath, struggling with the lump that formed in her throat the moment she spotting Tucker crossing the street toward the livery. "Morning," she replied, keeping her back to him. After fretting for over an hour, she still wasn't ready to face him. "If you've paid the livery master we can get out of here."

She continued tying down the supplies she'd taken the liberty of buying. When Tucker didn't respond and she didn't sense any movement behind her, Skylar looked back at him. She noticed he hadn't taken time to shave. His stubble-coated jaw was tight, his stance wide, his arms crossed over his chest. Irritation burned in his eyes as he continued to stand there, silently staring at her as though she'd somehow offended him.

"What?" she muttered when she could stand no more of his silence.

"I don't like this cycle we've gotten into. I don't expect you to throw your arms around me and smother me with kisses. Just to be civil, friendly. What do you say we give that a try?"

The painful tension in Skylar's body tightened. She didn't know if she could. The problem was, from the moment she'd spotted his gilded hair in the morning sunlight and watched his long leisurely strides as he walked toward the livery, she wanted to throw her arms around him and smother him with kisses. Even now, she ached to reach out and touch him.

A smile curved his lips as he walked toward her and Skylar had to suppress a wince. How could she be nice to him and suppress the rush of emotion she felt whenever he looked at her like that. He was making her soft. She never should have stayed in town with him.

"Com'ere," he said, holding out his hand.

Skylar stepped into his embrace. She sighed as his arms closed around her, a mixture of relief and exhilaration flooding her body.

"What's this?" he asked, easing back. His hand slipped inside her coat, tugging at the folded paper sticking out from the inside pocket.

"Newspaper. Garret needs some new reading material."

"You've been busy this morning," he said, nodding toward her saddle.

"When I picked your shirt up from the floor, a pouch of money fell from the pocket." She shrugged her shoulders.

"We were in need of a few things." Skylar dug her hand into her pants pocket. Retrieving the leftover coins, she held them up. "You really shouldn't keep such large sums of money in your shirt pocket."

Tucker smiled and pulled her back against the length of his body, ignoring the money in her hand as he brushed a light kiss across her lips. "You sound like Chance. Just tell me you got a receipt. He's worse than a harping wife if he can't document everything in his damn ledgers."

Tucker's lips moving softly over hers didn't hold back the sadness that crept into Skylar's heart. In Tucker's mind there was nothing worse than being bound to a wife. She was putting her trust in another illusion. No matter how badly she wanted him, it would never be enough. Tucker would never want her for a wife.

She had to distance herself from him.

Tomorrow, she told herself as she allowed Tucker's tender kiss and gentle embrace to ease her pain, filling the emptiness of her heart. *Tomorrow I'll end it.*

Within the space of a breath, she wasn't concerned about anything beyond returning Tucker's kiss.

Chapter 20

By the time Skylar made it to the top of the cliff a bright orange sun was cresting the eastern rise of mountains. Having left Zarad at the base of the hill, she'd climbed the giant pile of dirt and rocks, needing a good clear view of the surrounding area. When she stepped to the edge of the massive stone, she saw that she'd found it. She could see for miles. A number of valleys ran between low-range mountains, many of which Randal could be traveling through.

She should have scouted for Randal a few days back, but this was the first time she'd been able to leave camp before dawn without Tucker following her. In the past few days she'd discovered that long kisses and muffled laughter were an enjoyable way to start off a day. She thoroughly enjoyed every second of her time alone with Tucker.

That's beside the point! her better judgment shot back; a voice she'd been ignoring in the past few days. Tucker was a distraction, not to mention a bad influence. If she was going to get her mustangs back she had to stay focused.

Reaching into the deep pocket of her coat, she pulled out her father's spyglass. Lifting the brass scope she began scanning the valley farthest to the west, knowing he'd be coming from that direction. Although, even if she did spot Randal, she didn't know how she'd get her horses back on her own. She prayed Duce and the others were well, and could assist her.

In the last few days she'd discussed the possibility of running into Randal with Tucker. He'd even brought it up with Chance. Both seemed confident that Randal would beat them to Wyoming, but that their ranch hands could handle him.

Their lack of concern annoyed her. If they were plotting any strategies for dealing with Randal, she wasn't being included in their plans. Neither had mentioned paying her for her mustangs, should they manage to recover them.

They have their agenda, and I have mine, she reminded herself. If it came to that, she'd have to pray that Duce and the others still loyal to her would stand behind her.

Her mouth twisted into a frown as her gaze swept over the next valley, seeing no signs of rising smoke that would give away a large camp.

Hearing an approaching rider, Skylar lowered her scope and glanced down toward the base of the hill. She spotted Tucker as he rode into the clearing below. He stopped beside her horse and stepped down from his saddle.

"Skylar, where are you?" he called, glancing toward the cliffs. His lips stretched in a wide smile when he spotted her. "There you are. What are you doing up here?"

"Just scouting the passes," she said as she stepped down from one slab of rock to another.

"Watch the sunrise with me." He leaped onto a boulder and started toward her.

"The sun is right behind you, Tucker. We should get back. Garret and Chance should be up by now."

Tucker continued climbing up the rocky cliff and pulled her into his arms. Skylar sighed as his hand caressed her back.

"I can't argue with you when you're holding me like this."

"I know," he said, his smiling lips pressing against her ear. "Why did you sneak away from camp this morning?"

She tensed, surprised by his whispered question. "I didn't sneak away."

Tucker eased back. His steady gaze showed he didn't believe her. "Honey, a shadow leaves more of a trail than you did, so either you're playing hard to get or you were trying to elude me."

"You found me," she pointed out, kissing his smooth, recently shaven chin.

"I'm a damn good tracker."

Obviously. Fresh out of excuses, Skylar leaned up and pressed her lips to his, a distraction that turned out to be enjoyable for both of them. He tasted of coffee and smelled of clean, rich shaving lather—a delightful combination.

"So, show me what you were looking at." Taking her hand, he stepped around her and led her back up the stairs of stone. "Would you look at all that color," he said, his voice filled with awe as he reached the top. "Beautiful."

Skylar smiled, watching his emerald eyes shine with appreciation as he took in the vast landscape. Following his gaze, she realized he was right. The variety of seasonal changes was *beautiful.* The deep aspen-lined valleys looked like channels laden with gold and copper woven beneath the surrounding evergreen forests. The higher ranges, covered with snow-dusted pines, led up to brilliant snowcapped peaks that glistened in the morning sunlight.

How could she have missed such beauty? Yet she'd stood in this very spot just moments ago and hadn't truly noticed any of it.

Feeling a tug on her coat, Skylar looked back. Tucker sat behind her on the rocky perch. He pulled her down, situating her between his raised knees.

"Tucker—"

Her protest died in an involuntary moan as his grip closed over her shoulders. His large hands kneaded her shoulders and the back of her neck. She pulled in a deep relaxing breath as he skillfully worked the tension from her body.

"I smell rain," she said a moment later, detecting the faint scent in the brisk air.

"Rain? You sure?" He brushed her hair aside as he raked his teeth across the side of her neck. "I smell roses. I can taste them, too."

"Cut it out," she said, laughing as she swatted at him.

Tucker retreated and glanced up at the sky. "There's not a cloud in the sky, sweetheart."

"It's coming." She turned her face toward the cool northern breeze, breathing in the faint trace of impending rain as she leaned back against Tucker.

He folded his arms around her, eagerly accepted her weight, enjoying the contentment he felt as she relaxed against him.

"We should be picking our way through that maze of rock by tomorrow afternoon," she said in a dull tone, gazing toward the distant northern rise they had already studied in her journal.

"You don't sound happy about that. Do you have grievances you didn't tell us about last night?"

"No. I agree that it appears to be the fastest route. I just don't want to be stuck in some stone canyon with a storm brewing overhead."

"How do you know so much about mountain passes you've never ridden?"

"Same way you do. Experience. When you spend your life roaming, you learn to read the terrain."

Tucker was pleased by her acknowledgment. Skylar wasn't as domineering and pigheaded as he'd first thought her to be. She was bossy and stubborn all right, but she'd also taught him and Chance loads about working the mustangs and was always open to their suggestions. She didn't discredit anyone's opinion, Garret's included.

"Can I ask you a question?" she said, breaking the peaceful silence.

"Fire away, angel."

"I've been wondering why a man with a ranch in Wyoming would be rustling mustangs in New Mexico instead of his own backyard. Not that you don't have a band of fine horses, but you did hire us to supply you with your stock, so why travel so far out of your way?"

What a question. One he was reluctant to answer. One he wasn't sure he could answer. "I needed a breath of fresh air," he said after a moment.

"They don't have any of that in Wyoming?" she asked, smiling as she glanced over her shoulder.

For once, Tucker didn't return her smile. "I was thrilled to death when we got the land and started building our ranch. But…it just…I didn't…"

As he pondered his hand moved up from her hip and began to burrow beneath her warm flannel and wool underwear. He smiled at the feel of her soft camisole, then slid his fingers beneath that, too. Skylar drew a deep breath as his fingers grazed her waist. Watching her lips curve into a smile, Tucker felt the tension in his muscles begin to melt away. Odd how holding her could fill him with a sense of calm.

"We've spent our whole lives working toward having our own ranch," he said, taking more of her weight. "All that time and work focused on one goal, yet once I got it…it wasn't as satisfying as I thought it would be. It's got nothing to do with the ranch. The second I saw that green valley backed by snow-covered mountains, I knew it was the perfect location. Wait till you see it, Skylar."

He hugged her against him, realizing only now how much he was looking forward to seeing that valley again.

"It's the most beautiful stretch of land this side of heaven. We worked our tails off pulling our place together, building bunks, barns, stables and houses. But by the end of winter I was feeling—"

Hell, how am I supposed to describe what I don't understand? He stared out at the distant mountains, annoyed by the clash of emotions he normally did his best to suppress.

"Restless?" Skylar offered.

"I suppose," he said with a slight shrug, his fingers combing across her smooth abdomen. "I stayed until the end of spring. The day after we finished framing our house, I packed my saddlebags and couldn't ride fast enough. I just needed a change of scenery, I guess."

"You're just like my father. Driving cattle and horses was never about the money. He loved the adventure. I think he was in love with the land. You could see it in his eyes when we'd finish a drive and he began to chart a new course to the next job, always a new stretch of ground we'd never ridden."

Perturbed by the deep sadness he heard in her tone, Tucker shifted Skylar sideways, lifting her long legs over his thighs as he turned her toward him so he could see her pretty face. She laid her head against his shoulder, completely relaxed in his arms, and Tucker's chest expanded with a burst of odd sensations.

"Why do I get the feeling that's all you ever discussed with your father?" he asked. "Work, the next job, distribution of chores."

"What more is there?"

"Plenty. Your own aspirations, hopes and dreams."

"Dreams are for children, Tuck."

He knew firsthand how motivating dreams could be. Seven months in prison camp had nearly killed him and Chance. But they'd spent those days of pain and darkness planning for their future, dreaming about the horse ranch they would build someday. He looked at the sad curve of her mouth and thought about the few glimpses he'd already seen of what Skylar dreamed of having.

"Do you really believe that, honey, or is that your father talking? There were times when dreams were all that kept me and Chance going."

"My father helped me to see that you can't put your trust in illusions. You've had your ranch for more than a year, yet you're still not content. Perhaps dreams are just that, not meant to be had. Nothing ever has the same luster in reality as it does in our minds."

"It does for some," Tucker said, recalling Chance's expression when he told his twin he wanted to hunt mustangs in New Mexico. Chance had called him crazy, unable to fathom why he'd want to leave what in all respects was a paradise. "Our ranch is Chance's idea of heaven. He's right at home nestled in that little valley."

"But *you* don't feel at home."

"Sure I do," Tucker said, the lack of conviction in his voice sounding obvious to his own ears. "I'm just not accustomed to letting grass grow under my feet. It'll take some getting used to."

"Do you really think you can be happy staying in one spot?"

Tucker looked into Skylar's wide, questioning eyes, and

smiled. For the first time he could recall, he wasn't in any hurry to go nowhere. He wasn't a damn bit concerned about the ranch, the weather, their horses, their brothers.

"No question about it," he said as he kissed her. He was happy right where he was. It was a damn good feeling.

Skylar's breath unraveled in a long sigh as he caressed her long, slender side. But the moment his hand cupped the full satiny swell of her breast, she grabbed his fingers through the layer of clothing.

"Tucker, we can't."

"I know, angel. It's been forever since I've touched you."

"It's been four days."

"Feels like forever," he whispered against her lips, leaving his hand where it was as he proceeded to kiss her until she was again relaxed in his arms. The moment he caressed her breast, she broke off the deep kiss and quickly wiggled out of his arms.

"Now why did you have to run off?" he complained, already missing the feel of her warmth and weight pressed against him.

"Because I don't have a speck of sense when you're touching me like that."

Tucker smiled as he watched her shuffle quickly down the hillside. "Practical to the core," he said as he stood.

"And that smile of yours is just one more illusion," she called back.

The steady rainfall a constant hush in his ears, Tucker sat in his saddle before his anxious mustangs, helping to keep them contained between the deep canyon walls.

Garret and Chance were doing the same at the tail end of the idle herd. Tucker glanced warily toward the swirling black mass above them.

Thunder rumbled through the thick blanket of clouds, vibrating through him, echoing off the canyon walls surrounding them.

"Easy," Tucker murmured, talking more to the angry storm brewing overhead than his pack of nervous horses. This day was steadily going from bad to worse. The dark pitch and deep grumbling above them gave clear warning that the gentle showers raining down were only a prelude to the floodgate that was about to bust wide open.

Rock didn't absorb water. If those clouds opened up and dropped their heavy load, their canyon trail would fast become a riverbed with a torrent of water streaming through its narrow walls, and washing out anything in its path. Water was already tumbling at them from all directions, pouring off the high cliffs on either side and rolling down the rocky slope before him, swirling around the horses' hooves. The same slope Skylar had ridden over nearly half an hour ago.

An increasing surge of adrenaline and impatience ate at Tucker's nerves as he peered through the thin veil of water, searching for her return. Skylar had left them behind to scout ahead for the quickest route out of this death trap. If she didn't get her tight little butt back here quick, they'd soon be facing the reality she'd been fearing all morning. It was Skylar's intuition that had put the first kink in Tucker's day.

During the past few days he'd become accustomed to

stealing a few moments alone with her in the evenings and at sunrise. This morning, however, he'd walked into camp after his watch to find everything packed up. Worried that they'd be caught in the impending storm before they could get the horses through the canyons, Skylar had awakened their brothers well before dawn.

Her fear had been a valid one.

Tucker glanced again at the shifting clouds above him. He released a deep sigh of relief as he heard Skylar call his name and he caught sight of her riding toward him. She reined in beside him. Noting the worry in her gaze, he cursed under his breath. He grabbed her horse's harness and leaned toward her until the brim of his hat touched hers, shutting out the rain falling around them.

"That bad?" he asked.

"The quickest way out of these canyons is steep enough to raise hairs on the back of my neck," she reported, her unhappy tone matching her expression.

That couldn't be good. She wasn't squeamish about taking steep inclines and had sent them over a few in the past couple weeks that had raised the hairs on the back of *his* neck.

"This vein splits in two a half mile up," she said. "The horses will need to bank a hard right. The left pass leads to another long riverbed of rock. You'll have to block off that trail to get the horses to take the right turn. The channel opens up about a quarter mile down, before it drops off into a wide valley."

His gaze locked on the tender side of her neck where

her pulse beat rapidly. She was scared. "Just how steep is this *drop-off?*"

"*Steep.*"

"Hell."

"Would be on horseback. I wouldn't charge down that wet slope in a saddle. We'll pick our way down same as the horses. On foot."

"You're sure about this?"

"Sliding down that slick hillside won't kill us, but I won't guarantee the same for all your horses. If we don't get out of these canyons, we'll get washed clear back to the Colorado border. That's guaranteed to kill us all."

That hadn't been the answer he wanted. His muscles flexed with the urge to pull Skylar off her horse and soothe the fear in her eyes.

An irrational response.

Skylar eased back and glanced toward the horses.

"We'll keep a close watch on Garret," he assured her.

She nodded and urged her horse back. "I'll send the packhorses down first and hope for the best."

She no sooner disappeared into the dreary gray distance with the packhorses than a deafening crash of thunder rolled across the black sky in a ground-shaking roar. A few seconds later, the ground began to rumble, telling Tucker that somewhere farther north the sky had fallen and was rushing straight toward them. Putting his fingers to his lips, he pierced the air with a sharp whistle, telling Chance it was time to set off.

By the time they were all moving, water was rising beneath them. Tucker found the fork in the stone just as

Skylar had said. The path was already blocked by a heavy flow of rushing water. The horses didn't hesitate in turning right toward higher, dryer ground. Tucker held back and waited until Garret rode by in a cluster of mustangs.

"The hill is too steep to ride down," he shouted as Garret reined beside him. "You'll have to go down on foot. Make sure you stick to the *outside* of the herd."

Garret nodded then continued on.

Tucker and Chance guided the last of the horses toward the wide ridge. Half the herd crowded around the lip. Tucker jumped from his saddle and approached the edge.

Hell, no wonder they didn't want to go over. Unprotected by the high, stone walls, hard gusts of wind whipped across the hillside. Rainwater was pouring down the jagged face of the rock-strewn cliff. Although the scattered rocks could be helpful with the slippery footing for the horses, large boulders pushed out from beneath the hard-packed soil which could trip them up.

The kid was halfway down, keeping to the far side just like he'd told him and out of the path of the horses. Looking out toward the base of the hill, he saw obscure images of his mustangs trotting toward the short grass and groves of trees that stretched across the wide valley floor.

"Go on down so you can help the kid," Chance called from beside him. "I'll make sure this lot doesn't decide to backtrack."

Tucker didn't hesitate. When he was about halfway down, a stationary dark spot near the center of the slope caught his attention. Looking closer he saw that it was one of the pack animals. The mule had to be caught up somehow.

The stranded mule could very well trip the other horses. Tucker started edging his way toward it when he saw another patch of movement, something popping up on the other side of the trapped animal.

Oh God.

Tucker sucked in a burning gasp of air and held it as he watched Skylar's long frame move up past the mule, apparently attempting to free it. She drew her knife from the scabbard at her waist. He glanced up at the ridge as four of his mustangs came barreling over the mountainside, two of them headed directly toward Skylar. Slick gravel crumbled, scattering like marbles, sending them right down on top of her.

Her name burst from his burning lungs as he lost sight of her in a distorted blur of figures. The two dark mustangs skidded past the mule and continued down the hill. Tucker's gaze moved over the gray slope, praying Skylar had managed to avoid the mare's sharp hooves. He spotted her below the pack mule, clinging to the steep hillside. She lifted her head, and he released a hard breath.

"Keep going down," Tucker urged.

Tension closed over his body as he watched her reach a hand up, again climbing toward the pack mule. Another dark shadow of stumbling horses barreled down the cliff.

"Skylar!"

Thunder crashed overhead, drowning out his voice. The dark sky opened up and he lost sight of her in the heavy rainfall.

* * *

Skylar's gloved fingers gripped frantically at the slick slab of rock above her. Ice-cold water sleeted across her face, drenching the clothes beneath her coat as she struggled to keep her footing. Hard gusts of wind whipped at her wet hair. Her hat hung across her back from the long cord, having been knocked off as she slid across the hillside. She'd almost had her blade on the rope when she'd been forced to let go of the rock to avoid being trampled.

Clenching her knife between her teeth, she lunged to her left. The tender scar on her shoulder burned with pain as she pulled herself across the rough surface toward the rope jammed tight in a deep crack. She slid her blade beneath the thick braid of fibers stretching down from the large stone and cut the frightened animal free. As it disappeared into the blur of rain, Skylar released her hold on the rock and slid across the slick surface.

Another horse came down hard beside her, missing her by inches. Skylar screamed and rolled to her right. She continued sliding down until the ground angled out enough to get her feet beneath her. She shoved herself up, descending as fast as she could, trying not to worry about what was coming down behind her.

The second her boots hit solid flat ground, she started running. It wasn't long before she came upon the unmoving herd. Approaching them, she shivered from the cold wind whipping at her wet clothes.

"Guess we're making camp," called Chance from behind her. "We can't see a damn thing in this rain."

Skylar hugged her arms tightly around her middle to

calm her shivers as she looked past the water running off the rim of her hat.

Chance walked briskly toward her, leading his horse by the reins. "Nice job with that pack mule," he said as he stopped beside her.

"Not really. If I had checked them for loose ropes, it wouldn't have gotten hung up in the first place. We'll need the tarpaulins to stretch between a few of these trees so we can get a fire started."

Chance nodded in agreement. "You pick the spot while I round them all up and get— *What's wrong with him*?"

Skylar followed Chance's gaze. Tucker marched straight toward them, unbridled rage burning in his eyes.

He grabbed her by the hand, not pausing as he tugged her after him. "Excuse us."

"Tucker!" she shrieked.

"You're crazy, you know that?" he shouted, his powerful strides showing no sign of slowing as he led her deeper into the thick grove of aspen.

"What are—"

"You couldn't stick to the outside of the herd!"

"I did, but—"

"You had to be right there in the thick of it, damn near getting yourself killed!"

Skylar dug her heels into the wet ground and tugged at his hold on her. "If you dragged me off to tell me—"

Tucker hauled her against him, ending her words with a gasp. His arms locked around her like steel bands. "I dragged you out here because I need a moment alone with you, damn it!"

"To shout at me?" she asked, confused by the anger she saw in his eyes and felt in his tight muscles. Some of his mares had obviously sustained injuries. She was just as upset over any harm inflicted on his mares, but things could have been worse. Much worse. "Tucker, I warned you that your mares could get hurt. It was the safest way out of that mountain pass I could find. Did you see the amount of water pouring down after us?"

"All I saw was *you* in the path of those stumbling mares, risking your life over a damn mule!"

"That damn mule would have tripped every horse that—"

"*To hell with the horses!* You nearly got yourself killed!"

Skylar flinched at his hard tone. Tucker shut his eyes and strived to regain a shred of control. Even as he told himself she was in his arms, safe and unharmed, he couldn't force himself to ease his hold. She could have died and he couldn't have done a damn thing to save her!

"You ever do anything like that again," he managed to say in a milder tone, "and I swear I'll…"

Skylar felt his shudder, saw the wash of emotion in his eyes, just before he took her mouth in a hard kiss.

The realization that he'd been afraid for her dissolved her defenses. His kiss softened, and Skylar decided she liked his idea of punishment. Threading her fingers into the damp hair at his collar she returned his fervent kiss, smiling as he groaned in response and held her tighter still.

"You'll kiss me?" she breathed against his lips when they paused for breath.

"You'll wish," he said, his expression completely void of humor. "How's your shoulder?"

"It's fine." Her wet skin was too darn cold to feel any pain, a chill that was fading with every passing second of being wrapped in Tucker's arms. But standing in the rain wasn't going to help dry her clothes, and kissing Tucker wouldn't get the work done.

"If you've finished scolding me, we need to start setting up camp so we can get out of this rain."

"In a minute," he grumbled, nuzzling her cheek, holding her with a fierceness that was as comforting as it was confusing. As minutes passed, she could feel the tension slowly leaving his body. There was a distinct shift in the pressure of his hands on her back. Her breath caught as Tucker's teeth grazed her ear.

"Time's up." She broke away from the sensual embrace and turned in the direction of camp, forcing herself to start walking while she still had the strength to do so.

Chapter 21

Raindrops pelted Tucker's back as he staked his white mustang beneath the light shelter of aspens. With the collar of his long coat flipped up and his hat tugged low, he had managed to stay reasonably dry.

He glanced through the veil of falling raindrops toward the tarpaulin Skylar and Garret had stretched between four neighboring trees so that Skylar could start a fire. They would all be crowded under that flap of canvas for the remainder of the evening, which meant he wouldn't be getting any more time alone with her. He looked forward to that little bit of time more than he wanted to admit.

Frowning, he started toward the shelter. He stepped beside his brother as he ducked beneath the heavy tarpaulin. Noticing Chance's odd expression, Tucker followed his wide-eyed gaze, which collided with Skylar, on her knees beside the small fire she'd started. She had dug a pit and already had the wild turkey Garret had shot early in the day roasting over the low flames. Her rain-soaked shirt revealed the tight, rosy-tipped evidence of her chill. Skylar obviously didn't realize her wet clothes were practically see-through, or that Chance was presently taking advantage of the view.

He had no right to gape at her! Tucker stepped in front of his brother, blocking his view as he shrugged off his long coat. He began to unbutton his heavy wool shirt as he walked toward Skylar. Stepping behind her, he pulled off the thick shirt and draped it over her shoulders.

Focused on the turkey, Skylar looked up at him with wide eyes. "Tucker?"

"Look down, honey," he whispered near her ear.

"Oh!"

Tucker smiled at her look of surprise as she straightened away from the fire and quickly shoved her arms into the sleeves of his shirt. When he began to fasten the buttons, she slapped his hands away.

"Thanks, Tuck. I can handle the buttons." Her cheeks flushed as she turned away from him to finish closing the long shirt.

"What do you have stuffed up that bird?" Chance asked, now crouched on the opposite side of the fire, his expression full of perplexity as he inspected the herbs sticking out the back end of the turkey.

It occurred to Tucker that Chance's gaze may not have been fixed on Skylar, but on their supper.

"Thyme and rosemary," Skylar answered as she knelt beside the warmth of the fire.

"Looks like weeds," Chance said, lifting his skeptical gaze to Skylar.

"It'll taste good," she assured him.

"I don't doubt it." Chance straightened, his lips quirked

in a grin. "If I'd known all it took was a bullet in your shoulder to have us eating so good, I would have shot you myself back in New Mexico."

Tucker never knew a woman who blushed so much. *Or a woman half as stubborn*, he thought, seeing the fine trembling of Skylar's body. She was chilled to the bone.

"I'm gonna check on a couple mares I saw limping," Chance said, turning to leave.

"Right behind you," Tucker answered, but kept his gaze locked on Skylar as he shrugged his coat back on. "Honey, you're soaked from head to toe."

"I'm fine." Her gaze flickered past him before meeting his gaze. The wariness in her expression told him Chance was still standing behind him. Tucker didn't give a damn.

"I'm starting to wonder at your definition of *fine*," he said as he reached down, took her by the arm and hauled her up. "You're going to catch pneumonia in those wet clothes. Garret finished putting up your tent. Grab your gear and go change into something dry, I can watch over the bird and the fire."

"Only clean thing I have is the skirt and—"

"Go get it on," he instructed, ushering her away from the fire as she tried to dig her heels in the ground.

"Tuck, I need to—"

"No arguments." Gripping her shoulders, he turned her toward the packs and saddles piled on the far side of the shelter. "Go change into something dry before you catch your death."

She glanced over her shoulder, her expression full of

annoyance, then walked toward their gear and pulled her saddlebags from the pile. Tucker watched as she stepped from the tarpaulin cover and darted toward her tent.

"You sure that judge wasn't in Greeley."

Tucker met Chance's sober gaze. "Yes, I'm sure. Skylar wouldn't have let me out of that town without an annulment if he had been."

"You two seem to be on particularly good terms lately, and that quarrel in the woods sure sounded like a bickering married couple."

"Just because she hasn't been at my throat day and night doesn't mean she's not anxious to be rid of me. We'll get the annulment."

Chance lowered his gaze, frowning at the ground for a moment before he shook his head and turned away. "Don't burn our supper," he said in a warning tone, and stepped back out into the rain.

A short while later Skylar appeared beneath the shelter, dressed in her wrinkled gray skirt and his long wool shirt buttoned up over her waist. Judging by the fullness of her skirt bulging out beneath his green shirt, she'd pulled on all five petticoats. She hadn't worn the dress since the night he'd given her the new pair of Levi's. He couldn't say he blamed her. All those layers had seemed a cumbersome hassle in the saddle. Not that her attire made any difference to Tucker. She was just as stunning in her denims and chaps.

"Feel better?" he asked.

Skylar dropped to her knees beside him. The moment

she had stripped off her wet clothing and pulled on her first petticoat she had felt quite thankful of Tucker's insistence. "Yes," she admitted, and snatched her fork from his hand. "Now move aside, you're burning our supper."

He didn't budge an inch as she crowded in beside him to rotate the turkey. The warmth radiating from his body warmed her blood far more efficiently than her dry clothes had.

"Listen," he said after a moment of silence. "I may have overreacted a bit earlier."

"Just a bit?" Skylar asked, glancing up at him.

"I'm not taking back what I said, just the way I said it."

"Is that an apology or a statement?" she asked, amused by the sudden sternness of his handsome features.

"Both," he said, dipping his head and brushing his mouth lightly across hers.

She didn't pull away when his lips returned, lingering as his arms slid around her. She closed her eyes and leaned into the kiss, allowing the heady rush of sensation to thoroughly warm her from the inside out.

"Lordy, but that's a cold rain!"

At the sound of Garret's voice, the hands resting on Tucker's chest nearly knocked him over as Skylar spun back toward the fire.

Garret stomped in out of the downpour, his gaze dropping toward his wet boots. "A few degrees lower and I'll bet it'd be snowin'."

She was becoming careless!

"I know it's early," Garret said as he shook his head and arms, knocking off the excess water, "but I feel like we worked a whole day and then some." His tired hazel eyes met Skylar's gaze. "You changed your clothes."

Realizing he hadn't seen her wrapped in Tucker's arms, relief broke through Skylar with a force that shook her. "They were wet," she managed to squeeze past the lump constricting her throat.

"Take a load off, kid," Tucker said as he stood and walked toward Garret. "Your sister has hot coffee brewing. I'm sure you can talk her into pouring you a cup."

"I'm not trying to cut out on my work, Tuck."

"I know that. Chance and I can handle the horses. Find a spot to hang your gear so it will dry out."

"I'll need to use your long coat if I plan to keep dry tonight," Skylar said to Garret.

"I'm taking first watch," said Tucker.

"It's my watch."

"Not in this weather. You don't have another change of clothes and my gear is heavier than Garret's. I don't mind going out. You can have my watch tomorrow night—if it's not raining."

Tucker seemed to be in a take-charge mood this evening. Skylar smiled then shrugged her shoulders. "If you're sure, I won't complain about staying out of the rain."

"I'm sure," he said before stepping out of the shelter.

When Skylar glanced up, Garret was staring at her with

a wide grin. "What?" she asked, afraid he may have seen her in Tucker's arms after all.

He plopped down beside her and folded his long legs in front of him. "I'm just glad to see you and Tuck finally gettin' along."

"Are we?" she asked, digging a tin cup from the sack sitting on the other side of her. She filled the cup with steaming black coffee and handed it to her brother.

"Thank you, sis." He wrapped his hands around the warm tin. The grin he flashed warmed her chest. Impulsively, she leaned over and pressed a light kiss to Garret's damp white hair.

His smile broadened.

Lord, she was blessed to have Garret in her life. During the past several weeks she had felt a closeness with him she hadn't realized she'd lost.

"You like him, don't you, Sky?" Garret asked a moment later.

"Who?"

"Tucker."

"Sure," she answered, managing to keep a neutral tone.

"And he likes you."

A wave of dread prickled across Skylar's skin. Garret may not have seen her with Tucker, but his young mind definitely suspected something. "Garret, our plans haven't changed. You know why we're going to Wyoming."

"Yeah," he said, his expression glum. "To get the horses back and sell 'em so we can get us a home. But what good is a house gonna do us without the horses?"

"We'll still have the Arabians."

"What if we don't get the mustangs back, Sky?"

They'd be in a world of hurt. She was counting on the money from the mustangs to buy them a place of their own, as far away from Tucker Morgan as she could get.

"Tuck and Chance wouldn't turn us out," Garret insisted.

Skylar didn't doubt the confidence in her brother's gaze. Chance and Tucker wouldn't turn their backs on them when they reached Wyoming, but staying on their ranch wasn't an option. She couldn't be so close to Tucker without wanting more than he was willing to give her.

"I was sorta hopin'," Garret said, his voice slow with caution, "that maybe you and Tuck would—"

"We'll be parting company with the Morgans once we reach Wyoming. Accept it, Garret."

Garret's mouth flattened at her sharp response. "I think you're being stubborn," he grumbled under his breath.

"I think you're being naive." The sooner he realized the way things had to be, the easier it would be, for both of them.

"Maybe I just like seeing you smile."

Her head whipped back toward her brother, stunned by his softly spoken words.

"You've been happier lately," he said. "I like seeing you smile, Sky."

"So do I."

Skylar glanced up at Tucker standing beneath the tarpaulin shelter and instantly felt a warmth in her cheeks. *Criminy sake!* How long had he been standing there? And how was she supposed to convince Garret that there was no chance of Tucker wanting her for a wife when he spouted off such comments in his presence?

How was she supposed to convince herself?

Relieved from night watch by Chance, Tucker returned to camp and stretched on out on his bedroll. He folded his arms under his head and listened to the steady tapping of rainfall against the thick tarpaulin and Garret's steady breathing a few feet away. His thoughts centered around Skylar's warm body lying in the shelter on the other side of the campfire.

The woman was damn infectious. She'd infected every ounce of his being with her sensuality. He'd never known a woman with such passion—or had so much trouble controlling his own. Four days without being able to feel her skin against his was driving him crazy. In another day or so he wouldn't be able to make love to Skylar without putting her at clear risk of pregnancy.

He needed her *now*.

Sitting up, he glanced through the darkness where Garret was sleeping. The kid was dead to the world and wasn't likely to be venturing out into the rain in the middle of the night.

Tucker reached for his coat, barely shrugging it on as he stepped out into the rain.

"Skylar?" he whispered, lifting the edge of her tarpaulin.

"Tuck?" she said, with an alertness that told him she hadn't been sleeping.

He slipped inside and shrugged off his coat. Seemed

she was having just as much trouble sleeping. They might as well pass the time together. "Evening, sweetheart."

"What are you doing in here?"

Tossing his coat into a pile at the corner of her tent, he dropped to his knees beside her. "I'll give you one guess," he said, his hands already unbuttoning the heavy flannel. "It's driving me mad to be near you and not kiss the daylights out of you."

Skylar stared into the darkness of her tent, stunned by Tucker's sudden materialization. As much as she wanted to spend the night in his arms, there were obvious reasons why she couldn't. "Tuck, Garret's only a few yards away."

"I know," he whispered. "As much as I love your passionate cries, you're gonna have to keep it down."

"Tucker." She slapped at his nimble fingers.

"Garret is snuggled up in his bedroll and sound asleep," he said, feathering kisses across her face. "Let me hold you, Sky. Just for a little while. I promise to clear out before daybreak."

Tucker's masterful hands were no match for her half-hearted resistance, the pitch of night not hindering him one bit as he peeled away layers of clothing. His warm mouth caressed her neck with fiery kisses, distracting her, until she felt the consuming warmth of his body moving over her, his gentle fingers sliding across her sensitive skin, burning her from the inside out.

Chapter 22

Tucker woke to the sound of Skylar's whispering voice and her hand rubbing across his chest. His body awakened to her touch, her scent, the promise of the intense pleasure they'd already shared several times. Lord, she was everything a man could hope for in a lover—and more.

"Tuck, wake up," she whispered again.

"You are tenacious," he mumbled, his eyes still closed as he rolled on top of her, his lips easily finding the sensitive cove of her neck. "Not that I'm complaining, honey."

Hell, who needed sleep when they had a passionate woman yearning to be loved. But…for some reason, her hands seemed to be combating his attempt and fabric was covering her soft skin.

When had she gotten dressed?

"Tucker, the sun is up," she whispered in a harsh tone. "You have to get out of here before Garret wakes up and Chance comes into camp."

Tucker opened his eyes and lifted his head. Just as she'd said, the sun had risen, and just as her stern whisper had indicated, her sweet face was set in a hard frown.

Nothing he couldn't fix. "Damn, but you're beautiful in the morning."

Tucker felt a ring of victory as her lips tipped upward in a slight smile.

He wasn't blowing smoke. She truly was beautiful in the morning. He lowered his lips back to the sweet skin of her neck, not the least bit worried about anything beyond the woman beneath him. Spending the winter right here in this tent with Skylar would suit him just fine.

"Tuck, stop." Skylar moaned as his caressing lips sent shivers across her body. "You've got to get out of here before Garret wakes up."

If he heard her softly spoken plea, he gave no indication. He continued to nibble on her ear, her neck, her shoulder. Skylar groaned as his hand slipped into the shirt he'd already unbuttoned, knowing the direction he was headed, fully aware of the overwhelming passion he so easily evoked in her.

Instinctively her body shifted, allowing him to settle deeper into the cradle of her thighs. They'd already coupled more times in one night than she thought possible, yet her body ached for him.

But they couldn't!

She would die if Garret found out she had allowed Tucker to spend the night in her bedroll like some harlot. She forced her hands to drop away from him. "Tucker, you promised to leave before sun up. *You promised.*"

He braced himself up with his arms. "You're not an easy woman to leave, Skylar. Each time I tried to say good-night, well…" His lips twisted wryly. "You know what happened."

Yes, she knew what had happened. He'd awakened her, kissed her good-night, and then neither of them made any effort to end the kiss, not until he was locked deep inside her, until they both collapsed, temporarily sated as they fell back asleep wrapped in the warmth of each other's arms.

"Tuck, just go."

He started to push away from her.

"That you, Tuck?" called Garret, his voice not far from her tent.

Skylar's frantic eyes locked with Tucker's. *Oh, no.* Garret couldn't find her with Tucker's naked body looming over her!

"Nope," Chance replied from somewhere not far beyond her shelter.

Tucker collapsed against her, his head dropping to her shoulder as both released a silent sigh of relief. It was then Skylar realized she could smell smoke. Chance had started a fire.

"Oh. Morning, Chance," Garret corrected. "Have you seen Tuck?"

"I believe he's checking on the horses," came Chance's easy response, obviously covering for his brother.

If Chance had been sitting in the center of their camp long enough to build a fire, he'd surely heard their whispering. Skylar shut her eyes as complete humiliation washed through her.

"Sky's usually up by now," Garret said, his shadow casting across her tent.

"Why don't you let her sleep," said Chance. "We're in no rush to move out today. She might like to wake to some fresh trout for breakfast, though. There's a swollen stream about a half mile east of here. Think you could catch us some fish?"

"Sure!"

Skylar held her breath as she listened to her brother's departing footsteps.

The thought of facing Chance sent a shiver of dread down her spine. What had she been thinking, to allow Tucker to share her bedroll? How could he do this to her? He promised to leave before sunup!

She waited a few more minutes, motionless under Tucker, ignoring the fingers gently caressing her hair. Once she was sure Garret was out of hearing range, she shoved her hands against his chest. "Get off!"

Tucker quickly moved off of her. "Sky, I—"

"Get out!" she cried as she snatched up his scattered clothing.

Tucker blocked his face from his belt buckle as his pants came flying at him. "You don't have to get violent." He shook out his pants and stepped into them.

"I am the biggest fool!" she raged. "Well, no more! Do you hear me, Tucker Morgan? Keep away from me! You and your fallen-angel smiles, shining green eyes, and *big, bulky body*!" Her hands slammed against his chest at the last three words, shoving him from her tent.

Before Tucker could spit a word out, he was standing

barefoot in the sunlight, holding the rest of his clothes, and wondering how he'd suddenly become the bad guy.

"You weren't complaining about my bulky body last night," he said in self-defense, annoyed by his brash dismissal. This was no way to part after the night they'd shared!

His second boot shot out from between the crack of canvas. The square heel clunked hard against his forehead.

Swearing profusely, he picked up his boot and turned away from her tent before bullets started to fly in his direction. Skylar's fury ran as deep as her passion.

As he walked barefoot across the wet ground he spotted Chance crouched by the low fire, watching the entire spectacle with a concerned frown.

"Don't say a damn word!" Tucker warned as he walked past him toward their tent.

"Hadn't planned on it, little brother," Chance called after him.

Chance caught Garret's gaze from across the evening fire and knew the kid could sense the tension clogging the air like smoke from a locomotive. The kid's wide eyes silently asked him what was going on. Chance shrugged his shoulders and shifted his gaze toward the fire.

What a muddled mess. It was bound to happen, Chance thought as he glanced at his brooding brother, then Sky sitting on the opposite side of the fire. It had been a long day, pushing the horses through the high ranges, followed by a silent, tension-filled supper.

Picking at her food, Sky looked as though she were chewing glass. She hadn't made eye contact with him since she emerged from her shelter early this morning.

Chance was used to his presence causing discomfort to those around him, but hell, he liked Sky. He hated seeing her eyes dark with a misery that was damn near tangible. Tucker just couldn't take his advice and leave her be.

But he had to admit, he'd been shocked by his brother's newfound sense of discretion. For a man known to brag about his romantic escapades, Tucker had been surprisingly tight-lipped about his involvement with Skylar.

"Sky? You feeling all right?" Garret asked, eyeing his sister with concern.

"Yeah, Sky," Tucker put in. "Didn't you sleep well last night?"

A lethal glint flashed in Skylar's eyes. Tucker was treading on some mighty thin ice, which happened to be cracking fast.

Skylar shot to her feet and Chance figured his little brother was about to receive some enlightening on humility and tact. To his disappointment, she merely walked out of camp, her eyes glazed with tears. Chance silently cursed his brother's flippant tongue.

Short, sharp gasps echoed back from the trees she'd walked through. *Hell.* He knew this would happen. He'd warned him!

"I think she's crying," said Garret. He sprang up. "She never cries. Not even when our pa died."

"Hold up, Garret," Chance said as the kid started to go

after her. "I think Tucker should go apologize for being a horse's ass."

"I'm going," Tucker said as he got to his feet.

"Might help if you pretended you have some manners."

Tucker ignored Chance's barb and hurried after Skylar. Her slender body moved easily through a tight forest of aspen. For every step he took, her long legs carried her two more steps ahead of him. Long, powerful legs that had been wrapped around him most of the night.

He didn't get it. She couldn't get enough of him last night, yet all day he couldn't get her to say five words to him. What had he done that was so horrible? Garret hadn't caught them together, and Chance had better manners than to make an issue of it in front of her.

Skylar's sniffles echoed back through the trees as he began to gain on her. A twinge of guilt festered inside him.

Hell, he hadn't meant to make her cry. He'd only been teasing, but somewhere between last night and this evening Skylar had lost her sense of humor. He increased his strides until he was running after her.

"Skylar?" he called, at last only a few feet behind her.

"Go away, Tucker." She wiped roughly at her cheeks while keeping her fast pace.

Tucker lunged forward and grabbed a fistful of her coat. "*Talk to me*, damn it! What are you so peeved about?"

"It's got to stop," she said as she spun on him. "I want you to stay away from me." She stepped back, putting distance between them.

"*Why?* Garret doesn't—"

"Because it's wrong!"

"Wrong? Does it feel wrong when we're together? I was under the impression you fully enjoyed last night."

Her narrowed gaze blazed with anger, and Tucker mentally kicked himself for being such an ass, *again*.

"A bit of humiliation can do wonders to clear one's perspective."

"If you're worried about Chance, don't be. He's suspected about us from the beginning."

She blanched, her expression revealing such pain Tucker could hardly stand himself. "You *told* him?"

"Of course not! He just—"

"Thinks I'm a harlot."

"He does not! He's crazy about you."

Skylar huffed her disbelief.

"It's true. My brother never compliments anything, let alone a *woman*, but he's the first to sing your praises. We're both adults, Skylar, and besides, *we're married*."

She flinched as though his words had been a blow. Hell, he couldn't seem to open his mouth without hurting her.

"Don't use that excuse. You have no intention of following through with any vows of marriage and I've just realized I have no desire to be your whore."

Tucker's stricken expression almost made Skylar regret the comment, but what was she supposed to think?

"You know that's not true, Skylar."

"Isn't it?" He'd not spoken any words of love for her. He'd done nothing but seduce her and buy her gifts.

"No. I shouldn't have made light of what's happened between us. If I've made you feel shameful, I'm sorry. God as my witness, Skylar, I have nothing but respect for you."

"If that's true, you'll do the right thing and leave me alone. I do have a conscience, and a brother to raise. If Garret had found you in my tent…I would have died of humiliation."

"Sky—"

She pulled away as he reached for her. "Don't touch me. Just…*don't*."

"All right," he said softly, taking a step back, stuffing hands into pockets.

Skylar turned away from his hurt expression. Tears burned at her eyes. She knew this was coming. She knew she'd have to be the one to end it. But she hadn't expected such physical pain, so deep it took her breath.

"Skylar—"

"Go away, Tucker."

"Sweetheart, that's not rightly possible with us traveling together."

She glared up at him. "You know what I mean. No more teasing, no more kisses."

"Is that really what you want?"

What I want? When had life ever been about what she wanted? She wanted him to love her enough to want her for his wife. But what they had wasn't real. And what she wanted didn't matter. Tucker didn't believe in marriage; she'd known it from the beginning. If she'd lost sight of reality in order to soothe her own conscience, it was no one's fault but her own.

"Skylar?"

"It's what I want," she said, looking him straight in the eyes. There was no sense in prolonging the inevitable.

Chapter 23

Randal was close. *Too close.*

Tucker crouched beside his brother, inspecting the wide stretch of heavily rutted dirt. He touched the deep-pitted earth, still soft and damp. The number of unshod horses and accompanying riders couldn't be a coincidence.

"He came in from the West. Can't be a full day's ride ahead of us." Tucker straightened and glanced back at their camp, where he'd left Skylar and Garret, suddenly not comfortable with the mile gap between them.

"We're only a day and a half from the ranch," said Chance.

"What do you suggest?"

"We avoid 'em. We're outnumbered, three and a half to fifteen. Zeke will have hired on extra men to help fight off Randal. We head out early. If they rush the ranch tomorrow, we could get there in time to attack from the rear."

"Skylar might have—"

"We're not telling her," Chance cut in.

"She should know. If I'd known Randal was this close,

I wouldn't have left her and Garret alone in camp. For all we know, she's already out searching for signs of him."

"Until we know she's found any, this stays between you and me. The man double-crossed her and killed her father, Tuck. Suppose she doesn't want to wait a day and a half to get her revenge—what then?"

He had a point. Once Skylar set her mind to something, she was a force to be reckoned with. Not that he knew anything about the workings of Skylar's mind. She hadn't spoken a single word to him in three days and refused to look at him. "We better head back and find an excuse to keep her in camp. She's been doing perimeter sweeps, searching for signs of Randal ever since we reached Wyoming."

"I'll take the east trail back, you take the river."

"Let's hope she's in camp or on the east side," Tucker said as he swung up into his saddle. "She won't listen to me."

"Whose fault is that?" Chance mounted his horse. "I warned you."

"And you were right. Feel better?"

"I'll be feeling great once we get our deed back."

Tucker gave a nod of agreement and started in the direction of the river. A half mile from the stream, he spotted Skylar walking in the direction of camp, the skewbald mare at her side. She spotted him too, and veered right in an effort to avoid him.

Damn it. He was sick of being ignored. If she hated him, well fine. He'd take her anger over being invisible.

"Skylar!"

She kept walking. Tucker spurred his horse. He stopped beside her and leaped from his saddle. "Sky—"

"*What?*" she spat, spinning to face him.

Her gaze locked with his and Tucker couldn't remember what he'd been about to say. The sadness in her expression seemed to amplify the sense of loss he'd kept at bay the past few days. His irritation fled, replaced by a longing so strong there wasn't room for anything else.

Before Skylar realized what hit her, she was surrounded by the warmth of his arms. She tensed as his lips tentatively touched hers. She'd gone too long without his touch not to respond. She trembled as she tasted him and was tasted in return.

When he released her mouth, Tucker drew a ragged breath and held her tight against his body. Skylar rested her head against his chest, her mind tangled in a haze of confusion. She needed to pull away, but Tucker's embrace wasn't so easy to shrug off.

"Tucker, what do you want from me?"

Tucker shut his eyes, the desperation in her tone clawing at his flesh. He was still trying to figure that out. He'd been miserable these past few days. Holding her was like a healing balm, soothing the emptiness he felt deep inside. He wanted to see her smile, he wanted to hold her close and have the freedom to kiss her whenever he felt the notion.

Skylar pulled away and cautiously stepped beyond his reach.

Tucker had to fight his urge to pull her back into his

arms. "You can't deny that what we have between us is good."

"I can't live in the moment because it feels good, Tucker. I have to think about tomorrow. I have to think about building a future Garret can depend on."

Skylar turned away, and he was swamped in an unfamiliar rush of sensation. *Panic.*

"You know, we still need someone on the ranch to oversee the training of our horses. You're damn good at what you do."

Skylar stopped walking, the mare halting beside her. "Are you offering me *a job*?"

Unable to see her expression, Tucker wondered if anger or surprise strained her tone. She wanted a home and they needed a trainer. He knew she enjoyed working with the horses. No reason they couldn't set her up in a small place on their land. The thought of having Skylar on the ranch settled real well with him.

"I'm just saying we need someone skilled with horses, which you are. I know you like what you do. I was thinking if you had a place to call your own, you may be interested in staying on at our ranch."

"A place to call my own."

"Yeah," he said, stopping behind her, certain her flat tone was a definite sign of negativity. "You want a real home. Plenty of ranches build houses for their foremen and such."

"Sounds like a bunkhouse to me," she said as she turned to face him.

Tucker frowned. She wasn't going to accept his proposal. He could tell by the cold void in her eyes. "No it's not. We built a house for Zeke and Margarete. No reason we can't build one for you and Garret."

"Wouldn't that be too convenient? Horse trainer and mistress all wrapped up in one neat package."

"That's not what I meant!"

"No? So this would be strictly a business arrangement? You want me to work with your horses, *not* to warm your bed."

Hell. Of course he'd want her in his bed! "Skylar—"

"No thank you, Tucker. I could never work for you."

Moisture burned at her eyes. She turned away, refusing to shed more tears in his presence.

"Damn it, Skylar, wait!"

"For what?" She imagined in Tucker's mind he'd offered her a fair deal. He didn't love her, but the sex was good, so why would he assume she'd be hurt by his proposition?

"Would you wait a minute," he shouted, tugging her to a stop. "Why won't you even consider it?"

"Because I'm not like you," she said, shrugging his hand from her arm. "I thought I could be. I wish I was, but I'm *not*."

"Like me how?"

"I can't give myself to you and not feel…*things*."

His expression slackened. "You feel things, *for me*?"

He had his nerve to ask her that after he'd blatantly expressed that her feelings weren't reciprocated. She'd be damned if she'd bare her heart to a man who'd just offered her *employment*.

"I don't *need* you or any fancy clothes to get by. I can

take care of myself and Garret the way I always have. Living on your ranch or marrying *the first Wyoming man I come* across aren't part of that plan."

Tucker's heart sank in his chest. Had she heard him and Chance talking all that time ago? "Skylar, I said that before—"

"Don't." She lifted her hand to stop his words. "It didn't matter then, and it doesn't matter now. I don't need that dress you bought me to trap a husband to take me and Garret off your hands."

"Damn it, Skylar, I didn't buy you those clothes because—"

"I tried to take care of our entanglement in Greeley, but that didn't work out." She pulled a piece of folded paper from her jacket pocket and held it out to him. "Take it," she insisted. "I intended to give it to Chance this evening, but now is as good a time as any."

Tucker unfolded the stiff paper. He stared at the deed to his valley, but somehow couldn't muster the relief or excitement he was sure he should be feeling over its recovery.

Why was she giving this to him now?

"You got me to Wyoming and I've given you what's yours."

Her crisp tone cut through his surprise.

"I don't want our farce of a marriage getting in the way of me claiming what's mine. I'm getting my horses back. If you want my mustangs, I expect you to pay me for them."

She really doesn't trust me. The revelation hit him with

stunning force. "My God. You thought I'd steal your god-damn horses!"

"It crossed my mind," she said, confirming the truth he could see in the chilling depths of her eyes. Her cold gaze pierced his chest with a shaft of pain. Not only did she not trust him, she thought him to be a thief and a coward.

"You must think I'm a real bastard."

"No, I don't."

"The hell you don't! What else could you call someone who uses you for their own selfish needs while robbing you blind?"

"A *man*."

The finality in her quick response reminded Tucker of something he'd understood right off about Skylar. She didn't trust men. After what he'd learned about her father, he couldn't say he blamed her. But he sure as hell didn't appreciate being compared to a man who'd manipulated her and lied to her. He'd done neither.

Before he could say so, Skylar leaped onto the spotted mare and raced over the hillside without looking back.

Skylar didn't slow her pace until she neared their camp. She needed to calm down, to dry her eyes before facing their brothers. She veered toward the tree-lined stream. Dismounting, she approached a gently flowing river.

Her heart still racing, her skin clammy with sweat, she dropped to her knees at the water's edge and shrugged off her coat, tossing it onto the grass beside her. Her eyes burned as her lungs pulled painfully for a calming breath. She leaned forward and dunked her hands into a shallow pool of calm water, splashing the cold liquid across her face. She sat back and closed her eyes, allowing the light breeze to cool her damp skin. Slowly, the tension tearing at her body began to ease.

She opened her eyes and gazed up at gently swaying limbs of tall birch trees. Light gray clouds were scattered across the pink sky. She was wasting her time and energy by brooding over a man she couldn't change. Things were what they were. He wanted her, but he didn't love her. He deserved the pain she'd seen in his eyes before she turned and fled. The truth hurt.

It hurts like burning hell.

She lowered her gaze to the water. The still pool had settled, creating a smooth mirrored surface. She frowned at her reflection. She needed to focus on what really mattered. *Garret.*

The mustang beside her whinnied. The grass rustled.

Damn but Tucker was light on his feet. His reflection moved across the water as he stepped behind her. Skylar gasped at the unfamiliar face reflected there. She reached for her revolver just as something cracked against the back of her head.

In a flash of pain, her world went dark.

As the distant sound of murmuring voices grew louder Skylar slowly became aware of the hard ground beneath her cheek. Her head throbbed. Pain radiated from her shoulders.

She shifted slightly and realized her hands were bound behind her back. Wherever she was, she hadn't been taken there gently. Her ribs ached, she imagined from being tossed over a horse.

"I said fetch the boy if you found their camp, not the woman!"

Skylar's eyes flew open. Her body crowded with fear. She'd have to be dead not to recognize Wade Randal's rage-filled voice.

"She looked like the kid from behind," said an unfamiliar voice. "By the time we noticed it was the girl, it was too late. She'd seen us."

"Where's the Arabian?"

"She wasn't riding one."

"I want those horses!"

With some effort, Skylar lifted her head. She blinked, trying to clear her vision as she gazed up at the three blurred figures standing a few feet away.

"How many men did Morgan have with him?"

"Didn't see no sign of Morgan. We saw the woman before we found the camp."

Skylar pinched her eyes shut, trying to summon her strength as Randal's curses echoed in her throbbing skull. Suppressing a groan, she forced herself onto her knees and again opened her eyes.

She swallowed a gasp as her gaze collided with Wade Randal. His large shadow loomed over her. The lantern hanging from the center of the canvas tent shone brightly on his raven-black hair, the long straight strands reaching the faded black shirt stretched across his broad shoulders. Her eyes widened as she focused on the damage she'd done to the chiseled features of his face. An angry red scar began at his right temple and ran clear across the corner of his lips to the deep cleft in his chin. Crusted scabs clung to the thick red seam, some areas festering with infection. He'd obviously not troubled himself to keep the wound clean.

His cold dark gaze snapped toward her, and Skylar's breath lodged in her lungs. Fear shivered through her. He took a step forward then crouched down, resting his long arm on a raised knee.

"Take a good long look at your fancy work, *princess*."

The eerie endearment hissed through his crooked teeth. He had called her *princess* once before, right after he'd murdered her father.

It's time for a shift in the hierarchy of this outfit, princess.

His unblinking eyes held her gaze as he waved his hand toward the two men standing behind him. "Get out! Now that she's here, I'd like some time alone with my woman."

Her eyes flared. *His woman?* Surely he didn't still hold an interest in her after she'd refused him by lashing her whip across his face.

The measuring gaze sweeping down her body and his rippling grin contradicted that thought.

Skylar lunged to her feet, ignoring the biting pain in her ribs. She tugged against the rope binding her hands as she backed away from him.

A sharp smile sliced across his face as he stood, blatantly enjoying her startled response. "Going somewhere?"

Hatred welled up inside her. "Murdering bastard!" she shouted, yanking at her restraints.

"Now that's no way to greet a man who spared your life. Twice. If anyone has the right to be hateful, *it's me*."

"You murdered my father!"

"I did you a favor," he snarled, his eyes growing dark with anger. "Your old man was a fool, too blind to see the fortune within his grasp. You've got twice the skill he ever had. He and that kid never did nothin' but hold you back. I had the guts to take what should have been yours and was willing to share it with you! And just look what my thoughtfulness got me," he shouted, thrusting his chin forward and slanting his head.

Bright light spilled over his face, giving her a clear view of the puckered pink skin and rotting flesh. "Guess that goes to show it don't pay to be kindhearted."

Skylar could hardly fathom the insanity of his words. *Kindhearted?*

Randal's hand lashed out and grabbed her by the front of her shirt, hauling her toward him until her face was inches from his. She cringed as his breath washed across her face. His other hand snatched a fistful of hair at the back of her head, his fingers twisting the stands until they began pulling from her scalp, preventing her from moving away.

"You're more trouble than you're worth, you know that? I should have saved myself some grief by shooting you in Arizona."

Skylar struggled to tamp down her fear as she held his steely gaze. *Don't panic.*

"But something about you makes me go against my better judgment," he said, his hold on her hair easing.

"You're not like other women. You're good with horses, a hard worker, and damn nice to look at. Even nicer to touch."

His hand slid around her waist as he hauled her flush against his body. Panic sparked at her nerves. Bile rose in her throat as she felt the evidence of his arousal, as well as the sheer strength of his body.

Oh, God, Tucker. Please hurry.

She couldn't stop Randal. She knew it.

"You play your cards right and I might even give you a chance to reconsider."

"Never." The refusal exploded from her mouth.

Randal eased back. His dark brows furrowed. "Never? You were nearly mine in Arizona. Surely you haven't forgotten about our little tumble in the grass."

Her naivete of men had been severe. She hadn't had the first clue as to his intentions when he'd followed her out of camp that evening, nor had she asked for or enjoyed the liberties he had taken with her. No doubt Randal would have raped her if Garret hadn't come looking for her.

"Hell, you didn't even know how to kiss a man, much less please one. I can't say I'll be patient with you. I've wanted you for too damn long."

"Raping me won't make me yours," she said, amazed her fear hadn't closed her throat.

"Rape you?" he said with a bark of laughter. "Warming a man's bed is a wife's duty."

Wife? "You can't marry me."

"When I want something, I take it. You might be mustang wild," he said in a low growl, his hips shifting against her, "but I can break you. A bit of kicking and gnashing will only make it interesting."

"You can rot in hell," she forced through clenched teeth. "I'm married to Tucker Morgan."

Randal's arms dropped away from her so fast she stumbled sideways. His dark eyes narrowed. "You're lying."

"We were married in New Mexico."

His chilling smile sickened her stomach. "Then you're married to a dead man. By this time tomorrow you'll be a widow, free for the taking, not that I intend to wait."

Skylar made a dash for the opening of the tent. Randal's hand bit into her arm. A shriek escaped her throat as he swung her against the wall of his body.

"Don't start acting like a little girl." His other hand fisted the front of her shirt, yanking it from her waistband. He tugged at the closure of her pants, and Skylar panicked.

With a fierce twist of her body, she rammed her knee into his groin. Randal yelped, stumbling back as he bent forward. Skylar kicked her leg up, her boot catching his chin, rattling his jaw.

Finding his balance, Randal dragged the back of his filthy arm across his split lip. "You bitch!"

His fist cracked against her left cheek with such speed she didn't see it coming. The heavy blow knocked her off her feet and through the opening of the tent. A scream ripped from her lungs as she slammed against the hard ground, landing on her back and bound hands.

Her shoulders burning with pain, Skylar rolled to her side, then onto her knees as she tried to catch her breath.

She saw a group of men clamor up from beside a campfire a few yards away. Striving to pull a gulp of air into her aching lungs, she leaned forward and rested her forehead on her folded legs, her mind still registering the pain in her face.

"Wade, what the hell are you doing?" one of the men shouted.

"Stake her out on the west side of camp," Randal said from behind her.

When no one spoke or moved to take her, Skylar lifted her head. Five gaping sets of eyes moved between her and Randal.

"How'd she bust yer lip while she's tied up?" one of them asked.

"Same way I'm gonna bust yours if you don't do what I said," Randal shouted.

Skylar screamed as he yanked her bound hands up from behind her. Forcing her to her feet, he grabbed her hair and tugged her head back. "My gentling tactics are a tad more aggressive than yours," he whispered against her ear. "But effective just the same."

Keeping a firm hold, he guided her through the camp. He yanked her to a stop then tripped her, knocking her to her knees.

"Stake her," he instructed.

"You sure you want her here?" asked whoever was driving the stake into the ground behind her and securing it to her roped hands. "It's bound to rain shortly."

"Good." Randal turned and started walking back to his tent. "A night out in the rain ought to take the fight out of her. By tomorrow she'll have learned to be a little more grateful."

I've proven to be a slow learner.

Her father's death should have taught her not to allow her focus to be muddled by men, yet she'd repeated the same fatal mistake. She'd let her affair with Tucker distract her from what was important. Keeping Garret safe. And now her foolishness was going to cost them all.

"Sky?"

The sound of Duce's voice sparked a glimmer of hope.

"I told you she'd make it to Morgan," said Mitch's gruff voice, another of her mustanging companions.

"Sky?" Duce whispered again. "Are you all right?"

"Is *she* all right?" said another man. "Hell, we're all as good as dead now."

"Shut up, Lance," Duce snarled. "You've been sniveling since Arizona."

"These ropes have been cutting into my wrists since Arizona! Once Randal gets those Arabians, he won't need us to herd the mustangs."

"I swear," said Mitch, "if someone would give me a gun, I'd shoot you myself."

Pain radiated through her body. Groaning, Skylar lifted her head. Duce sat with three others just six feet away under a small shelter of canvas. All four looked worse for wear with their hands bound in front of them. Each was filthy, having shaggy full beards. Duce's burnt-orange hair set him apart from the others.

Feeling cold drops of water against her face, Skylar looked up at the round patch of dark sky revealed through the clearing of tall evergreens. Cold raindrops began soothing the ache in her cheek.

"At least get her out of the rain," Duce shouted to his captors.

"Pipe down, Duce, unless you want to go hungry tonight. Wade says she stays put."

"Don't," Skylar said, imploring her friend not to cause trouble for himself.

"At least give her a damn coat!"

"If you're so worried about her, give her yours."

Duce rose to his feet and began walking toward the other group of men. He stopped beside the fire and held out his bound hands. "You'll need to remove the rope so I can get it off."

Taking his time, the other man stood, drew his revolver and pulled the hammer back. "You better hold real still," he said as another man began untying the rope around Duce's wrists. "You so much as twitch and you're a dead man."

Once his hands were free, Duce shrugged off his coat then allowed the man to replace the restraints, his eyes flinching as he knotted the rope. When the gun was lowered, Duce knelt down, picked up his coat and started toward her.

"Wish I could say I was glad to see you," he said as he knelt down, dropping his coat over her shoulders.

"Thanks. Me, too."

He reached for the side of the coat with his bound hands and pulled one side over her shoulder, then the other. "Garret okay?"

Skylar cringed at the sight of the deep rope burns and raw skin of his wrists. "He is for now."

"Morgan with you?"

"Both of them. Brothers," she said, seeing the question in Duce's eyes.

"How many others?"

"Just Garret," she said with reluctance.

"*Damn.* Do you think they'll come after you?"

"You've done your good deed, Duce," called a harsh voice. "Get back where you belong."

Skylar nodded as Duce stood, not doubting for a moment that Tucker would come for her.

Chapter 24

Tucker watched a streamer of clouds float across the glowing face of the moon. A sigh broke from his lungs, sending a swirling mist of white vapors into the cold air. It was well past midnight, yet he hadn't left his post, content to freeze as he sulked and watched over their camp and the horses. He hadn't gone back to camp for supper, his gut too full of self-contempt to have room for any sort of appetite.

He couldn't get the image of Skylar's cold gaze out of his mind. Their conversation played over and over, amplified by the nighttime silence.

He'd had plenty of time to realize he'd messed up.

Messed up *big*.

I can't hide from her forever, he thought as he turned his horse away from the quiet herd and began riding the short distance toward camp.

When Tucker ducked under the tarpaulin sheltering their campfire, the scent of coffee washed through his senses. Chance sat before the small fire, pouring a steaming trail of the black liquid into a cup.

"Morning." He held up the tin cup.

"Thanks."

"It's nearly two in the morning. Any particular reason why you didn't wake me?"

Sipping at the strong brew, Tucker sat beside him. "Guess I wasn't paying attention to the time." He flickered a glance at Skylar's shelter only a few yards away.

Why couldn't he just admit he wanted to be with her? The thought of not having Skylar in his life sent an instant lash of denial ripping through him, yet the realization of being legally bound to any woman had once put ice in his veins.

What am I so afraid of?

He wasn't his father and Skylar sure as hell wasn't Winifred. If there was ever a woman who contradicted everything he despised in his lazy, whining stepmother, Skylar was that woman. Skylar put her responsibilities and those she loved above her own wants, and even her basic needs, without a word of protest. Hell, even he and Chance had made their share of complaints in the past few weeks about the cold, the heat or being plain exhausted. But he couldn't recall Skylar voicing a single one.

He could, however, remember his father's complaints about all the travesties of marriage. During the seven months he and Chance had stayed with him in the rebel camps he'd filled their heads full of damning words on marriage. He had warned them about beguiling women who baited men with coy smiles and silken gowns, only to make their lives a living hell once they slipped a wedding ring onto their pretty little fingers.

Winifred Morgan didn't give them any reason to doubt their father's words. Having no memories of their own mother, they'd begun to worry that she had been no different from Winifred. Their father never spoke of his first wife, nor had Tucker ever seen a portrait of her. One evening, he and Chance had mustered up enough courage to ask if their birth mother had trapped him with smiles and fancy dresses.

A chill washed over Tucker's skin as he recalled his father's shaken response. He'd pulled a thin chain from beneath his shirt which held a slender band of gold. Their mother's wedding ring.

Don't ever compare your mama to Winifred, he had said in a stern tone. *Your mama wasn't an ordinary woman. She was an angel. Once the Good Lord realized she was too good to grace this earth, He snatched her right back up to heaven. You boys have her golden hair. Too bad you didn't get her blue eyes.*

His father's green eyes had grown misty as he'd looked at each of them. *Pure as sapphires,* he'd said. *They touched a man's soul in a way that made him want to be better than he knew how to be.*

His father had died in battle the next day. Tucker had taken solace in the fact that he'd gone to heaven to be with the angel he loved.

His lungs ached from the breath trapped inside as his mind flooded with the first image he'd ever had of his mother.

A blue-eyed angel with gilded hair.

My God. No wonder Skylar had blindsided him.

Yet, what he felt for Skylar went beyond any fascination for an image in his mind or simple physical attraction. Just as his father had said, something in Skylar made him want to be better than he knew how to be. He'd never cared about pleasing anyone beyond himself until he'd met her. He'd never allowed himself to love anyone beyond his brother, *until Skylar.*

She had loved him with an honesty and trust that shook his soul, yet she didn't trust him completely. Not with what mattered. Her dreams. Her future.

And who can blame her?

My father taught me not to put my trust in illusions. Your smile is just one more illusion. You're just like my father...it was never about the destination...he loved the adventure.

The memory of her words sent a sharp pain ripping across his chest. At the time he hadn't noted the comparisons that now struck him like a jolt of lightning.

Tucker was tempted to crawl into Skylar's tent and convince her that he wasn't a damn thing like her father, and that she was the only adventure he needed, but he knew he wouldn't try to convince her with words alone. He couldn't be close to her and not give in to the powerful yearning to hold her, to love her.

"You look like hell," Chance said, glaring at him over the rim of his coffee cup. "Must have been rough, balancing Sky and the horses in all this rain."

"What the hell are you talking about? I've been on watch."

"Stop treating me like I'm an idiot."

"I haven't been with Skylar. She's barely talked to me since she tossed me from her tent."

"Then where's she at?"

Tucker gaped at him. "She's not here?"

"No. I figured you ran into her near the river and—"

Tucker's coffee dropped to the ground as a rush of panic welled up inside him. He sprang to his feet and ran toward the shelter Garret had put up for Skylar. He pushed back the canvas flap, his gut twisting into knots at the sight of Skylar's supplies sitting in the dark shadows of her tent, exactly where Garret had tossed them this afternoon. Her bedroll was still wrapped up in a tight tube.

He dropped the flap and spun on Chance as he walked up behind him. "Why didn't you come tell me she never came back to camp?" he demanded.

"I figured she was out romping somewhere with you."

Tucker closed his eyes, trying to calm the fear crashing over him. They should have told her about Randal. "Dear God, she's gone after the horses," he said, certain she'd gone to face Randal alone.

"Whose horses?" asked Chance.

"Hers."

"You told her about the tracks? We agreed we wouldn't tell her!"

"I didn't tell her! That doesn't mean she didn't find the tracks on her own."

"You think she'd go it alone?"

Tucker didn't take the time to answer. He was already in a full run back toward his saddled horse, pausing only to grab a lantern. He rode out to the hillside they'd been on earlier and carefully followed her tracks leading toward the river. He found a place where her horse had stood idle, along with unfamiliar boot prints leading to, and away with the horse.

A sense of dread coiling up his spine, he followed Skylar's smaller boot print to a grassy embankment beside the river. Her tan coat stood out like a warning beacon on the damp grass.

She wouldn't have left her coat. He picked it up and swept the light across the ground. A few yards away a patch of mud revealed the tracks of three horses. His heart thundered with the sound of Chance's approaching horse. Clutching Skylar's jacket, panic constricting his chest, Tucker knelt beside the meshing of footprints.

They took her.

Chance crouched beside him a moment later and inspected the imprints in the soft mud. "Who the hell—"

"God, Chance, she didn't go after Randal. He took her!"

"He's baiting a trap."

"Trap or not," Tucker said as he straightened, "I'm going after her."

"We're only a day away from the ranch. The sole reason we've deliberately avoided Randal is so we wouldn't be outnumbered."

Chance's reluctance stunned him. "She could be dead before we reach the ranch!" Tucker put out the lamp then swung back into his saddle and started racing back toward camp to get the supplies he needed. Chance followed close behind him.

"You're going to track her in the dark?" he asked, on his heels as he rushed into camp.

Tucker crouched beside a pile of supplies. "It's how I made my living, remember?" He reached into one of the sacks, retrieving a rifle and another revolver.

"What about the mustangs we've been busting ass to drive this far?"

"I don't give a damn about the horses," he shouted as he straightened. "What's wrong with you? Randal has had her since nightfall. The man backshot her father!"

"What's going on?" Garret asked, emerging from his tent. Barefoot and dressed in the red one-piece woolen underwear Tucker had bought for him, he rubbed at his eyes.

"Randal has your sister," Tucker said flatly.

The boy's body snapped to full attention. Tucker tossed the kid a rifle, saying, "She was taken before sundown. We're getting her back. *Now*."

"Yer damn right we are," said Garret. He turned and ducked back into his shelter.

"If he's baiting us," Chance said as he shoved a bullet into the chamber of his revolver, "he's likely after the deed."

"But I don't know where she put it," Garret called out from inside his tent.

"I have it," said Tucker.

Chance's eyes widened a fraction as his brother dipped his hand inside his coat. He swore under his breath when Tucker held up the deed. "How long have you had that?"

"Skylar gave it to me earlier this evening."

"Were you planning on telling me?" Chance all but shouted.

"It slipped my mind."

His brother's eyes widened with disbelief. "Slipped your mind? She gave you our deed and it slipped your mind?"

"What the hell are we standing around for?" Garret said, stepping from his tent fully dressed.

Tucker turned away from Chance. "We'll need the lanterns."

A few hours later Tucker was at the crest of a hill, crouched between Garret and Chance, their gazes locked on a herd of horses too large to hide. A hillside spotted with evergreens sloped down to a thick grove of tall trees. High jagged cliffs rose up on the far side. They needed to move fast. The sun would soon be peeking over that eastern rise and stealing their cover. In the last bit of moonlight, they saw two men on horseback guarding the herd on fairly open ground at the northern end of the grove.

Randal's camp had to be in the trees.

"We'll have to leave the horses," whispered Chance, who'd finally come to his senses.

Tucker nodded in agreement.

"We still need some sort of plan," Chance continued.

"I say we stick together," said Garret, "find Skylar and get the hell out of there before anyone sees us."

Tucker glanced over Garret's head. Chance was looking at the kid with a measure of bewilderment. "Remember bein' that young, Tuck?" he whispered.

"No," he answered honestly.

Their attention was drawn to movement in the shadows below them. Tucker's eyes narrowed as he spotted a man riding through the trees. One of Randal's men.

The camp was well guarded. It was going to take them twenty minutes or better to get down to that grove while having to sneak their way past guards. By then, the sun would be fully up.

"I got him," Chance whispered, and drew his knife from the scabbard at his waist.

"I can get him from here," Garret said, raising his rifle toward the man clearly visible as he rode into another patch of moonlight.

Tucker put his hand over the barrel. "No guns. We don't want that camp full of men to know we're coming to call."

"And put your damn hat on," ordered Chance. "All that white hair glows like a lantern."

Garret nodded at Tucker, then cast a frown at Chance as he tugged his hat on.

Chance started stalking down the hillside.

"I'm comin' with you," Garret insisted as Tucker moved to follow his brother.

"Sit tight, kid. We won't descend this ridge without you, I promise. Remember, no gunshots. Got it?"

Garret took a deep breath, controlling the adrenaline they were all struggling to contain, and gave a sharp nod.

Skylar fought not to give in to the dark relief of unconsciousness. Never had she experienced this type of cold. Sitting on her knees, crumpled forward with her hands bound behind her, her body was consumed by a combination of numbness and stinging shafts of pain.

Sometime during the long night she had stopped shivering, her muscles too exhausted to twitch. Intermittent showers had kept her hair dripping wet and clothes damp as moisture drizzled beneath Duce's coat. The last time she'd opened her eyes, the dreary gray sky held a translucent glow—signs of the sun beginning to rise behind the dark clouds. Her time was running out.

Tucker, where are you?

"Morning, princess."

Skylar didn't move as Randal knelt beside her. She couldn't, her body was too sore and stiff. The warmth of his fingers sliding beneath her chin burned against her chilled flesh. He lifted her face, forcing her to meet his gaze.

"I trust you slept well?" His bruised lips shifted into a smug grin.

"*Coward,*" she seethed with a shallow breath.

Randal's expression stoned over as he snatched his hand away from her face. He released her bound hands from the stake. Skylar cringed as his warm palms closed over the sides of her shoulders. Pain sliced through her cramped muscles as he hauled her to her feet, ripping a sharp cry from her lungs.

She heard the sound of her feet hitting the ground as her legs unfolded, but she couldn't feel them. The moment Randal eased his hold, she began to slump back to the ground. His arm banded her waist.

"Don't worry, princess," he said, lifting her. "I know

just the thing to warm you up. Being the gentleman that I am, I've even managed to find us a honeymoon shack."

Skylar barely registered his words, unable to focus beyond the sharp talons of pain ripping at her skin with each shift of her body as he hoisted her over his broad shoulder. Her teeth chattered as her muscles began to awaken and quiver. Holding her like a sack of potatoes, Randal turned on his heel and her world spun.

He seemed to walk for a mile before he finally lowered her, letting her slide down the front of him.

"Wake up, princess." He set her feet on the ground and shook her until she made an effort to stand. Skylar opened her eyes. They were surrounded by granite cliffs reaching high into the thick gray sky. They stood before the wooden door of a tiny cabin wedged into a crack in the stone mountainside. A wide piece of metal banded the door, a lock securing the latch.

"This little ole rat hole ain't worth locking," Randal said as he slammed the butt of his gun against the metal. The lock fell open. Randal's eyes snapped toward her. "You're mine."

He was wrong. Dead wrong. Tucker would come for her.

"I plan to break you in good," he said as he yanked open the flimsy door.

A film of white covered the open doorway. Intricate patterns of silken thread, several webs overlapping with one another. Spots of black scattered to the edges of the door frame as daylight spread across the entryway.

Spiders.

Skylar's body stiffened. Her feet suddenly braced beneath her.

Randal's hand shoved against her back.

Sticky white fibers clung to her face as she stumbled forward, breaking the thick webbing away from rotted wood, pulling the spiders down—*onto her.*

Skylar's lungs expanded with a deep gasp of primal fear.

Chapter 25

"Shh," Tucker instructed as he knelt behind the broad shoulders of a man with flaming red hair. The man Garret had identified as Duce.

"Morgan?" he whispered.

"Yeah," Tucker answered, peering over his shoulder at the quiet campsite. A few yards away, five men sat around a campfire talking amongst themselves. Tucker imagined there were more in the five tents spaced throughout the trees.

"Lift your hands over your head, real slow like you're stretching."

Duce followed his instructions. When his hand dropped back behind his head, Tucker cut through the rope then moved on to the second man.

"How many men?" Chance asked as he and Garret moved in beside him.

Duce's eyes widened as his gaze shifted to Chance. "Twelve," he whispered.

"Only nine now." Chance slid a revolver beside Duce

then glanced at the other three men. "The rest of you will have to find your own."

Tucker cut the ropes of the second man then handed him the knife. He studied each of the four faces, not wanting to shoot one of his allies by mistake if all hell broke loose. "Where's Skylar?"

"He took her from that stake a short while ago," said the gruff voice of the second man.

Tucker's heart constricted as he spotted the stake on the open wet ground and the small dry patch in front of it where she'd obviously been sitting. *Oh God, Skylar. I'm sorry.*

"She couldn't even walk when he dragged her off," said Duce, his whispered voice filled with disgust. "He said somethin' about a honeymoon shack."

"That ba—" Chance's hand clamped over Garret's mouth, cutting off his angry words.

Cursing under his breath, Tucker's body coiled with rage. *"Which way?"*

"East, toward those high cliffs."

Tucker glanced toward the high rocky peaks rising up beyond a stream on the other side of the camp.

"I reckon he found a miner's—"

"Tucker!"

The bloodcurdling scream tore through the crisp morning air. The sound of Skylar shrieking his name raised every fine hair across Tucker's skin. Reflexively, he drew his revolver and answered her call, shouting her name as he leaped past the seated men and began running in the direction of her voice, barreling through the camp full of armed men.

The five men by the fire seemed just as startled by the shrilling voice echoing off the granite cliffs. Tucker shot the first one who reached for his gun. The others threw their hands into the air, their gazes looking past him.

Trusting that Chance had his back, Tucker ran toward the stream on the far side of the camp. He splashed through the water, his gaze moving over the jagged cliffs that rose up on the other side. Jumping onto a wide boulder, he bypassed the winding path that lead to a break high on the stone mountainside. He was at the top of the pass with a few leaps.

Skylar's screams hadn't stopped.

His heart raging, Tucker paused as he came to a three-way split in the maze of rock.

Keep calling me, angel.

Gunfire erupted from the valley behind him as he chose the channel to his left. He followed the narrow path and rounded a bend to his right. A small shack came into view up ahead. The wide frame of a man with long black hair filled the doorway. Randal struggled with Skylar who was thrashing and screaming on the floor beneath him. His filthy arm swung back, preparing to strike her.

"I wouldn't!"

The large man turned, his expression gaping as Tucker charged toward him. "How the hell did—"

The mangy bastard reached for his gun as Tucker's fist slammed into his jaw, knocking him away from the cabin.

Somebody had already whupped him hard with an ugly

stick, Tucker noted as his gaze swept over his mangled face. *Not nearly hard enough.*

Tucker laid into him, slamming a fist into his gut as Randal's knuckles cracked against the younger man's jaw. The pain exploding through his face made him think of Randal using those heavy fists against Skylar. Randal's size and strength better than equaled Tucker's.

In a blur of murderous rage, Tucker swung wildly, delivering blow after blow, accepting a few punches in return as he drove Randal back, farther away from Skylar.

As sun broke from the cloud cover, blasting them with a blinding dose of intense sunlight, Randal lunged at him, clamping an arm around him, and trying to knock him to the ground. From the corner of Tucker's right eye, he saw a valley open up beside him. He hadn't noticed the sheer drop-off hidden in the gloomy gray haze. Randal's weight shoved him toward the edge.

He's trying to toss me off the cliff!

Tucker dropped low and kicked his leg out, sweeping it against Randal's heels.

Randal fell back, his head slamming against the rock surface with a fierce crack. Tucker bent forward, planting his hands on his knees as his lungs pulled for a full breath.

Randal didn't move.

Behind him, Skylar screamed at the top of her lungs. He pushed to his feet and ran back to the cabin. She was still on her knees inside the shadows of the cabin. Tucker crouched behind her and had to work to capture her bound hands as she thrashed in full hysterics. The second he cut her hands free, her fists started swinging.

"Skylar," he said, trying to capture her flailing arms. "Angel, it's *me!*"

"*Spiders!* They're on me!"

Realizing she wasn't fighting *him,* but the sticky film of spiderwebs clinging to her head and shoulders, he grabbed her by the waist and yanked her out into the increasing sunlight. He pulled at the webs and knocked a large spider caught in a clump of its own web from the back of her tangled hair.

"They're gone," he said as he peeled the rest of the sticky mass from her damp hair and clothes. "Relax, honey, they're gone."

She stopped twisting, her lungs gulping for air as she glanced up at him. "You're sure?" she asked, her voice trembling as violently as her body.

The stark fear in her glistening blue eyes twisted into his heart like a dagger. "I'm sure," he said, pulling her into his arms. The chill of her body stung him through his clothes.

"Don't let me go," she sighed.

"I don't plan to." *Not ever again.*

She sagged against him, nearly slipping from his grasp.

"Sky?" he said, afraid she'd passed out.

"Where's Garret?"

As if on cue, Garret shouted Tucker's name from somewhere behind him.

"Over here," Tucker called back, glancing over his shoulder as Garret rounded the mountainside.

"Skylar!" the kid shouted, his face brightening.

"Now, ain't that sweet."

At the sound of Randal's cold, gritty voice, Tucker let Skylar slide gently to the ground before he turned to face him.

I should have kicked him off the mountain when I had the chance. Randal stood in the very spot Tucker had left him, his revolver trained on Garret who had backed up against the cliff, his eyes wide with fear.

Randal's thumb slipped over the hammer of his gun and clicked it back. "Now walk on over here," he said to Garret.

"Don't move, Garret."

"Back off, Morgan," snarled Randal. "He can mosey on over here or he can die."

"Stay where you are," Tucker said to Garret, and pulled the deed from his jacket pocket. He held up the worn folded paper as he took a step toward Randal. "Isn't this what you're really after? What's more important, the woman and the boy or the horses and the land?"

Randal's dark eyes shifted toward the deed. "What if I said I was more interested in the woman and the horses?"

Tucker's gun was drawn and cocked with such speed, Randal blinked hard as his eyes focused on the other man's hand.

"I'd say over my dead body."

A smile slid across Randal's swollen lips. "Know what I think? I think you're fool enough to care for this kid. Throw your gun down, Morgan. You can't win. You shoot me. I'll shoot the boy."

"What about me?" boomed Chance's voice.

Tucker followed Randal's gaze. His brother stood at the entrance of the passage Garret had used, his rifle raised, aimed at Randal's head.

Randal's aim faulted as his eyes peeled wide.

Tucker started to take a step forward.

"Don't," Randal warned as his gaze moved between them.

"You can't shoot us all," said Chance.

Randal's eyes narrowed as he turned his cold gaze on Garret backed against the hillside. "Then I'll take my one shot."

"No!"

Tucker heard Skylar scream as she streaked past him and leaped at Randal. "Skylar!"

Skylar shoved against Randal with all her weight, grabbing for the gun aimed at her brother.

Randal shouted a curse. The ground shifted beneath her feet. A gunshot exploded in her ears as Skylar felt herself being drawn over the edge of the cliff. Red flashed across Randal's neck just before she pounded against the mountainside. Randal's heavy body slammed on top of her before they began tumbling down the steep slope. She grasped at the jagged rock, trying to slow her fall. Her back pounded onto a hard surface, rattling her aching bones and forcing all the air from her lungs.

"Skylar!"

Disoriented, she distantly heard Tucker repeatedly shouting her name. Dirt and gravel began pelting against her, forcing her to open the heavy lids of her eyes.

Tucker was skidding down the steep hillside.

"Skylar? Honey?" He dropped over her, his knees straddling her hips.

Fear slammed through Tucker, shaking him as he saw the amount of blood glistening against the bright sunlight. Her neck and chest was covered. *He shot her!*

Buttons scattered as he ripped open her blood-soaked shirt and shoved up the wool undershirt.

"Tucker—"

"I've got you, angel," he soothed, his hands frantically searching for the bullet wound.

Skylar tried to push his hands away and sit up. "I can—"

"Lie still, damn it!"

"Tuck, I—"

"I said lie still!"

The raw emotion in his tone seized Skylar's full attention. The intensity in his eyes spooked her. She stilled, allowing his hands to move over her aching body.

"You weren't shot," he gasped a moment later, sounding surprised.

"No. I think Randal was hit. I saw red. Is he—"

"He's facedown at the bottom of this cliff." Tucker grimaced as though the words tasted sour on his tongue. But as he shifted her clothes back into place and met her gaze, warmth flooded his eyes. "Can you sit up?"

"Yes."

"You sure?"

"I'm sure," she said, hiking herself up on her elbows.

A hard sigh of relief broke from Tucker's chest as his strong arms encircled her and hauled her against his body.

"God, Skylar. I've died a hundred times over in the past few hours."

She could feel his rapid heartbeat against her chest and wasn't sure which one of them was trembling more.

"I swear I came as soon as I found you gone."

She smiled. "I knew you would."

"That was one hell of a tumble," Chance shouted from up above.

Tucker eased back to see his brother scrambling down the hill.

"Thank God this ledge broke her fall," he said, stopping beside him. "Is she—!"

"She wasn't shot," Tucker assured him, and clamped her back against his chest.

"You need help getting her up this hill? It's a hell of a climb."

"We can manage."

"All right. I'll head back up and make sure Duce has everything under control."

"We'll be right behind you," Tucker said as Chance began picking his way back up.

Tucker spotted Garret's worried face peering over the sharp edge. He nodded, giving the kid reassurance that his sister was all right. The change in Garret's features was immediate.

"Can you stand, sweetheart?" he asked a moment later.

"I can stand," she said, yet her eyes still seemed dazed, unfocused.

Tucker got up and helped her to feet. "Careful," he said,

wrapping his arm securely around her waist to keep her steady. "This ledge isn't much wider than you."

Skylar winced, her expression contorting with pain.

"Honey, are you going to be able to make it up?" he asked, already supporting most of her weight as he held her against his side. "I can carry you."

"I can make it," Skylar insisted. Her body, however, wasn't being as cooperative as her mind. Standing upright was taking far more effort than it should. "Can you hold me for a minute?" She couldn't think of anything she wanted more than just to be in his arms.

"Gladly." Tucker leaned back against the mountainside, opened the front of his coat and pulled her against him, fitting her to his long body.

Skylar shoved her hands inside his jacket, feeling his warmth seep into her bones as he wrapped his arms around her. She buried her face against the bend of his neck, filling her senses with his musky scent. His hands moved over her back in long, steady strokes, soothing her pain, easing her tension, relaxing her cramped muscles.

"Don't fall asleep yet, angel."

Skylar blinked her eyes open and realized she *had* been half-asleep. She couldn't help it. He was so warm and she couldn't feel any safer than she did at this moment.

"Ready to move, sweetheart?"

"No." She was content to stay right where she was. She didn't want to be disturbed—but eventually, she was.

Skylar wasn't sure how he'd managed it, but a short while later she was standing at the top of the cliff, again wrapped in Tucker's arms.

Dear God, she was happy to see him. To *feel* him.

"Skylar?"

"Hum?" She sighed, doing her best to melt into the length of his body.

"Sweetheart, you're shaking. We need to get you by a fire."

She didn't feel as if she was shaking. She didn't want to go anywhere, but Tucker began to pry her hands from around his waist. Her protest died on her lips as she was lifted into his arms. Her eyes drifted shut. Being held was even better than being hugged.

A few moments later, she was jarred awake and found herself sitting before a campfire.

"Stay here," Tucker said as he released her shoulders. He shrugged off his coat and draped it around her. He tossed a few chunks of wood onto the low flames of the fire. "I'll find you some blankets," he said as he turned away.

Skylar stared into the orange glow, dismayed by Tucker's absence. She didn't need blankets. She needed *him*.

Bothered by the feel of her shirt clinging to her neck, she wiped at something sticky on her throat. Her breath caught at the sight of her bloodstained hand. Glancing down at her chest, air rushed from her lungs. Her stomach lurched.

Blood! Randal's blood. It was everywhere!

She peeled the saturated wool shirt away from her skin. Thick trails of scarlet streaked clear down to her stomach.

Bile burned at her throat.

She had to get it off!

* * *

When Tucker returned with an armload of blankets, only his jacket was lying in the spot he'd left Skylar. He turned in a full circle, scanning the campsite. She wasn't anywhere in sight. Dropping the blankets, he started through the cluster of tents and spotted Chance and Duce standing over the men they were securing with ropes. "Chance?" he called, running toward him. "Have you seen Skylar?"

"No," Chance said as he straightened. "I thought she was with you."

"I turned my back for two seconds and she was gone. I think she's in shock. She wasn't—"

"Tucker." Chance's eyes widened as he looked past him.

Tucker follow his brother's gaze. In the space between two tents he could see a stretch of the stream—*and Skylar.*

She was in shock all right, and shedding every damn bit of her clothing as she walked toward a wide section of the stream.

Tucker set into a hard run just as Skylar kicked her pants aside and walked into the water. He tugged his shirt up over his head as his boots splashed into the freezing stream.

"Skylar?"

She turned, looking up at him with wide, glistening eyes. "It's everywhere. I don't want his blood on me."

Tucker's gaze moved over the scarlet dots spattered across her cheek. Her neck and chest were smothered with a thick trail of red that went past her waist. "All right," he said as he tossed his shirt over his shoulder and took the shirt she'd dunked into the river from her hand. "Let me help you."

He squatted down and pulled Skylar against him, setting her bare backside on his thigh. He thoroughly rinsed her shirt in the shallow stream then he swabbed the blood from her face, neck and chest. Skylar didn't so much as flinch as he smoothed the ice-cold cloth across her skin. Her mind may have been unaware of the frigid temperature, but her prickling skin showed that her body was well aware of the cold.

Pain mingled with rage as he carefully rinsed the rope burns on her wrists and dark bruises across the left side of her ribs. Randal had died too quick a death.

Finished, he dropped her shirt into the stream, letting the current take it as he tugged his shirt over her head. The blue cotton covered her to her thighs. He helped her slip her arms into the long sleeves, then carried her from the river. She laid her head against his shoulder, completely relaxed in his arms. Not at all like Skylar, he thought, disturbed by her passive behavior.

As he approached the others, every man had their back to them, including his brother and Garret.

Damn.

She wouldn't like knowing Garret had seen her in such a state. Although, she was hardly aware of anyone or anything around her. To his amazement, she was asleep.

"She all right?" Garret called after him.

"She'll be fine," Tucker said as he strode back to the campfire.

Minutes later he had Skylar bundled in the blankets.

He sat by the increasing warmth of the fire with Skylar on his lap, snuggled against him as she slept.

"She really okay?" Chance asked as he knelt beside him.

"She will be."

Watching Tucker hold his sleeping angel with such possession, Chance continued to be astounded at how deep his brother's feelings had grown for her.

"She's just worn-out," Tucker said. "I don't know how she found the strength to tackle Randal. She could barely stand."

Chance knew how. He'd seen his brother show the same protective endurance for him. "Remember the night that sympathetic soldier sneaked us out of the prison camp? You were a shivering, bloodied-up mess after taking the beating that was meant for me. I hardly had a scratch, but you outran me as we sprinted toward those train tracks. You were the one who dragged *me* onto the freight car when I stumbled trying keep up with you and that moving train."

"Can you go back and get our horses?" Tucker asked, his gaze never wavering from Skylar. "She won't want to wake here. Once she's warmed up a bit, I'm taking her back to our camp."

"I'll take care of it," Chance said, shrugging off the tangle of ill emotion that came with memories of the past. "We've got six men restrained over there, all guilty of horse thieving. There's only one penalty for horse thieves here in Wyoming. We've also got four men willing to carry out that sentence and I don't see any reason to prolong their fate. Do you?"

"They made their choice," said Tucker. "So be it."

Chance nodded in agreement and stood.

"Chance, I don't want Garret to witness the hangings."

"Understood," Chance said, agreeing wholeheartedly. He hadn't intended to be present, either. A man didn't witness the loss of a life without losing a part of his own soul. He didn't have enough of his soul left to spare. "Me and the kid will go fetch our horses."

A few hours later they were all riding toward their camp, Sky tucked snugly across Tucker's lap. If she'd stirred once during the long ride, Chance wasn't aware of it.

He quickly jumped from his saddle and went to help Tucker. "I'll take her while you dismount," he said, reaching up for Sky.

"She's not leaving my arms." Tucker tossed a leg over his saddle and dismounted, holding Sky protectively against his chest.

Chance's eyes widened, but he didn't say a word.

"Tucker?" Skylar said, lifting her head from his shoulder.

"I've got you, angel girl," he assured her in a tender tone Chance had never heard from him.

"Garret—"

"Garret's fine, sweetheart."

"I need—"

Tucker silenced her with a kiss on the lips.

Damnation. Apparently Tucker no longer cared who witnessed their affection.

"You need sleep," he said in a firm tone. "And I'm going to make sure you get it."

Chance didn't hear any sound of protest after Tucker ducked into her tent and figured Sky must have consented to his demands or fallen back asleep. He looked at the kid and was surprised by Garret's grinning face.

"I knew he was sweet on her," he gloated.

"Yeah, but is your sister sweet on him?"

"She likes him, all right. I've never seen no one rile Sky the way Tuck does. Think he'll marry her?"

"He already did." Tucker had lost his damn mind, and didn't show any signs of coming to his senses. There wasn't anything he could do but support him and pray for the best.

Chapter 26

Feeling something warm and fuzzy beneath her cheek, Skylar bolted upright.

A sigh of relief broke from her lungs as her gaze locked on Tucker's sleeping face in the shadowed glow of early morning. No wonder she'd slept so soundly.

Shivering as the cold morning air swirled around her, she hunkered back down beneath the blankets, nuzzling close to Tucker, pressing against the warm skin of his bare chest. The man was better for warming than a cook fire, the warmth from his body incredibly soothing against her sore, aching muscles. She pulled the heavy fur blanket back over them and laid her head against his shoulder.

Releasing a deep sigh, she placed her hand on his chest.

He had come for her, risked his life for her, risked his ranch for her. Tears burned in her eyes at the memory of him holding his deed out to Randal in exchange for Garret's safety. Skylar knew she'd never love anyone as she did Tucker. She wished that was enough.

Skylar shifted over him, loving the feel of his body stretched out beneath hers. Her bare legs rubbed against the long underwear covering his muscular thighs as she pressed her cheek against the steady beating of his chest.

"Does your heart belong to me?" she whispered, turning her lips to his warm skin. He cared for her, but she wanted more. Tears stung her eyes. She couldn't settle. She wanted Tucker, but she deserved a husband.

Tucker mumbled her name in his sleep and banded his arms around her. Smiling, she ignored the pain in her ribs as she allowed him to pull her against him. She wouldn't give up this time with him. Right now, it was enough to be in his arms. She turned her lips to the solid contours of his chest, kissing and tasting as she made a slow ascent.

"Skylar?" Tucker said, with an alertness that told her he was waking up.

She moved up his body and feathered soft kisses across his lips. Tucker's hands slid up from the blanket and framed her face as he returned her kiss. When she eased back, his tender smile touched her heart.

"Definitely better than all my dreams of waking with you in my arms and kissing you good morning."

Skylar smiled. "You dream of kissing me?"

"Every time I close my eyes and plenty of times in between." He hugged her close and gently raked his fingers through her hair.

Maybe this was enough. To love and be loved.

"How are you feeling?"

"At the moment, wonderful."

"Then we'll have to have lots of these moments," Tucker said as his hand slid under her shirt to caress her back.

Her eyes again heavy with sleep, she sighed, giving

in to her drowsiness. Even as she absorbed his warmth, she knew she was only fooling herself. Tucker had been honest from the start.

Leaving him was going to kill her, and she couldn't even hate him for it.

"Skylar?"

When she didn't respond, he pushed her hair away from her face. Her long lashes rested against soft warm skin. Her breath grew deep and steady.

Tucker pressed his lips to her forehead, cherishing the feel of her weight in his arms. He could hardly believe he hadn't been dreaming, but had actually awakened to Skylar's kisses.

Assuming she'd fallen back asleep, he began to gently roll her onto the blanket beside him.

"Don't."

Tucker froze, surprised by the sharp command.

"I want to hold you," she whispered.

"Only if I can hold you in return."

Pain closed over Tucker's chest when she immediately sat up, pulling away from his embrace. She reached down, gathering up the bottom of the blue shirt. She winced as she tugged it over her head and tossed it aside, a pain Tucker felt as his gaze swept across a number of dark bruises on her light skin.

He shuddered with a rush of emotion when she laid her head back against his shoulder, her soft skin brushing his chest as she pressed her lips to his throat. Her deep, contented sigh vibrated clear through his soul.

"Much better," she purred, stretching as she shifted, settling perfectly on top of him. "You make everything better."

Tucker grabbed the edge of their blankets and pulled them up, tucking the edges around Skylar's bare shoulders, thankful to have her in his arms, smiling and warm.

When he awakened again the sun was boldly shining through the canvas tent. Skylar slept soundly in his arms, her warm rosy cheek resting against his shoulder, her expression soft and peaceful. His stomach growled as he breathed in the scent of bacon. He could hear his brother talking to Garret. The night before, he'd smelled the supper Chance had cooked, but hadn't been willing to leave Skylar.

This morning, however, he was completely famished. He hadn't eaten anything since before he'd skipped supper two nights back. He doubted Skylar had, either, but at the moment, she needed rest more than anything. They'd been curled up in their nest of blankets since yesterday afternoon and aside from Skylar's surprise kisses, she hadn't stirred once during all that time.

"Skylar?" he whispered, brushing his lips across her forehead.

When she didn't rouse, Tucker carefully eased her onto the blankets. "Be right back, love," he whispered, then slid from their warm cocoon into the cool air and quickly shrugged on his clothes.

Garret's head shot up the second he stepped outside.

"How's she doing?" he asked, jumping up from his spot by the campfire.

"Sleeping," Tucker said as he stepped up to the warmth of the fire. "But she woke a short while ago," he added, seeing Garret's brow still creased from worry. "She's feeling just fine, she even said so."

"Hell, that don't mean nothin'," Garret complained. "She always says she's fine."

"Yeah," Tucker said with a smile, "but I believe her this time."

"How long do you reckon she's gonna sleep?" Chance asked as he handed Tucker a cup of coffee.

"As long as she needs to. I won't wake her."

"Put your ruff down, little brother." Chance laughed softly as he shook his head. "I have no intention of disrupting your angel's beauty sleep. Your mustangs have scattered so we're riding out to round them up."

"I can't leave Skylar."

"I know that," Chance said with exasperation. "I'm just letting you know where we'll be. We should be back in a few hours."

"Are you gonna stay married to my sister?"

The kid fired the question like a gunshot. Tucker smiled at the protective concern in Garret's expression as he stepped toward him, his shoulders squared. He supposed it was a fair question for a man who'd just openly spent the night in her bed.

"Would you object if I tried to talk her into being my wife?"

Garret gave a shriek of excitement as his long arms clamped around Tucker, nearly cracking his ribs. He immediately jumped back, appearing chagrined by his burst of affection.

"I'll take that as a no."

"Go mount up, kid," said Chance with a low chuckle. "We've got work to do."

Tucker watched Garret hurry off toward the horses and noted that Chance hadn't moved to join him.

"I left you some breakfast there in the skillet," Chance said.

Tucker glanced at the cast iron covered with a tin plate sitting off to the side of the fire. He nodded. "Thanks."

Chance shrugged his shoulders, and continued to stand there, staring at him. The measuring look in his eyes told Tucker he had more on his mind than breakfast and horses.

Lord, he knew this was coming. The strain between his loyalties to Chance and his love for Skylar had been driving him crazy. But he'd made his choice and hoped to high heaven that Chance would understand. Chance was fond of Skylar and even Garret, though he'd probably not admit it.

Even so, that didn't mean Chance would want to share his home with them. The two-story house they'd built had been for the both of them.

"So what about you?" Tucker finally asked. "Any objections to my marrying Skylar?"

"I just hope you know what you're doing."

"She's good for us."

"Us?" Chance's lips tipped slightly.

"Yeah," Tucker said. The ghost of a smile on his twin's

face was proof of the change he'd seen in Chance over the past several weeks. Skylar had been good for both of them. Tucker hoped his brother saw that.

"Hell," Chance groaned. "If you're bent on ignoring any sense of caution, as you usually are, there's nothing I can do to stop you." He dipped his hand into the inside breast pocket of his coat. "You still ought to give her this."

Sunlight glimmered on the small golden circle sitting in his brother's callused palm.

Tucker's mouth dropped open. He recognized the smallest speck of a diamond channeled into the slender band. "Mama's wedding ring."

"I never thought either of us would have use for it," he said, the bafflement in his expression showing he clearly didn't understand Tucker's interest in marriage. "I can't guarantee Sky won't throw it back at you. You sure picked one feisty angel to fall for, but I suppose that's what you need to keep you in line."

He was giving her their mama's ring? "Are you sure?"

"Would you just take it?" He shoved the ring into Tucker's palm. "I'm tired of harboring the damn thing. It would be just your *dumb luck* to accidentally marry a fine woman. I doubt we'd ever find a woman more deserving than Sky to wear our mama's ring."

He couldn't have given Skylar a greater compliment. "Thanks, Chance," Tucker said, a huge weight lifting from his chest as relief swept through him.

"You go gettin' all teary-eyed on me," Chance said in a tone of warning, "and I'm gonna have to knock you to the ground and relearn you how to behave like a man."

Tucker smiled and slipped the ring into his pants pocket. "If that's a threat, I'll need to set my coffee aside."

"I wish I had the time to pound on you," Chance said as he moved away from the fire. "But I've got horses to round up and you have a pretty woman to tend to."

"You do know they'll be living with us?" Tucker called after him, wanting to be sure they had a clear understanding.

Chance's eyes fairly sparkled as he glanced back at his brother. "And your wife will be cooking for all of us. Sounds like a sweet deal to me."

Two down. Tucker sat by the fire and sipped his coffee. *One to go.*

Skylar emerged from her tent nearly an hour later, holding a blanket tight around her shoulders.

Crouched by the fire, stirring a skillet filled with potatoes and venison, Tucker instantly set it aside as she approached him. With not a cloud in the sky, the bright sun shone boldly on every bruise and scrape marring her pretty face. There were still streaks of dried blood in her tangled blond hair.

She glanced around the campsite. "Where is everyone?"

"Garret and Chance are tending the horses. I'm going to tend to you," he said. "So why don't you come over here and eat some breakfast." He dumped the contents of the skillet onto a plate. "We can enjoy each other's company while we're still alone."

The wariness in her eyes as he stood stung at Tucker's nerves. "Honey, you don't have to act like spending a little time alone with me is a death sentence," he said in a light tone as he put his arms around her.

Her soft laughter eased his tension.

"I didn't mean to give that impression," she said, leaning into him while keeping her firm hold on her blanket. "I enjoy your company very much, Tucker."

He hoped so. An explosion of warmth shot through his chest when she smiled up at him.

"You shaved." Her gaze moved over his bruised jaw. "That must have hurt."

"It looks worse than it feels." He hoped the same went for her banged-up face, not that she'd say otherwise.

Keeping an arm around her shoulders, he led her toward a log and guided her down beside him. Skylar grimaced as she crossed her ankles.

"Where do you hurt?" he asked.

"Everywhere." She released a long breath then glanced up at him. "Don't look so worried. I'm just stiff. Probably from sleeping for so long." She squinted as she looked up at the bright sky.

"Probably from tumbling down the face of a cliff," he said drily as he handed her the plate of warm food.

"It must be near nine o' clock and I know the sun was well up in the sky when you tucked me into those blankets yesterday."

"I'm surprised you remember."

"Not much. But I do remember seeing you every time I opened my eyes."

Tucker smiled as she leaned against him and began to eat. She scooted closer, pressing against his side.

"Are you making a stew?" she asked a while later, noticing the water he had warming over the fire.

"No. We're going to have a morning sponge bath."

Her gaze whipped up. Tucker nearly laughed at the excitement that lit her face.

"Do we really have time?"

"Hell if I care. Finish up, because once you're through eating, I'm taking you back inside that tent. We'll see if I can't rub some of the stiffness out of those sore muscles."

Skylar felt a rush of excitement as she stared at Tucker's determined gaze. "Tuck—"

"Don't worry, honey," he said with a wink. "I'll be a perfect gentleman."

She smiled at his words of humble intent, knowing there was no way on this earth she'd settle for having his hands on her body without touching him in return. She couldn't think of anything that could make her feel better. She needed this last bit of time alone with him.

Anticipation bubbling, she hurried to finish her breakfast.

They stopped the large herd at a river for a short rest before continuing on. Tucker held Rosie by the reins as he watched Skylar. He'd noticed the transformation in her the moment they caught up with her crew and herd. She'd ridden beside him for the past five hours, her expression guarded, her eyes unsmiling.

She stood a few yards away talking to Duce and Mitch, her grey skirt billowing in the breeze. He knew she was fond of the burly men filling her in on the condition of her horses, yet he couldn't tell by her firm expression.

Chance had been right. Skylar was used to being treated like one of the men. A few had raised their eyebrows at seeing her in her feminine attire, but they hadn't uttered a word about the change. All four men from her crew had greeted her with shoulder nudges and back slaps. The entire time her mask of indifference had remained firmly in place, leaving no trace of the sweet, wild, sensual woman he knew her to be.

What a strain, he thought, *to have to constantly suppress the woman she wants to be.* The woman she *is*.

This morning she had blatantly seduced him. For the first time in his life, he'd actually been prudish. He hadn't intended to make love to her, not wanting to hurt her bruised body, but Skylar had been relentless in her seduction. They'd barely made it into their clothes when Chance and Garret came back into camp. Despite all her passion this morning, she hadn't so much as flashed him a smile since. Nor had she made any attempt to be near him.

Perhaps she was mad at him for threatening to tie her behind his saddle if she attempted any of her fancy riding tricks. She hadn't been too happy about his imposed restrictions, but she'd stayed at the back of the herd and kept a nice, easy pace.

Tucker sensed her distance from him was more than sheer stubbornness. That thought made him nervous. He didn't like being treated like just one of the other men. She'd been damn careful not to give anyone the impression that he was her man. Yet she'd staked her claim this morning, when she settled over him, taking his body as completely as she'd taken his heart. And he'd let her, knowing he could have made her pregnant.

His skin prickled. He warmed at the thought. Skylar had him wanting all sorts of things he'd never dreamed of before. He stuffed his hand into his pants pocket and touched the smooth band of gold.

Well, hell. He hadn't exactly had time to woo her this morning, with their brothers damn near catching them in the buff.

He glanced again at his woman who appeared to be in a serious conversation with two men from her crew. Duce caught his gaze, the look in his eyes bordering on lethal.

What the hell was she telling them?

Tucker swung into his saddle and began riding toward them. He reined in close beside her, catching everyone's attention.

"Climb up here with me, honey," he said as he reached for her.

Skylar's eyes flared in surprise.

"Come on," he urged, smiling down at her, thinking she'd better get used to the endearment. "I want to show you something."

"Show me something?"

He took her hand in his. "Trust me, sweetheart."

Red splotches flagged her cheek. "Tucker," she said, her teeth clenched.

"Quit stalling." He tugged her toward his horse and glanced at the two men clearly struggling to bite back their smiles. "Y'all don't mind if I steal your ramrod for a time, do you?"

Duce beamed a grin. "Not at all."

Having no choice in the matter, Skylar reached up and allowed him to set her across his lap. He carefully draped her skirts over her legs then glanced at the other men. "We'll meet you at the ranch."

"The ranch?" Surprise distracted Skylar from the lecture steaming in her mind. "Are we really that close?"

"Yep."

"Why didn't you tell me?"

Tucker leaned forward and brushed a quick kiss across her lips, right there in front of everyone!

"I wanted to surprise you," he said, smiling as he urged his horse into motion.

"Tucker, you can't—"

"Patience, honey," he interrupted. "It's not far. Once we get there, you can rip into me all you like."

Skylar held her tongue, certain he misunderstood the type of ripping she had in mind. This was the reason she couldn't stay on at his ranch. She imagined the others knew of their involvement, but that didn't mean she wanted to make a spectacle of herself. She'd just finished making all the arrangements. As soon as Chance and Tucker paid her for her mustangs and the marriage document was annulled, she and Garret would be riding out with Duce and a couple of the others.

Tucker's arm tightened around her waist, and Skylar shut her eyes, pain piercing her chest at the thought of leaving him. She settled against him, finding strength in his touch. He stopped a short distance later at the base of a grassy knoll, and Skylar was certain he was stealing more time to be alone with her.

"Tucker," she said as he set her on her feet.

"Hold your horses," he teased, dismounting and taking her by the hand. "It's right up here."

A cold breeze tugged at Skylar's skirts as she followed him up the grass-covered hill. As they neared the top, a green valley backed by huge, snowcapped mountains came into view.

Skylar's breath stalled in her lungs as she caught sight of the ranch in the center of the rippling valley, her eyes taking in the large farmhouse standing among the stables and outbuildings.

"A little slice of paradise, huh?"

"Tucker," she said, struggling to find her breath. "Is that your ranch?"

"Uh-huh. See that?" he said, pointing at the two-story farmhouse that had caught her attention immediately. "That's our house. I haven't actually seen the finished product. Chance and I had just finished framing it when I took off to New Mexico, looking for wild mustangs."

"It's so big, and beautiful."

She shivered as he moved behind her and wrapped his arms around her middle. "Welcome home, Skylar," he whispered against her ear. "If you weren't already my wife, I'd ask you to marry me."

Her sharp intake of air told Tucker his words surprised her. The intensity of what he felt for this woman continued to surprise *him*.

She pulled back, turning slowly in his arms. "Tuck?" she whispered, her voice barely audible.

"I love you, Skylar," he said in a rush. "I don't want to sneak around to make love to my wife. I want you in my arms every night, every morning, and all the time in between." He leaned down and brushed his lips across her gaping lower lip. "Will you stay with me, share my home, be my wife?"

Her tense expression didn't waver as she stared up at him.

Tucker began to panic.

"Damn it, Skylar, *you love me*!"

"I know."

"You know?" he repeated, bewildered, elated, *in love*. "You love me?"

Skylar's lips quirked with a smile as she gave a nod.

"Would it kill you to say so?"

She slid her arms around his neck. "I love you, Tucker."

"I knew you did."

Joy bursting through her soul, Skylar laughed at his smug grin. "No you didn't. You were downright scared."

"I know now. You could say it again, honey." But he didn't wait for her to speak. His mouth settled over hers and he kissed her until she sagged against him.

"Tell me that you'll be my wife," he said when they paused for breath.

"Tell me you love me," she countered.

"I love you," he said, his voice fraught with urgency.

"Then I'll be your wife."

His eyes shimmering with excitement, Tucker stepped

back and dipped his hand into his pocket. Skylar gasped as she saw a shimmer of gold. Lifting her hand, he slid the ring onto her finger. "This makes it official, Mrs. Morgan."

Tears stung her eyes as she stared down at the band and small twinkling diamond. It was beautiful, *perfect*. "Where did you—"

"Chance gave it to me. It was our mother's. Do you like it?"

Oh God. She couldn't breathe.

Just like the man standing before her, it was so much more than she had ever hoped to have, exceeding her wildest dreams.

"I love it."

"Then why are you crying?" he asked as he stroked his thumb across her tear-streaked cheek.

"I don't know," she answered truthfully, laughing as he pulled her into his arms. Apparently happiness could also trigger a tearful response. She'd never been so happy in all her life.

"You ready to go see your new home?" Tucker asked, anxious to show her the spacious seven-bedroom house. *Wait till she sees the view from our bedroom window*, he thought, glad now that he'd chosen the master bedroom facing the east instead of the west. This year he'd get to spend long winter mornings in bed with his wife, watching the sunrise and keeping warm.

"How could you have left this place?" she asked, staring out at the valley. "It's perfect."

"I told you it was the most beautiful stretch of land this

side of heaven," he said, hugging her against him. "It just took an angel to make it feel like home."

His angel turned, giving him the smile that melted his heart.

Epilogue

Tucker stood at the door of the large barn, staring out at two feet of freshly fallen snow, freezing as he waited for Chance to retrieve Garret's Christmas present from the loft. With the sun barely into the sky, streams of smoke swirled up from the stovepipes of the bunkhouse and Zeke's home a little farther down the road. Tucker imagined their foreman would soon have everyone shoveling snow and breaking ice.

A few extra chores wouldn't put a dent in Tucker's Christmas. He'd already had the best Christmas morning a man could have, and had taken his time unwrapping and unraveling the greatest gift he'd ever been given. He tucked his cold hands into his armpits and thought about the warm woman he'd left in the house.

"What's that stupid grin for?"

"Nothin'," Tucker said as he glanced up at his brother.

Chance stepped away from the ladder with a burlap sack under his arm. "You're so far gone," he said in a solemn tone as he shook his head. "You can't stand still for two seconds without thinkin' about her and getting that dopey look on your face."

It was true, and Tucker didn't give a damn. He'd never imagined a man could love anyone the way he loved Skylar. Chance didn't know what he was missing. "We might have to find a woman to put the same look on your face," he suggested.

"Like hell! I'd sooner have a woman skin me alive with nothin' but a spoon. Besides, your woman is one of a kind, and I've never had your dumb luck."

Laughing, Tucker followed him through the snow. He reached over and grabbed the whimpering sack squirming in Chance's arms. "So what does this mutt look like?" He pulled out a ball of black fluff with four white paws. The big red bow tied around its neck gleamed against the morning sunlight. "Nice touch," Tucker said, smiling at his twin.

"It's a Christmas gift," Chance grumbled, thumping his booted foot against the bottom step of the back stoop to shake off snow. "They're supposed to be wrapped."

"Uh-huh." A gift for a kid Chance swore did nothing but annoy him. Yet he'd insisted on riding thirty miles through the snow to make sure the kid got a hound for Christmas.

"Stick the damn dog back in the sack."

Laughing, Tucker put the pooch back in the bag and followed Chance into the kitchen. Skylar stood by the stove, sliding a turkey into the oven, looking lovely as ever in the fancy pink gown he'd bought from Miss Kelley in Colorado. With her golden hair swept up in one of the braided hairdos Zeke's wife had taught her, she appeared wholly out of place in the plain kitchen. The sight of her in that pink satin still took his breath.

Closing the oven door, she turned, flashing a bright smile as she wiped her hands on the red apron tied at her waist. Her eyes darted toward his wiggling captive.

"You found one!"

"Chance did," Tucker said.

"Oh, Chance!" Skylar snatched up her brother-in-law before he could dodge her arms and gave him a tight squeeze.

Tucker laughed quietly as his brother endured her embrace, then he shifted the dog into Chance's arms in exchange for his wife.

"I did help him bring it in the house."

"He's going to love it," she said as she wrapped her arms around Tucker's neck.

"He better," Chance grumbled. "Let's get this over with." Coffee cups clanked as he picked up the tray Skylar had prepared with rolls and a pot of coffee.

"I think he's warming to us," Skylar whispered.

She turned away before Tucker could get a kiss. He followed them through the dining room into the great room where a monstrous ten-foot pine trimmed with red and white ribbons reached toward the high ceiling. Garret stood at the far end of the room, shoving another log into the stone fireplace.

As Chance slid the tray of cups and coffee onto a table before a long sofa, the dog let out a sharp bark. Garret's gaze whipped around and locked on the bundle under Chance's arm.

"Merry Christmas, kid." He shifted the gift into his arms. White paws pounced against Garret's chest as the pup squirmed from the bag.

"He's great!" He beamed a smile at Chance. "Thanks!"

"Thank your sister and Tucker."

"Not for the pup," Tucker said as he sat beside Skylar on the sofa. "Our gift is still wrapped under the tree. Chance bought you the dog and tied that fancy bow around its neck."

Chance shot Tucker a disgusted look as he dropped into an oversize chair.

Half an hour later Skylar snuggled against her husband, sipping her coffee as Garret romped across the paper-strewn floor with the puppy he'd named Boots.

"There's one more here," Garret said, pulling a package from behind the tree. "It's for Skylar."

Skylar glanced at the man cuddled against her side. He grinned as Garret set the festively wrapped box on her lap. She had already opened more presents than everyone else, the crate of fine china having brought her to full-on tears.

She quickly peeled off the paper and lifted the lid. Tears stung her eyes at the sight of the tiniest clothes she'd ever seen. Tucker had realized she was expecting before she could have suspected. At three months along, she was still absorbing the shock. A baby was a whole new transition, one that would affect the household, not to mention her work with the horses.

"Well, are you gonna show us what it is?" asked Garret.

Tucker nudged her shoulder. Reluctantly, she lifted one of the tiny white gowns from the box.

"Baby clothes?" asked Garret. "You gonna have a baby?"

"Round the first of June," said Tucker, his voice beaming with pride.

"Did you hear that, Chance? We're gonna be uncles!"

"I have ears, kid."

Skylar's stomach burned with tension as she met Chance's gaze. They had already imposed on him so much. He tolerated all of them quite well considering he hadn't bargained on getting an instant family.

"A baby, huh?" His lips eased into a gentle grin. "Now, that's somethin' special," he said as he rose from his chair.

Skylar stood as he crossed the room, and felt a flood of relief as she stepped into the first embrace he'd ever willingly given her.

Garret was next, practically squeezing the life out of her. "Maybe it'll be twins!"

Skylar's heart lurched.

"I don't think so," Tucker said, glancing at the flat of her stomach, the tiny rise in her belly not yet noticeable beneath her full skirt.

"Let's get out of here," Chance said to Garret after congratulating his brother. "We've got work to do."

"Can I bring Boots?"

"Sure. He can help you muck out the stables."

"See?" Tucker said when the door closed behind them. "You were worried for nothing. I told you Chance would be happy for us. I know my brother."

Chance's approval was no small relief. Tucker shrugged on his coat then pulled her into his arms. Before he could kiss her the front door popped open.

"Tuck, are you—" Zeke's mouth snapped shut as the older man's gaze collided with Skylar wrapped in Tucker's arms. "Pardon me." He flashed a smile, wrinkling the skin at the corners of his blue eyes. "Merry Christmas, Skylar."

"Merry Christmas, Zeke."

He shifted his gaze to Tucker who'd not relinquished a smidgen of his hold on her. "There's not a trough or watering hole that ain't froze over. You comin'?"

"After I kiss my wife."

"Newlyweds," Zeke mumbled before pulling the door shut.

"A man's got to have priorities," Tucker said as his hand slid beneath her chin and tilted her face up. Before his lips reached hers, the back door slammed as a shriek echoed through the house.

Margarete raced through the dining room. Her arms opened wide as she saw them. "I just heard! A baby!"

Skylar was wrenched from Tucker's arms as Margarete squeezed the breath out of her. For a tiny woman in her late fifties, she had an amazing amount of strength.

"Zeke and I wanted children, but it wasn't to be," she said as she released her hold, her eyes shining with tears.

She turned to Tucker and gave him the same bone-crushing embrace. "This is exciting! We have so much to do."

Tucker laughed as they watched her whisk back into the kitchen. "She's definitely happy for us."

Skylar sighed as he gathered her close. Hearing the back door slam again, she paused before reaching his lips.

"We just heard!" boomed Duce's voice. "Where's the little mamma-to-be?"

"Oh, Lord." Skylar pressed her face to Tucker's shirt. Garret was obviously announcing to the world.

"Com'ere." Tucker took her hand and led her to the front door. Stepping outside on the wide covered porch, he shut the door and gathered her close. "Can't believe I have to stand on the porch in the freezing cold to get a minute alone with my wife."

"I love the baby gowns, and the dishes," she said, smiling up at him.

"I love you."

Unable to wait a second longer, Skylar reached up and kissed him, long and thorough.

"Damn," he breathed when he lifted his mouth from hers. "You're gonna have to stop kissing me like that before I have to ride out. Makes it hard not to take you back inside."

Skylar laughed. "Later," she promised.

"Later always takes too long," he complained. His hand slid between them and covered the small rise in her abdomen.

"I can still hardly believe it, Tuck."

"I know the feeling, angel. You sure I'm father material?" he asked, holding her gaze.

"Yes. I've never known a more responsible and caring man."

"If I possess either of those qualities, it's because of you. I've been a mess my whole life. Just ask Chance."

"I don't have to. I knew you were a decent man before I married you."

"Your memory's not too good, honey," he said through his laughter. "You married me because I won our marriage document in a card game and tricked you into signing it."

"That's not how I remember it," she said, and smiled at his look of surprise. "You had already gotten to me. The moment I met you. You still get to me."

Tucker's smile broadened. "Yeah?"

"Yeah."

"Then I guess we'll have to have us a passel of kids." He lifted her against the length of him and spun her around. "Should be fun, huh?"

"It'll be heaven," she said, knowing their children would grow up in a home filled with love and laughter.

* * * * *